THE INTERVIEW

THE INTERVIEW

By: Karol Seydel

XULON PRESS

Xulon Press
2301 Lucien Way #415
Maitland, FL 32751
407.339.4217
www.xulonpress.com

Paperback ISBN-13: 978-1-6628-4170-5
eBook ISBN-13: 978-1-6628-4171-2

"Let me know you, O you who know me; then shall I know even as I am known. You are the strength of my soul; make your way in and shape it to yourself, that it may be yours to have and to hold, free from stain or wrinkle."

— St Augustine, *Confessions* Book 10

Prologue

THE OLD MAN SLUMPED IN HIS CHAIR. HE WAS TIRED and his guest had long worn out his welcome.

"Do I have your word?" the guest asked.

The old man stared back at him, then floated his gaze around his study. Amid the numerous books occupying the shelves were two picture frames: photos of him shaking hands with the previous and current pope. When he was ordained a priest he never dreamed he would later become a bishop, much less a Cardinal who carried the responsibility of electing the leader of the Catholic Church.

His guest continued, "You know those within the pontiff's closest circles do not expect him to make it through the summer. He is very ill."

The old man saw through the false pretense. A conclave wouldn't start for at least two or three weeks after his death; but the vultures were already circling.

The election of the next pope would be monumental for the future of the Church. Five years ago, the Church had unofficially split into two camps. The rupture followed a fateful decision by the current pontiff to allow married priests and female deaconesses. The camp supporting the decision attended the *Novus Ordo*: the Mass promulgated in 1965 after the closure of the Vatican II

Council. Those in the other camp were known as traditionalists' for their orthodox views on the liturgy and the priesthood. They flocked to churches celebrating the ancient Latin Mass: the Mass as it had been celebrated for centuries and up to the Council. The priestly orders in these parishes did not allow women to be ordained and retained the discipline of celibacy.

The old man sighed heavily, considering the fallout. The Latin Mass parishes had grown exponentially in numbers, revealing an unspoken schism within the Church had occurred. The gossip mill coming from the Vatican was churning out dire projections of future restrictions upon the Latin Mass. The traditionalists were concerned the next pope would strip away the worship they understood as authentic and beautiful. Tensions within the Church hierarchy and between the factions were at a fever pitch, and the incoming pontiff would either exacerbate or heal the divisions.

The old man had once been a champion for progressive changes but the flourishing Latin Mass population as compared to the dwindling *Novus Ordo* parishes made him second guess his original stance. He had discussed the reversal of his convictions with a few close confidants. Whispers that he was likely to support a more traditional candidate in the next papal election had reached the ear of his visitor, and was the reason his guest had dropped in unannounced.

"I'll ask again," the guest said, his voice piercing the silence, "do I have your word that you will vote as before?"

The inquisitor knew full well that the old man's "conversion" could have a devastating effect and cause many to jump ship to the other side. The last conclave six years ago nearly elected an Italian cardinal who would have never allowed for such progressive changes to take place. It had been a close call and the old man had championed alongside him to ensure the Italian did not wear the papal white cassock. He would not stand to see all of his hard work undone. He waited with anticipation to hear the old man's decision.

The elderly Cardinal peered over his steepled fingers at his sharp-eyed guest. "Do you remember the advice of Gamaliel to the Pharisees? He warned that if the plan of Peter and the Apostles were of men they would fail. But if their works were of God, and it was true that Jesus of Nazareth had risen from the dead, then no one could overthrow them. I give you the same advice. You can continue down the path you have chosen; but if it is of men and not of God, it will fail."

The guest glared at him through narrow eye slits. His voice dripped with disdain, "You have succumbed to trifle sentimentalism." He rose without uttering another word and left the room.

The old man knew he had made a formidable and dangerous enemy within the highest ranks of the Church. It was time to repent of his past sins and clear his conscience. He took out a pen and paper and wrote a letter to Cardinal Nicolo Menconi in Rome.

Chapter 1

FRANCESCA MENCONI PULLED HER CARRY-ON BAG behind her as she sailed through the terminal at JFK International Airport. She had just purchased a large iced herbal tea to relax her before her long flight to Rome. From the time she was young, Francesca had traveled to Italy nearly every summer to visit her family and her famous uncle, Cardinal Nicolo Menconi.

When she was a little girl he had been Father Menconi, a priest in the diocese of Rome. Having a relative who was a priest living near the Vatican made her a near celebrity in Catholic grade school. Her celebrity status only increased as her uncle's titles elevated to Bishop of Viterbo then Archbishop of Genoa. Archbishop Menconi later moved to Rome when he became part of the Roman Curia. By the time Francesca was in college, he was named a Cardinal and made prefect of the Congregation for Divine Worship and the Discipline of the Sacraments.

Francesca's trips to visit her uncle had become less frequent since his newest appointment at the Vatican. He had planned to attend her college graduation six years ago, but the death of a pope and seclusion in the conclave prevented him.

Last week, she received a call from her uncle asking her to come for a visit. It was as if he had sensed her inner conflict and need for his guidance across the ocean. She and her *Zio*, as she tenderly called him, were exceptionally close. After the tragic death of her father when she was ten, *Zio* had become a father-like figure.

She eagerly accepted the invitation; a dose of her uncle's wisdom and the charm of Italy were exactly what her soul needed.

Now, reaching the end of the terminal, Francesca stopped in front of the overhead monitors to double check her gate number. As she turned to head in the direction of the concourse, a man collided roughly with her, toppling Francesca, the bag, and her tea to the floor. She shrieked as the cold drink soaked through her shirt, shocking her with an instant ice bath.

"Oh, my gosh!" the man exclaimed.

She glared up at her offender. He was about her age and struggling to put his phone in his pocket.

He held out his hand to help her up. Francesca brusquely waved it away.

"I got it. Let me guess," she accused as she stood up, "you were texting and walking instead of looking where you were going."

"Guilty as charged," he replied. "I really am sorry." He dug out his wallet. "Here's fifty dollars for a new shirt and a new drink."

Francesca opened her mouth to wield additional insults but stopped. It wasn't worth it. If she was going to purchase something clean and dry to wear she had less than an hour to do so.

She took the money. "Thanks."

The man barely looked at her and headed off.

"Unbelievable," she muttered.

Within thirty minutes she had changed into a clean but hideous New York souvenir T-shirt, and bought a fresh cup of tea. She had some money left over which she happily pocketed for punitive damages. When she arrived at the gate, she read the dreaded words, "delayed" under the departure time.

"This just keeps getting better," she grumbled out loud.

She stormed towards a chair but came to an abrupt halt. The man who had started her cascade of misfortunes was sitting in the waiting area for the same flight. He pounded away on his laptop, a set of headphones plugged in his ears.

I bet he won't even recognize me, she mused.

She parked herself in a chair directly across from him, wondering if her penetrating gaze would make him look up. He was immersed in his work and didn't even budge.

If he hadn't been such an insensitive twit she might have found him attractive. His hair was the color of dark coffee with hints of auburn red. The light brown freckles sprinkled on his nose contributed to his boyish good looks. From her memory his hazel eyes were marbled with specks of blue.

She sighed haughtily at his obtuseness and pulled a book out of her bag and began to read.

⚜

Daniel Fitzpatrick heard a loud sigh and glanced up from his laptop. His earbuds were just for show. He didn't want to talk to anyone and the headphones usually prevented random strangers from trying to strike up a conversation.

The book held by the woman sitting across from him instantly grabbed his attention. It was the most recent work by Cardinal Nicolo Menconi: *From Whence Comes My Help.* The Cardinal was the reason he was traveling to Rome. His eyes drifted from the book to the woman holding it. Her long, dark-brown hair and attractive face set his recognition in motion: she was the woman he had knocked over.

He desperately wanted to ask her about the Cardinal. Anyone reading his book was bound to have an opinion on the controversies in the Catholic Church. It wasn't exactly the type of book most people would bring along for light reading on a flight.

This is awkward, he thought. He mulled over the best opening line to get her attention and chimed out, "We just keep bumping into each other."

Francesca barely lifted her eyelids in his direction. *Well, well. He did remember me.*

Daniel ignored her non-reaction and continued, "I'm the one who ran into you earlier. I'm glad you were able to find a new shirt."

She lifted her chin to look him fully in the face. *Is this guy for real or is he on something?* He spoke as if they had lightly bumped shoulders rather than him running her over like a linebacker.

"Yes. That is kind of hard to forget," she stated dryly.

"I am sorry. Really. Can we start over?" He smiled and held out his hand. "My name is Daniel."

Despite his sincere and handsome smile, Francesca held tightly to her grudge.

She reluctantly shook his hand. "I'm Francesca."

"You're going to Rome, too?" he asked.

"Yes. Visiting a relative."

"Business trip," he offered as an answer to the question she didn't ask. He wondered if he had engaged in enough small talk to ask what he really wanted to know. He pointed towards the book in her hands.

"So, do you think it's true? The papal conspiracy?"

Francesca's guard instantly went up and she became leery of this stranger's motives. She would protect her uncle at all costs. She decided to force him to ask the real question that was obviously on his mind.

"What do you mean?" she asked evenly.

Daniel studied the woman more closely. Her deep green, almond shaped eyes were alert and intelligent. He had a feeling she could easily give a dissertation about the conspiracy upon request. For some reason, she was being coy with him.

"I'll be more straightforward. Do you believe Cardinal Menconi was deliberately thwarted from being elected pope?"

"I think people love conspiracy theories. Especially when ideologies are divided." Francesca was well aware of the division in the Church and wondered what side her interlocutor was on.

"Are you a Trad?" she asked, using the slang for Catholics regarded as traditional in their beliefs and who attend the Latin Mass.

"I was raised Catholic. I prefer not to classify myself with other labels."

"Fair enough," she conceded. "Do you attend the *Novus Ordo* or the Latin Mass?" she asked, taking another route to ask the same question.

"I said I was raised Catholic. I didn't say I was practicing," he stated flatly. Daniel had been an investigative journalist long enough to know when someone was holding back information. Francesca was crafty and definitely knew more than she let on. He circled back to his original inquiry, "Do you think the division of ideologies made its way into the conclave and determined its outcome?"

"What goes on in the conclave is secret, so we will never know will we? It does appear the people are speaking with their feet, as they say. Latin Mass attendance continues to increase while the *Novus Ordo* parishes are in decline."

"And Cardinal Menconi is an outspoken proponent of the Latin Mass and for those who attend it," he countered.

His persistence to return to the conspiracy surrounding her uncle made Francesca even more leery. For someone who didn't practice Catholicism, Daniel knew a lot about the turmoil going on inside of it.

"I believe the Cardinal to be a good man. Maybe you should read his book," she offered, lifting it up slightly. "It gives you a glimpse inside his heart. Maybe his words would inspire you to return to the faith."

Daniel smiled politely. It would take more than words from Cardinal Menconi for him to ever want to go back to the Catholic Church and organized religion. He could tell the conversation was over. "It was nice talking with you," he said. "I hope you enjoy your trip."

Just then, the airport speakers crackled with the announcement that their flight would be boarding soon. Francesca was glad to have an excuse to leave. She gathered her things and made a bathroom stop before getting in line to board the plane.

Daniel watched her from a distance. It was obvious that she was strikingly beautiful, even in a cheap souvenir T-shirt. Most guys would have used the fortuitous chance meeting with a woman like Francesca to get her number and weasel a dinner invitation. But Daniel Fitzpatrick wasn't like most guys; he didn't have time for superficial dating games. He had played the game of love more than once and lost. After typing a few more notes he shoved his laptop into his carry-on and turned his thoughts back to papal conspiracies and Cardinal Menconi.

Chapter 2

FRANCESCA LIGHTLY STEPPED ACROSS THE COBBLE-
stone streets of Borgo, a district of Rome nestled in between
Saint Peter's Basilica and Castel Sant'Angelo. She had stopped by
Saint Peter's Square on the way to take in its glory. The colonnades
stretching out in a semi-circular fashion from either side of the
domed basilica were designed by Bernini to represent the Church
extending her arms in a mother's embrace to welcome her pilgrims. Standing in front of the Vatican certainly made Francesca
feel like she had come home. She had been away from her parents'
homeland far too long.

Her spirit soared as she entered the Ristorante Velando to
meet her uncle for dinner. He was easy to find in his long black
simar: a black cassock with cardinal red piping, red buttons and
black elbow length cape. A wide sash of scarlet red silk tied at the
waist and his red zucchetto, or skull cap, clearly identified his office
of Cardinal. A large smile lit up his face at seeing his niece come
through the door.

"*Mia passerotta*, you have finally flown home."

His warm greeting tugged at Francesca's heart. He had called
her "his little sparrow" for as long as she could remember.

She hugged her uncle tightly. "*Ciao, Zio!* I have missed you so
much!"

The waiter was quick to find the well-known Cardinal a table.
"You sounded sad on the phone," he said after the waiter brought
wine and a basket of bread. "Tell me what is troubling you."

Francesca unloaded everything: her dissatisfaction with her job at the local television station, and her disastrous love life of one failed date after another.

"*Zio*, I didn't get a degree in journalism to mindlessly turn out someone else's agenda or cover some brainless story on a dog that can water ski. Not that I expected to instantly become the news anchor for a national network, but this is ridiculous."

"Maybe you are in the wrong line of news, Francesca. There is more to journalism than television."

She sulked a little. It had always been her big dream to be a news broadcaster on TV. It was hard to admit that her uncle was probably right. She was learning fast that making a career in broadcasting required her to sell her soul in ways she hadn't anticipated.

"And," he continued, "maybe you are looking in the wrong places for romance. Do you belong to any young adult bible studies?"

Francesca fidgeted uncomfortably in her seat. Her work hours did not allow her to attend evening bible studies. Most of her dates were late night meetings at bars after work.

"It's the east coast. Life is just different there."

Her uncle shook his head. "Child, you are lost and unhappy. You need to find your compass. I have a favor I need to ask of you. Maybe it will be the beginning of putting you on your path."

"What favor?"

"Someone else is meeting us for dinner. I will explain everything when he arrives. Ah! I believe that is him coming in now."

The Cardinal stood up and motioned to his guest. Francesca pivoted towards the door and watched in gaping horror as Daniel, the linebacker from the airport, approached the table.

Cardinal Menconi noted the jaw-dropping surprise that occurred when they saw each other, but made the introductions anyway.

"Mr. Fitzpatrick, this is my niece, Francesca Menconi. Francesca, Daniel Fitzpatrick. It appears you two know each other?"

Daniel's intuition was affirmed; the woman had definitely known more than she was letting on. She was the Cardinal's niece! He wasn't sure how to react to her presence at his business meeting with the Cardinal. He guessed the most prudent course of action was to be as charming and cordial as possible.

"We met briefly at the airport." He saw Francesca stiffen and her mouth opened to give what would surely be an unflattering description of the event. He quickly continued, "Actually, your Eminence, I am embarrassed to say I wasn't paying attention and knocked Miss Menconi to the ground, causing her to spill her drink all over her shirt. But, she was gracious enough to forgive me."

The Cardinal lowered himself into his chair and gestured for Daniel to take a seat. He glanced at his niece. From the look on her face it appeared she had neither forgiven nor forgotten.

He clapped his hands together. "It appears all turned out well. Now we are here together so we can start over with a—how do you say—a clean slate?"

Francesca forced a smile. Her mind was in a spin wondering what in the world her uncle could want with the likes of Daniel Fitzpatrick.

"Mr. Fitzpatrick," the Cardinal began, "when your magazine reached out to my office for an interview, I did some research on you. Your essay on the scandal of the Church was fair. It was hard to read, but fair." The cardinal closed his eyes and took a heavy breath. "Wolves have been devouring the sheep." After a brief silence he continued, "Your magazine is friendly to Christian principles, and I need to be among friends."

"Thank you, your Eminence. I am honored that you read my work. Please call me Daniel."

Francesca stared in disbelief. "You're Daniel Fitzpatrick from *The Classic Journalist?*"

She was well acquainted with the magazine and its top writer who had garnered much fame several years ago for his article on the sex scandal that had rocked the Catholic Church. While it painfully uncovered the clergy's abominable and sinful behavior, Daniel's investigation was unique in that it included stories of priests who were falsely accused. He and the magazine were criticized for the inclusion, and accused of attempting to assuage the seriousness of the offenses. She was shocked that the buffoon from the airport and the highly respected author of an award winning essay could be the same person.

"You look surprised," he said.

She quickly recalled their conversation at the airport and his persistent digging for information. "I'm just wondering if my uncle knows you are interested in conclave conspiracy theories and if he should trust you," she fired at him.

"I think I have proven in my work to be fair and balanced," Daniel replied, bristling at her accusation. "But, yes, your uncle does know because it is precisely why I have been sent here to interview him."

"Why don't we order?" the Cardinal interrupted, attempting to lower the escalating tension. He gave them both a smile. "I'm sure you are both hungry from your long flight."

Daniel and Francesca brooded over their menus. Once the waiter had taken their food orders and left, Cardinal Menconi took command of the conversation.

"I said I needed to be among friends. And I need my friends to get along with each other." He looked sternly at his niece and then at Daniel. They got the point but still refused to make eye contact.

"Daniel, I will grant an interview with you but I first need you to do some investigating for me. I need someone from the outside who will not raise suspicion from within the Vatican." He turned to Francesca. "And he will need help. Someone who can speak the language and knows her way around Italy. You also have a degree in journalism and I expect your talents will complement his."

"Wait," Francesca said, "you want me to work with him? That's why you asked me to come and visit you?"

The Cardinal lovingly placed his hand under her chin. "I'm sorry, *mia passerotta*, I couldn't risk being overheard on the phone. Forgive me."

Francesca was more confused than upset. "*Zio*, what is going on? What is all this about?"

He took an envelope out of his inner breast pocket. "Two weeks ago, I received a letter under my door." He handed each of them a single sheet of paper. "I have made a copy for each of you. Daniel, I gave you a translation in English on the back."

The waiter returned with salads for each. Cardinal Menconi blessed the food and began to eat. Francesca and Daniel opened their copies. The words were penned in elegantly handwritten Italian.

Cardinal Menconi,

I write these words with a contrite heart, laden in sorrow. When we are young, we easily follow the throng of those heralding a cause for change. What is assumed as boldness and bravery can actually blind a person to what is True. Some Truths are never a cause for change, since they have been established by the One who is all Truth.

Now, as I reflect on my life, I am forced to make an examination of my conscience.

I write to you, Cardinal Menconi, because I fear for the Church, the Bride of Christ. Not that she will perish, for by our Lord's assurance she will withstand the gates of hell. I fear for those who will suffer because of my poor decisions, and for the souls of those who ignite and fan the flames of destruction. It is no secret that Our Mother has warned us on more than one occasion.

Unlike myself, you have been a bastion shepherd for the flock. A guardian and protector, never betraying the Sacred Tradition entrusted to us. Now, dogs are round about me and a company of evildoers encircle me, and I am alone in my own potter's field. It is important to know one's friends from one's enemies.

I pray the key will not slip from your fingers when the chalice is poured out, lest the fissure be beyond repair.

May God forgive me, have mercy on my soul, and grant me a peaceful death.

In desperation to be His Faithful Servant and Hers,

Giuseppe Cardinal Baldano

Daniel refolded the letter and peeked at Francesca. Her face was drawn and serious. He could tell from her intensity she was quickly assessing the meaning in Cardinal Baldano's message.

Daniel was the first to speak. "It appears Cardinal Baldano is switching sides to a more traditional way of thinking."

Francesca tutted lightly in disgust. "Is that your complete assessment?"

Daniel ignored her critical tone. "No, he writes as a harbinger of doom."

"That's putting it mildly," she muttered.

"Francesca," the Cardinal chided, "don't be so arrogant and puffed up with knowledge. Just tell us your interpretation."

"Cardinal Baldano is doing more than switching sides," she began, trying not to sound full of herself. "He is stating he hopes *Zio* will be the next pope. That's the reference to the key. Jesus gave Peter the keys to the kingdom."

The Cardinal slowly nodded. "In the conclave the cardinals place their twice folded votes in a chalice and the ballots are read aloud. Once a candidate receives the two-thirds votes that are required, he is asked if he will accept. If he does, he becomes the next successor of Peter, the first pope appointed by Christ himself."

Daniel remarked, "His reference to the keys slipping through your fingers sounds like he believes you were almost elected the last time." He raised his eyebrows in Francesca's direction, challenging her to deny Cardinal Baldano's insinuation about a papal conspiracy. She remained silent, but her green eyes returned his comment with a stony glare.

The main dish arrived bringing a brief interruption. Francesca leaned over and whispered in Italian in her uncle's ear, "*Zio*, why do you think you can trust this man? He told me at the airport that he is not a practicing Catholic. The other clues in this letter went right over his head. If things are this serious—"

Her uncle cut her off sternly but quietly, "*Basta!* Enough! I need you to trust me." He added tenderly, "Please, Francesca."

Francesca saw the sorrow in his eyes and it pierced her heart. He wasn't asking her as a shepherd of the Church. He was pleading with her as her uncle.

Daniel didn't need an interpreter to figure out what had transpired between the prelate and his niece. Daniel felt as much aversion to working with Francesca as she obviously did with him; he worked alone and preferred it that way. But he needed this interview. His career had become stagnant since his bombshell essay and a good conspiracy theory was just the boost he needed. He had high hopes of getting enough information from the Cardinal to write a book. He would have to play along. Given the look on Francesca's face, they would be working together whether they wanted to or not.

"How is your dinner, Daniel?" The Cardinal asked.

"It's probably the best lasagne I've ever had," Daniel replied.

Cardinal Menconi grinned. "Have you been to Italy before?"

"No. This is my first trip."

"Well, one more reason my niece will be of great help to you. She has visited Italy nearly every summer since she was young."

Daniel glanced at Francesca and attempted to smile. He looked at the Cardinal. "What, exactly, do you want us to do for you?"

The prelate laid his fork on his plate and leaned forward. "The day after receiving Cardinal Baldano's letter, a young man approached me as I was walking from my apartment to Saint Peter's Square. He handed me an envelope and said, 'The sender wants me to tell you that he entrusts to you what has been entrusted to him.' He quickly disappeared before I could ask any questions." He handed another piece of paper to Francesca and Daniel.

Daniel opened the paper and scowled. It was a list of seven prominent clergy with a bible verse next to each one. "What did this young man look like?" he asked.

"He appeared to be in his mid-twenties. He had light brown hair, blue eyes, muscular build, and was wearing a Milan football shirt."

Francesca had been quiet since being reprimanded by her uncle, but her usual boldness had returned. "Back to Daniel's original question: what do you want us to do?" she asked.

"I would like you to research the men on this list. I know a lot about each one, and some I have known for a long time. I need fresh and unbiased eyes to investigate them: to see why they would be listed together on this paper." He lowered his voice and glanced at Daniel, "I would begin with their money transactions."

Francesca stared at the names on the list. She recognized them all, meeting some of them at charity dinners with her uncle. Her heart sank. She had a feeling she wasn't going to like what she and Daniel would uncover.

A wave of exhaustion from her day of travel crashed over her. "I need a good night's sleep before I start investigating anything."

She looked up at Daniel. "Why don't you and I meet tomorrow for dinner? We can investigate the list independently and compare notes before hatching a game plan."

She wants time to form her own theories before hearing any of mine, he thought. He respected that. "That's fine with me. When and where?"

They exchanged phone numbers and Francesca said she would text him the details. When she got up to leave, the Cardinal rose and gave her a kiss on the cheek. Daniel pushed back his chair to leave too, but felt a hand on his shoulder. "I need to talk with you just a bit longer about the interview for the magazine," the Cardinal said.

Francesca and her uncle exchanged a few words in Italian, then she left, throwing a reluctant glance and smile to Daniel. He waved awkwardly. "See you tomorrow night."

After she exited the restaurant, the prelate lowered himself back in his seat and let out a deep sigh. "I am going to ask you something that may seem very odd coming from someone you just met." He met Daniel's eyes and leaned forward, keeping their eyes locked. "Francesca is like a daughter to me. I need you to be her guardian; to watch over her."

Daniel slowly rolled his fingertips on the table as he mulled over the request. From what he could tell, Francesca Menconi did not need a babysitter. And wasn't she supposed to be helping him? He studied the strained face of the Cardinal. His fingers stopped when he came to his conclusion.

"How many death threats have you received, your Eminence?"

The Cardinal didn't blink. "None. An informant who is well connected warned me to be careful. I don't think they would come after Francesca. As strange as this sounds, I think she is safer here under my watch than in America. Don't misunderstand, she will be of great help to you."

"They?" Daniel asked, picking up on the plural pronoun. "Is it a group of people?"

The tired Cardinal squeezed his shoulder. "Follow the money transactions."

He waved to the waiter for the check. Daniel reached in his wallet to settle his portion of the bill.

"I'll take care of it," the prelate said. "I'm grateful you have agreed to help me. One more thing, please don't tell Francesca there is speculation about my safety. I don't want her to worry."

"You have my word, Your Eminence."

Daniel walked back to his rented apartment, immersed in his thoughts. There was an authenticity to Cardinal Menconi that Daniel rarely encountered in people. He knew the clergyman wasn't playing him. For whatever reason, he trusted Daniel to investigate the puzzling letters and watch over his niece. His business trip had taken an abrupt turn. He had come to Rome for an interview and found himself thrown into detective and protection services. The Cardinal's gratitude was undeserved; something big was brewing and Daniel was thrilled to be the first on the ground to break the story. If all went well he would be writing about more than a Cardinal who might have been deliberately thwarted from the papacy.

He could be on the brink of the story of a lifetime.

Chapter 3

FRANCESCA ARRIVED AT SAINT PETER'S EARLY IN the morning before the cruise liners docked and unloaded their tourists upon the Eternal City. She passed through the large bronze doors and stepped inside the vast Basilica.

She veered to the right side of the church and paused for a moment in front of Michelangelo's *Pieta*. Francesca had visited many churches and museums, but nothing paralleled the beauty or magnificence of this depiction of Mary holding the body of Jesus after it was taken down from the Cross. Despite the countless times she had seen it, the *Pieta* still evoked a visceral response within her.

Another few steps brought her to the altar of Saint Sebastian and the tomb of Saint Pope John Paul II. This was another usual stop for her, but a small group of pilgrims were celebrating an early Mass so she didn't disturb them. Just a few feet away was her destination; the Blessed Sacrament Chapel.

A sign written in six languages stood at the entrance instructing visitors the chapel was only open to those who wish to pray. *Zio* had told her that Saint Pope John Paul II worried Saint Peter's was becoming more of a museum and less and less of a church. He reserved the chapel as an exclusive place for prayer and Adoration of the Blessed Sacrament: the Body, Blood, Soul and Divinity of Jesus Christ in a consecrated Host. Francesca always considered it a well-kept secret; simply passing by, you would never know there was a beautiful chapel enclosed behind the marble wall. She approached the doorway, framed by a wrought iron grate and a thick velvet smoky-gray curtain for the opening. Francesca stepped beyond the curtain, and entered the sacred space.

She walked toward a pew in the middle, and kneeling down in the aisle on both knees, bowed to her Lord and her God. Moving into the pew, she knelt for a while longer before sitting back and taking in the surroundings. Her eyes scanned the ornate decorations and paintings on the walls and ceiling but her main focus was the altar and tabernacle of gilded bronze, designed by Bernini, one of the main architects of Saint Peter's. The tabernacle reminded her of a mini domed basilica with statues of the twelve apostles around the roof and a statue of Jesus atop the dome. Golden angels knelt on either side of the altar, offering their adoration with those who came to visit.

Francesca closed her eyes and began to silently speak to the Lord with her heart. She complained about her job, her failed relationships, and her frustration at being twenty-eight years old and still single. Tears burned her eyes as she expressed her longing for a family; a husband and children.

Her litany of troubles escalated to her present situation. *I came here to be comforted by Zio,* she continued to rant, *only to be asked to investigate a list of bishops and cardinals. And to top it off, he's asking me to work with the rudest, most self-absorbed human being on the planet!* Francesca had sized up Daniel Fitzpatrick as a poster child for the narcissistic, self-involved journalist who didn't have the time of day for anyone but himself.

And why does Zio seem to trust and like him so much? He wouldn't listen to anything I had to say.

She let out an audible sigh. *I really am lost and unhappy. About everything.*

Francesca opened her eyes. Behind the altar and tabernacle rose a rounded arch suspended over a golden curved framed canvas of the Trinity: God the Father, with cherubs peering from underneath his flowing robes; Jesus the Son on His right, with cherubs also supporting his garments; and the Holy Spirit represented by a dove hovering between them. The Father's hand raised outstretched, as if in a blessing.

Blessing.

Francesca's conscience chastised her for wallowing in self-pity. She was blessed to be praying in a beautiful chapel at the Vatican in Rome. Her uncle was a Cardinal who had taken her more places than most people would see in their lifetime. She would eat a wonderful dinner tonight, complemented with delicious wine. She had a large and loving family. And when she left to go back home to the United States, she had a small but nice apartment in Boston. A job that paid the bills. Her body was strong and healthy.

I'm sorry, Lord. I have a good life. I know I do.

She sat in quiet gratitude before redirecting her thoughts back to having to work with Daniel Fitzpatrick. Her mind replayed the scene of him knocking her over in the airport and her resentment flared, but was quickly replaced by the memory of her uncle pleading with her. She had always trusted *Zio*, and she knew he must have a good reason for retaining the services of Mr. Fitzpatrick. He must see something in him that she didn't.

The Lord looks on the heart.

She moaned internally. The Bible verse recalled what God said to Samuel regarding the young shepherd boy David, who would later slay Goliath and become the revered King of Israel. David was described as being handsome, but that was the only similarity Francesca could find between him and Daniel.

Are you so quick to see the splinter in his eye, and not the plank in your own?

Her stomach lurched. A battle began between Francesca and her conscience. The last two years had been the lowest of her life, and for each transgression that surfaced as she prayed, she hurled back every rationalization and justification imaginable to defend her actions. Yet as her sins became exposed to the light she saw them for what they were, and she had no excuse.

There were the parties where people openly mocked her uncle and Church, and she remained silent; fearful of being exiled from the crowd she thought she needed in order to succeed. The gossip, ridicule, and lies she told to deconstruct her reputation of being a goody-goody, and show her co-workers she could be just as ruth-less and power driven as anyone. A date she went on after her last—and worst—breakup where she almost let things go too far before putting on the brakes. The horrible names he called her on his way out the door still made her sick to stomach.

Francesca didn't like who she had become. She was unrecog-nizable, even to herself. The woman driven by ambition and fix-ated on a television career was not the same woman who led Scripture studies at the Newman Center in college or who had consecrated herself to the Virgin Mary while accompanying her uncle on a pilgrimage to Fatima.

And through it all, she attended Mass every Sunday and received Communion without a second thought. This was the greatest source of her guilt: receiving the Eucharist unworthily with so much sin in her soul.

The plank in her eye was large and it was painful. She crossed her arms tightly across her stomach and began to slowly rock and back and forth. She knew what she needed to do: like the repen-tant woman who knelt before Christ, it was time to break the ala-baster jar of her heart and shed her tears of contrition upon the Savior's feet.

She stepped outside her pew, went down on both knees again, and this time tears of sorrow fell as she bowed. She slowly rose, exited the chapel, and walked to the right transept. After standing in line, she asked the attendant for a priest who spoke Italian. The attendant pointed to several ornate wooden confessionals.

Francesca took a deep breath, and approached the closest one, preferring to enter the side for anonymity, rather than a face to face encounter.

The priest greeted her and asked the Lord to grant her a good confession.

"Bless me Father, for I have sinned," she began. "It's been—" her voice cracked. Her last confession had been two years ago; her last trip to Rome.

"It's been two years since my last confession, Father. And so much has happened. I don't even know where to start." And her tears began to flow freely and she was openly sobbing.

"My child," the priest said gently, "do not be afraid. Our Lord wishes to embrace you, bind your wounds and restore you to your dignity as His daughter. Whenever you are ready. Take your time."

Strengthened by the priest's compassion, Francesca opened her heart and let Jesus, the Font of all mercy, wash away her sin and shame, resolving to leave behind the life she had been living. When she left the confessional, she felt lighter and freer, ready to give her life a fresh start; even if that start meant working with Daniel Fitzpatrick.

Chapter 4

THE *PIAZZA SAN PIETRO*, OR SAINT PETER'S SQUARE, bustled with people taking pictures and buying souvenirs from vendors. The sun had descended in the sky and begun to relinquish its dominion as the source of heat for the day. The evening promised to be pleasantly cool for the end of May. Francesca escaped the swarming crowd to find refuge underneath the Bernini columns that lined the piazza.

Although she had resolved to give her unexpected pairing with Daniel Fitzpatrick a fair trial, the situation still puzzled her. What mostly preoccupied her was the secret conversation that had occurred between the two men after she had left the restaurant. She could sense her uncle was keeping something from her. There was more lying beneath all the mysterious letters he had received.

Trust me, mia passerotta, he had said, just before he kissed her goodnight. She had always trusted him and she wouldn't stop now.

As she looked out over the piazza, she saw Daniel approach the fountain where they had agreed to meet. He was dressed in a pair of khaki trousers and a blue polo shirt. She couldn't help but notice his tall and fit physique. As she watched, two American college age girls asked Daniel to take their photo. They looked at each other and giggled as they walked away. Obviously, they were not immune to his athletic build and good looks.

Daniel saw Francesca walking toward him. He tried to ignore how pretty she looked in her white eyelet summer dress. It was modestly fit; a round neck and knee length, but still showed off her toned arms and slender figure. When she stopped, he realized she was only a few inches shorter than his six foot one inch frame.

"Hello," he said.

"*Ciao!* Doing your good deed for the day?" she asked.

He wrinkled his brow. "What? Oh, the picture?" He shrugged. "Sure. So, where are we going?"

Daniel wasn't used to letting someone else be in charge but he had no other choice.

"One of my favorite places. Follow me."

They headed south along the Tiber River towards Trastevere: a Roman district full of restaurants and lively pubs. As they walked, Francesca took the opportunity to clear the air.

"I want to apologize for my rudeness yesterday. I hope we can start again, as *Zio* suggested, with a clean slate."

Daniel was impressed by her magnanimity. In his experience, it was a rare occasion to get an apology from someone. "I'm sorry we got off on the wrong foot," he said. "I could have handled the situation at the airport differently. I can have a one-track mind sometimes."

"Apology accepted." After they walked a little further, she asked, "Do you prefer 'Danny' or 'Daniel'?"

He paused; very few people called him Danny anymore. "The only people that call me Danny live in my hometown and knew me when I was a kid. I generally go by Daniel. What about you? 'Frannie' or 'Francesca'?"

"A lot of people here call me Francesca. But in the States, my friends call me Frannie. Either is fine. Where is your hometown?"

"Jackson, Georgia. A small town about forty miles south of Atlanta. I live in Chicago now."

"Ah. I heard a hint of a southern drawl in the way you said 'Atlanta.'"

He uttered a short grunt. "Some things you just can't exterminate." He had worked hard to distance himself from his backwoods roots.

Frannie's head turned at his comment. She found the sound melodiously smooth and charming and wondered why he found it so detestable. Their arrival to the restaurant prevented her from making any further remarks.

"This is it," she said, pointing to her right.

The Osteria da Zi Umberto had a large seating area extending into the street. The tables were nearly full, but Francesca secured a small one under a large tree growing in front of the establishment.

Daniel glanced at the one page paper menu. The only word that looked familiar was *spaghetti*. He flipped it over but the other side was blank.

"Do you want any help or recommendations?" Francesca offered, eyeing Daniel's reaction.

"No," he said, setting the menu on the table. "I'm going to order lasagne."

Francesca almost laughed but didn't want to be rude. "That's what you had last night. Don't you want to try something different?" she asked, trying to give him a way out without embarrassing him.

"It was good. Why change?"

She saw the waiter approaching. "Because lasagne isn't—" she started but Daniel didn't let her finish.

"Thank you, but I know what I want to order," he said gruffly.

Francesca's annoyance at having to be in the company of Daniel Fitzpatrick was back in full force. *Fine*, she thought. *Be a dolt.*

The waiter looked at Francesca, who spoke in Italian and ordered the spaghetti carbonara and a bottle of red wine. She propped her chin on her hand and watched the waiter as she waited for Daniel to order.

"I'll have the lasagne, please."

The waiter glanced at Francesca then at Daniel. "We don't have lasagne this evening, sir." he said in English.

Daniel crossed his arms and glared at Francesca. "Well, that would have been nice to know."

She threw him a petulant look. "I tried to tell you but you cut me off." In Italian, just to irritate Daniel further, she fluidly ordered Daniel the *gnocchi spuntature*, and added a course of *saltimbocca alla Romana*.

After the waiter left, Francesca said, "You know, it's ok to ask for help. It isn't a sign of weakness."

Daniel exhaled loudly through his nostrils. If he wanted a possible book deal and the interview with the Cardinal he was going to have to find a way to work with his niece. A way that did not include fighting all the time.

"I usually work alone," he said apologetically. "This is all a little new for me."

His conciliatory tone helped dissipate Francesca's temper. "I wasn't expecting any of this, either," she said. "I came here to be on vacation."

Her irritation was quickly forgotten as the realization of being back in Italy washed over her. Italian laughter and conversation floated across the nearby tables. A smile spread across her face. It was like music to a song she hadn't heard in years.

"And it feels so good to be back! Isn't it just fantastic?" She gestured with her hand, "The charm of the picturesque narrow cobblestone streets, the old stone and brick buildings with green ivy cascading down the sides, the piazzas, the art of eating a laid-back-no-rush dinner, the food and wine...Ahhh. My soul needed this. It needed Italy."

Francesca blinked back the tears that were forming. Her soul needed the spiritual healing that took place earlier in the Vatican, too. The spiritual cleansing from the grace of forgiveness allowed her to fully appreciate the present moment.

For the first time, Daniel could not prevent himself from being enchanted by Frannie. He had no interest in dating anyone, but he was still a man; and the woman sitting across from him was alluringly beautiful. It was not simply skin-deep, but a beauty that was authentic and genuine. The radiant smile on her face reflected a soul that was kind and sincere. Her jasper green eyes were like changing chameleons that could shoot flaming darts or emit the warmth of the sun. When she wasn't looking at him with complete disdain, she was breathtaking.

Daniel felt a twinge of heat in his chest and glanced away. He took a piece of bread from the basket left by the waiter and spun it around between his fingers. "So, what's the story? How do you have an uncle living in Italy?"

Frannie's peaceful moment ended and she refocused on her dinner date. "*Zio*—that's the Italian word for uncle—is my father's brother. My parents moved from Italy to Boston when I was four years old to work in the office of the Italian Consulate General. We would come back here once a year to visit family. I've always considered Italy my home away from home."

"You and your uncle seem especially close, for only seeing each other once a year."

Frannie eyed Daniel suspiciously. He was being his nosy-reporter-self again. "We have a special bond," she said slowly, affirming his astute observation. She reminded herself *Zio* trusted this man and of her promise for a fresh start.

She continued, "When I was ten, my father died in a car accident. I thought we would move back here, but my mother was determined to stay in America. She was concerned about the high Italian unemployment rate and thought she had a better chance as a single mom if we stayed in Boston. My mother, my two older brothers, and I became US Citizens within the year to ensure that we could stay in the country.

"My father and I were very close, and I was lost without him. My brothers were close to Papa, too, but they were older and getting ready for college. I started traveling to Italy every summer to spend time with *Zio*. He wanted to fill the void left in my heart and became a surrogate father to me." She smiled. "I rely on his counsel and lean on him a lot."

The wheels turning in Daniel's brain stuck in gear, and he couldn't think of anything to say. He didn't expect to learn Frannie had experienced something as tragic as losing a parent. What really amazed him was how she talked about it with graceful acceptance. Daniel had not fared as well when dealing with his own childhood tragedies.

The arrival of their dinner shook him out of his trance. He realized he had no idea what had been ordered for him. Whatever it was, it looked and smelled amazing. Small, round lumps of pasta covered with a red meat sauce filled the plate. He picked up his fork and was about to take a bite when Frannie exclaimed,

"Wait!"

"Wait for what?"

"I was going to offer you some of my spaghetti and see if I could have some of your gnocchi."

He blinked rapidly. "You want my food?"

Her shoulders dropped and her chin jutted out. "No. It's called sharing. You were supposed to learn how to do it in preschool. *Zio* and I do it all the time. Besides, the meal is served family style with more than one course."

Daniel rarely ate a meal with anyone. He frequented the same places for takeout or cooked at home. Sharing food was a little too intimate for his taste. He shrugged. *Oh well, as they say, when in Rome...*

He moved his plate so it touched hers and she divided the meal between each. He stabbed a gnocchi with his fork but before it reached his mouth he was interrupted again.

"Hold on!"

He lowered his fork and it made a clanging noise on the edge of his plate. "What other ritual do we need to engage in before we can eat?"

"Grace." she said evenly. Praying before meals was a practice she had casually discarded but after today, she wanted to bring the simple gesture of gratitude back into her life. She crossed herself and softly prayed the traditional blessing in English. She noticed Daniel made a half attempt to cross himself at the end but didn't look happy about it.

"*Mangiamo!*" she said enthusiastically.

"Does that mean I can eat now?" he asked with sarcastic politeness.

Frannie ignored his snarkiness. "That's exactly what it means!"

Only a few bites in, Daniel pointed his fork at the lumpy pasta and asked, "What is this?"

"It's gnocchi: a homemade potato pasta, like a dumpling, and the sauce is made out of pork sausage and short ribs. Do you like it?"

"It's freaking spectacular," he said, stuffing his mouth with another bite.

"Don't eat too fast. Italians like to eat with leisure. I ordered saltimbocca for the second course. It's veal wrapped in prosciutto."

He noticed she was taking a break from her pasta to enjoy the wine so he followed suit. The wine brought out even more of the flavors from the meat sauce. Guilt crept into his conscience for being so abrasive. Despite his pigheadedness, Frannie had been very gracious in ordering a delicious meal for him. He wasn't used to being on the receiving end of unsolicited kindness.

He made a clearing noise in his throat. "Thank you, Frannie, for helping me order. The food and wine you chose are delicious."

"You're welcome." *Whaddya know. He isn't a complete neanderthal.* "Should we start talking about the list?"

Daniel pulled his copy out from his back pocket and she took hers out of her purse.

"Did you see any pattern as to why these men would all be listed together?" she asked.

Daniel shook his head. He had only researched five of the seven listed. "Not yet. Cardinal Donati's name stood out immediately, though. I came across him while conducting research for my essay. Allegedly, he is involved in some shady business at the Vatican Bank."

Frannie remembered the inflammatory headlines, but hadn't followed the story. "Are you referring to his possible connection with the Italian mafia?"

He nodded. "In recent years, the Vatican Bank has been under scrutiny for money laundering with possible ties to the mob. When Cardinal Fortino Donati was appointed the President of the Commision of Cardinals of the Vatican Bank, he was charged with cleaning up the corruption. Allegations abound that he instead channeled mafia money through the bank to embezzle and misappropriate funds."

"Funds for what?"

"My guess is payoffs or blackmail. They claim the Vatican hid the mafia's money in their bank and used a percentage fee to fund their increasing debt, as well as payment for silence to avoid any inconvenient scandals."

Frannie's heart sank. "That explains the Bible verse next to his name." She dug out her phone to pull up the verse on her Bible app and read it out loud. "'The love of money is the root of all evils.' I guess that's why *Zio* mentioned an investigation into money transactions."

"What about you?" Daniel asked. "Did you find a pattern?"

"Possibly. But, isn't it odd that *Zio* would ask us to investigate every man on this list?"

"What do you mean?"

Frannie was surprised that she had to explain. "Mr. Fitzpatrick, you must not have done all of your homework. One of these men has been *dead* for over a year."

Chapter 5

D ANIEL STARED AT THE LIST OF CLERGYMEN, TRYING to process Frannie's news flash. The two men on the list he hadn't given a quick internet search for were Cardinal Baldano and Cardinal Jozef Vidmar from Slovenia. Giuseppe Baldano was obviously alive and well and writing letters.

"Cardinal Vidmar?" Daniel asked.

"Yes. He passed away rather suddenly, if I recall."

"Do you know what side he was on?"

"You're still assuming there was a conspiracy with the pope's election."

Daniel let out a cynical laugh. "We have a cryptic letter from Baldano and a list of high ranking church officials that your uncle— another high ranking official—wants us to secretly investigate. I think it's safe to say we are knee deep in conspiracy territory."

Frannie absently swirled the wine that was in her glass. She knew Daniel was right. It pained her to admit corruption had made its way into the highest offices of the Church. "It's rather unlikely that Vidmar would have cast his vote for the current pontiff," she offered. "He was one of the bishops that composed the Letter of Opposition."

"That was the letter that came out condemning the decision to allow married priests and women deacons, right?"

Frannie scrutinized him through a squinted eye. "For not being a practicing Catholic, you know quite a bit about what's going on within the Church."

"Working for a conservative news outlet keeps me somewhat up to date on Catholic politics. But refresh my memory."

Frannie explained, "A council convened to tackle the abuse crisis in the Church. They composed a list of drastic changes to centuries of Catholic teaching and discipline for the clergy, recommending female deaconesses and allowing priests to marry. In protest, a group of bishops walked out of the council and wrote a statement of dissent against the decision. The bishops not only dissented but urged Catholics to return to the Traditional Latin Mass. It worked. Latin Mass parishes have really grown in number. And so began the unofficial schism we find ourselves in."

Daniel remembered Frannie asking him at the airport which group he had allegiance to.

"What did you decide?" he asked. "Latin or the other?"

"I'm TLM." She watched Daniel scrunch his face in confusion. "It's an acronym for Traditional Latin Mass."

The saltimbocca arrived and Frannie tried to take a pause from the heavier conversation to immerse herself into the scrumptious dish.

"Mmm. This is really good," Daniel observed as he reached in for a second helping. But his thoughts prevented him from completely shifting his focus away from their discussion. "I have a question. Why do you bother being a part of an institution that is so patently full of corruption?"

Frannie clenched the napkin in her lap. She was used to being at the receiving end of these types of taunts—especially when people found out she was the niece of a Cardinal. A pang of guilt returned over the times she remained silent, but she didn't allow it to fester. She had confessed and been forgiven. After today, her days of silence and fear were over. She attempted to speak the truth with charity.

"I'm not going to leave Peter because of Judas. If anything, the story of Judas proves that there was conspiracy and deceit within the top ranks from the very beginning of the Church. I mean, it's not like Jesus didn't know what would happen. But it didn't stop Him from calling Judas as a disciple or telling Peter to head up the Church. Maybe that's why He reassured Peter that the gates of hell would not prevail against it."

Daniel found himself at a loss for words, which was a rarity for him. He always had a comeback, whether it was a rebuttal based on evidence or merely a snide comment. He had chastised a lot of religious people, but no one had ever given him an explanation that seemed so reasonable and thought out. It challenged Daniel's conception of religious people being mindlessly led along like a puppy chasing a butterfly.

"You said you saw a pattern in the list?" he asked, changing the subject.

"Maybe. I reread Baldano's letter. He said it was important to know one's friends from one's enemies. I think that's the key to this list. Archbishop Karl Kratzer from Austria, Vidmar, and *Zio* are on this list and all of them signed the Letter of Opposition so they are of a different association than the rest and probably the 'friends' mentioned by Baldano. That's why I'm confused about the timing. Vidmar can't be a friend or an enemy if he is no longer living.

"I agree with you about Donati," she continued, "Archbishop von Eichel is from Germany and his Bible verse from Ezekiel is less than flattering: 'Princes in the midst of her are like wolves tearing the prey, shedding blood, destroying lives to get dishonest gain.' Which leaves Cardinal Constantini; the parable of the dishonest steward next to his name doesn't paint a pretty picture there, either."

She picked up the list and began pointing at each one. "That's another thing. All of these men have a Bible passage that is only one verse long. Constantini gets a whole parable. I'm not sure what that means yet. But, I do think von Eichel, Donati and Constantini are shady and make up the group we should study first, along with Baldano. He may appear to be a friend because of his letter, but we should still take a closer look."

"What does the verse say next to his name?" Daniel asked.

Frannie accessed the verse on her phone app. "'You brood of vipers! How can you speak good things when you are evil?' It's from Matthew's Gospel. Jesus is laying into the Pharisees."

"That definitely sounds like a condemnation for Baldano." Daniel didn't care where the passage was from or what it was really about. It didn't surprise him Jesus was raking someone over the coals. He assumed the Bible was full of God's chastisements and wrath.

He wondered about the others and inquired, "The verses next to the friends list are more flattering?"

"Yes," Frannie answered. "Kratzer's is from Revelation, 'He who has an ear let him hear what the Spirit says to the churches.' I assume that is because he was the primary author of the Letter of Opposition. Vidmar's is Jesus telling his disciples, 'I send you out as sheep in the midst of wolves; so be wise as serpents and innocent as doves,' And *Zio's* is," she paused, knowing it would confirm Daniel's bias, "Jesus giving Peter the keys to the kingdom."

"Hmm. Yeah, no indications of a papal conspiracy in that list," he mumbled sarcastically. He leaned back in his chair and lightly strummed his fingertips on the table, digesting Frannie's hypothesis about friends and enemies. Her arguments were sound and made sense. But there was something about the list that had been bothering him since he received it.

"I don't disagree with your analysis. My question is, who gave the Cardinal the list? A friend? Or foe?"

Frannie cocked her head to the side. "I assumed Baldano had it delivered."

"By a random delivery guy dressed in a soccer shirt and not in a courier's uniform? Why not just include it with his letter?"

Frannie rested her chin in her hand. "I admit I hadn't thought much about it. But, you're right. That doesn't add up."

"And the most intriguing part is Constantini. I assume you know who he is?"

Frannie slowly straightened and smoothed her dress. His name had been the most disturbing to her. She had attended charity dinners and auctions with him and her uncle several times. He was charming, charismatic, and a high profile cardinal-celebrity of sorts. But that wasn't the most troubling part, and it was obvious Daniel had made the connection.

"Cesare Constantini is the Dean of the College of Cardinals." she answered heavily. "In the event of a pope's death, he presides over the conclave."

Her words hung in the air as the two sat with their own thoughts. A papal conspiracy was seeming less crazy and a plausible theory needing further investigation. The realization of how far wickedness had wrapped its tentacles in and around the Church made Frannie remember the warnings in Baldano's letter. She wouldn't talk to Daniel about that tonight. *He's going to scoff at you when you give him the second half of your hypothesis.*

The waiter appeared and asked Frannie something to which she smiled slightly and nodded. Daniel assumed he would be bringing the check.

"So, what's our plan?" she asked.

"I spent most of the day getting reacquainted with Donati and the Vatican Bank so I would like to do some digging tomorrow into the three men you identified. Would you mind meeting me at my apartment in the morning?"

"Sure." She added his address into her phone. It was near the Vatican and not far from where she was staying.

The waiter arrived with two shot glasses filled with a yellow liquid. He sat one in front of Frannie and the other in front of Daniel.

"What's this?" he asked cautiously.

"Limoncello!" she said brightly, happy to divert her attention to something good.

Daniel lifted the glass to his nose and took a whiff. The smell of lemon and alcohol were so strong he jerked his head back. "We're doing shots?"

Frannie laughed. "Not really. It's a *digestif:* an alcoholic drink served after dinner to help digest your food. You don't down it like tequila. Just sip it."

Daniel looked at her skeptically and took a small sip. "Mmm," he said, raising his eyebrows. "That's really refreshing."

"Have I steered you wrong yet this evening?"

He chuckled and shook his head. "No, Menconi, I guess you haven't."

Their eyes met briefly but Daniel didn't allow himself to gaze too long. *Sooner or later she would steer you right down heartbreak alley. They always do.*

She asked for the check and they threw in enough paper Euros to cover the bill.

They walked back to Vatican City along the street above the Tiber River. The golden lights shining on Castel Sant'Angelo provided a stunning backdrop against the navy blue night sky.

Daniel stopped and looked down to the river. "Is that a pedestrian trail?"

"Yes. It's used for biking and running."

"Sweet! Let's make our morning meeting at nine. That will give me time to go for a run."

"Do you run any races?"

"No. I just want the exercise. I don't need to run with a hundred other people."

His answer didn't come as a shock. She had already concluded Daniel Fitzpatrick wasn't a social butterfly.

As they neared Saint Peter's Square, Frannie stopped and pointed down a side street. "My flat's down there. I'll see you in the morning."

"Thanks again for helping me with dinner. It really was delicious. I've had more carbs and alcohol in two days than I've had in the last month."

"And we've only scratched the surface. You haven't had pizza yet!"

"Will you let me know if there's a salad on the menu?"

Frannie laughed out loud. "I can do that. I'll be sure to hook you up with some leafy greens and vegetables."

"Umm...*grazie?*"

"*Brava!* Very good!"

Daniel wasn't sure what to do next. Despite the professional nature of the evening, it was the closest thing to a date he had experienced in a long time.

He stuck out his hand. "Good night."

Frannie shook it firmly. "Good night." She turned and headed down the street toward her apartment. Despite the rough start, the dinner went much better than she anticipated. Daniel Fitzpatrick wasn't too awful to be with. *But, he is as awkward as a teenager,* she laughed to herself. Her mind drifted to when their eyes met briefly at dinner and the sound of his laugh. He might be the most handsome, awkward man she had ever met.

Chapter 6

DANIEL HURRIEDLY PICKED UP THE FEW THINGS scattered around the small round dining table so Frannie would have a place to sit when she arrived. His morning run had taken longer than he expected, but it had cleared his mind. He was sure the courier who delivered the letter to Cardinal Menconi was the key, but he had no idea how to find him. In the meantime, he would explore Frannie's pattern and hope the mysterious delivery man would show up.

A knock came at the door precisely at nine. When he opened it, he was greeted by a smiling Frannie holding two paper cups in her hand and a large bag strapped over her shoulder. She handed him one of the cups as she entered.

"*Buongiorno*! I brought you a cappuccino."

Daniel stared at the cup. His attempt to make coffee in the pot provided by the apartment had been an epic fail. It tasted like dirty water. The nutty aroma of real coffee filled his nostrils. He wasn't sure what to make of Frannie's considerate gesture to bring one for him.

"Thank you. That was really thoughtful."

Frannie noted the surprise in his voice and found it odd. It seemed only natural to purchase a cappuccino for him, too. "Next time, we need to meet at the café," she said. "I had to explain I was meeting an American friend. Italians don't get their coffee to go."

Daniel rated an hour at a café just to drink a cup of coffee as a complete waste of time, but he didn't argue. "You can set up your laptop here," he said, pointing at the table, "It's the only flat surface I have except for the coffee table."

Daniel watched her dig out her laptop, a notepad, and a small paper bag. She wore tan linen wide-leg trousers with a white cotton shirt. Even in casual clothes, Frannie looked like a million bucks.

She took a pastry out of the bag and tore it in two. "I gathered you are a carb-counter but you're going to have to forget all of that while you are here." She handed him half of the pastry.

Daniel reluctantly took it from her hand. "A croissant for breakfast?"

"No," she said firmly. "That is not a croissant. It is a *cornetto*. It's sweeter and has a more cake-like consistency than a croissant. It's going to go great with your cappuccino."

Daniel took a bite. It melted in his mouth. He gave it a closer look. "How does something so plain taste so good?"

Fannie grinned. "Italians know their food." She opened her laptop. "Which person are you starting with?"

"I want to look at Constantini. Your uncle mentioned to follow their money transactions. I want to start there with him."

"I'll take von Eichel. And I have another avenue I want to examine as well."

They spent the morning in silence, immersed in their own research. Frannie's dive into Archbishop Martin von Eichel proved uninteresting and predictable. The Archbishop had been sowing seeds of discord all around Germany, vocalizing his desire to see progressive changes in the Church. It was von Eichel along with Constantini who led the charge to insert female deaconesses into the all-male clergy.

With little effort, she found images of von Eichel with Constantini at various fundraising events. The numerous photos she found of them together reeked of a suspicious collaboration.

Bored with von Eichel, Frannie shifted her focus to the line in Baldano's letter that really got her attention: *It is no secret that Our Mother has warned us on more than one occasion.* The only Mother he could have meant was the Blessed Virgin Mary. Frannie was familiar with several Marian apparitions in which Mary had appeared to people and delivered messages—or warnings—about the fate of souls and of the world. She began reacquainting herself with the Virgin's appearances at Fatima, Portugal; La Salette France; and Akita, Japan. She dug in her bag for her headphones and listened to a video documentary on Akita, taking copious notes. At the end, she pulled her earbuds out and threw them aside. She leaned back in her chair and rubbed her forehead.

"Need a break?" Daniel asked.

"Yeah." She glanced at her phone. It was way past noon. "Do you want to go get lunch?"

"I found a supermarket and bought some salad greens. I thought we could make our own."

"You were serious about that salad, huh?"

"And time." Daniel opened the small refrigerator and set the vegetables on the counter. "Did you know it took us almost three hours to eat dinner last night?"

"Yes, and it was grand! Most days I am cramming my meals in my mouth in under twenty minutes. It's a sacrilege to the civility of the human race and the digestive tract."

Daniel sputtered out a laugh. "That is quite a colorful diagnosis." Frannie joined him in the kitchen and washed the vegetables. He started chopping up the lettuce and dividing it between two plates.

"If you hand me a knife, I'll cut these," she said, motioning to the vegetables she rinsed. He handed her a knife and she continued her critique of American dining as she sliced. "It's true!

Americans don't know how to slow down and enjoy anything. We really don't know what leisure means."

Daniel reached over her and picked up a cucumber. He acknowledged the truth in her statement. Life as he knew it growing up in a small Georgia town was night and day compared to the fast rat race he was living today. His Grandma Mae used to chide him about it all the time. He could almost hear her say with her southern drawl: *at the rate you're a-goin', life is fixin' to pass you by quicker than green grass through a goose.* The corner of his mouth curved in a half grin at the memory of Grandma Mae.

Frannie's arm brushing against his interrupted his thoughts as she divided peppers and tomatoes onto each bed of lettuce. "Okay, Chef. Anything else we're putting on these?" she asked.

He looked down at the two salads. He was caught off guard by how effortlessly they had worked together. "Aside from some oil and vinegar, that's it."

Since the dining table was full of papers and laptops, they sat on the floor and used the coffee table to eat. Frannie crossed herself and said grace for both of them. Daniel politely waited but she noticed that this time, Daniel didn't even bother crossing himself.

"How was your run?" she inquired as they began eating.

"Good. It's a great route. I went to the Olympic stadium and back."

"That was about five miles. Is that your normal distance?"

Daniel shrugged. "Probably a little farther than usual."

"I'm a runner, too. I like to run the trails in Villa Doria Pamphili. It weaves through a beautiful park and you can run up Janiculum Hill, where you get a fantastic view of the city. You really should run it at least once while you are here. It's not hard to pick up the trail from my apartment. If you're interested, we could run it together."

Daniel stopped eating mid-bite and stared at her.

"What?" she asked defensively.

He finished chewing and swallowed slowly. "For someone who doesn't like me very much, you're being very cordial."

Frannie glanced away and pushed the food on her plate around with her fork. She wasn't going to divulge anything about splinters or planks in eyes and her own faults. "*Zio* likes you. And for whatever reason he trusts you. As I said last night, I'm trying to put our mishap of a beginning in the past and start fresh. We could be working together for a month or more. We might as well be friends."

Once again, Daniel was at a loss for words. He tried to look for an angle that Frannie might be working but couldn't come up with one. Her radiant smile made it unthinkable that she could be manipulative.

"The Villa trail sounds nice. Maybe next week?"

Frannie nodded. "Just let me know."

When they finished eating, they took their plates to the sink. "You can leave them," he said, "I'll do them later. We should get back at it."

An hour later into their research, Daniel called over his laptop. "Hey, Frannie?"

"Yeah," she said distractedly. She was reading an article about Mary's appearance at La Salette. The dire words given by the Blessed Mother were unsettling to her given the current state of the Church.

"Have you ever heard of a charity called—I'm not going to pronounce it right, 'com-passion-ee?'"

"*Compassione*," she corrected, then pronounced it slowly, "com pas sió ne. The *i* has an *e* sound, and the *e* has an *a* sound. And you draw out the *o* a little."

"Okay, *Compassione*," he repeated with some semblance of its proper Italian pronunciation. "Have you heard of it?" he asked again.

"Yes, it's a European Catholic charity organization. Why do you ask?"

"Constantini and Donati are on their board and a popular fundraising duo for them. I just wondered if you thought the organization was on the up and up."

Frannie's brow furrowed and she stared off in deep thought. The organization was mentioned in an article she read earlier. It came to her like a flash. "Wait! Hold on a second." She frantically typed into her search engine and found the article she was looking for. "Come here and check this out."

Daniel got up and stood beside her. When he saw what was on her screen, he knelt down on one knee next to her chair and leaned forward to read the article. It was from a news outlet in Vienna. Frannie had used the translation feature so they could read it in English.

Benefit Rock Concert Tour Begins in Controversy
Archbishop Kratzer Sides Against Vienna and
Munich Archbishops

Archbishop Kratzer of Salzburg refuses to host a benefit concert for *Compassione*, the European charity organization sponsored by many Vatican prelates. The concert, which has taken place for the last three years in Vienna's Saint Stephen Cathedral, has not been without its critics. Conservative Catholics cite blasphemous costumes and behaviors in front of the high altar of the church.

One protestor said, "The singers are half-dressed and allowed to stand on the altar rail. One performer dressed up with horns on her head. It's sacrilege."

During the concert, many demonstrated their disapproval by praying the rosary outside the cathedral.

Daniel reached over and used Frannie's keyboard to scroll through the pictures provided in the article. Even as a non-practicing Catholic, he was disturbed by what he saw taking place within the historic church. The description made by the protestor regarding the performers was highly accurate. He quickly scanned the article and found why Frannie wanted him to read it.

Archbishop von Eichel of Munich and Vienna's Archbishop Lechner praised the concert and the charitable contribution made by *Compassione* all over the globe. They urged all bishops to welcome this group of entertainers who are doing "the work of the Lord within the vineyard of the world." The tour begins in Munich, stopping in Vienna, and continues into Italy. Cardinal Constantini is to host the final concert in Milan.

Archbishop Kratzer refused to allow the concert in any church in his jurisdiction of Salzburg. This isn't the first time the Archbishop of Salzburg has taken issue with his fellow bishops. Kratzer was the author of the Letter of Opposition, written in response to the Council in Rome...

Daniel quickly scrolled through to the end. The rest of the article gave details that he already knew about the council and pope's decision. At the end was information on how to get tickets for the performance.

Daniel got up and went back to his seat. He rolled his fingers slowly on the table and stared at his computer screen. When his fingers came to a stop he looked up at Frannie.

"I think your assessment of the shady men on the list is correct. And, I think they are linked together by the Vatican Bank, though I'm not sure exactly why."

"What made you look into *Compassione*? It's just a charity organization."

"Your uncle instructed me to follow the money transactions. I decided to see if Constantini was connected to any large corporation or organization. Finding him on the board of *Compassione* was easy. When Donati was there, too, it raised a flag, so I looked further. They rake in millions of Euros. Millions," he repeated. "If it's true Donati is misappropriating funds via the Bank, maybe this is his cover."

"As a non-profit organization, don't they have to make their financial report public?"

"I looked at it. It's pretty basic. They report the amount of funds collected by external donors, organizations, and so on, but that doesn't mean they don't have ways of hiding money."

"So where does the Vatican Bank come in?"

"Some of the clients of the Vatican Bank are involved in missionary work. The Bank manages the client's investments, and it's a tax haven. Where better to hide money laundering than under the guise of an innocent charity? Throw in an incentive for a low tax liability, and we have the perfect setup for fraud."

Frannie sank in her chair. She crossed her arms, visibly irritated. "Why would *Zio* ask us to do this? He could have someone at the Bank look into books and records for him. He has enough friends."

Daniel rubbed his hand over his mouth. He had promised not to say anything about the Cardinal being tipped off that he could be in danger. It was his opinion her uncle had lost trust in anyone close to him. Frannie's words resurfaced in his mind: *For whatever reason, he trusts you.* The prelate's unfounded trust was a mystery he hoped to solve when he finally got his interview.

"Maybe after getting these two letters, the Cardinal isn't sure who his friends really are. That was Baldano's warning, right?"

The message of Our Lady at Akita rang in Frannie's ears. She warned of a time where cardinals would oppose cardinals and bishops against bishops. But could such a dire prediction be solely about money?

"The Vatican Bank connection is reasonable," she said, "but what does a papal conspiracy and a possible money laundering scheme have in common?"

Daniel shrugged. "I guess that is what we are supposed to find out." He buried his head in his laptop and returned to his work.

Frannie's heart was troubled by the implications of Daniel's theory. The idea of digging further into the Bank's operations was not the slightest bit appealing. The wooden image of Our Lady of Akita stared back at her from her computer screen. One of the Lady's messages was to pray for the Pope, bishops, and priests. Frannie knew there were still faithful clergy within the hierarchy of the Church; her uncle wasn't completely without friends.

It is important to know one's friends from one's enemies, Baldano had advised.

Frannie decided to leave the enemies list to Daniel. She would turn her efforts to getting to know the clergy on the mysterious list she identified as friends. Inspired by the courage of Archbishop Kratzer, he seemed like a good place to start.

Chapter 7

A SMILE ERUPTED ACROSS FRANCESCA'S FACE WHEN she saw the tall and handsome Italian stand to greet her at the restaurant. She ran toward him and jumped into his arms.

"Alessandro!"

Alessandro squeezed her tightly, lifting her up off the ground. "Francesca! You are terrible for staying away so long. Over two years!" He let her down and they greeted each other with an Italian double cheek kiss.

"It's so good to see you," she said.

Alessandro pulled the chair out for her then took the seat across the table. The waiter appeared and they ordered wine and antipasti. Francesca got comfortable. She and her childhood friend had much to catch up on.

"Why so long since your last visit?" he asked.

"I've been busy."

"Yes, so I'm told. Big time television news star. That makes you too busy for your *Zio* and old friends?"

"Oh, don't start," she scolded light-heartedly.

Over the next course of food they caught up on each other's lives. By the time the second course appeared Francesca was getting around to the bizarre circumstances of her working arrangements with Daniel and the investigation into the letters *Zio* received. When she gave him her viewpoint on the names on the list, including the clergymen under suspicion he let out a low whistle.

"That is a bombshell of a list, Francesca. I don't like you looking into these matters."

"You make it sound like these men could be dangerous."

He leaned forward and spoke in a low whisper, "There were rumors at the time that Vidmar's death was unusual."

Francesca's face blanched. "You're not saying—"

"I'm saying that he received a clean bill of health from his doctor, and less than a week later he died of an apparent heart attack."

"Apparent? Couldn't they identify the cause of death with a fair amount of certainty?"

"Only if you do a complete autopsy. By all accounts he died alone so it didn't look like foul play. He was in his late seventies and no one saw a need to request anything further. They embalmed him quickly so he could lie in state at his cathedral."

"Then why suspect anything?"

"His housekeeper said he had been unusually distracted and anxious. She suspected it had to do with a guest he was expecting that evening for dinner but no one ever showed up. When she offered to clean up the trays of food she had laid out he refused and sent her home. She was also quite adamant that he was as healthy as a horse."

Francesca narrowed her eyes. "Who was the guest?"

"She wasn't sure. His appointment book disappeared."

"You think someone arrived after the housekeeper left?"

Alessandro shrugged. "Vidmar had enemies. He wanted an investigation into the Vatican Bank. He didn't exactly get along with the Cardinal who is the president of the Cardinals' Commission."

"Donati?" she asked, knowing full well the answer.

"Yes, I think that's his name. Anyway, tensions have been high since the papal election."

"Do you believe the rumors about the conspiracy?" she asked.

"It was a contentious conclave, Francesca. And look at what's happened in its aftermath. All I can say is, something's not right."

She squirmed in her seat. Now someone she trusted was hinting at papal conspiracy. She would have to share all of this with Daniel tomorrow.

Alessandro read the anxiety on her face. "I'm sorry. I didn't mean to worry you. Just be careful."

"Well, I'm not alone, remember?" she asked dryly.

"Oh, yes. Daniel. Is he nice?"

"I guess. I mean, it's only been a couple of days. We actually met on the flight here." She proceeded to tell the whole story of Daniel literally running into her at the airport and the shock of him showing up at the restaurant. By the time she finished, Alessandro was holding his sides in a fit of laughter.

"That's a really funny story. I'm kinda hoping he's 'the one.'"

Francesca made a face. "The one?" she repeated in disgust. "What on earth would make you say that?"

"So your mother will stop calling me to tell me about your love life. She calls me whenever you have a breakup with a serious boyfriend. There was Eric, Jordan—who was the last one? Oh, Brandon."

Francesca covered her face with her hands and groaned. "I think our parents betrothed us when we were six years old." Her mother constantly reminded her about Alessandro: still handsome, still single, and just a flight to Italy away.

Alessandro grew serious. "Francesca, there is something I want to tell you."

She peeked through her fingers. "What?" she asked apprehensively.

"After all my talk about conspiracy within the Church, you're going to think I'm crazy. But I've made the decision to join the seminary."

Her hands fell to the table. "To be a priest?"

"That's usually what you go to a seminary for," he said, grinning.

His news didn't really come as much of a shock. Francesca had always sensed a restless longing within him. He had only dated a handful of girls and seemed more content when he wasn't in a relationship. When they were kids, Alessandro would suddenly disappear but she always knew where to find him; in the church by his house, just sitting there in the silence. She asked him once, *What do you do in there for that long?* He answered, *I just listen.* Alessandro must have been hearing the call for some time.

"What happened to make you choose this?"

"I've been an EMT for many years now, and I've seen a lot. But something happened a couple of months ago that changed everything. We were called to a car accident outside the city. A young man had flipped his car multiple times and we had to pull him out. It was obvious his body had been severely crushed and he could barely breathe. He used every ounce of energy he had left to tell me he had never been baptized. And he wanted baptism. I grabbed a bottle of water out of the truck and administered an emergency baptism for him while he lay in the middle of the street. A sense of peace came over the young man like I have never seen. He thanked me, and then he gave up his last breath.

"Francesca, it was the strangest thing. I've rescued people, performed CPR and brought people back we thought would never breathe again. But, at that moment, I realized I wanted to bring back people who are spiritually dead. I'm being called to something more. Except for my parents, you're the first to know."

Francesca smiled sweetly at her old friend. She wasn't surprised he would confide in her. If her mother only knew she called

Alessandro after every one of her break ups, too. He had always been her confidant. And she had been his.

"When will you go?" she asked.

"I'm leaving for a month-long retreat in a couple of days. I need the time to fully surrender myself and to come to terms with my decision. I'll be gone most of the time while you're here." He added with a grin, "But, it sounds like you'll be busy, anyway."

She reached over and took his hand. "I don't think you're crazy, by the way. I wish I knew what I was being called to do. I'm a little jealous."

Frannie recounted how she had been losing a piece of her soul a little at a time. "Even though my time in adoration and the illumination of my conscience before confession helped me put things back in focus, I'm still unsure what to do about my career."

"Maybe that's why you are here in Italy. Pay attention to what brings you peace and what doesn't. You will have to discern the feelings further in prayer, but God will lead you where he wants you to go."

"Well, well. Father Alessandro," she said teasingly. "That's going to take some getting used to."

He looked down at their hands and placed his other on top of hers. "Do you remember when we were fifteen, and you were here for a visit? We were mad because our parents wouldn't let us date anyone, and we wanted to know what kissing was like."

Frannie knew where this was going. "Oh, boy. You're going to bring that up?"

"I remember that first kiss like it was yesterday," he said. "It is one of my most special and favorite memories. And I knew at that moment, I would always love you, Francesca. And yet, after every break up you had, after every call from you or your mother, I tried to convince myself to get on a plane and come to you. But

I couldn't. I think I've always known deep down that I love you but—" he broke off.

Francesca finished his sentence for him. "But in a different way."

They shared a look and neither had to say anything. The love between them was as strong as any married couple, but not romantic. It was a deep friendship that bonded them in a way few people experience.

Tears spilled down Francesca's cheeks. "I will always love you, too. Alessandro. You are truly my best friend."

She pulled her hand away and wiped at her tears. "But," she said, regaining her composure, "I'm never coming to you for confession."

They both laughed out loud.

"I think that's probably a good idea," he said. "I hope you and Daniel are still here when I get back. So I can meet him."

"Ugh. If I haven't strangled him."

"I think you like him," he teased.

"I do not!" Francesca spent the next half hour over coffee and tiramisu telling her friend the reasons why Daniel Fitzpatrick could never be "the one" for her.

Chapter 8

THE NEXT MORNING, DANIEL WAITED FOR FRANNIE at a small table outside the coffee shop near his apartment. He glanced at his watch and irritably scanned the street. He had received a text from her last night telling him she had something big to tell him and to meet her at the café at nine in the morning. *If this has something to do with food, I'm going to be furious.*

She suddenly came into view, smiling as she walked, as if she were the happiest person on the planet. The pink dress she wore was stylish without being too short and skimmed her curves without being too tight. Her long hair was pulled up, with a few strands left down, framing her face. He watched a few men turn their eyes in her direction, but Frannie was oblivious. When she sat down, she was still smiling.

"*Buongiorno!*" she said.

Daniel attempted to repeat the Italian morning greeting, "*Buongiorno.*"

She looked down at the empty table. "You haven't ordered yet?"

"Are we eating or talking? I thought you had some news to share."

Frannie flicked her gaze upward. Daniel's grumpy nature was reason number one why she could never date him. He didn't even stand up when she approached the table or pull the chair out for her. It didn't come as a surprise. She had only met one living and breathing male who knew how to treat a woman like a lady and he was going to be a priest.

"I am perfectly capable of eating a pastry, drinking a cappuccino, and talking at the same time," she said with a huff. "Do you want something?" she asked, more politely.

"Sure," he waved his hand. "Whatever you get is fine." He resigned himself to the fact that they would be at the café for a while. He reached down and pulled his laptop out of his bag. "Can you find out if they have a wifi password?" he asked.

Frannie returned with the password plus two cappuccinos and two pastries: one filled with an almond paste and the other with fruit jam. She prayed quickly, and cut the two pastries in half. Daniel assumed this meant they were sharing food again.

"I met a friend of mine for dinner last night," Frannie began as she reached for the almond half. She glanced around and was grateful there was no one sitting around them. She lowered her voice anyway. "He said that Vidmar was no friend of Donati's and very suspicious of the Vatican Bank." She proceeded to give Alessandro's account of the strange circumstances surrounding his death.

Daniel slowly digested the information. Frannie didn't seem like the type that would have friends that were off their rocker, but he found himself asking, "Do you trust this friend of yours?"

"With my life," she said firmly and without hesitation.

"If Vidmar's—" he made quotes in the air with his fingers— "heart attack was really foul play, then someone saw him as a threat. Given his suspicions of the Vatican Bank, maybe we should start there."

Frannie nodded. "Agreed."

Daniel began typing on his laptop. Frannie scooted her chair a little closer to watch. He did a quick search to see if he could find any stories of Vidmar and the Vatican Bank. The search came up with nothing of real interest.

"Can I try something?" Frannie asked.

He willingly turned the computer toward her and reached for half of the jelly pastry.

Her fingers traveled to the website for the newspaper, *Il Giornalista*, or, *The Reporter*. She searched their archived articles using Daniel's same key words. A list of hits popped up on the screen. When she engaged the translation feature, the Italian headlines appeared in English for Daniel to read:

> *Vidmar Accuses Vatican Bank of Scandal—Calls for Review*

> *Vidmar vs Donati? Vatican Downplays Rumors of Internecine Feud.*

> *Was Vidmar's Death by Natural Causes? Skeptics Claim Autopsy Part of Cover-Up*

Daniel numbly chewed his food as his eyes scanned the words displaying on the screen. He let Frannie click the article links and they bent forward towards the screen, their heads nearly touching.

After a quick rummage through the journal pieces, it was clear Cardinal Vidmar had been quite vocal about his disapproval of Donati and the administration of the Bank. And according to the sources at *Il Giornalista*, there was enough circumstantial evidence to suggest foul play was involved with Vidmar's death.

Frannie finished reading the last article and stole a glance in Daniel's direction. This close, she could see how the light freckles on his nose met up with a few that were sprinkled along his cheekbone. His freckles added a cherubic innocence to his appearance. If his personality ever reflected his good looks, she could easily find him irresistible.

Daniel leaned toward Frannie, turning his head to speak, and realized his lips nearly brushed her cheek.

He jerked back. "Sorry," he said, quietly.

Frannie flushed slightly, mortified that she had been the only one aware of their close proximity to each other.

Wishing to detract from his embarrassing moment, Daniel asked, "What type of journal is this?"

Frannie quickly gained control of herself. "It's a conservative outlet, but not widely known. Their editor in chief used to work as a reporter for the Vatican newspaper but got into a tiff with the editor and left to start his own magazine. I read some of their editorial pieces from time to time and I wouldn't say I always agree with them. I think what they report is factual but sometimes with a flair for the sensational."

"So what's your take on what we just read?"

Frannie was both shocked and flattered that he wanted her opinion. "I would guess that Vidmar was on to something within the workings of the Vatican Bank, but the feud could be some of the sensationalism I'm talking about. And yet, it looks like there are legitimate holes in the 'death by heart attack' claim. What is of interest to us is their suggestion that Donati has ties to the Garone family. That's a new lead; and a big deal."

Daniel nodded in agreement. "When I was researching Donati a few years back, I stumbled upon a few sources linking him to the Garone name. From what I know, the Garone family is a front for the Fratelli Mafia. They own businesses and restaurants and by all appearances keep their noses clean while they use their storefronts to export stolen art, jewelry, and firearms for the Fratellis. All the money made from their criminal transactions is hidden in their accounting books or paid under the table."

Frannie's mind was spinning. She had a theory but it made her stomach churn to think about it. "Do you think," she started hesitantly, "the Garone family is helping Donati with extra funds to pay off debt the Church has accrued, and they're using the Vatican Bank to do it?"

Daniel rubbed his hand across his face. "I'm not sure. I think you are right to form a triangle between Donati, Garones and the Bank. I feel like there's still more to it than Church debt. We still don't know why this would have anything to do with the conclave."

Frannie heard her phone vibrating in her bag. She expressed surprise when she saw who was calling her. "*Ciao, Zio!*" she said brightly.

Daniel could hear the Cardinal's muffled voice speaking in Italian.

"Yes, he's with me," Frannie used English as she spoke into the phone. She set it on the table and switched it to speaker mode. They had been at the café so long they were the only ones sitting outside. No one was around to eavesdrop.

"Hello, Daniel," the Cardinal greeted in a genial tone.

"Hello, your Eminence."

"I would like it if you two could come and see me this afternoon at my residence. Could you be here in three hours?"

Daniel glanced at his watch. It was already eleven o'clock. They had been there longer than he thought. He nodded his acceptance.

"Yes, *Zio*, we'll be there," Frannie answered for them.

They said goodbye and hung up.

Frannie closed the laptop. "Did you run this morning?"

"No, I had a conference call with the office."

"I'm going for a run on the Villa Doria Pamphili route. We should take a break and wait to talk to *Zio* before we go down any rabbit holes. Do you want to join me?"

"You mean, run together?" he asked.

"If you can keep up," she asked with a smug grin.

Daniel stared blankly at her. Her invitation caught him off guard. He was glad she had chosen to ignore his misstep earlier. He had miscalculated just how close they were sitting together. Before he jerked back, he caught a whiff of Frannie's perfume; a light jasmine. It reminded him of his grandmother's flower garden. He had forgotten how much he loved the smell.

"Relax, Fitzpatrick. I'm asking you to go on a run, not a date."

"I'm just surprised you are questioning my athletic prowess," he replied, trying to cover for his brief stupor. "I can keep up," he added, answering her challenge.

"Meet me at my apartment in twenty minutes?"

"I'll be ready."

Daniel glanced over at Frannie, jogging effortlessly in stride with him. They had been weaving through the trails of the park for nearly thirty minutes, and Daniel had to admit she was right; it was a beautiful place for a run.

The park was a delightful medley of meticulous gardens, a lake, unique water fountains, and large umbrella pines along the pathways. Daniel almost stopped to stare at a pristine white villa towering over a sea of green shrub labyrinths that stretched out in front of it. Frannie noticed it caught his eye.

"That's the *Casino del Bel Respiro*," she said, not slowing down. "It means, 'beautiful breath.'"

Daniel nodded, "That's a good name for it." He noticed Frannie spoke easily while she ran. Her stamina was impressive.

"You run at a good pace, Menconi," he said.

She shot him a smile. "Are you ready for the finish?"

Daniel heard a hint of taunting in her voice. "I said I could keep up."

He continued jogging next to her as they came to the end of the park and turned onto a street leading toward the top of Janiculum Hill. Daniel wasn't expecting a steep climb after the long run and pushed through the flare of an old nagging knee injury. He persevered enough to land at the top first, barely a step ahead of Frannie.

It took both of them a minute to catch their breath. She punched his arm lightly. "Good run, huh?"

"Yeah, it was!" he said, still a little out of breath. He looked up at the larger than life monument in front of him. On the top was a statue of a man who looked like a general on a horse.

"That's Giuseppe Garibaldi," Frannie said. "He was a nationalist and fierce guerilla warfare leader during Italy's wars of independence in the late 1800s. When a French army attacked, he led a battle that pushed them back on this hill. He was instrumental in the unification of Italy under Victor Emmanuel II, who became the first king. The king unified the country, but also left the pope landless with nothing but the Basilica, his residence, and a few other buildings. Basically, what we know today as Vatican City."

Frannie did a few stretches as Daniel walked around the monument. "Come on," she said, "let me show you the real reward for jogging up the hill."

She led him over to a populated terrace. Daniel could see over the tops of their heads why they were gawking: it opened up to a panoramic view of the city. Church domes, spires, a maze of buildings, and the massive monument of Victor Emmanuel II, all prominent in the historic Roman skyline.

They waited for a group of tourists with selfie sticks to disperse so they could move closer.

"Wow!" Daniel said. "You can see for miles."

Frannie stared out over the Eternal City. "It's amazing, isn't it?" she said quietly.

Her heart was heavy as she thought about the message in Baldano's letter: *It is no secret that Our Mother has warned us on more than one occasion.*

Secret. She was sure Baldano's word choice referred to the apparition of the Blessed Mother to three shepherd children at Fatima, Portugal. The Blessed Mother showed the children three visions accompanied by three "secrets," or explanations. The first two urged for the repentance of sinners and a command to consecrate Russia to her Immaculate Heart. If her command was ignored, Our Lady warned that "Russia would spread her errors throughout the world, causing wars and persecutions of the Church." The third secret was not released until the year 2000 by the Vatican. It revealed a vision of a "Bishop in white," which they assumed was the Holy Father. He was walking up a steep mountain, where there was a cross at the top. Before getting to the top, the Holy Father "passed through a big city, half in ruins." The Holy Father was accompanied by bishops, religious women, and others. The Bishop in white is described as being "afflicted with sorrow," and praying for the dead that he passed on the way. At the end of the vision, the Holy Father and the others were killed at the top of the hill, and angels were seen gathering their martyred blood.

Rome is known as the city built on seven hills, Frannie thought to herself. The thought of the pope walking through Rome in ruins made her stomach turn. According to the Vatican, the third secret was fulfilled when Pope John Paul II survived the assassination attempt on his life in 1981. Other theorists weren't so sure. Our Lady of Fatima had made it clear, "The good will be martyred; the Holy Father will have much to suffer." Did Baldano believe the suffering of the pope in the vision was yet to come? She shuddered at the thought.

A loud group of tourists startled her out of her trance. She glanced around for Daniel. He had moved on around the terrace and was taking in the view of St Peter's.

She hurried over to where he was standing. "We should start heading back."

"I was thinking," he said, "this is Rome; as in the Rome of Julius Caesar and Nero. This place can fill the pages of history dating farther back than the battle that occurred on this hill. I've never been to a place this old, and I'm realizing just how old the world really is. And what little time I spend on it in comparison."

"I know what you mean. You can visit Mamertine prison where Saints Peter and Paul were jailed, and the place where Paul was beheaded," she pointed toward Saint Peter's, "and Peter is buried underneath that Basilica. When you're here all of a sudden you realize these aren't just stories. It's real."

"And it's all still here," Daniel said.

"Yeah," Frannie said wistfully. "It's still here." Rome had endured fires, wars, and multiple invasions that sacked the city, and it survived them all. Whether or not the third secret of Fatima had been fulfilled, Frannie knew God had a plan. Either Rome could be damaged and rebuilt and the Blessed Mother's Immaculate Heart will triumph, or Jesus will come back for His Bride, the Church. And the Heavenly City will be far grander than even her beloved Rome. She needed to have hope and trust in the Lord. And Daniel was right. Her time on earth was short. Two years was way too long between confessions. She vowed to make it a regular habit.

She glanced over at Daniel. *Who knew Daniel Fitzpatrick could be so thoughtful and introspective?*

She grinned. "You've given me an idea for where we should have dinner tonight."

Daniel had returned from his musings and was back to business as usual. "We're going to dinner?"

Frannie shook her head disapprovingly. "Seriously? *Zio* must have something he wants to tell us."

"True. And heaven forbid we don't discuss it over food," he added sarcastically.

They started their way back down the hill. "When are you going to trust me? You're going to love this place."

"Do they serve salad? My body needs something other than pasta and bread."

She laughed. "You'll see."

Chapter 9

CARDINAL MENCONI'S RESIDENCE WAS NESTLED IN the Borgo district, only meters from the Vatican. The Cardinal reclined in a patio chair on the small balcony of his apartment, the dome of Saint Peter's dominating his view. He often implored the help of the impetuous fisherman when he felt his courage and faith wavering. How many times he had ventured out of the boat, hearing the call of Jesus to come to Him on the water, only to sink and cry out, "Lord, save me!" Even at the last conclave as he heard his name being read among the votes as a possible successor to Peter, the Cardinal silently echoed Peter's words, "Depart from me Lord, for I am a sinful man." While he was relieved he lived in Borgo and not the papal apartments, he regretted his prayer. If it had been a test, he failed miserably. His supplication should have echoed Jesus' words in the garden, "Not my will, but yours be done." *Saint Peter, pray for me; that I don't deny our Lord again.*

His reaction to Baldano's letter was a mixture of anger and sadness at the current battle within the Church. He took out his phone and read a mysterious email he had received for what felt like the hundredth time. It was yet another reminder that he was going to be hurled into the fray whether he wanted to be or not. Just like Peter.

Do with me what you will; but please protect Francesca from harm.

A knock at the door let him know his guests had arrived. He opened the door and welcomed them in. Francesca gave him a kiss on the cheek, and he extended his hand to Daniel. He liked the young man, and was grateful he had willingly agreed to watch over his niece.

"Can I offer you two a drink?" he asked.

"I could use a water," Daniel said.

"I'll get it, *Zio*," Francesca offered. "I need one too. Daniel and I went for a run and we are still thirsty."

The Cardinal raised his eyebrows at the news they had spent some leisure time together, but didn't draw attention to it. He motioned for Daniel to have a seat on the couch.

Daniel was a little intimidated to be in Cardinal Menconi's personal home. He surveyed the room, noting its modest size. The furniture and decorations were elegant, but not overly lavish. Most of the pictures on the wall were either sacred art images or pictures of religious sites. A picture frame on an end table held a photo of the Cardinal with a young girl. It took Daniel only seconds to recognize it was Frannie. They were standing in front of an altar in what appeared to be a small cave. She must have been thirteen or fourteen at the most.

Cardinal Menconi saw him looking at it and picked it up and handed it to him. "That's my favorite picture of us from our pilgrimage to the Holy Land. That's in the bottom level of the Basilica of the Annunciation in Nazareth, where the angel Gabriel appeared to Mary."

Daniel stared at the girl in the photo. The warm green eyes, the radiant smile, and the exuberant spirit remained unaltered in the woman Frannie had grown to be. Francesca Menconi was who she had always been. It was hard for Daniel not to like her for it.

Frannie appeared with two glasses of water. Daniel smiled and handed the photo back. "You look the same," he said to her as she handed him a glass.

She wrinkled half of her nose. "Thanks...I think."

Turning to her uncle, she changed the subject. "What do you have to tell us, *Zio*? I'm sure you have a reason for inviting us here."

Francesca could read him like a book. "I do, but tell me what you two have discovered so far."

Francesca gave him a summary of their suspicions regarding Donati and the Vatican Bank, and his involvement with Cardinal Constantini on the board of *Compassione*. "Our search also revealed speculations that Donati has connections to the Garone family. Do you know if that's true?"

"I know the rumors about mafia connections to the Bank. Since they are only rumors I will leave that up to you two to investigate. However, Donati does have a direct connection to the Garone family."

Daniel dug in his bag for a pad and pen. "What kind of direct connection, sir?"

"Fortino Donati is the oldest of seven children. His youngest sister Elena, being a rebellious adolescent, fell in love with Massimo Garone when she was sixteen. She ran off with him, and came back two years later with a baby boy," he paused a beat, "and bruises all over her body. He brutally beat her routinely but somehow Elena managed to escape with her son, Giovanni. When Massimo showed up at the Donati home demanding Elena and his child return to him, Father Fortino Donati met him at the door. How he came to an agreement with the Garone family, I do not know. But Massimo left Elena alone and Fortino stepped in as Giovanni's godfather to be a father-like figure to his nephew. Massimo died a few months later. In a drunken state, he attacked a family member, and they got into a struggle. A gun went off accidentally while the cousin tried to wrestle the gun away from him."

"Where are they now?" Frannie asked.

"By the time Fortino was appointed the Archbishop of Milan, Elena had married a respectable businessman and Giovanni was graduating college. Elena and her family decided to follow Fortino there and they took over management of a restaurant."

Daniel perked up. "A restaurant? One of the Fratelli ventures, perhaps?"

The Cardinal shook his head. "I understand that Giovanni and Elena separated from the family."

Daniel's eyes narrowed. "What do you mean, 'separated from the family?'"

"They removed themselves from the Garone family and their illegal operations; they have never associated with the Fratelli Mafia."

"And you believe this?" Daniel asked.

The Cardinal shrugged his shoulders. "That's what I was told by Cardinal Donati himself."

He saw his niece's eyes widen. "Yes, Francesca, I used to be friends with Fortino." The Cardinal eyes were sad. "I find it very hard to listen to the rumors about him and the Bank. The Fortino I knew would never be involved in such corruption. Or, for that matter, go along with a progressive agenda."

"What about Cardinal Vidmar, sir? He was a friend of yours. But he apparently butted heads with Donati."

The Cardinal took a deep breath. "Jozef Vidmar was an honest and good man. He wouldn't allege something just to ruin someone's reputation. I'm sure he had his reasons."

Daniel and Fannie exchanged looks. Both knew from the Cardinal's reaction he thought there was more to the story. They watched him get up and retrieve a piece of paper lying on his dining table.

"I asked you two here because of an email I received." It was obvious he didn't want to discuss Donati's family history any further. "I have been invited to a charity benefit at the Duomo in Milan. The *Cappella Musicale del Duomo* will be in concert with cocktails beforehand at the *Veneranda Fabbrica*. Cardinal Constantini has invited me for dinner afterwards."

Daniel scooted toward the edge of the couch. "Did he say why he wants to meet?"

"I'll translate his words." Cardinal Menconi read from the paper he held. "Although we hold different opinions about the direction of the Church, we must come together to lead the flock. It is prudent for both sides to be unified. We cannot afford a quarrelsome conclave."

"A conclave?" he asked. "Aren't those only convened upon the death of a pope?"

"It is rumored the pope is not well."

"And Constantini's already preparing for the election?" Daniel asked rhetorically. "Are any of the other clergy from the list being invited to benefit?"

"Donati will probably be there, but no others I am aware of."

"You can't go, *Zio!*" Frannie blurted out, interjecting into their conversation.

The Cardinal looked at her quizzically.

Frannie retreated from her dictatorial tone. "I mean, I don't think it is a good idea. We uncovered something else. We read about the theories surrounding Vidmar's death. Based on what you just told us about Donati, I don't think you should be alone with either of these men."

She locked her eyes with her uncle for several seconds. He knew the rumors about Vidmar's death. Seeing the anxiety in Francesca's eyes gave him pause. The idea that meeting the Cardinal for dinner would be dangerous hadn't crossed his mind.

"So you think I make an excuse not to go?"

Frannie glanced at Daniel, then back to her uncle. "I think you should send two ambassadors in your place."

The Cardinal shook his head emphatically. "Absolutely not! If you think it is dangerous for me, why would I send you into the dragon's lair?"

"You gave us this job, so trust us to do it!" she fired back. She began speaking passionately in Italian and within seconds the two were yelling over each other.

Daniel stood up and held out both hands. "All right, all right! Hey—*Basta!*"

His use of Italian shocked them both into silence.

Daniel sat back down. "Pardon me, your Eminence. But, I think Frannie is right. It smells fishy. What would Constantini hope to gain by meeting with you? He knows where you stand; does he really think he is going to change how you would vote? Trying to convince you otherwise seems like an exercise in futility. And, I hate to say it, but there is a hint of a threat in between the lines. It is as if he is accusing you of trying to organize dissent among the cardinals."

Daniel continued, "Accept his invitation. When we show up in your place, he will either graciously extend the dinner invitation to us, or decline. Whatever happens, he won't harm us. It would be unwanted publicity that would send conspiracy theorists spinning stories for months."

The Cardinal patted his hand on his chin. Daniel's arguments made sense. "I will write him back and suggest a restaurant in a popular area just in case. If I claim it is my favorite he shouldn't question it."

Daniel smiled. "Good. It's all settled."

Frannie dug out her phone and opened up her calendar. "When is it, *Zio*? Tomorrow I'll make a hotel reservation under your name."

He gave her a brochure of the event. "The second week of June."

"Can I see that?" Daniel asked.

Frannie entered the date and time in her phone and handed it to him. "It's in two weeks. We have some planning to do." Her head was already turning. Constantini was no fool. Their plan would need to be well thought out prior to leaving for Milan.

"What a surprise," Daniel said dryly. "It's a benefit for *Compassione*. I really hope he extends that dinner invitation to us. I would love the chance to ask him a few questions."

"Speaking of invitations," Cardinal Menconi directed toward Daniel, "has Frannie invited you to Sunday dinner?"

Frannie's face went blank. "To—*Zia* Rosa's?" she stammered. "Er, no. I haven't," she added, a bit embarrassed her uncle assumed she would have already invited him. It seemed odd to her that he would want Daniel at a family gathering.

Daniel felt as uncomfortable as Frannie looked. "That's okay, really. I'm sure Frannie would like some time alone with her family."

The Cardinal waved his hand. "Nonsense! You are like family now. You'll join us for Mass Sunday morning, yes?"

Frannie raised her eyebrows and looked expectantly at Daniel. *How was he going to get out of this one?* she thought.

Daniel fiddled with the brochure he was still holding. "Would it be possible, your Eminence, if I only joined you for dinner?"

Cardinal Menconi nodded. "Of course, *mio figlio.* I'll send my driver to pick you up."

Frannie stood up. She was still a little miffed at her uncle not warning her about his intentions for Sunday. "We should probably go, *Zio.*"

They exchanged goodbyes and left the apartment building in silence. Once on the street, Daniel said, "I'm sorry about Sunday. I didn't want to offend him. You can tell him I'm not feeling well," he offered.

Frannie felt a pang of guilt for outwardly showing her displeasure. She smiled politely. "No, he wants you to come or he wouldn't have asked you."

"What did he say? Something about a fig?"

"*Mio figlio*. It means, 'my son.' Like I said, he wants you to come to dinner because he likes you."

Daniel felt a tug on his heart. No one had ever called him 'son' before. If his mother did he couldn't remember it. The Cardinal had said it with such tenderness. He replayed the words in his mind: *mio figlio.*

"It's a little early for dinner," Frannie said, "but there's a lot to see along the way. Do you have something else you need to do?"

Daniel whipped his head around. "What?"

She thought she saw a brief flash of pain in his eyes. "Are you okay?"

"Yeah, why wouldn't I be?" he asked defensively.

"Do you want to do a little sightseeing on the way to dinner?" she repeated, ignoring the fact that he was obviously lying.

Daniel shook off whatever weird sense of emotion he was feeling. "Lead the way."

Chapter 10

A GAGGLE OF TOURISTS SWARMING ROME'S FAMOUS Trevi Fountain required Daniel and Frannie to wait at the back of the crowd for their turn at the front. Daniel gaped at the number of people trying to get close enough to throw a coin over their shoulder and into the water.

"Are you going to do it?" Frannie asked, giving him a little nudge with her elbow.

"Fight all of those people to throw a coin in some water fountain? No thanks!"

"It isn't just some water fountain," she said with slight indignation. "Its source dates back to the Roman aqueducts that provided the citizens with water. The current design and statues were commissioned by the pope in the mid-1700s."

"It is rather majestic, I'll give you that," he said, in awe of its grandeur and crystalline blue water. In the center, a tall male statue stood regally upon a sea shell chariot, led by two winged horses. A Triton flanked each of the horses; one blowing a seashell like a trumpet, the other wrestling the unruly steed. Water flowed from underneath the chariot, cascading down a three-tiered waterfall.

"Is that Neptune?" he asked

"Oceanus, actually. He was seen as the god of fresh water rather than the god that ruled the sea."

Several people were beginning to leave, freeing up some space. "Oh come on," she said, "have a little fun!"

Frannie grabbed his arm and pulled him through the crowd until they were within coin-throwing distance at the base of the fountain. She dug in her purse for some change.

"The legend is, if you throw one coin, you will return to Rome quickly. Two coins, you will find romance." She gave him a playful smile, "Three coins and you will find romance and get married."

When she opened her hand, three Euro coins lay inside her palm.

"Choose your own fate, Fitzpatrick."

Daniel couldn't help but laugh. "You're a piece of work, Menconi."

He took one in his right hand, held it up in front of her nose, and then tossed it over his left shoulder. "There. Are you happy now?"

She giggled. "What a chump. There went your chance for romance and happily ever after."

"Ha! I'll take my chances." People were starting to crowd in again. "Can we go now?" he asked.

The next stop was the Pantheon. Daniel stood on the steps staring up at the triangular pediment and columns. The awe of the ancient history that took hold of him at the top of Janiculum Hill washed over him again.

"When was this built?"

"This structure was completed in the early second century. It sits on the site of a previous pagan temple constructed by the son-in-law of Augustus Caesar."

"Whoa. And it's still here," he said, echoing his words from earlier.

"It started out as a pagan temple, but now it's the Basilica of Saint Mary and the Martyrs."

Inside he got a look at the oculus, the nearly ten-yard diameter hole at the center of the dome. Frannie explained the floor was slightly curved so that any rain flows away from the center and down a drainage system.

"There are no windows," she said, "so the hole is the only light source of the building."

He shook his head. "It really is incredible."

She then led Daniel to their final destination: Largo di Torre Argentina. She stopped on the sidewalk, overlooking ruins of Roman columns and steps. "Those," she said, "are the ruins of Pompey's theater complex where Julius Caesar was killed."

"No way!" he exclaimed.

"This end was the Roman Senate House, and at the other end, separated by a long portico, was the theater. Its original walls are still visible in Da Pancrazio, the restaurant where we're going to have dinner!" she stated, proud of her surprise reveal. "You were so reflective about ancient Rome at Janiculum Hill, I knew you had to see this."

Daniel turned, his eyebrows squished together.

Frannie could see he was totally perplexed. She repeated his words from earlier, "The filling of the pages of history...the world being so old and ancient but still here...I thought it would be even more surreal to stand so close to an event that happened before the time of Christ."

Daniel realized his reaction must seem eccentric. His confusion wasn't why she brought him here; it was because somehow she knew he would like it. The pounding in his chest alarmed him.

He let his face relax into a smile. "Thank you for bringing me here." He looked back out over the ruins. "It's one of the nicest things anyone has done for me in a long time."

Frannie found herself feeling sorry for him. Her mini ancient Rome tour didn't seem like a big deal to her. How could Daniel not have any friends? He wasn't such a horrible person that he shouldn't have at least one or two good ones.

Daniel interrupted her thoughts, "How do you know all of these historical facts?"

"I worked as a guide for a Catholic tour company for a couple of summers during college."

"Hmm. You must have had fun doing it."

"It was an easy gig. All I had to do was be excited to tell the groups about Rome, the Vatican, and all Italy has to offer. I made a killing in tips."

I bet you did, he mused. Frannie's bubbly personality combined with a genuine love for the culture would have been contagious. Add in her lovely face and glowing smile and she could win the heart of anyone.

"So, where's this restaurant?" he asked. He needed to distract himself from his meandering thoughts.

They arrived at Da Pancrazio in less than five minutes. Frannie asked the waiter for a table in the basement, where the walls of the theater had been preserved. Daniel looked around at the historic Roman hallway, now lined with dining tables. The bottom half of an old pillar stood at the end of the room, a remnant of the empire that once ruled the world.

"You're right. This is surreal," he said. "Like I've stepped back in time."

"Italy is good for the soul." She smiled, "And the stomach. I'm hungry."

Daniel opened his menu. "Hey! They have pages in English!"

"I recommend the vignarola soup for you as a starter. It's full of green vegetables."

Daniel peeked at Frannie over the top of his menu. A medal of the Virgin Mary hung around her neck, reminding him of a painful childhood memory. The dull ache vanished quickly; she had on the pink dress she wore to the café that morning, when he learned she smelled like jasmine. The sensation of heat flared in his chest again. *Don't get pulled in,* he warned himself.

"I'm getting the artichoke ravioli," she announced. "What are you getting?"

"The lamb special."

"Are you up for sharing plates?"

"I didn't know I had a choice," he said, smirking.

She threw him a look for his sassy comment. "I'm offering to share the eggplant parmigiana with you, if you're interested."

The waiter appeared. When Daniel ordered, he added the soup she suggested and the eggplant dish. He had never had it before but Frannie seemed to have a talent for selecting delicious food.

Frannie held up her wine glass. "*Salute!*" she said.

Daniel imitated her, "*Salute!*" and clinked his glass to hers.

"Thank you, by the way," Frannie said after taking a drink, "for helping me convince *Zio* not to go to Milan."

He felt a little guilty for not telling her about the warning her uncle received, but he had given his word to the Cardinal. Regardless of being kept in the dark, Frannie's intuitive instincts were on the money. "Between Donati's family history and Vidmar, I think you were right to advise him to stay away."

Daniel's readiness to treat her like an equal colleague astounded her. She had pegged him as the arrogant, chauvinistic type.

"Your uncle mentioned you had a degree in journalism. Are you a writer?" he asked.

"No. I went into television. I grew up watching the Boston evening news with my dad. He would explain what was going on in the world to me in a way that I could understand, but taught me at an early age how to think critically about what was being reported. One of the evening news anchors was Suzanne Thompson. I thought she was the most elegant woman on television. I wanted

to be just like her when I grew up. I'm working for the same local station, but I'm light years from being an anchor."

"What do they have you doing?"

"I'm an on-the-scene reporter. You know," she sat up straight, painted a plastic smile on her face, and added a lacquered gentility to the timbre of her voice. "Reporting live from the capitol, I'm Francesca Menconi, 9 news." She rolled her eyes. "Actually, I rarely report from the capitol. I get sent to cover the dumbest news stories. I think it's because Will Kelly doesn't like me."

"Is he the station owner?"

"No, he's been their lead anchor for thirty years. Suzanne Thompson has retired, but he is still there. And he may not be the owner but he certainly calls the shots. The running joke is that he is the biggest 'ass-set' at the station. I have been busting my butt at that place since I graduated from college six years ago. From intern, to writer, to a few TV spots on the weekends and now, finally, on-the-scene reporter. There was an opening for the morning show, and I nailed the audition. Everyone said so. But they chose some young upstart who had only been at the station for two years. I think Will was behind the decision."

"What makes you think he doesn't like you?"

"One of my first assignments as a reporter was to cover an altercation that happened in front of a Planned Parenthood Clinic. A family that belonged to one of the pro-life groups was praying peacefully across from the facility, within the required boundaries, and a car drove by and threw a metal pipe at them, hitting their teenage daughter. She was injured pretty badly.

"At first, it was reported that the attack was from the pro-life group on a girl trying to enter the Planned Parenthood clinic. When it was revealed what really happened, pro-life advocates from all over the area came to pray where the accident took place and at the capitol, asking the local and national news to report the truth and rescind the original story. So, they sent me—the girl with a Catholic Cardinal for an uncle—to cover it. I still think it was on purpose," she added bitterly.

"They had certain questions they wanted me to ask. Most of them were politically charged from the pro-choice point of view, and none of them got to the heart of the matter. So, I asked a couple of the questions they wanted, then asked follow up questions that allowed them to tell their side of the story and a true account of the events. It just so happened the father of the girl who was assaulted was there, and I was able to get him on camera for the interview. By the time he was done telling his side, no one was going to belittle him. He told his story from the heart and wasn't afraid to shed tears over his innocent daughter.

"Needless to say, Will was livid. I was accused of putting my own religious agenda ahead of the job. Which is nuts because they sent me to interrogate rather than interview. The exchange with the girl's father is what saved me. By all accounts I was reporting the truth as it was being told to me by an eye-witness. I wasn't fired but I've been basically blocked from any advancement at the station."

The waiter had arrived with Daniel's soup and a salad Frannie had ordered. She crossed herself and said grace aloud. Daniel waited patiently for her to finish.

"It's funny isn't it?" he asked, allowing his soup to cool. "We are supposed to report the truth, but sometimes no one really wants it. Or they want their own slanted version. I ran into the same thing several years ago. I submitted an article I had been asked to write about the gender gap between the salaries of men and women. I incorporated the results of a study out of Harvard that found that women tended to work less hours and were less likely to volunteer for overtime than men. And for most, it was their choice to do so; women with children wanted to be home at a certain time and not at the job. I got called into the editor's office where I was told I needed to reconsider my position." He shook his head. "My article cited several other studies, but I included the one from Harvard because it presented a whole different point of view. I wasn't going to change what I wrote, so I told them where to go and walked out."

"And that's how you got to *The Classic Journalist?*"

He nodded and swallowed his bite of soup before replying, "It's been a good move for me. Have you considered a different area of journalism?"

Frannie sighed. *Not until this week,* she thought dryly. *Zio,* Alessandro, and her time in Adoration all seemed to be pointing her to a career change. Having Daniel Fitzpatrick mention it was even more annoying.

"Everyone makes it sound so easy," she said, irritably. "Have you ever had a dream of something you wanted more than anything, so you work your butt off for it, and just when you thought it was about to become a reality, it's yanked away from you?"

Daniel stared blankly at her. There had been more than one dream yanked away from him. He knew the pain all too well.

Frannie took his silence as a "no" to her question. "I don't expect you to understand. It's just hard for me to let it go."

They finished their salad and soup in silence. When the waiter brought the main course, Frannie tried to sound more upbeat as she took some of Daniel's eggplant dish.

"What should we do about the connection between Donati and the Garone family? Is a story that old worth looking into?" she asked.

Daniel was glad to have something to talk about besides deep personal matters. "You know what I thought about when your uncle told that story?" He didn't wait for an answer. "*The Godfather* movie."

"Which part?" Frannie lowered her voice and produced a thick New York accent, "'I'm gonna make him an offer he can't refuse,' or 'leave the gun, take the cannoli?'"

Daniel chuckled. He was impressed she could recite quotes from the iconic film. "You would make a good mobster, Menconi, but I wasn't thinking about either of those. In the first film, it was revealed there was a rule that the mob didn't make hits on cops because it would draw too much attention. I wonder if the Garone family was upset that Massimo drew negative attention from the Church. Massimo's death could have been an inside job."

"And if Massimo was as big of a hothead as he sounds, no one would second guess the story." She gasped and dropped her fork, barely catching it before it fell to the floor. "Do you think Donati would have made an agreement with the family in exchange for vengeance for his sister? A deal to protect them and shield the real nature of their business?"

Daniel shrugged. "It would explain the long history between him and the Garones. And how Giovanni, his godson, has been able to remain detached from the family mob business. It makes sense." He let out a cynical laugh. "The godfather made them an offer they couldn't refuse."

Frannie's heart sank. Catholic clergy ensconced in greed and embezzlement were bad enough; to be complicit in a murder sounded much worse. She wanted to be wrong. "We're just speculating. Maybe it was just an accident."

Daniel didn't want to douse her hopes. While the details were a speculation, he was fairly certain Massimo's death was not an accident.

After dinner, they began their trek back to their apartments. All of a sudden, Frannie turned off the sidewalk. Daniel didn't know exactly where they were, but his sense of direction was always on point. He knew she was headed the wrong way.

"Where are you going?" he asked. "The Vatican is over there," he said, pointing in the other direction. Both of their apartments were located within blocks of Saint Peter's Square.

"My favorite gelato place is on this side of town. I haven't been here in two years and I am going to enjoy it all."

"Of course it's food related," he muttered.

The line was long but they finally reached the counter. The freezer case was filled with mounds of creamy clouds of gelato: vanilla white, chocolate brown, and bright pastel colors in tantalizing fruit flavors. Frannie ordered a cup with lemon and pistachio.

"What do you want?" she asked Daniel.

"I'll pass."

"Seriously?"

"Yes."

She reached in her purse to pay the clerk, then shook her head. "No, you can't. He'll have a small cup of stracciatella."

Daniel growled out loud. "You are so bossy."

"Here," she said, handing him a cup of what appeared to be the Italian version of chocolate chip ice cream. "Enjoy."

Daniel made a face and followed her to a side bench. He sat down with a huff and angrily shoved the plastic spoon in the cup and took a bite.

Frannie watched him engage in a war with his dessert, then settle into a cease fire. "Well?" she asked, noticing he was eating more slowly and no longer using his spoon like a weapon.

Daniel wasn't sure what annoyed him more: that she ordered for him like he was a four-year-old or that the gelato was the most delicious type of ice cream he had ever tasted. He waited until he finished his last bite before answering.

"Yes. You are still bossy."

Frannie giggled, guessing he couldn't bring himself to admit he liked it. "It's that good, huh?"

"I plead the Fifth. What do you plan on doing tomorrow?"

They rose from the bench and started walking. "I have something I want to look into. Why don't we research on our own? We can discuss our findings at *Zia* Rosa's on Sunday."

Daniel agreed. He had a few things he wanted to look into himself.

They came to a stop at Frannie's street.

"Good night," she said.

"Frannie, I—" he stopped. It was hard for him to say what was on his mind. "I really had a good time today. The run, the ruins; all of it was great. Thank you."

Frannie felt a pang of sadness for him again. It was satisfying to know she had been able to bring him some amount of happiness.

"I'm glad, Daniel. You're welcome."

"I'll see you on Sunday."

She nodded and watched him walk away. She wasn't sure what to make of Daniel Fitzpatrick, or the fluttering that was occurring in her stomach.

Chapter 11

Daniel stood on the corner of his street waiting for Cardinal Menconi's driver. Frannie had texted him, telling him the driver would be arriving shortly. He wished she would have taken him up on his offer to excuse himself from going to the Menconi family dinner. He was sure he was going to feel more like an intruder than a guest.

There was a small part of him that was anxious to see Frannie. He buried it, dismissing it as nothing more than wanting to share what he had unearthed in his digging around yesterday.

A black sedan appeared and slowed to a stop at the corner. A man hopped out wearing a black suit and a buoyant smile. He was tall and burly, with jet black hair, accented by thin threads of silver on his temples. Daniel guessed him to be in his late fifties.

"*Buongiorno!*" the driver greeted, "*Signore* Daniel?"

"*Sì*, that's me."

The driver walked around the car and opened the back passenger door.

Daniel was a little embarrassed to be chauffeured in such a manner. "*Grazie*," he said, attempting to use what little Italian he had picked up from listening to Frannie.

The driver climbed in and quickly pulled away.

"How is your visit to *Roma* so far, *Signore*?" he asked.

"It's been great. The food is fantastic."

The driver bobbed his head enthusiastically, "*Sì, sì!* You have been able to see some of the city?"

"Yes. Frannie–the Cardinal's niece–took me to Janiculum Hill, the Pantheon, and the ruins of Pompey's theater. It's incredible."

"You are lucky, *Signore* Daniel, to have the Menconis as your host while here. They are a wonderful family."

Daniel hadn't thought of the Cardinal and Frannie as his "host," but the driver was right; they had assumed the role graciously. "They have been very kind. What's your name, sir?"

"Paolo."

"Nice to meet you, Paolo. How long have you worked for Cardinal Menconi?"

"Twenty-five years," he answered proudly, "I owe Cardinal great debt. He saved my son's life." Before Daniel could inquire, Paolo continued, "My son, Emilio, got in with a bad group of boys when he was a teenager. He was doing and dealing drugs, and it almost killed him. Cardinal Menconi dropped everything to come and see him in the hospital. He took care of the cost of his," he fumbled for the English word, "the place where addicts go."

"Rehabilitation center?" Daniel offered.

"Yes. Rehabilitation. And Cardinal went and saw him every day. Talked and prayed with him. All of this for the son of his driver! Now Emilio is married with three good kids. Cardinal has baptized each one! He now works in the same rehabilitation place helping others with addiction. I told Cardinal I will work for him until I cannot work anymore. I give my life for him."

Daniel was moved by Paolo's heartfelt testimony. Daniel was still cautious of those in charge of organized religions but had come to believe Cardinal Menconi was one of the good guys.

"We are here, *Signore*."

The car stopped in a residential area of homes and apartments. Daniel looked out his window at *Zia* Rosa's house: an old two-story salmon-colored villa. A solid half wall fence lined the perimeter. The entry point was a black wrought iron gate.

Daniel tried to exhale the apprehension out of his body. By the time he opened his door, Paolo was beside him, holding a bouquet of flowers.

"Here, *Signore*. Give these to *Signora* Rosa." He chuckled. "I thought you might not think of flowers for your hostess!"

Daniel felt like a heel. It never occurred to him to ask if he should bring anything. He reached in his back pocket for his wallet. "Thank you, Paolo. You probably just saved me from a lifetime of embarrassment. Let me pay you for them."

Paolo waved his hand. "No, no! Cardinal told me to take good care of you. So I take care of you." Before Daniel could argue further, he bounded around the front of the car. "I'll be back later to pick up you and *Signorina* Francesca. *A presto!*"

"*A presto*," Daniel repeated robotically, assuming it was some form of goodbye. He opened the latch to the black gate and found himself in a large tiled terrace-like patio, greeted by the sound of children's laughter. Seven children were chasing another who was on a kick scooter. Straight ahead was an old wooden door, half open. He dodged his way through the children and entered hesitantly.

He heard voices and made his way down the short hallway. At the end, to his left was the kitchen, where most of the family was gathered. A few others were in the combined living and dining room to his right. A young woman left the living room and came to greet him. She wore more make-up than necessary, heavily coating her otherwise pretty face. Her yellow dress left nothing to the imagination of her curvy and well-endowed figure.

She smiled seductively at him. "*Ciao.* You must be Daniel. This is a pleasant surprise." The way she looked him up and down made him very uncomfortable.

Daniel was relieved to see Frannie walking towards them. "Hey there," she said, "You should have texted me when you arrived.

I would have met you out front." She gave the young woman a cursory glance. "Daniel, this is my cousin, Lorena," she said flatly.

"It was nice meeting you," Lorena said, giving him a sultry look before going back to the living room.

Frannie pretended not to notice her cousin's unabashed flirtation. "Flowers?" she asked.

"For *Signora* Rosa," he said, stealing the phrase from Paolo.

Frannie tilted her head. "That was very thoughtful of you."

Daniel heard the surprise in her voice and felt a twinge of guilt. *Yeah, that's me, Mr. Thoughtful.*

Frannie motioned towards the kitchen. "Come on. I'll introduce you."

Rosa Morelli was a joyful and vivacious woman with gray hair pinned up on her head; a few natural curls framed her round and pretty face. She beamed at the flowers and greeted Daniel as if he had been a friend of the family for years.

"Nico is outside," Rosa said. "He has been waiting for you. But not as anxiously as Frannie," she added, laughing.

Frannie's jaw tightened and she felt her face get hot. She spewed out a rapid sling of Italian words at her aunt. "Italian relatives," she muttered to Daniel, "they say everything they think, whether it's true or not."

A sliding door from the kitchen led outside to the rear patio. It had taken Daniel a few moments to realize "Nico" was Cardinal Nicolo Menconi, Rosa's brother. He was sitting in a plastic chair, dressed in his black cassock and cardinal red piping, with a beer in his hand. He stood up to greet Daniel and Frannie.

"Ah! *Buongiorno!* Can we get you a beer, Daniel?"

"Just water for me, please."

The Cardinal looked a little embarrassed. "I don't think we have any water in the cooler out here."

"I'll get you a glass," Frannie offered, and headed towards the kitchen.

The Cardinal gestured towards an empty chair, "Have a seat."

Daniel took the chair next to him. "Thank you again for the invitation, your Eminence."

"It's good to have you. No business talk today. Just relax and enjoy. Let me introduce you." Daniel was introduced to Rosa's husband, Berto, and their three sons. The eight children running around the terrace were also introduced, all grandchildren of Rosa and Berto. By the time he was introduced to Lorena's parents, Daniel had so many names in his head it was like a bowl of Italian alphabet soup.

Frannie returned with a glass of water for Daniel and sat next to her uncle.

"I'm sure you've made the connection," the Cardinal said, "Francesca's father, Franco, was my brother. I'm the oldest. Rosa and I have another brother and sister but they live in Venice and Florence."

Frannie laughed. "When all the Menconi brothers and sisters and their children get together, we have to book a wing of a hotel out on the coast. No one has a big enough house to fit us all!"

"What about you, Daniel?" the Cardinal asked. "Do you have a big family?"

Daniel's mouth went dry. "No," he said quietly.

Frannie saw a flash of pain in his eyes again; like when she told him *Zio* had called him "son."

Rosa came out and announced it was time for dinner. Frannie watched Daniel's cheeks puff out slightly as he exhaled, obviously relieved he didn't have to answer any more questions about his family.

Frannie let *Zio* and the others file into the house ahead of her, so she could walk with Daniel. She shot him a reassuring smile. "Dinner can be a little intimidating. I'll help you navigate."

"I can't believe your aunt cooked for this many people."

"The women in the family help and pitch in. I hope you're hungry!"

The Morelli dining room table was actually two tables put together with a large white tablecloth covering them both. It was just big enough to get all the adults and children crammed around it. Daniel and Frannie sat next to each other with the Cardinal on Daniel's other side and Rosa next to Frannie. To Frannie's delight, Lorena was seated way down at the other end.

The table was set with Rosa's nice dishes, silverware, and wine glasses. Daniel's flowers were in a vase and placed in the center of the table. Once everyone was seated, Cardinal Menconi gave the blessing and everyone raised their glasses of wine in a toast. Then bowls of salad, pasta, meat sauce, and baskets of bread were passed around the table. Daniel had never been to a family dinner so large and with so much food. The loud and boisterous members all spoke Italian so he didn't know what the conversations and laughter were about. Frannie was right; it was a little intimidating.

Frannie and the Cardinal took turns translating a few of the stories for him. After the second pass of food and fill of wine glasses, Rosa's son, Tommaso, asked Daniel some questions about America; mostly regarding the tech job market and what it was like living in Chicago. Frannie was lightly paying attention to their conversation while visiting with Rosa. Daniel was telling Tommaso about downtown Chicago and the waterfront along Lake Michigan. A comment from Daniel tickled her ears.

"My favorite place in Chicago is Wrigley Field where the Cubs play. There's nothing like it." He saw Tommaso's blank face. He remembered soccer, known as football in Europe, was the main sport in Italy. "It's a baseball fan thing."

"Oh, baseball," Tommaso said. "That's Francesca's sport. We can't get her to watch football. We tease her about not really being Italian." His brothers overheard and chuckled along with him.

Daniel turned to Frannie. "You like baseball?" he asked.

Her face was serious. "I am a Boston Red Sox fanatic. And I get what you're saying about Wrigley Field. I feel the same way about Fenway Park."

"There's something about the old fields, right?" Daniel became animated with passion, "There's history in the soil, in the bleachers that just infuses the whole park. It's timeless; like a goodness that has been preserved and not dismantled in the name of progress."

"Totally!" she exclaimed. "The new mega parks are just not the same." She held up her palm in a halting stop. "Wait a minute, I have an important question to ask you. Do you like the Yankees?"

Daniel made a face. "The Yankees? I can't stand the Yankees."

"Oh thank goodness," Frannie sighed. "I didn't know if I could continue working with you otherwise."

For a second, Daniel sank into Frannie's twinkling green eyes that smiled playfully at him. He flashed her a mischievous smile. "That makes two of us."

They spent the rest of the dinner reminiscing about the seventh game in the 2016 World Series when the Cubs won in the extra tenth inning. Frannie knew every player and could recall with Daniel every moment of the memorable inning. When they finished, Frannie glanced up to find they were some of the last remaining at the table.

Frannie's back straightened and she awkwardly finished her last bite of food. She was suddenly aware she had gotten lost in a conversation with Daniel Fitzpatrick about baseball. She couldn't believe they held something in common. She stood up and picked up his plate with hers.

"I should help Rosa and the others clean up," she announced and headed for the kitchen.

Daniel was a little startled at her abrupt departure. He stared at her empty chair, still reeling that they shared a love for baseball. He got up and headed outside with the rest of the family, trying to distract himself from daydreaming about sitting with her at Wrigley Field enjoying a hotdog, and how cute she would look in a Cubs baseball cap.

Paolo came back to collect the Cardinal, Frannie and Daniel. He dropped off the Cardinal first, then rolled to a stop in front of Frannie's apartment.

Glancing at the clock on her phone she said, "Wow. It's pretty early yet." She looked over at Daniel, silently wondering what his plans were for the remainder of the night.

He glanced absently at his watch. "Do you want to meet tomorrow?"

Her heart sank a little at the non-invitation to spend the rest of the evening together. "Sure. We should start planning for Milan."

After Frannie exited the car, Daniel noticed Paolo didn't pull away. He leaned over in the back seat and saw Paolo staring at him in the rearview mirror.

"Is something wrong, Paolo?" he asked.

"*Signore* Daniel. If I were your age, and a beautiful *signorina* said to me the evening was still young, I would have taken the hint."

"What?"

"I would ask her to go for a walk. Enjoy the moonlight! Enjoy being young and romance!" He shook his head disapprovingly and muttered in Italian as he drove Daniel home.

Enjoy romance? Is that even still a thing? Daniel asked himself. He had believed it was once. But society and experience taught him romance had progressed into a dating scene that resembled the shallowness of a baseball mega park. He closed his eyes. There was something timeless about Frannie; a preservation of what was good and true. Almost like Wrigley Field.

Paolo interrupted his thoughts. "We're here, *Signore.*"

"*Grazie*, Paolo. It was nice meeting you."

"I hope you have a wonderful evening," he said with a hint of sarcasm, before he drove away.

Chapter 12

FRANNIE ENTERED HER APARTMENT, THREW HER purse to the side, and collapsed on the couch. She cringed thinking about her overly flirtatious overture to Daniel in the car. Luckily, his awkwardness came in handy; the proposal shot right over his head, saving her the embarrassment of being turned down.

She quickly calculated a time zone conversion; it was only noon in Boston. She spoke into her phone, "Call Jen."

Within seconds, she heard her friend's voice chime, "Hey, girlfriend!"

"Hey."

"You sound depressed. Is Mr. Linebacker still driving you nuts?"

"Not in the way you think."

Jen perked up, "Okay, spill."

Frannie recounted their run and ruins tour, her surprise at his treatment of her as an equal colleague, and the revelation that he was a die-hard baseball fan. "But there's this sense of sadness about him. Like, he's had a rough go of it. I think he's been burned by someone before—or maybe multiple people. He seems surprised by most remedial acts of kindness. I swear I saw pain in his eyes when *Zio* asked him about his family. I feel sorry for him."

Jen was quiet on the other end.

"Hello? Are you there?" Frannie asked, wondering if she lost the connection.

"Yeah, I'm here. Frannie, I Googled Mr. Linebacker and found images. Is he really that good looking or are the images photoshopped?"

Daniel's handsome profile and boyish freckles flashed in her mind. "They're not photoshopped."

"That's what I was afraid of. You fly across the world to Rome and you manage to find another adorable stray dog."

"Thanks, Jen," she said irritably.

"Hey, you called me because you knew I would tell it like it is. You have an unfortunate habit of finding and falling for guys in trouble. You pour your kind spirit upon him, he grows confident and strong and then—he leaves you. I have three words for you: Eric, Jordan, and Brandon."

Jen was right about Frannie's past boyfriends. Each had some deep-seated issue from their past and Frannie had been more of a counselor than a girlfriend. Each break up was nearly the same: "It's not you, it's me. You're a wonderful person, Frannie, and I've grown so much from our relationship. I hope you have, too." Brandon was the most recent; he had broken up with Frannie to go back to his old girlfriend.

"I know Jen," Frannie moaned, "and I tell myself to stick only to conversations about the work *Zio* wants us to do, and then the next thing I know I'm inviting him on a run and ordering him gelato."

"That's because you're the most generous person I know," Jen said gently. "I'm just saying be careful."

A text appeared on Frannie's screen. It was from Daniel.

"Uh oh! Daniel just texted me."

"What does he want?"

"He wants to know if I want to go for a walk," she said, dazed by the message. She opened the full text. "Oh. He said he didn't get a chance to tell me about something he found yesterday. See? He may be a stray, but it's obvious he's all business."

"Mm-hmm." Jen sounded unconvinced.

"I should see what he uncovered."

"Mm-hmm." Jen repeated in the same tone.

"I'll be careful," Frannie pouted, "I promise."

"Ok...later."

"Later."

Frannie texted Daniel back. He would be at her apartment in fifteen minutes.

Daniel and Frannie strolled among the locals and tourists enjoying Rome's Lungo il Tevere summer festival. Each night, the festival converted the banks of the Tiber River into a nighttime celebration. Tents and umbrellas lining the river came alive with various restaurants, bars, and craft vendors. Live music and DJs created outdoor dance clubs under the stars. The walkways were filled up with people out relishing the Rome nightlife and pleasant evening weather.

Daniel stuffed his hands in his pockets to prevent them from fidgeting. In hindsight, his decision to ask Frannie to go for a walk seemed rash. Paolo had been so sure she was fishing for an invite; he worried his curiosity to see if Paolo was right had gotten the better of him.

They approached a bar that wasn't overly populated. "Should we stop here for a drink?" he asked.

Frannie nodded. They ordered a glass of wine and selected two bar stools that overlooked the river.

"Don't keep me in suspense," Frannie said, "What did you find yesterday?"

Luckily, he had a legitimate reason he could use as justification for calling her. "I did some more digging into money transactions. Guess who bankrolled Elena and Giovanni's Milan restaurant?"

Frannie's eyes widened. "Not the Garone family!"

"It doesn't look that way on the surface, but I think so."

"What do you mean?"

"The loan is managed by an offshore bank in Switzerland. The records are all in Elena and her husband's name, but the Swiss bank holds other accounts listing the Garone family as the primary account owners."

Frannie squinted one eye at him. "How did you find this out?" she asked suspiciously.

Daniel shifted uncomfortably. "I've had to acquire relationships with some contacts over the years that, shall we say, provide services under the radar."

He held up his hand at her disapproving face. "They're the good guys," he said reassuringly, "but they are able to snoop in valuable ways and remain undetected."

Despite Frannie's skeptical look, Daniel moved on, "I think we should go to Milan a few days early to stake out the restaurant and see if we can talk to Elena."

"A stake out? As in, sit in a car on a dark street all night drinking coffee?"

"I've done it before. It's not that bad."

"What do you think's gonna happen? We'll see an unmarked delivery truck pull up at three in the morning and witness mysterious boxes being unloaded by the back door?"

"No," he paused, stifling a snicker at her witty sarcasm. "I have a knack for identifying shady characters and situations. If I get the tiniest feeling there is something suspicious going on, I can use it to lean on Elena and get her to talk."

Frannie stared at him intently. He never flinched; he was dead serious—and confident. Perhaps her uncle had placed his trust in Daniel for his detective's nose and intuition. Every avenue he had tested so far provided a solid lead.

"Okay," she said, "I'll make reservations at another hotel before the concert and get a rental car."

Her willingness to agree to his plan surprised him. "Good idea. I'm sure it would be easier for you to make those arrangements than for me to attempt it."

Daniel glanced over Frannie's head and spotted an older man sitting three bar stools down from them. He was short, round, and balding, with gray hair only on the sides and back of his head. What struck Daniel was that he was alone. Most of the patrons participating in the river festival were couples and groups of friends out for a night on the town. This wasn't a single scene for older men. His first thought was the man was waiting for a female escort. The bald man glanced at Daniel and quickly looked away.

Daniel's instinct for shady characters kicked in. He saw Frannie's wine glass was empty. He finished the rest of his in one gulp.

"Let's walk down a little farther. What else is down there?" he asked, knowing it would get her talking and distracted. Sure enough, she started listing all the different venues and eateries available. Daniel observed the bald man leaving when they did, keeping about a three person distance between them. He needed to put his gut feeling to the test.

He spotted a gelato stand. "Hey, let's get some gelato!"

Frannie gaped at him. "Mr. Low Carb Man wants a second dose of sugar? After having cookies at *Zia* Rosa's?"

Daniel shrugged. "You were right. It's the best ice cream I've ever had. I'll take the same kind you got me before if they have it."

Frannie eyed him warily but placed an order for two small cups. Daniel watched the bald man stop and browse the goods at a jewelry vendor close by. Once Frannie had the gelato, he instinctively placed his hand on her back, to ensure she stayed close to him, and led her to a table under an umbrella. The bald man entered the tent next door and sat on a barstool, still within eyesight.

Daniel's unexpected warm hand on her back caused Frannie's heart to beat wildly. Once they were seated, she noticed he was busy canvassing the area and barely touched his gelato.

She scooted her cup to the side and folded her hands on the table. "Okay. Fess up. What's going on?"

He took two bites of his gelato and leaned forward on the table. He looked into her eyes and gave her the warmest smile. She thought her heart was going to explode in her chest.

"Frannie, do you see the bald man sitting at the tent to your right? He followed us from the wine bar. I need you to pretend we are on a date, so that he doesn't suspect we are talking about him."

She followed his lead and leaned in toward him, and gave him the same type of sweet smile. "I see. And why would this man be following us?"

Daniel chuckled, pretending she had told a joke. "I have no idea."

Frannie glanced to her left and saw a merchant selling large straw hats. "I have an idea," she said, still grinning. "Give me a couple of minutes, and then meet me at the hat seller two vendors down." She finished her gelato and handed him her empty cup.

"Two minutes," he said. "If this guy follows you, I'm not waiting."

"Deal."

Daniel watched her chat with the salesperson, then duck behind another customer, out of sight. He got up and tossed the gelato cups in the trash. As soon as he headed down the street, the bald man followed not far behind. When he reached the hat vendor, Frannie appeared and put her arm around Daniel, and he took her cue and placed his arm around her. He looked down and saw she was holding a ladies' straw hat with a wide brim and black sash over her chest.

He heard pop music coming from a few feet away. "Did you say there was a dance club up ahead?"

"Yep."

"Got it."

The dance club was in an open area in front of a small raised stage with a DJ. Once they reached it, Daniel grabbed Frannie's hand and moved quickly through the crowd to the side of the stage, so that they were surrounded by other dancers. Frannie placed the large hat on her head and Daniel pulled her close and lowered his head near her neck. Her heeled sandals made them close to the same height, making it easy for the hat's wide brim to shield him from sight. He made a small adjustment so he could peek underneath it, and have a view of the street. The DJ was playing a song which didn't match their slow dance but they tried to sway with the beat while using the hat as a cover.

"Do you see him?" she whispered.

The man approached the dance club area scanning the crowd, then glanced to his left and his right. He looked over the dance crowd again, and stood up on his tiptoes.

"Yes. He can't find us."

The man frowned, irritated, then walked away. Daniel closed his eyes and breathed a quiet sigh of relief. The smell of jasmine filled his nostrils and he realized he was holding Frannie in his arms. The warm feeling in his chest resurfaced.

"Is he gone?" she asked.

He allowed himself one more moment before he released her and stepped away. "I think we lost him."

"Daniel, please don't tell *Zio*. It will just worry him."

He nodded in agreement, but wasn't sure he should hide it from the Cardinal. "Let's head out," he said. "It looks like the streets and tents are getting even busier. We should be able to get lost in the crowd. But keep your hat on, just in case."

They plowed their way through the throng of people and exited the festival to the upper street level. They headed back, in silence. He wasn't used to Frannie being so quiet. Her hat made it difficult to see her face.

"The hat was a great idea," he offered, fishing to see if she was all right.

She turned and gave him a smile. "Thanks. You read my mind about the dance club."

Her smile looked a little forced. He wondered if she was unnerved by being followed or by how closely he had pulled her to him. That probably wasn't part of her plan.

When they reached the street to her apartment, she stopped in the middle and looked it up and down.

"I've been watching, Frannie. I haven't seen him."

"It's not that. I'm just wondering when he started following us. Did he follow us from *Zia's* house, yours, or mine?"

"It's a good question. But, I'm walking you to your apartment and checking it out."

Frannie gave him the key. He stepped in and peeked around the rooms. "It's empty."

Frannie entered and sat her purse on the coffee table. "Wow. That was an eventful evening."

"No doubt." *Certainly not the romance Paolo had in mind,* he thought dryly.

"You weren't kidding about your instinct for shady characters."

"I don't think he would have hurt us. But someone is curious as to what we are up to."

An alarm went off in Frannie's mind. "If Donati has connections to the mafia—" her voice trailed off.

Daniel didn't want to admit he had the same thoughts. "I don't want to jump to conclusions yet, but we should keep our guard up."

Frannie decoded his response to mean he didn't want to worry her. She almost called him out for it, but refrained. To her amazement, he had been very protective of her. A chivalrous Daniel Fitzpatrick contrasted starkly with the man who tackled her at the airport. The mere notion caused her heart to skip.

"Let's meet tomorrow," she said, shaking it off. "I had something I was going to share with you before the stalker appeared. Is here ok? I'll make lunch this time."

"Sure. I'll see you tomorrow." He turned toward the door.

"Hey, Daniel?"

He spun around. Frannie met him with eyes that were just as warm as they were when she was pretending to be his date.

Was she not faking it earlier?

"Thank you for coming in to make sure everything was okay. I really appreciate it."

He knew her thanks were sincere; no strings, no ulterior motive. She was just being Frannie. "You're welcome."

She insisted he text her when he got home, then they said good night. He waited outside her door to listen for a click of the bolt, making sure she locked the door.

Daniel did a sweep of the street with his eyes. He didn't expect to see anyone, and all looked clear. He moved at a swift pace, his thoughts bouncing between whether the man had been following them or the Cardinal, and occasionally, the warmness of Frannie's eyes.

Chapter 13

FRANNIE STARED BLANKLY AT THE SCREEN ON HER laptop. Two cups of coffee weren't enough to clear the brain fog resulting from her restless night of sleep. Alessandro's concern that she could be placing herself with dangerous company seemed more plausible now. She comforted herself with Daniel's assessment; there would be nothing to gain in harming the niece of a famous Cardinal and an American journalist.

A knock brought her to her feet. The morning had slipped away. It was already nine o'clock and Daniel had arrived.

When she opened the door, he frowned and scolded her from the entryway, "You open the door without even asking who it is?"

"Well, 'Good Morning' to you too!"

"I'm serious, Frannie. I told you to keep your guard up." He hastily brushed past her and into the apartment.

She held her hands up. "Okay, okay, I got it." Her eyes focused on the two to-go cups he held in his hands. "Did you bring coffee?"

"Cappuccino," he answered grudgingly, still irritated at her lack of vigilance.

Frannie's lips twitched into a smile. She was flattered by his consideration for both her safety and her need for caffeine. She took one of the cups from his hand. "Thank you."

He unloaded the bag off his shoulder onto a dining chair. "I knew you wouldn't be productive without some food," he said, trying to ignore her radiant smile by poking fun at her, "so I picked up some of those cornette things."

Frannie giggled. "You mean *cornetto*."

"Yeah, those."

They sat down at Frannie's dining table. Daniel set up his laptop while Frannie ate her pastry. "Did you sleep okay?" he asked, no longer showing signs of annoyance.

She shrugged. "Off and on. You?"

"Same."

"I'm worried about *Zio*. I'm beginning to think he was the one initially being watched. Maybe we should tell him, so he can think about hiring protection."

Daniel reached for a pastry to dodge making eye contact. A phone call to the Cardinal was unavoidable. He would need to reach out to him today and tell him everything.

"I'm not sure your uncle was the target. Last night, I realized something. I'm an outsider to the Menconi family. Whoever is watching knows you, I assume. They don't know me. And depending on how long they've been tracking, they could have seen me with your uncle after you left the restaurant the first day we met, and us sitting at the café pouring over our laptops the other morning."

Frannie's heart sank. Jen had Googled Daniel's name and found images. It wasn't hard to do a search in reverse using a picture. Someone could have taken their picture without them knowing it. Once they found out who Daniel was, it would raise a red flag.

"You make a good point. Maybe we restrict our research meetings to one of our apartments." Frannie took a drink of her cappuccino and stared out the window. It was time to share what happened on Saturday, the day before dinner at *Zia* Rosa's.

She began, "I know we jumped to investigate the names we assumed were the 'bad guys,' but I decided it wouldn't hurt to know more about the 'good guys,' too. I started with Kratzer. I have an idea that I want to run by you, and since it looks like the Menconi family is under surveillance, it might be quite timely."

"He's the one from Austria, right?"

"Yes. He's the Salzburg Archbishop that didn't support the rock concert and spearheaded the Letter of Opposition. Vidmar was a dear friend of his. Before Vidmar died, they were working together to restructure something called the *Traditio* project.

"*Traditio* was initially developed to research population trends in parishes all over the world that celebrated Mass in the Extraordinary Form and those that did not." She added for clarification, "Extraordinary Form is another term for the Latin Mass. The project was halted within its first year. Vidmar and Kratzer saw other benefits in the data collected by the project so they decided to keep it going. They wanted to extend it beyond Mass attendance to consider other religious practices of the Catholics being surveyed. The Vatican got wind of this, and guess who was asked to go in and shut it down?"

She didn't wait for an answer. "Cardinal Baldano, prefect of the Congregation for the Evangelization of Peoples.

"And in a strange twist, it was American Catholic news outlets that first published the data, not Austria. I won't bore you with the details, but it made a case that the Latin Mass Catholics not only disapproved of the progressive changes, they were also more likely to have flourishing families and increased vocations to the priesthood."

Frannie's face read like she had dropped a bombshell but Daniel didn't understand why this was important. "I get that you've made a connection between some of our players, but why do we care about a survey of where Catholics go to Mass?"

"Because, I've been communicating with someone who might be able to get us an audience with Archbishop Kratzer."

"Don't we already know what the good guys think? What additional information would he have to tell us?"

Frannie fiddled with the last bite of her cornetto. This was the part she was dreading.

"I went to Adoration on Saturday." She quickly explained, "There's a side room in Saint Peter's where you can sit and pray in front of the Blessed Sacrament."

She glanced up to see his reaction. It was wooden and unreadable. She decided to lay it out there. "I've been conversing with this contact for a few days. After some discernment in the Adoration chapel, I feel strongly that we should go to Salzburg after Milan. We might learn something from the Archbishop. And, we won't have to worry about being watched," she threw in to win him over.

Daniel thought maybe his lack of sleep had affected his hearing. "Salzburg," he repeated. "You want to go to Austria?"

Frannie could tell this was going to be a hard sell. "Yes."

"How far is it?"

"About eight hours by train."

Daniel's eyes bulged out of his head. "Eight hours? On a train?"

"This isn't like riding the Amtrak in the US. European trains are super comfortable and fast."

"Eight hours doesn't sound fast."

"It's two hours to Venice then about six to Salzburg so it's broken up," she pointed out, trying to make it sound like a quick jaunt.

Daniel shook his head. "I need more information to convince me to get on a train for eight hours."

Frannie sighed and crossed her arms. "I've trusted your gut instincts, why can't you trust mine?"

Daniel's jaw clenched. He didn't like where this conversation was going. "You said you came to this decision after some—" he paused to interject air quotes–"discernment. Are you saying God is telling you to go to Salzburg?"

The dismissive tone in his voice was unmistakable. "Oh, I see. Because my instinct may have come from talking with God in prayer it must be invalid, is that it?"

Daniel looked away. He wasn't sure what to think. Francesca was the most clever and intelligent person he had met in a long time. That fact that she relied on faith and religion seemed contrary to her reasonable nature.

Frannie noted his refusal to answer and continued her interrogation. "What will you think if it turns out *Zio* was told by God to trust you?"

Daniel's head jerked up. "Is that what he said?"

"No," she said irritably, "I have no idea why he trusts you like he does. But, what about your instincts for shady people? How do you know God isn't speaking to you and blessing you with proper discernment in those moments?"

Daniel let out a scoffing laugh. "Because God doesn't bless me."

He saw Frannie's eyes widen and her brows go up. He instantly regretted the slip, but changed his mind. *Maybe she needs a strong dose of reality*, he thought.

"My life story isn't like yours. I never knew my dad. Fitzpatrick isn't even his last name; it was my mother's. My mom died when I was seven and I was raised by my grandmother. So, tell me," his voice dripped with cynicism, "how does God bless a child by leaving him without a mother or father?"

Frannie's mouth fell open but she quickly closed it. She had never met anyone close to her age that could share her sense of loss of losing a parent. "I'm sorry, Daniel. I think I shared with you my dad died when I was ten, so I understand–"

Daniel abruptly cut her off, "No. You don't. I didn't have an uncle living in Jackson, much less Italy, to step in and be a father figure. You have a family; a mother, brothers, uncles, and cousins. I wasn't blessed," he expressed the word scornfully, "with that."

Frannie flinched slightly. The flashes of pain she detected in Daniel's eyes were real. It was a pain he carried deep within him. *You're so bitter*, she thought sadly. *You're not practicing Catholicism because of the Church; you're mad at God.* She closed her eyes. *Lord, I don't know what to say*, she prayed.

Memories came flooding back to her; how even in the midst of her sadness she discovered she could be grateful for the time she and her father had together. The virtue of gratitude had been indispensable in helping her heal.

"What was your grandmother's name?" she asked softly.

Daniel's features relaxed slightly. "Mae. Grandma Mae."

Frannie heard the affection with which he uttered her name. *Keep going.*

"What was she like?"

Daniel was flustered. His line of attack was supposed to make her doubt whether God could talk to her; not ask questions about his past. He thought of several snide comments but Frannie's openness drew him in, and he couldn't get a single one to come out.

"She was a spit-fire," he heard himself saying, his Georgia drawl escaping. "She had to have been, to raise me," he added dryly.

Frannie chuckled softly. "I'm sure."

The return to her usual grittiness relaxed him. He wasn't looking for anyone's pity.

"Did she stay in Jackson or move with you to Chicago?"

He shook his head. "Grandma Mae would never move from Jackson. She came to visit me a few times, but she wasn't the type to be impressed by fancy restaurants and 'big-city-life' as she called it." He paused, deep in thought. "She did enjoy her last trip to

Chicago. I was receiving an award for my essay from the Chicago Headline Club. She was so excited to go to the banquet with me."

He glanced up to find Frannie's eyes glistening warmly at him. He took his phone out of his pocket and within a few seconds handed it to her.

On the screen was a picture of a short gray haired lady with kind eyes and a proud smile. Daniel had one hand around her shoulder and held his award with the other.

"That's a great picture," she said, handing the phone back.

"She passed away the following year," he said sadly. "I'm glad it wasn't sooner. It meant a lot that she was able to be there at the banquet."

"I bet it meant a lot to her, too." Frannie added gently, "Sounds like it was a blessing for both of you."

Daniel stiffened. He felt like the victim of a bait-and-switch scam. But deep down he knew Frannie wasn't that devious. And she was right. It was one of his fondest memories, which for Daniel, were few and far between.

He grunted and turned to his laptop. "We should probably figure out our game plan for Milan. Constantini will be expecting the Cardinal and we need him to extend the dinner invitation to us."

Frannie let him change the subject, hoping she gave him something to ponder. "Yep, we will need to be on our toes. Constantini won't be easily duped. What about Salzburg?" she asked, not missing a beat.

Daniel tried to come up with a way out but couldn't find one. He blamed reminiscing about Grandma Mae; his memories of her must have softened his heart. "Fine. We'll follow your gut on the long train to Salzburg."

Frannie didn't hide her elation. "Fabulous! I'll confirm with my contact right now. Look at the bright side, they have some of the best beer in Europe!"

"Are you going to order food for me there too?" he jabbed.

"If you try to order lasagne instead of snitzel I might," she shot back.

"Ha ha, Menconi," he said, absent of any real mirth. "Let's get to work."

They spent the rest of the day planning their trip to Milan, and to Daniel's chagrin, Salzburg, Austria.

♔

Cardinal Menconi's phone vibrated. The caller ID displayed on the screen was completely out of the blue.

"Hello, Daniel. This is a surprise. Is everything all right?"

"Yes, your Eminence. I'm outside your apartment building. Are you home? I have the item you asked Frannie to deliver. I offered to bring it over since it was on my way."

The Cardinal paused. Everything was not all right. He wasn't expecting a delivery from Francesca. "Oh, yes of course. Come on up."

Daniel entered the apartment and folded up an empty paper grocery bag he was carrying as a prop. He had put on the charade in case anyone was following close enough to overhear his conversation. He wanted to talk to the Cardinal in person. "Sorry to call unannounced," he said.

"What's wrong? Is Francesca okay?"

"She's fine. But, something did happen." Cardinal Menconi motioned to the couch while lowering himself in his armchair. Daniel took a seat and proceeded to recount their escapade from the previous evening. "I think I was the mark," he said when he had finished. "They probably want to know who the stranger is with you, with Frannie, and at the Menconi home. It's quite possible they have found out who I am and what I do for a living."

The Cardinal leaned back heavily in his chair. "Is that what you told Francesca?"

"Yes. But, she's worried about you. She may talk to you about getting protection for yourself. You already have that, don't you, sir?"

"I have Paolo. He is all the eyes and ears I need. And you don't need to suspect him. He knows why you are here."

The thought had crossed Daniel's mind. It was on Paolo's suggestion he had even called Frannie. "I'll take your word for it. Did he report anything suspicious last night?"

"No. I'll let him know to watch next time."

"We leave for Milan next week, then Frannie wants us to go to Salzburg. I don't think anyone will follow us but we will be cautious."

"Salzburg? Archbishop Kratzer?"

Daniel nodded. "She has convinced someone to get us an audience with him. I'm not sure why." He tried not to show any disdain for the unexpected trip.

The Cardinal rubbed his chin. "Francesca is smart not to ask me to call Kratzer for a meeting. That would get out and raise suspicion. The fact that she has found a way to contact him without my assistance means she must think it is important."

Daniel's stomach twisted in a knot. He should have seen the obvious; a quick call from a Cardinal in Rome would be the easy and sure way to get an audience with the Archbishop of Salzburg. He regretted being so antagonistic simply because her faith prompted her to devise a well-reasoned plan.

"Regardless," the Cardinal continued, "maybe I should send Paolo with you."

"No, that won't be necessary. They may have been interested in me, but you are still their main target. Keep Paolo close, sir."

Cardinal Menconi sighed. "Thank you for telling me. I'll be ready if Francesca says anything."

Daniel stood up to leave. The Cardinal followed him to the door announcing, "I'll have Paolo pick you up on Sunday for dinner at the same time. Unless you want to change your mind about Mass?"

"Um, no. I mean, I don't want to keep intruding on your family." He hadn't even considered that he would go back to *Zia* Rosa's.

Cardinal Menconi waved his hand. "It is the least I can do to make up for your unpleasant experience last evening." A large smile spread across his face. "Let us be your family while you are here in Italy."

A pain serrated Daniel's chest. *Family.* When he left Italy, he wouldn't be going home to any family.

"Thank you, your Eminence. The same time as last Sunday will be fine."

They shook hands and Daniel headed off to his apartment. He looked around and didn't see anyone following him. When he entered his apartment, he checked around and all was clear. He fell onto the couch.

Frannie had invited him to dinner but he had declined. He needed some time alone. The memory of Grandma Mae and the banquet touched something within him. Somewhere he couldn't pinpoint, and it stirred up a restlessness he couldn't shake.

He opened his laptop and typed in the search bar, "catholics and god's blessings." The first article in the list of results referenced a paragraph from the Catechism of the Catholic Church:

> In blessing, God's gift and man's acceptance of it are united in dialogue with each other. The prayer of blessing is man's response to God's gifts: because God blesses, the human heart can in return bless the One who is the source of every blessing.

Was the Church implying that God's blessing required a response on his part? Why would God want or need a response from Daniel Fitzpatrick?

He slammed his laptop shut. It didn't matter. God hadn't given him anything to respond to other than disappointment and hurt.

Except Grandma Mae.

He closed his eyes. If she hadn't taken him in and raised him, who knows what his fate might have been.

Okay, Frannie. I'll give you that one. God blessed me with Grandma Mae.

"So what do you want in response, God?" he muttered. "A thank you note?"

An old memory resurfaced of a Bible story Grandma Mae liked to use in her many teaching moments. The details of the story were fuzzy, but he recalled a group of lepers were healed by Jesus but only one came back to thank Him. As a child, he thought Grandma Mae just wanted him to learn proper manners. Now he realized she was trying to teach him the lesson of gratitude for the gifts he received. He pushed the thought away, made dinner, and watched the highlights of a Cubs baseball game on his computer.

When he went to bed he tossed and turned for hours; his mind crowded with thoughts of blessings, Grandma Mae, Frannie, and ungrateful lepers. He longed for sleep and decided to give the ridiculous a try.

Okay, God. Thank you for blessing me with Grandma Mae. I don't know what I would have done without her. I miss her. Tell her hello for me. And, I don't know what else to say, so I guess that's it. Um...Amen.

He was surprised by how un-ridiculous it felt to say what was on his mind. His eyelids began to droop. He could almost hear Frannie say, "Don't look now, Fitzpatrick, but you just prayed." He imagined the smell of jasmine, smiled faintly, and then drifted off to sleep.

Chapter 14

ARCHBISHOP KRATZER SAT ALONE IN THE DARK AND empty Salzburg Cathedral. A few hanging lamps and burning votive candles left by pilgrims offering prayers provided the only faint glow in the church. In the dim lighting he could make out the large painting in the Baroque high altar depicting the Resurrection of Christ; Jesus draped in white, suspended in mid-air over the empty tomb with angels around him. The Roman soldiers cowered in fear and awe at the God-man who in His resurrected body proclaimed victory over death.

The Archbishop prayed for the day the Church would rise victorious from the current scourge she currently faced. But even he grew weary and tired and wondered if God was hearing his pleas.

How long, O Lord? How long will you hide your face from me? But I will trust in your merciful love; my heart will rejoice in your salvation.

The sound of footsteps on the marble floor interrupted his prayer. Each step reverberated a hollow echo in the vacant church. The old wooden pew creaked loudly as the late-night guest sat down beside him.

The visitor stated flatly, "I am usually the one that calls these late night meetings."

"Yes, but there has been an unusual development," Kratzer said. "Francesca Menconi has asked to see me. She is bringing a journalist from the United States with her."

"Nicolo's niece? Have you talked with him?"

"No. She used one of the previous *Traditio* project workers to make the contact."

"Interesting. She bypassed all Vatican routes of communication." The guest mulled over the information. "Did she say why she wants to see you?"

"She is helping her American friend make contacts for a story on the state of the European Church. He wants to know more about *Traditio* and the data that was collected."

"And you believe her?"

"Not at all. It is obviously a cover. That's why I called you. She must be on an errand for Nicolo." He slowly turned toward his guest. "What do you think it means?"

A knowing smile spread across the visitor's face. "It means Nicolo is investigating. Let's see what *Signorina* Menconi and her friend want to know."

Chapter 15

"Hello, *Signore* Daniel!" Paolo greeted cheerily as Daniel climbed in the back seat of the Cardinal's black sedan.

"Hello, Paolo. How have you been?"

"Good, good. I understand a man followed you and *Signorina* last week?"

Daniel leaned over to check Paolo's reflection in the rearview mirror. Paolo's eyes were serious and strained. Daniel's intuition led him to believe that Paolo was nothing short of trustworthy.

"What did he look like?" Paolo asked.

Daniel retold the story and gave as good of a description of the bald man as he could.

"I am sorry, *Signore*. The Cardinal told me to take care of you and I got lazy. It will not happen again."

"You don't have to apologize. It wasn't your fault."

"What about the rest of the evening?" Paolo asked with a lift in his voice. "With *Signorina*? You took my advice, yes?"

Daniel felt his face get a little warm. "We were discussing our work for the Cardinal, Paolo. There wasn't any romance."

He grunted in disappointment, then turned optimistic. "I bet *Signorina* was grateful you were so interested in her safety. I bet your *cavalleria* made an impression!"

"*Cavalleria?*"

"Yes. The code of men with armor that served king and country."

"Knights? You're not talking about chivalry are you? That's long since died out. Women don't want to be treated like that anymore."

Paolo pulled up to Rosa's villa. He peered at Daniel from the rearview mirror. "*Signore,* a good woman, one with, eh—*virtù,* expects to be treated like a lady. And when you find that kind of woman, you will want to treat her that way. And you will find it has not died out at all."

Daniel didn't respond. Paolo obviously lived in a past era that had slipped away. Grandma Mae had taught him the same old-fashioned ideals. When he tried them, he was laughed at and scorned.

Paolo opened the passenger door and Daniel hopped out. "Oh wait," he said, reaching across the backseat and retrieving a bouquet. "I brought flowers this time."

Paolo smiled. "Very good, *Signore. A presto.*"

"*A presto.*"

Daniel entered the villa and casually made his way to the kitchen, assuming it was where he would find Rosa and Frannie. The amazing smell coming from the pots on the stove hit his nostrils and he was unexpectedly glad to be there. Rosa greeted him first with a loud *buongiorno* and warmly patted his cheek. She joyously received the flowers and went immediately to fetch a vase.

Frannie waved at him from the stove.

"Hi," he said, taking a peek inside the large pot she was monitoring. It was full of chicken bits simmering in a sauce with onions, tomatoes, and bell peppers.

She flashed him her radiant smile. "Want a preview of dinner?"

She took a spoon and scooped up a bite of chicken and sauce and handed it to Daniel.

"Mmm. Tastes as amazing as it smells."

"It's *pollo alla romana,* and no one makes it like *Zia* Rosa!"

He handed the spoon back. Frannie pointed toward the patio. "The rest of the family is outside. We'll be ready to eat in a few minutes. I put a few bottles of water in the cooler for you."

"Thank you. For the water and the uh–taste test," he said, awkwardly.

Rosa walked by with a stack of plates and bumped into him, pushing him uncomfortably close to Frannie.

"Sorry," he mumbled, "I'll get out of the way." He stepped by her before she could reply and walked outside, taking in a deep breath of fresh air.

Daniel shook off his embarrassment and looked around at the Menconi clan. He recognized the faces but wasn't certain of everyone's names. He said hello to a few and glanced around for Cardinal Menconi but didn't see him. Unsure of what to do next, he walked to the cooler and grabbed a water bottle. He held it a moment, musing how Frannie went out of her way to make him feel at home when a sultry voice spoke his name.

"*Ciao*, Daniel."

Lorena had appeared beside him. Her clothing choice was the same as the Sunday prior, except her tight dress was blue instead of yellow.

"*Ciao*. Lorena, right?"

"Good memory," she said, obviously flattered. "I was hoping you would be here."

Daniel glanced up for any sign of the Cardinal but saw none. He was stuck.

Lorena took a small step closer. "We weren't able to talk last Sunday. Francesca didn't let you out of her sight."

Daniel didn't respond, hoping she would walk away.

"You are a reporter, like Francesca?" she asked.

"More of a journalist," he said curtly. "Someone who writes stories rather than reports them."

"I hear her television career isn't going anywhere," she said, shamelessly delighting in the misfortune of her cousin.

Daniel glanced up and saw the Cardinal stepping out onto the patio. *Oh, save me from having to talk to this mindless twit.* "Your Eminence," he called, leaving Lorena by herself at the cooler, "*buongiorno!*"

"*Buongiorno*, Daniel! Sorry I am late and holding up dinner. Someone who has been away from the Church for years wanted to make a confession after Mass. No one else was around so it was my honor to do it."

Daniel gave him a quizzical look. "You hear people's confessions? Isn't that a little beneath your rank?"

The Cardinal laughed and patted Daniel's back. "I am a priest, first. I just happen to be a priest who was ordained a Bishop, then appointed a Cardinal." His eyes turned misty and sad. "I miss being a parish priest. My days are mostly meetings and politics. Parish priests have their share of that, too. But at least they are able to live out their vocation by hearing beautiful confessions and baptizing the little *bambini*."

"How can a confession be beautiful? Isn't it a laundry list of what the person has done wrong?"

The Cardinal smiled. "Ah, *mio figlio*. A prodigal son or daughter, a Zaccheus, someone shedding the bitter and contrite tears of a Peter; these are beautiful in the eyes of God. Saint John Paul II said that a man who goes down on his knees in the confessional because he has sinned, adds to his own dignity as a man. Today, I got to exercise my true vocation. And it was a blessing for me to be the priest that restored someone's dignity as a son of his Heavenly Father."

Great. More talk about blessings. And did he call me his son, again? Daniel was about to ask him how a sinful man on his knees could possibly be considered dignified when Rosa came out and announced dinner was ready.

Daniel and Frannie took the same seats at the dinner table as last Sunday. Lorena snuck in behind Daniel and craftily slid onto the chair on his other side. Frannie rolled her eyes. The two cousins had been rivals since they were kids; mostly instigated by Lorena. Lorena's incessant flirting with Alessandro only occurred when Frannie was visiting from the States. Frannie had no doubt Lorena's interest in Daniel was part of her childish obsession to be in competition.

During dinner, Frannie couldn't help but gloat internally as she eavesdropped on Lorena trying to strike up a conversation with Daniel. Her blatant flirtations were met with a short response that bordered on rudeness. As the plates were being cleared, Lorena tapped Daniel on the shoulder.

He looked at her with a set of dull eyes. She leaned her elbows on the table, further accentuating her low cut dress. "Daniel, my friends and I are going down to the summer festival by the river this evening. I'm sure Frannie wouldn't mind if you took a break from working. I could show you the night-life of Rome."

I bet that isn't all you want to show me, he thought. It was obvious her suggestive advances were out of a deep-seated jealousy. He almost borrowed from Grandma Mae's southern wit and said, *Darlin', you're so far out of the same league as Frannie, you're playin' a different sport.*

"Actually, Frannie and I walked the river festival last Sunday," he said loudly enough to ensure Frannie could hear. "It was a memorable evening," he added, shooting a glance at Frannie.

She had been staring ahead, blasting silent insults at her cousin. His remark caused her head to snap around. He winked at her and asked, "Don't you agree?"

Frannie's heart banged so hard in her chest she was sure he could hear it. She smirked, "Definitely. It was a night of unexpected surprises."

Lorena glowered at her but she didn't flinch.

Daniel pivoted back to Lorena. "Frannie and I leave for Milan tomorrow but maybe we can join you and your friends some other evening?" He knew it was an invite that would never come.

"Sure," Lorena said, a fake smile plastered on her face, "that would be fun." She got up from the table and left.

Frannie was stunned. Daniel Fitzpatrick, the same linebacker from the airport, had character. It was obvious what Lorena was willing to offer and he flat out rejected it. And to top it off, he led Lorena to believe they were romantically involved, making it crystal clear he wasn't remotely interested.

"Hey," he said, drawing her from her thoughts, "thanks for playing along. No offense, but your cousin is kind of a—"

"Floozy?"

He chuckled. "That's a nice way of putting it."

"A memorable evening, huh?" she teased.

His memory recorded every moment: holding her close while they pretended to dance, her perfume, and her arm around his waist.

"Well, it's not every day you're tailed by someone who could be part of the Italian mafia," he said half-jokingly. Her green eyes were as warm as when she thanked him for inspecting her apartment. He quickly looked away.

"Yeah, that's kinda hard to forget," she said, wondering if that was all he remembered.

"Francesca," Rosa called, "can you help with dessert?"

Frannie excused herself and helped Rosa carry trays of cookies to the table and take orders for espresso.

The Cardinal moved to Lorena's empty seat next to Daniel. "I understand you leave for Milan tomorrow."

Daniel nodded.

Frannie returned with two cups of espresso in one hand, and one in the other. She placed them on the table, and the three of them chatted about their Milan trip.

Cardinal Menconi's lips quirked into a grin; the ire between Daniel and his niece at their first meeting contrasted greatly with the ease in which they spoke to each other now.

"I would like to talk with you and Francesca before you go," he announced. "I'll ride along when Paolo takes you home. We are going to make a stop on the way."

Chapter 16

Paolo rolled the sedan to a stop in front of Saint Peter's.

"Have you been inside yet, Daniel?" the Cardinal asked.

"No, I haven't."

"Ah, wonderful!" The old man had a gleam in his eye. "I'm going to show you the basement, first! Paolo, we will be inside for a little while."

"Take your time, your Eminence."

When Daniel entered the doors of the basilica, the sensory input nearly overwhelmed him.

The interior was a sea of columns, arches, and statues in rose, gray, and cream colored marble. Geometric shapes on the marbled floor directed Daniel's eyes down the massive main aisle to the altar at the far end. He quickly assessed that it was the length of at least two football fields. His gaze floated upward to the golden ceiling, taking in the array of gilded squares that ornamented the long tunnel vault that stretched all the way to the altar.

Frannie pulled on his elbow, "I know it's jaw-dropping, but we need to keep up with *Zio*."

Daniel expected to follow the Cardinal toward the front, but instead he turned left. They moved so swiftly he could only glance at the statues and larger-than-life paintings that seemed to fill every space of the walls yet astonishingly, not appear cluttered. They arrived at the top of a set of stairs where a guard was stationed. The guard greeted the Cardinal with a nod and the three descended the steps to the basement of Saint Peter's.

At the bottom of the stairs, they followed a tight corridor that curved to the right. Statues filled small niches along the hallway. Painted frescos of cherubs, leaves, scallops and flowers covered portions of the walls and ceiling. This ceiling was much lower, making Daniel feel like he was walking inside a kaleidoscope. The Cardinal came to a halt in front of an entrance to a tiny chapel.

The chapel was extremely small and narrow, lined with a few wooden chairs and kneelers capable of only seating one person in each. Three cameo-white marble steps veined with amber and gray led up to the altar. Behind it was a metal grate of gold open circles welded like a honeycomb, serving as a screen for a slab of marble. The slab was cream, with a piece of red marble running vertically and another horizontally, forming an upside down "T."

Cardinal Menconi placed his hand on Daniel's shoulder. "Francesca told me you enjoyed seeing the Roman ruins of Julius Caesar. I wanted to show you some of the ancient ruins we have at Saint Peter's."

The Cardinal pointed toward the altar. "The marble behind the altar was built by the Emperor Constantine to protect the burial place of Saint Peter."

Daniel recalled Frannie mentioning something about the bones of Saint Peter when they were on Janiculum Hill but it hadn't sunk in. "You're saying, you know where Saint Peter was buried, and it's behind that wall?"

"Yes," he paused, "and no."

Frannie saw the confused look on Daniel's face. "Oh, *Zio*, you're always trying to bring an essence of drama to your tours. Let's have a seat inside and you can tell him the story."

"She is so bossy," the Cardinal whispered to Daniel.

Daniel smirked and followed him into the chapel. Cardinal Menconi lowered his voice in respect for the sacred place they had entered.

"The story is long with much history, but I will give you the shortened version. Before Pope Pius XI died in 1939, he requested to be buried down here, next to the other popes. The incoming Pope, Pius XII, decided to clean up and renovate this level, making it more suitable and dignified so that other popes could be buried here, too. They decided to lower the floor, to give the area more room. When they tore it up, they found ancient bricks. Traditional legends alleged Constantine built the original basilica over Saint Peter's grave, so naturally, they wanted to dig and see if they could find the actual grave with his bones."

"The original?" Daniel asked, pointing up. "This isn't the first?"

"After Emperor Constantine legalized Christianity in 313 AD, he began building churches so the Christians had a place to worship."

"He's a complicated character," Frannie chimed in. "While a champion for the rights of the early Christians, he refused to publicly accept baptism until he was on his deathbed."

The Cardinal continued, "The Constantine basilica was in a dilapidated state by the 1300s from years of sieges, raids, and neglect. In the early 1500s, the pope decided to start afresh and commissioned a new design. Some of the most famous Renaissance artists are responsible for the basilica as you see it today."

He clapped his hands together. "Back to our story. When the archeologists started digging in 1939, they uncovered the ancient Roman Necropolis, an ancient burial ground for the dead. They found a grave encased in marble, which, from historical accounts, they suspected to be the memorial to Saint Peter built by Constantine. They found human remains inside and naturally, assumed they had uncovered his bones, too. The remains from the grave were a mix of bones of a younger male and a female. They were disappointed since there was no way this could be Peter the Fisherman. But, this is where the story gets good!"

The gleam in the old man's eye was back and he rubbed his hands together. "Doctor Margherita Guarducci, a scholar of ancient Greek inscriptions, joined the excavation team in the 1950s. She was commissioned to decipher the ancient markings left by visiting pilgrims on a wall, known as the Graffiti Wall, which had been uncovered in the excavations. In this wall, was a mysterious hole, large enough for a small box to fit.

"She was given a piece of another wall, The Red Wall, believed to be built at Peter's tomb around 160 AD, that ran perpendicular to the Graffiti Wall. The chunk had fallen off and was found in the hole. A Greek inscription was scratched on it that said, *Petros Eni.* Doctor Guarducci translated it to read 'Peter is within,' or 'Peter is buried here.' This begs the question: what was this hole for, and did the excavators find anything inside?"

The Cardinal was becoming more excited and animated, building up suspense. "The answer is again: yes and no. By all reports, the hole in the Graffiti Wall was found mostly empty, with only a little debris.

"It was by sheer accident–if you want to call it that–that ten years later, Doctor Guarducci met an assistant to one of the priests overseeing the excavation. According to the assistant, the priest would patrol the site after the workers left and remove any human remains. He was convinced the workers were not being careful and human remains would be unceremoniously discarded. He would place them in a box to be properly buried later."

"You can't be serious," Daniel said, anticipating where this was going, "The priest removed the bones from the hole and put them in a box and tucked them away to be buried? And nobody put two and two together that they might be Saint Peter's?"

Frannie chortled, "A woman did."

"Ah!" The Cardinal exclaimed. "It was not good for man to be alone. God created woman to be a helper fit for him. Doctor Guarducci was a helper indeed!"

Frannie pondered out loud, "Jesus sent Mary Magdalene, a woman who found Jesus' empty grave, to tell Peter and the others Jesus had risen from the dead. It seems fitting that two thousand years later, a woman finds Peter's empty burial place and tells the world where he was buried and uncovers his bones."

Daniel was still befuddled at the absurdity of the whole thing. "Why were his bones in a wall and not in the grave enshrined to him?"

Frannie answered, "Peter's bones were probably moved before Constantine built the basilica. The Red and Graffiti Walls were already there. The theory is they moved the relics to protect them. You have to remember, Christians were fiercely persecuted in those early days."

The Cardinal nodded. "Evidence suggests the grave was only known to Christians; the Red Wall and the facade built on it were designed to look pagan as a cover to hide the resting place of the highly regarded Apostle. It is known that Pope Sylvester revealed the location of Saint Peter's tomb to Constantine. It is speculated that he left out the fact that the tomb didn't contain his bones because he wasn't sure he could trust his newly Christian friend. History proves he was right to be cautious: when Julian the Apostate came to power twenty years after Constantine, he created discriminatory laws against the Christians and severely oppressed them."

Daniel crossed his arms. "So, a lot of this is a theory about a pile of ancient bones found in a wall. Is there anything scientific to substantiate this claim? I mean, it's not like we can check his dental records."

"Actually yes," the Cardinal said, "much scientific research was done. The bones were identified to be an elderly male of robust build, suitable for a hardworking fisherman. They were wrapped in a royal purple cloth that under examination, contained threads of gold. Gold and purple cloth for dignitaries was a common practice, indicating he was given the utmost respect and dignity at his burial. Soil was found in the bones, suggesting they had originally been buried in the ground. A chemical analysis test revealed the soil matched the ancient soil in the original grave, as found in the excavation. Most telling, the bones of both feet were missing. This attests to the tradition that Peter was crucified upside down; the feet were likely brutally cut off to remove the body quickly from the cross.

"And don't forget the marking of *Petros Eni*, 'Peter is here,'" Frannie added.

Daniel stared at the marble behind the golden grate. If nothing else, he was sitting on top of an ancient necropolis and staring at a monument that was built in the fourth century honoring the grave of a man alive at the time of Christ. And people still flocked to this spot with devotion to the One Peter followed. Like the Pantheon and other Roman ruins, it was still here.

"If we go through that door to the left," the Cardinal said, "we can look at the bones."

Daniel followed him and went up a few stairs and stepped into a dimly lit room surrounded by ancient ivory and honey colored brick walls. A platform had been made for a person to view an excavated area behind a glass. When Daniel peered in, he saw a large slab with old scratches on it that he assumed was the Graffiti Wall. And in the wall was the hole, just as described, which now held bones in clear containers, with a light shining on them.

Daniel felt his hair stand on end. He wanted to be skeptical, but looking in the repository at the bones, there was something believable about the story he had been told. The hypothesis couldn't be proven beyond a shadow of a doubt, but the archaeologists had used science and reason to their limits. It was very possible he was looking at the bones of Saint Peter the Apostle.

"I guess I never thought about the Church employing the sciences. I thought you were all about taking leaps of blind faith."

The Cardinal looked kindly at him. "Daniel, faith and reason are like two wings that lead a person to truth. If you continue to search, our faith is the most reasonable thing you'll ever study. It is far from blind. It is that which helps you see life most clearly."

Daniel took one last look at the old wall and relics, and went back down the steps to the chapel.

"My other reason for bringing you two here," Cardinal Menconi announced, "was to give you a blessing before you leave for your trip."

Daniel looked a little uneasy. There was that word again: blessing.

"A blessing?" he asked. "What does that entail?"

"Relax, Fitzpatrick. It's not an exorcism," Frannie remarked sarcastically.

Her uncle scowled at her, silently rebuking her.

"Sorry, I was just joking," she said, defensively.

The Cardinal turned his attention to Daniel. "Don't worry, it's quite simple. I am going to recite a short prayer, sprinkle you with holy water, and make The Sign of the Cross over you. Let us begin. *In nomine Patris, et Filii, et Spiritus Sancti...*"

They departed the chapel and went back up the stairs to the main level of the basilica. It was nearly seven o'clock and the last of the pilgrims were mulling around before the church closed. As they neared the main entrance, the Cardinal asked for a moment to talk to Frannie alone.

Daniel strolled across to the main center aisle and marveled again at the enormity of the church. He looked to the right, and an ivory colored statue caught his eye. It was on a pedestal, with a rose and brown colored marble slab behind it. On the marble slab was a white cross, positioned so that the statue appeared to be directly beneath it. Daniel moved toward it, as if being pulled by a magnet. When he got closer, he realized it was a depiction of Mary holding the body of her Son, Jesus, just taken down from the Cross in her lap.

There was something about the woman that captured his attention. Her beautiful face expressed a soft sadness as she looked upon her child. One of her hands wrapped under his arm, just touching his ribcage to support his dead body. As Daniel studied her more closely, he felt a sense of acquiescence within the woman to the moment; her other hand was held out and upward as if she was offering her Son to him. He became still as a stone, transfixed by the beauty of the statue and the woman's face.

On the other side of the church, Cardinal Menconi whispered to Francesca, "What do you hope to learn from Archbishop Kratzer?"

"I don't know *Zio*, I struck up a conversation with an American woman who lives there and then the trip was affirmed while in prayer. Daniel almost didn't agree to it when I told him."

The Cardinal chuckled, "Our friend has the heart for our faith. He just needs to get over whatever stumbling block is in his way."

The heart. She recalled her first visit to the Vatican chapel: *The Lord looks on the heart.* Her uncle jolted her back to the subject of the Austrian Archbishop.

"Tell Archbishop Kratzer I know you are meeting with him. We have a good relationship and I don't want him to think I am being deceitful. He is smart and will know that you have circumvented Vatican contacts on purpose."

"Is it safe to mention the letter from Baldano and the list?"

He took a moment to consider before answering. "Yes. If the situation presents itself." He looked across the church and turned his head toward the motionless Daniel. "I think the heart of our friend has been enchanted by the *Pieta*. He's been standing there this whole time. You should let him know they are ready to close and I am the reason we are not being rushed out of here." He added sternly, "But show more compassion and patience, Francesca."

She stiffened with indignation. "I am compassionate and patient with him, *Zio*," she said impatiently. "My joke earlier was just our usual banter with each other."

"Hmm. I see," he said, raising his eyebrows. "I have been sensing something between the two of you!"

She laughed nervously. "There is no 'something.' We are not–" she stopped, flustered at her uncle's suggestion. "I am not having this conversation with you!" she whispered angrily.

She spun around and stormed off, trying to calm herself with each step. When she arrived next to Daniel, she started to tell him it was time to leave but quickly closed her mouth. His gaze was riveted on the sculpture, his eyebrows pulled down in concentration. His arms were limp at his side, but his fingers were stretched apart, as if he ached to comfort the Woman holding her dead Son.

"It's beautiful, isn't it?" she said softly.

"It's so beautiful, it–it pierces you," he whispered.

Francesca's eyes widened in shock. How could he be so cynical at the tomb of Peter and yet be deeply affected by this statue? Her eyes darted back and forth between him and the *Pieta*.

It's Her, she thought. *She's the one who has captivated him.*

Historical facts she had to memorize as a tour guide came flooding back to her.

"It's called the *Pieta*. Michelangelo carved it when he was only twenty-four years old. He did it out of one slab of marble."

Daniel shook his head slowly. "Incredible."

"Mary would have been much older than he has portrayed her to be. He received criticism for it, but he said it was intentional; he wanted to impart the timelessness of the beauty and purity of the Blessed Virgin Mary."

Francesca hesitated before revealing another piece of Michelangelo history, but felt nudged to share it. "It is rumored he was thinking of his own mother's face; he was only five or six when she died."

Daniel's skin prickled as Francesca's words fell on him. He became unusually aware of the necklace hidden beneath his clothes and the medal that hung from it. His reason for wearing it was not out of any religious devotion. He rarely gave it much thought.

She loves you. Like a Mother.

Daniel heard the words loud and clear but was uncertain where they came from. His head whipped toward Frannie. "What?"

Frannie's throat went dry. Maybe she shouldn't have added that last part. "Um, Michelangelo's mother—"

"No, what did you say after that?"

Frannie's brow furrowed. "Nothing."

Daniel looked back at the art piece.

Francesca was hesitant to interrupt the silent conversation that was obviously taking place in Daniel's soul. The pacing guard reminded her it was past closing time. She lightly placed her hand on his shoulder.

"Are you all right?"

He knew what he heard. If Frannie didn't say it, there was only one other alternative, and he wasn't ready to consider it.

"Yes. I'm fine," he said, trying to sound normal despite the intense conflict inside his head.

"We need to go. The only reason they haven't kicked us out is because we're with *Zio*."

Daniel stole one last glance at the sculpture and followed the Cardinal and Frannie out the main entrance, down the steps, and onto the main street where Paolo was waiting for them. Daniel was quiet on the ride, speaking only to say good night.

Once in his apartment, he dropped onto his bed and buried his face in his hands, trying to make rational sense out of what happened to him at the *Pieta*.

God isn't going to speak to you, he told himself. *You must have imagined it.*

He concluded it had something to do with hearing Michelangelo lost his mother at a young age. He tried to convince himself there was a reasonable and psychological explanation; the stirring of an emotion stored somewhere in the recesses of his boyhood memories. But the burning he felt in his soul told him otherwise.

Chapter 17

DANIEL SLEEPILY REACHED OVER AND HIT SNOOZE on his phone alarm, hoping for a few more minutes of sleep. He and Frannie had arrived in Milan at ten o'clock in the morning. They'd forced themselves to stay up most of the previous night and through the three hour train ride so they could take a long nap at the hotel in preparation for the surveillance of Elena and Giovanni's restaurant that evening.

Groaning, Daniel willed himself to get out of bed. After a shower, he met Frannie in the lobby at six o'clock, refreshed and ready to head to the Donati establishment located northwest of the city center.

Frannie cruised up and down the street in front of the restaurant, trying to locate a parking place that could double as a stakeout point. After thirty minutes, someone finally left and she skillfully swung the compact Fiat in the vacant parking spot.

"We made it!" she happily exclaimed, turning off the car.

She glanced over at Daniel. He had both hands gripped on his knees and his eyes closed. She shook his shoulder. "Hey! We're here."

"I'm waiting for my equilibrium to return to normal," he said gruffly. "I don't know which was worse; your jerky driving or everyone else's."

"Ahem," she grunted. "I think what you meant to say was, 'Thank you, Frannie, for expertly maneuvering the small and narrow streets of Milan and finding the perfect place to park.'"

He opened his eyes. The street was lined with tall trees, giving them a perfect cover. "These trees are perfect," he admitted, surveying the area, "they will help block any street lights from shining into the car."

She repeated her faux politeness more forcefully, "You're welcome, Daniel. For expertly maneuvering the small and narrow streets of Milan and finding the perfect place to park for the stakeout."

"Okay, okay," he said, holding his hands up. "I'm sorry. You did a wonderful job, given that everyone here drives like a maniac." Her scowl remained in place. "I'll tell you what," he added in a conciliatory tone, "I'll buy your dinner this evening. However many courses, desserts and lemon-digest-your-food-drinks you want."

Frannie tried to hold onto her pout but was unsuccessful. His description of Italian dining made her snicker. "Since I have to stay awake, it will be an after dinner espresso, not limoncello." She opened her door. "Come on, *Zio* has arranged for us to get into Santa Maria delle Grazie. It's just a few blocks from here and the home of Leonardo da Vinci's *Last Supper*."

They crossed a piazza and approached the church and museum complex. At the entrance, Frannie handed a letter written by the Cardinal on his stationery to the attendant, and he waved them through without a ticket. They filed in behind the last group of tourists allowed in for the day.

As they waited, Frannie gave Daniel her five cent tour. "The church remains an active monastery and convent. Da Vinci painted the *Last Supper* on a wall in the refectory, or dining hall. He wanted to experiment, and made the decision to paint it on a dry wall rather than wet plaster. It was an epic fail."

They entered the humidity controlled room and Francesca lowered her voice to a whisper, "He had to repair it even in his own lifetime. Between that and the monks tearing up the bottom of the fresco to put in a door, damage from Napoleon's soldiers, and bombs from World War II, it's a miracle it has survived at all." By the time she finished, they were face to face with the famous painting.

Daniel placed his hands on his hips. "It really is just painted on a wall," he whispered with an incredulous grin. "I would have guessed it was framed and in a museum somewhere."

"Not much of what you see is actually Da Vinci's work; much restoration has been done because of the failure of the first painting technique. When *Zio* brought me here the first time, he told me it was a lesson that even the most brilliant minds make errors in judgement. But just as Da Vinci's life isn't defined by this mistake, our mistakes shouldn't define us; we have to be willing to try again."

Daniel's stomach dropped. His past was full of errors in judgement that he had allowed to shape him into a loner. The Cardinal's advice reminded him of one of Grandma Mae's favorite phrases: *You'd best get glad in the same britches you got mad in.* It was her way of telling him to get over it and move on. The phrase irritated him now as much as it did then.

"Your uncle and my grandmother would have gotten along well. She also had a knack for turning anything into a proverbial lesson for something."

"He thinks I'm in the wrong line of journalism. This was probably his way of reminding me I can change course. I know he means well but it's annoying."

Daniel started chuckling.

The tour guide hushed them. "What's so funny?" Frannie asked, turning around so the tour guide couldn't see them.

"We're looking at one of the most famous paintings in the world, and instead of being inspired or in awe, we're both annoyed."

"Why are you annoyed?"

Daniel didn't want to tell her the real reason so he embellished a random thought he had earlier. "I'm annoyed that it's on a wall in a cafeteria."

"It was originally commissioned by a duke to be turned into a mausoleum."

He raised his brows. "Wow, that duke was taking 'last supper' to a whole new level."

Frannie bent over in a fit of giggles and the tour guide made another announcement to be quiet. People were starting to stare so Daniel put his arm around her shoulders and ushered her out where they could laugh freely. Back on the street, Frannie regained her composure and held her sides. "Whew! Oh, my sides hurt."

"I don't think the attendant was too happy with us."

"I hope he doesn't tell *Zio*." She nodded toward the piazza. "Let's go eat."

The Donati's establishment, *Sotto l'Albero*, was a typical family eatery: white tablecloths covered the tables, bottles of wine lined the back wall, and waiters donned white dress shirts and black aprons.

Frannie asked if they could sit in the back corner for privacy, and the waiter agreed. The table gave them a panoramic view of the front door and most of the eating area.

"Well, what do you think?" she asked.

"I haven't even looked at the menu."

"So I noticed. I meant the restaurant."

"How old did the Cardinal say Elena and Giovanni would be?" he asked, oblivious that he never answered her question.

"Giovanni is in his mid to late thirties. Since she had Giovanni as a teenager, that would put her in the early to mid-fifties." She watched Daniel scrutinize every worker, hoping one of them would fit the mark. His menu still lay untouched on the table.

"Do you want me to order for you or do you want to know what the dishes are?"

Daniel gave it a cursory once-over. "I don't see the words *spaghetti* or *lasagne* so just order. I trust you." He scanned the area for a worker in Elena or Giovanni's age group. No one stood out to be anyone other than wait staff.

During their courses of salad and Risotto alla Milanese, Daniel constantly surveyed the room, hoping Elena or Giovanni would come out to greet the patrons. After the waiter brought the main dish, he caught something out of the corner of his eye. He almost dropped his fork.

"Frannie!" he whispered, "look at the kid who just walked in."

At the front counter, a young man with an athletic build and light brown hair sporting a Milan soccer t-shirt was handing over an insulated delivery bag and appeared to be waiting for the next delivery.

"What if that's the kid who hand delivered the list?" he asked.

Frannie scrunched up her face. "That seems like a long shot. But, there's one way to find out." She grabbed her phone. "Lean in and act like we're taking a selfie. Smile!" Daniel leaned in for the fake photo op, never taking his eyes off the target. Frannie kept the camera aimed at the front of the restaurant and snapped three photos of the young man. When she finished, he had taken another stack of food orders and was out the door.

She enlarged the photos so his face could be clearly recognized and texted them to her uncle, asking if it was the same person.

Daniel stared at the phone, waiting for the reply.

"He's probably at dinner, so he isn't going to answer right away." She gestured toward his plate with her fork. "Yours is getting cold."

Daniel reluctantly pulled his eyes away from the phone and to his dinner plate. "What is this?"

"Cotoletta alla Milanese. It's a classic veal dish."

Daniel stared at the fried meat cutlet with arugula greens on top. "It's fried," he stated flatly.

"I offered to give you choices but you told me to order," she retorted defensively.

"I'm sure it's delicious," he said to soothe her. "I was expecting pasta. Not something that looks like chicken fried steak."

"I can assure you, that is not chicken fried steak," she informed him, slightly offended at his food comparison.

Daniel took a bite. The meat was so tender, it nearly melted in his mouth. He took his wine glass and lifted it toward Frannie. "Thank you. For ordering another wonderful meal."

Frannie's limbs felt numb. Daniel Fitzpatrick's gracious manners made her head spin. She steadied herself and lifted her glass to his. "You're welcome." Their eyes met and for a brief moment Frannie wondered if this was the real Daniel rather than the one she met at the airport.

The sound of Frannie's cell phone vibrating and buzzing on the table caused them to jump, both slightly embarrassed and grateful for a distraction. *Zio* had responded to Frannie's text.

She translated the Italian message, "It looks very much like the young man who gave me the list, but I am hesitant to say for sure. The next time you—" Frannie stopped.

"What? Did he remember something else?" Daniel asked anxiously.

She groaned morosely and continued reading, "The next time you go visit a sacred destination it would do you well to remember you represent the Menconi family name. I love you and be safe." She plopped the phone on the table. "Can you believe he found out about that already?"

Daniel felt guilty for purposely inventing cheeky humor to distract from his personal moping. "Tell him it was my fault."

Daniel's growing list of noble character traits was too much for her to process. She avoided looking at him, afraid of being swept away by a gentleman hiding behind a pair of blue hazel eyes and lightly freckled face.

Frannie waved her hand. "He'll forget about it. More importantly, if a Donati employee is the secret delivery man, that shoots Baldano being the sender out of the water."

Daniel finished her thought, "And implicates someone in the Donati family."

After dinner, Frannie ordered a couple of espressos to help them stay awake. Daniel drank quietly, brooding over the delivery man. He finally broke the silence, "According to your uncle, the young man said something about entrusting to *Zio* what had been handed to him. What could that mean? And why would Donati, who we put on the enemy list, reach out to your uncle?"

She shook her head. "I'm at a loss. None of it makes any sense."

Daniel took up his habit of strumming his fingertips on the table. When he stopped, he said, "A possible link connecting the Donatis to the clergy list changes things. My idea to talk to Elena or Giovanni has to be aborted."

"Do you still want to do the stakeout?"

"Yes. You never know what we might see." He smiled mischievously. "Besides, I wouldn't want that perfect parking spot to go to waste."

Chapter 18

T HE STREETLIGHTS ALONG THE SIDEWALK IN FRONT of the *Sotto l'Albero* restaurant cast a pale illumination onto the road. The trees provided the shaded cover Daniel was hoping for, preventing the light from shining directly into the car. They were parked across the street and two parking spots down from the restaurant, giving them an unobstructed view of the front door. By half-past ten Daniel and Frannie were nestled in their seats and ready for the long night watch. Frannie reached behind the seat and pulled out a ball cap. She placed it on her head, and slid down slightly.

"What are you doing?" Daniel asked.

"We're on a stakeout. I thought we needed to be incognito."

He pressed his forefinger over his mouth to suppress the laugh that wanted to escape from his lips. It had been a futile exercise trying not to like Frannie; he had already conceded that much. But now she was just plain adorable. She was just as cute in a baseball cap as he thought she would be.

Don't go there Danny, he scolded himself. Struggling to keep a straight face he asked, "Do you think a Boston Red Sox cap with a big red 'B' will draw more or less attention here on the small and narrow streets of Milan?"

She angrily yanked it off her head and threw it in the back seat. "I was trying to avoid any recognition from the restaurant."

"I watched. I didn't see anyone paying much attention to us." He pulled a camera and a set of binoculars out of his bag. "Now it's just a matter of getting comfortable; we're going to be here a while."

Frannie settled back into her seat but quickly grew fidgety. After thirty painful minutes, she announced, "I need something to pass the time."

"I had a feeling you weren't going to handle the quiet well," Daniel muttered.

"This will help," she said, holding up a wireless speaker. "Some tunes!"

She chose a playlist on her phone she used for running. The first song was by New Kids on the Block.

"Ugh," Daniel grumbled as the first notes were sung, "you can't be serious."

Frannie put her hand over her heart. "You don't like New Kids? Were you dropped on your head as a child?"

She saw his eyes roll. "Fine," she huffed, scanning the songs. "How about something even more retro?"

The recognizable piano notes of "Don't Stop Believin'" began to play.

"Better," he said.

Frannie started to sing along but was interrupted by Daniel's protest, "Whoa! Stop! You are absolutely tone deaf. You're hurting my ears."

Daniel's charming manners had gone out the window. "You crap on my song choices and now my singing!" she spat. "I suppose you think you can do better?"

He took his eyes off the street for a brief second and shot her a devilish grin. When he started singing, Frannie's mouth fell open. His strong voice rang out in perfect pitch. Frannie waited for the instrumental break to stop the music.

"You have an amazing voice!" she declared.

Daniel felt sheepish for allowing himself to be goaded. He didn't sing in public anymore.

Frannie started the music again. "Come on, Fitzpatrick, drown me out."

Reluctantly, Daniel chimed in. It didn't take long for him to start belting out the notes with confidence. His chest was drumming like his heart would soar out of his rib cage. Singing was a part of him that had been buried for a long time, and it was as if his soul had taken flight.

When their car karaoke had ended, Frannie turned the music down. "Okay, you can't have a voice like that without a story behind it. So, what is it?"

Frannie's question brought Daniel down from the clouds and crashing back into reality. "There isn't a story. I can sing. That's it."

She lowered her chin. "You surely have done more with that instrument than singing in the shower."

There was no way out of his predicament; he was stuck in a car for hours with Frannie with no escape. He knew she wasn't going to let him off the hook. At least he could stare out the windshield as an excuse not to make eye contact.

"I sang at every neighboring and tri-county fair beginning at age twelve. When I turned sixteen, some guys wanted me to sing with their band at the local bar on Friday nights. Jackson is a small town and no one cared that I was under age. Grandma Mae made the guys promise that I wouldn't be given any alcohol." One side of his mouth tweaked up, "They kept their word; no one dared to cross Grandma Mae.

"The bar was also a restaurant and a popular hangout for most of the town. Singles and families would come out for the music and dancing. I sang every country and southern rock song you can think of. The crowd loved me; and I loved the crowd and the applause. When I was on stage performing," he said wistfully, "I wasn't Danny Fitzpatrick; the boy without a mom or dad who lived with his grandma. I was someone else."

He cocked his head to the side, "I guess you could say singing allowed me to define myself on my own terms. Kind of like the lesson in Da Vinci's painting."

Daniel's depth of introspection proved to Frannie once again he wasn't the shallow journalist she had pegged him to be.

"Do you play any instruments?"

"I play guitar but not very well. I learned enough chords so I had something to occupy my hands while I sang."

"A handsome boy who played the guitar and could entertain a crowd? I bet you broke a lot of young girl's hearts," she said playfully.

Daniel's nostalgic expression turned sour. "I only loved one girl in high school," he confessed. The trip down memory lane was snowballing down a hill he couldn't stop. "Heather and I planned to get married, but I didn't have any money for college. I knew a career in music would be a long hard road for a family. So I decided to join the Marines. The goal was for me to get a college degree on the GI Bill. Then, I got sent to Afghanistan for nine months."

His voice became lifeless, dead to any emotion. "I guess I wasn't worth waiting for. When I came back, I found out she had slept her way around town. I was humiliated. As the town enter-tainer, everyone knew me. There was nowhere to hide from the gossip or whispers. So I signed up for another tour in Afghanistan. I didn't care if I came back or not."

Frannie sucked in a breath at the disregard for his own life. "Daniel, I'm so sorry."

He shrugged. "I obviously came back. I have a knee that gives me trouble from time to time but that's about it. I know guys that came back missing limbs so I guess you would tell me God's blessed me there, too?" he asked with sarcasm.

Yeah, I would, she thought. Her mind drifted to his comment about Da Vinci. *He has allowed his past to define who he is.* Her heart sank. *Zio* didn't send her to Santa Maria to see the painting as a lesson for her. It was for Daniel. She began chiding herself, *Not everything is about you, Frannie.* She had the same narcissistic tendencies she accused Daniel of having.

"Frannie!"

She jumped, startled. "What?"

Daniel had his camera in one hand and was handing her the binoculars with the other. "We have company."

She held the optics up to her face and adjusted the focus to bring the fuzzy street into view. Daniel had snapped a half dozen photos with his zoom lens by the time he heard Frannie gasp out loud in recognition.

"It's the bald man that was following us!"

"It sure is," Daniel replied, continuing to shoot pictures at lightning speed.

"What is he doing in Milan?" she wondered out loud.

The door to the restaurant opened and a woman in her fifties came out with a brown sack. They had what appeared to be an unpleasant exchange. She handed the bag to the bald man who opened it and nodded. He turned and walked to the end of the street, where he got in the passenger side of a car, and was gone.

"The street was too dark for me to get the plates," Daniel said. "But, I got the man and the woman."

Frannie was still staring at the restaurant, stupefied.

"Well," Daniel said cheerily, as if he had finished a family photo shoot, "no unmarked delivery trucks unloading mysterious boxes, but I'll bet my bottom Euro our bald friend wasn't here picking up take-out."

Frannie finished her double espresso and was contemplating a caffè Americano. The combination of her heartache over Daniel's personal story and the scene that played out in front of the Donati restaurant had supplied a poor night's sleep. Daniel was on his way to join her at the café next to the hotel to discuss the events of the previous evening.

When he arrived, his tired eyes gave away the fact that his slumber had been as short and restless as hers.

"Do you need a double espresso, too?" she asked as he sat down at the table.

He nodded wearily. "Yes, please."

She flagged the waiter for Daniel's coffee order. He looked at the spread of meats, cheeses, and pastries on the table. It was mid morning and as usual, Frannie had anticipated his need for fuel. He had tossed and turned most of the night; it wasn't like him to share so much about himself and he worried it would make things awkward between him and Frannie. As he filled his plate and watched her silently say grace, he didn't feel awkward at all. Her usual routine made him feel oddly at ease.

"I sent the pictures to my contacts," he said in between bites. "They confirmed the woman is Elena, just as we suspected. She remarried, just as the Cardinal told us, to a man named Sergio De Marzo. The young delivery man is their son, Stefano. They weren't able to identify our stalker. The fact that they couldn't find him using social media or a broad internet search is a bad sign; it means he keeps under the radar." The bald man and the implications of him being in Milan was the other reason for his sleepless night.

Daniel continued, "I think I missed something really obvious that night at the river: the guy was horrible at tailing us. He actually made eye contact with me, and then looked away. That's way too sloppy to be a professional hired job. He also sat very close to us and got up as soon as I did. A rookie would have been more covert than that. I think his following us was a last minute decision, and he didn't count on us spotting him."

Frannie digested the information. "If Mr. Baldy is under the radar, we may have been right to suspect he is part of the Fratelli Mafia."

"I thought the same thing. He could have been there to collect a payment of some sort. That would explain the bag."

She wrinkled her nose. "There is something about this that doesn't add up. I watched Elena's reaction. She looked frightened."

"If the Garones bankrolled the restaurant, why would she be scared of one of their guys?"

"Maybe she doesn't want to be involved with them. Her first involvement with the Garones didn't fare so well." She leaned on her elbow and gave him a pointed look. "I'm a woman, Daniel. I can tell when a female is terrified."

Daniel rolled his fingers on the table.

"What are you thinking?" Frannie asked.

Daniel looked at her quizzically.

"You roll your fingertips when you're thinking," she said.

He stopped and crossed his arms, self-conscious that Frannie had been observing his quirky habits. "You make a good point. It would make sense Elena would be wary of the Garone clan and their business partners. One would think Elena would be hesitant to become involved with them again. But it doesn't appear they are as separated from the family as the Cardinal thought."

"Maybe they wouldn't let them out or they've found a way to bring them back in. Either way, she doesn't look happy about it."

"I guess we'll see what tonight brings." Daniel glanced at his watch. "We should go. We have to switch hotels so you can check in under the Cardinal's reservation, and I need a nap before tonight's concert. I scheduled an Uber to pick us up at six."

"I could use a nap, too. We need to be well rested and ready for our encounter with Cardinal Constantini. *Zio* said there was a possibility Donati could be there, too. We could get two for one tonight."

He grabbed a pastry for the road. "It's time to call the Cardinal and remind him to make his phone call."

Chapter 19

DANIEL KNOCKED ON FRANNIE'S DOOR AND WAITED. He brushed some lint off his jacket. He made it a point to always travel with a suit; he never knew when formal attire would be required. Little did he know he would need it for this concert fundraiser at a Catholic cathedral.

He checked the time and rapped again. "Frannie?" he called. The door opened. "The Uber is—"

Daniel stopped and stared at the woman standing in the doorway.

The top of Frannie's sleeveless cocktail dress was white with a round neck, embellished with black flowers containing a sequin in the center of each. It gathered at the waist, then flowed out into a black pleated skirt, hitting at her knees. Around the waist was a wide black sash, tied at the side. A pair of heeled black sandals accentuated her muscular calves, earned by years of running. Loose, cascading curls of dark brown hair rested on her shoulders and down her back.

She was stunning.

"You look—" Daniel started, then caught himself. "You look nice," he finished, sounding clumsy.

She blushed bashfully at his cumbersome compliment. "Thank you. You clean up pretty well yourself, Fitzpatrick." Frannie drank in Daniel's appearance. He was extremely handsome in his navy blue suit. He had stylishly paired a baby blue pin-striped shirt with a blue and gray diamond patterned tie. She noticed the colors brought out the blue in his eyes.

Daniel extended his hand toward the hall. "After you."

On the ride down the hotel elevator, Daniel had to fight the urge not to steal another look at the lovely woman standing next to him. Her dress revealed nothing but her natural beauty. Paolo's words about chivalry and a woman of virtue resurfaced: *when you find that kind of woman, you will want to treat her like a lady.*

At the Uber, he walked around and opened the door for her.

Her face beamed as she expressed her appreciation, "Thank you."

A warm sensation filled his chest as he rounded the back of the car and climbed in. *I think she liked that. One point for you, Paolo.*

The streets near the Duomo were lined with cars so Frannie asked the driver to drop them off a couple of blocks away.

As the car rolled to stop, Daniel handed the driver a tip. He saw Frannie put her hand on the door handle. "I've got it," he said.

He opened her door and took her hand, lifting her out of the car. "Which way?" he asked, offering her his arm.

Frannie tilted her head and looked dubiously at him.

"If we're supposed to be a couple tonight, shouldn't we act the part?"

She nodded numbly and looped her arm through his. "Straight ahead."

Frannie's head was light as a balloon. Act the part? Is this how he would treat a woman on a date? *Don't start swooning,* she scolded herself, *you need your wits about you. Besides, stray dogs can seem nice at first.*

They headed for the headquarters of the Veneranda Fabbrica del Duomo di Milano, where the evening would begin with cocktails and hors d'oeuvres. The Veneranda Fabbrica, or "Venerable Factory of the Duomo of Milan," was established six hundred years ago when construction for the cathedral began, and in modern times still remained responsible for the preservation and restoration of the iconic church. It was here they planned to meet Cardinal Constantini and, if they were lucky, Cardinal Donati.

Frannie gave her name to the attendant at the front booth and showed her ticket, but he claimed she was not on the list of attendees. She began to explain who she was and that she had come in her uncle's place.

"I'm sure Cardinal Menconi would have called and told someone," she said innocently. "You don't have my name, Francesca Menconi, on the list anywhere?"

"No, *Signorina*, I am sorry. You are not listed."

"There has to be some mistake," she pleaded. "Is Cardinal Constantini here? My uncle said to ask for him if there was any trouble."

The attendant spoke into a hand-held radio, and asked Frannie and Daniel to step to the side. Another man arrived and Frannie recounted the same story. He left and came back, followed by a tall man with ash gray hair wearing a Cardinal's simar, walking with an elegant gait. The tall man shook hands and greeted some people along the way. Within minutes, Francesca and Daniel stood face to face with Cardinal Constantini.

"Francesca," he said genially, taking her hands in his, "what a pleasant surprise! Nicolo called me with his regrets this morning. I am so sorry he has taken ill."

Frannie thought she heard a twinge of suspicion in the Cardinal's remark. "*Zio* was very disappointed. The *Cappella Musicale* is one of his favorites." She gestured toward Daniel and switched to English, "Cardinal, this is my friend, Daniel Fitzpatrick."

Daniel shook his hand firmly. "*Buonasera Cardinale.*"

The Cardinal smiled pleasantly at the greeting. "Nicolo told me you were accompanying Francesca. You are interviewing Nicolo for an American magazine?"

"Yes, your Eminence."

The entryway was getting clogged with people. The Cardinal waved his hand. "Let's get you inside."

He led Frannie and Daniel out of the foyer and into the rooms where the reception was well underway. "Enjoy your evening," he said.

"Your Grace," Frannie said as he was turning to leave, "we would be honored to have dinner with you this evening. I know we are a poor substitute for *Zio*, but I understand there is a reservation in his name at a restaurant across the street. Will you join us, please?"

Cardinal Constantini's eyes darted back and forth between Frannie and Daniel. She had spoken in Italian, but Daniel knew Frannie had just extended the dinner invitation. He watched the Cardinal mull it over, thinking it through. It was evident the Cardinal calculated his every move.

"*Grazie*, Francesca. I am sure you two are much more fun and entertaining than old Nicolo," he said, speaking in English. "It will be a breath of fresh air to have dinner with a young couple in love. I will meet you after the concert."

Daniel placed his hand on Frannie's back and smiled.

"Thank you, Cardinal," she said.

Daniel kept his hand on Frannie's back as they walked toward the bar.

"In love?" Frannie repeated. Her cheeks were warm. "*Zio* was just supposed to say we were dating."

"You didn't flinch, did you?" he asked.

"I don't think so. I may have blushed, though."

"Good. I think it was a test. He wanted to see my reaction. Why else would he switch to English?"

"I don't think he is buying that *Zio* is ill," she said grimly.

Daniel pressed his lips together. "We need to come up with a story before dinner; how we met and how long we've been dating. Just in case."

They quickly fabricated a narrative in the event the Cardinal pressured them for details about their relationship. As they went over their story one last time, a Cardinal simar caught Daniel's eye. He jerked his head in its direction.

"Frannie, do you recognize him?"

"I sure do. That's Cardinal Donati."

"Hmm. The pictures I found online must be old or he's lost a lot of weight. He doesn't look anything like I imagined him."

Cardinal Fortino Donati was a tall and thin man; almost sickly looking. His lanky frame combined with his close-set eyes and hooked nose gave him the appearance of an Ebenezer Scrooge character.

Frannie pretended to sip her wine and hid her mouth behind the glass. "What were you expecting? A robust Vito Corleone from *The Godfather*?"

He liked Frannie's quick wit. "Maybe. I just didn't think," he froze. "Holy—"

Frannie sucked in a loud gasp that barely drowned out Daniel's crude remark. She understood the reason for his exclamation; following behind Donati was Elena, Stefano, and two other gentlemen. The men had to be Elena's husband and Giovanni.

"Is it normal for the whole family to attend this type of thing?" Daniel asked.

"I don't know. I've attended many with *Zio* over the years. But, I was an out of the country guest. I don't recall ever being introduced to the family members of other Cardinals. Their guests are usually benefactors."

The Donati clan were inching closer to where they were standing. Daniel winked at Frannie. "Work your magic."

She wished he wouldn't have winked at her. It caused her heart to flutter and she didn't have time for that right now. With a smile on her face, she stepped forward.

"Cardinal Donati, my uncle said you might be here." She stuck out her hand, "Francesca Menconi. It's been a long time!"

A polite smile spread across the prelate's face, changing his countenance from Scrooge to a wise grandfather. "Francesca! How lovely to see you. Where is Nicolo?"

"He's not feeling well." She gestured in Daniel's direction. "He let my friend and I use his tickets for this evening."

Daniel moved to her side. He watched the Cardinal's polite smile fade into disappointment.

"I see," Donati said softly.

As Frannie was introducing Daniel, Cardinal Constantini appeared. His sturdy stature and charisma overshadowed the frail clergyman. "Fortino," he said, "I see you found Francesca. It's too bad Nicolo couldn't be here."

Daniel didn't understand the Italian conversations taking place, but he watched the other Donati family members. They all stiffened at the arrival of Constantini. Elena bit nervously on her thumbnail, then yanked it away when she noticed Daniel watching her.

"How wonderful you could bring the family, Fortino," Constantini said with a saccharine veneer. "Italians have the closest family ties, wouldn't you agree, Francesca?"

"Of course, your Eminence," she answered evenly. Frannie felt the tension between the Donatis and Constantini. They looked paralyzed with fear.

Cardinal Donati suddenly snapped to attention. "Yes Cesare, you are right." His pale eyes suddenly flashed with light. He met Francesca's eyes with an alert gaze. "In fact, I was hoping to introduce my family to Nicolo."

Elena, too, perked up. "Yes, it's been years since I've seen your uncle. This is my husband, Sergio, my son Giovanni, and my youngest, Stefano."

Frannie translated the family introductions for Daniel, who had been acutely observing everyone's expressions and body language.

A well-dressed woman, obviously a patron of the Duomo, came over to Constantini, wanting his full attention. He reluctantly excused himself, leaving Francesca and Daniel alone with Donati.

Donati's relief at Constantini's departure was palpable. He looked pointedly at Frannie, saying, "Nicolo and I share a similar family story. We both have been entrusted with the care of family members after a tragedy. It is something we have long respected about the other. Please tell him my family regrets that we missed him."

Daniel caught the nearly imperceptible nod he gave to Stefano, before saying goodbye and strolling away with the others.

Stefano approached Frannie and Daniel, and spoke in English, "Tell your uncle that I wish I could have formally met him this evening. He might not remember me; our first meeting was rather quick." He turned to Daniel, "How long will you be staying in Milan?"

"We leave in the morning," he answered as casually as he could. The young man was not shy about dropping hints.

"Mornings in Milan are quite beautiful." Stefano remarked lightly before his eyes drilled into Daniel's. "I hear the skies in the morning will be crystal clear." Stefano smiled pleasantly. "*Ciao.*"

"*Ciao,*" Frannie numbly repeated, watching him walk away.

Daniel stared into his wine glass and swirled it, pretending to care about enhancing its taste and smell. "Do you know what this means?"

"Yes," Frannie replied, taking a drink of her own.

"Donati wanted your uncle to see that Stefano is the one who delivered the list." The excitement in his voice was mounting, "He wants the Cardinal to know it came from him!"

"Yeah, I got that, Captain Obvious," she quipped. "I don't think Donati wrote it. So who did and how did he get it?"

"I don't know, but this is a game-changer."

Frannie said, "People are starting to head to the concert. We need to file in with the stream of people and look natural."

He smiled and made a show of extending his bent arm. "Then, I would suggest you wipe the fussy look off your face."

She blew out her cheeks and replaced it with a smile. "Better?" she asked, placing her arm in his.

"Much."

"Sorry," she whispered as they followed the throng to the Duomo. "His cryptic message about the morning having clear skies jarred me. What was that about?"

"I'm not sure." He lowered his voice, "But don't wander off. Stay by me tonight, please."

She nodded. Daniel's unexpected display of gentlemanly behavior had caught her completely off guard. Even if there wasn't a reason to remain by his side for safety, she would have wanted to stay there anyway.

Chapter 20

"Wow!" Daniel said under his breath. "They sure build big churches here, don't they?"

Frannie grinned at his reaction to the Duomo of Milan, one of the largest Gothic cathedrals of the world.

"This one took six centuries to finish. It was started in the late 1300s and not truly completed until 1965."

The church dominated the Piazza del Duomo, appropriately titled after its namesake. The cathedral's pinkish-white marble façade, illuminated by lights, shone brilliantly against the sapphire night sky. Spires of increasing heights gave the illusion of a triangular shape, ascending upwards towards the gold Madonnina, crowning the highest spire. Six large protrusions that reminded Daniel of thin skyscrapers were symmetrically spaced and projected from the front. Each one increased in elevation, with the two tallest framing the center.

Once in the door, Daniel marveled that despite the cathedral's massive size, it was inviting. Stained glass windows and artwork diffused the interior with light and color. The floor tiles created an impressive quilt-like pattern of geometric florals composed of white, black, and mauve marble. The tall columns and vaulted ceiling guided the eyes upward, flexing the mind toward a transcendent magnificence beyond that of earth.

Daniel let himself be immersed in the present moment. All thoughts of the Donati family and his reason for being in Milan melted away; the grandeur transported him out of the secular world and across the threshold to another place. The Vatican had spurred a similar reaction, but entering the Duomo stirred something within his inmost being. The spiritual experience caused him to reconsider what happened in front of the *Pieta*.

What I heard was real, wasn't it?

A light squeeze forced him to reorient his attention. Frannie's arm was still loosely looped in his, and she was gently trying to get his attention.

"We should take our seats," she whispered.

He noticed they were one of the few left in the main aisle. She must have let him stand there longer than he thought.

They scooted past a couple sitting on an end and positioned themselves in the middle of a pew. Daniel performed a quick sweep of the audience. There were more faces in the church than at the cocktail party, suggesting tickets for the concert were sold to the general public. His eye patrol landed back to his row and to Frannie, sitting beside him. She appeared completely at home in her surroundings, leisurely flipping through the concert program. He had attended a few theater events but this venue was unlike anything he had ever encountered.

Frannie felt the probe of his stare and returned it with raised eyebrows. "What?" she asked, suddenly feeling she was being examined under a microscope.

"This is normal for you, isn't it?" he asked with polite curiosity. "Concerts, large cathedrals, stained glass, art, and European restaurants are just a regular day in the life."

"Being able to visit *Zio* has blessed me with the ability to travel and enjoy unique opportunities. But, I enjoy a baseball game and a hot dog as much as the next person. I guess I'm a bit of a chameleon; I'm able to blend in and be at home in both."

The memory of her wearing the Red Sox hat flashed in his mind. Frannie's timeless beauty and character could shine through whatever she was wearing: a cocktail dress or baseball cap. She was the classic girl next door. His kind of girl.

She gave him a reassuring smile. "I was looking through the program so I could walk you through the concert. The songs will be performed by an all-male schola cantorum. It's a choir dedicated to chant music of the Church. Most will be young boys that attend a specific school for the purpose of musical training. They range in upper grade school to middle school. Since it is a schola, the songs will be in Latin. The majority of the compositions they are singing tonight are dedicated to the Blessed Virgin, but there are also Mass parts like the *Sanctus* and *Agnus Dei.*"

She recalled Daniel hadn't been to Mass in years and assumed the last time he did it wasn't in Latin. "You would know them as the Holy, Holy, Holy and Lamb of God."

A cynical laugh slipped from his mouth. "I don't remember much about Mass except the horrible guitar songs."

"With a voice like yours didn't you sing at church?"

Daniel shifted uncomfortably. Grandma Mae used to beg him to sing for the parish. "I stopped going to Mass after I was Confirmed. I made a deal with Grandma Mae that if I went through the preparation for Confirmation I wouldn't have to go to church anymore. I don't think she thought I would really stop going."

Frannie kept her face void of expression. Daniel's beef with God went back a long way.

A booming voice over a microphone drew their attention to the front. The schola took their places in front of the altar, dressed in magenta cassocks underneath a white surplice: a linen hip-length tunic. Daniel thought they looked like altar boys.

As the boys and men began to sing, Daniel didn't like the sound at all and was about to settle in for the longest concert of his life. But as the song continued, he could hear the deep bass voice of one of the adult males create a sorrowful undertone as the prepubescent voices of the boys blended a higher pitch tone into the mournful melody. He had no idea what the words were, but it imparted a tragic tale.

"What is this song?" he whispered.

"*Stabat Mater*," she quietly replied, "It means, 'The Mother was standing.' They're singing of the suffering of Mary at the Cross."

Daniel closed his eyes. He could detect the different vocal ranges providing layers of harmony. It was soothing and he felt his muscles relax. The image of the *Pieta* came to his mind. The chanting told a musical story worthy of the Woman, her beauty, and sorrow. Suddenly, the song was over and he was jolted back to his pew.

Frannie continued to give him the name of each song and its translation. She noticed that sometimes he shut his eyes and tilted his head, as if he was trying to listen more intently.

"Did you sing in choir at school?" she asked during a pause in between songs.

"Only at the persistence of my high school choir teacher. I figured it would be an easy way to earn my electives. I hated it at first. My status as a local celebrity made me a cocky teenager. I thought learning to read music and sing songs I branded as old and stuffy were beneath me. But a year in I realized she was disciplining my voice; growing and strengthening it like a muscle."

The next song started and he quickly whispered, "I'm in awe of these kids. They're incredible."

Frannie smiled inwardly. Despite his harsh first impression, Daniel Fitzpatrick was capable of being fair and open-minded. And a gentleman to boot.

He's still a stray dog, she tried to tell her pounding heart. The more time she spent with Daniel, it became harder to convince herself this stray was like all the rest.

The concert finished and they waited patiently for Constantini to visit with the people converging upon him to steal a moment with the famous Cardinal.

Daniel studied him from a distance. "He is quite the charismatic charmer, isn't he?"

Frannie rubbed her left temple and nodded.

"What's wrong?" Daniel asked

"I have a slight headache that I'm sure is due to lack of food. Our late breakfast was hours ago. And I'm dreading dinner this evening," she confessed. "Something weird is definitely going on. The Donatis were nearly squirming when Constantini joined us."

"I noticed," he said, clearing his throat. "Here he comes."

Francesca plastered a charming smile on her face and rambled on about the concert for the quick minute it took to cross the street to the restaurant. The waiter led them to their reserved table and Frannie pretended to read the menu. She already looked it up online and Daniel had practiced ordering for both of them. They made a show of discussing the dishes before the waiter arrived. Frannie asked the Cardinal to choose the wine, a gesture to give an appearance he was the head of the table. Daniel ordered pasta for the first course, the salmon for Frannie, and the beef filet for himself as the second. The words rolled easily off his tongue in Italian.

As the waiter took his menu, Daniel glanced at Frannie. He could read the approval on her face, and the warm feeling filled his chest again. Although it had been pre-planned with a lot of preparation, he liked ordering for her. The whole thing was Frannie's idea, since they were supposed to be dating. The suggestion had surprised him. He'd tried ordering for a girl once and received a tongue-lashing for his efforts.

Another point for you, Paolo. Maybe this chivalry thing isn't out of style.

Cardinal Constantini poured wine into their glasses. "What about you, Daniel, did you enjoy the concert?"

"Yes, your Eminence, very much. The talent of the young boys is quite impressive."

"Milan is proud of her cultural heritage. The *Cappella Musicale del Duomo* is our city's oldest cultural tradition. It began in 1402. It is a gift that enriches the Church and one that she can share with the world."

"You surprise me, Cardinal," Daniel said, leaning back casually in his chair. "I didn't think you shared the desire to preserve and protect the traditions of the Church like your friend, Cardinal Menconi. I read you were one of the more progressive clergymen."

Out of the corner of his eye, Cardinal Constantini saw Francesca nervously grab her wine glass and take a drink. Daniel Fitzpatrick was brazen, but relaxed and cool as a cucumber. They stared over the table, each making an assessment of the other.

The Cardinal broke the tension by chuckling lightly. "I see why Nicolo agreed to let you interview him. You are bold and straightforward. In answer to your question, I do not have a disdain for all traditions. But the Church cannot live in the past. She must be ever mindful of the future. In this, my friend Nicolo and I have agreed to disagree."

Daniel smiled reservedly. He had serious doubts about the depth of friendship Constantini felt toward Cardinal Menconi.

The Cardinal directed his attention to Frannie. "Now, tell me, Francesca, where did you meet this young man?"

With Daniel's help, Frannie managed to drag out their fictional storyline over the first course of the meal. The Cardinal's interrogation took a divergence to Daniel's journalism career over the second course. Daniel finished summarizing his essay on the Church scandal, and found a way to make his move.

"In my research, Cardinal, there were many indications that Cardinal Donati's management of the Vatican Bank may have included some outside investments that were, shall we say, dubious?"

The prelate watched Francesca's jaw tighten at her date's unabashed digging for information. This time, he didn't chuckle while answering.

"The Bank has had its share of scandals over the years. Unfortunately, Cardinal Donati has been the subject of unfounded rumors," he stated flatly.

"Are the ones about his ties to the Garone family unfounded?"

"Daniel!" Francesca scolded through her gritted teeth. "What are you doing?" Daniel pretended not to hear her.

"Do you think," he continued, "the Cardinal could be using a business, say—a charity organization—as a front for embezzling church funds?"

"You don't have to answer that, Cardinal!" Francesca exclaimed. She gave Daniel a piercing glare. "I'm so sorry," she said, looking apologetically at Constantini, "for such abrupt rudeness. I—"

"Francesca," the Cardinal said, patting her hand condescendingly, "don't get worked up, child. Daniel is a reporter so he likes to ask questions. I have nothing to hide," he added ominously.

Francesca looked like a volcano ready to erupt. She picked up her purse. "If you will excuse me," she said evenly, "I am going to get some fresh air." She pushed her chair from the table and stormed toward the door.

"So Cardinal," Daniel said, as if nothing had happened, "will you answer my question? Off the record, off course."

Cardinal Constantini eyed his interlocutor coolly. "It appears your lady friend is upset with you."

Daniel shrugged. "I'll apologize later. The Menconis are very forgiving," he said with a sneer.

The prelate flashed his teeth. "You are an ambitious one, aren't you?"

"I'm just a reporter who likes to ask questions."

"I cannot help you. I do not know anything about Fortino Donati's dealings at the Bank."

"And, *Compassione*? Is it purely a charitable organization?"

"I am on the board with Fortino. But I assume someone as shrewd as you knew that. Even as a member of the board I am not made aware of all the money transactions. My role is to act as a consultant for the areas of the world where the money is most needed," he said innocently.

Constantini casually took a sip of his wine and continued, "Unfortunately, the person that could answer your questions is Cardinal Jozef Vidmar, *buonanima*, God rest his soul."

"I take it that means he's dead?" Daniel asked callously.

"Yes. He had a contentious relationship with Fortino. I know for a fact he went to see Cardinal Vidmar the day he died."

Daniel raised his eyebrows. "What are you suggesting?"

"Nothing," he replied, a smug grin resting on his face. "I am simply answering your questions. Now, I would like you to answer some of mine."

"I don't know what I could possibly—"

The Cardinal didn't let him finish. "What are you writing about Nicolo?"

It was Daniel's turn to assess his interrogator. He maintained his confidence in answering, "His views on the current division in the Church and whether there was an underground movement that prevented him from being elected pope in the last conclave."

"And how did my friend answer the last question?"

Daniel didn't want him to know the interview had not yet taken place. He shook his head. "I can't answer that. There are publishing agreements I would violate."

Constantini's normally charismatic glimmering eyes turned to steel. "I see." He took out his wallet and handed Daniel a business card. "If your magazine is interested in a full disclosure interview,

I would be happy to give one. Perhaps you could print both: two Cardinals, two viewpoints, one Church. With your name under both interviews, of course," he added.

Daniel took the card. "I think I understand you, Cardinal." He lowered his voice as Francesca approached. "I'll be in touch when I can."

Francesca calmly lowered herself back into her seat. The waiter reappeared asking for dessert orders.

"I am ready to call it a night," she announced. "It's late." She gave the waiter her credit card despite the Cardinal's objections.

"*Zio* told me to take care of the bill for him." She gave Daniel an icy side glance. "And it is the least I can do in recompense of the boorish behavior you had to endure."

"Daniel and I came to an understanding while you were gone, Francesca. I promise, all is well. Let me offer my driver to take you to your hotel."

Cardinal Constantini was dropped off a few blocks from the Duomo, and instructed his driver to take Frannie and Daniel to where they were staying. Frannie faced the window, almost pressing herself against the door to be as far away from Daniel as possible. When they pulled up to the hotel, she thanked the driver, and hastily shoved the door open, not allowing Daniel to open it for her.

Daniel had to walk fast to keep up with her, angrily punching the up arrow on the elevator. When the doors closed, Frannie's head swiveled toward Daniel.

Her mouth twitched, and they both burst out laughing.

"That was some performance, Menconi," Daniel sputtered.

"Thanks. It worked then?" she asked anxiously. "He was willing to talk?"

"I didn't learn a lot, but it was interesting. He let his shady personality show when he thought I was ready to sell you and the Cardinal down the river."

"Let's have a drink at the bar on the terrace. I can't wait to hear what happened after I left."

She selected the top floor. When the elevator doors slid open, Daniel stuck his arm out. "May I?"

She smiled and placed her arm inside. "Lead the way," she replied, happy she no longer needed to pretend she was mad at him.

Chapter 21

THE HOTEL'S ROOFTOP BAR HAD A MIXTURE OF HIGH
top tables, casual patio chairs and couches. Daniel and
Frannie chose a cushioned loveseat at the far end away from the
crowd, nestled among a patio garden of green vines and plants.

"Constantini really dropped that Donati was with Vidmar the
night he died?" Frannie asked.

"Yep. He made it sound like he was giving me an exclusive tip."

Frannie swirled her Aperol spritz. "So what do you make of it?"

Daniel's gaze drifted over the view of Milan from his perch
on the roof. Modern glass skyscrapers in the distance forged an
anachronistic skyline, clashing against the classic architecture
in the forefront. Daniel loosened his tie, welcoming the fresh air
blowing through the terrace. Putting on a show for the Cardinal
had been more nerve wracking than he anticipated.

"He didn't want to talk about the Bank or *Compassione*—that
was evident. I'm not sure if his tip on Donati was bait for a real
story, or to deflect me from the money trail. One thing's for sure:
when I spoke disparagingly about the Menconi family, he relished
it. I think he's as devious as they come. My shady character radar
was off the charts."

Frannie squished one eye in thoughtful concentration. "To
sum up our Milan trip, we discovered Mr. Baldy has some connection to the Donati family, who by all appearances don't like him.
And there's no love lost between them and Constantini, either. The
Donatis were undoubtedly wanting *Zio* to know they were behind

the delivery of the list of names with Scripture references. And according to an unconfirmed tip by Constantini, Donati was at Vidmar's home the night he died. You want to know what I think?"

She didn't wait for him to answer. "I think Donati is crying out for help. Whether he's gotten in over his head, or was shoved into the deep, I don't know."

Daniel nodded slowly. "I think you're right."

Frannie finished her drink and set the glass on the table in front of them. "Are you sure you don't want anything?"

"I'm fine with water, thanks." He could tell she didn't want to talk about it anymore and he didn't either. They weren't going to solve anything tonight. "How's your headache?" he asked.

"It's gone. A lot of it was stress. I'm glad that's over."

"You played it well. Your anger with me seemed real enough."

"I imagined you were Will Kelly from the TV station. The rest came naturally after that."

Daniel's mind stalled. Their faux hostility masquerade bothered him more than he wanted to admit. Her admission she had to use someone else as a conduit for her anger piqued his attention.

"You didn't have enough animosity to conjure up for me on my own accord?" he teased.

Frannie reprimanded herself for being so transparent. *He's fishing to see if I will say no!*

She wasn't about to give him the satisfaction of knowing how easy she could fall for his charms.

"I've come to the conclusion you're an all right person. When you're not being a dolt."

He grimaced. "A what?"

"A dolt."

"What the—" he stopped himself from uttering his usual profanity. "What is a dolt?"

"A doofus bone-headed idiot." The explanation rolled off her tongue as if she was reading it right out of a dictionary. "But dolt sounds nicer," she added.

Laughter cackled from his mouth. "A nice insult?" He switched to a high girly voice, mocking her, "I may be calling you a stinking sack of dung, but I said it nicely."

Frannie crossed her arms, smacked at being made fun of. "Okay, you go from being a complete ass to gentleman quick as a fastball pitch. Is that easier vocabulary for you?"

Her down-home wit and adorable pout made Daniel howl in laughter even more.

Frannie's mouth quivered, trying hard to maintain a serious face, but it was no use. She broke down in spite of herself and joined in.

Daniel finally gained composure and wiped his eyes with the back of his hands. "Ahh," he sighed. "I can't remember when I've laughed so hard. You are a hoot, Menconi. A real hoot."

She was slightly nettled; her attempt at a backhanded compliment backfired and she became the brunt of the joke.

"Frannie, can I ask you something?"

All sarcasm in his tone was replaced with pure sincerity, but she eyed him warily. "I guess," she said cautiously.

"What did you mean by gentleman?"

This had backfired in a big way. *You might as well tell him,* she told herself, *but try not to be too flattering.*

"Unlike your behavior at the airport," she began, "you were a gentleman this evening. Opening the car door, offering your arm and," she added quickly, "you seemed concerned about my safety at one point." She tried to shrug it off as no big deal, "That's all."

"You didn't find any of those things offensive?"

Frannie carefully measured his question. Daniel wasn't fishing for anything. He genuinely wanted to know her answer.

She shook her head. "No, I didn't. Those 'things' used to be known as manners that show women are unique; to be guarded and deserving of respect, such as opening the door and so forth. What's offensive is the attitude that girls can't do, know, or handle anything. Or worse, ogling and cat-calls. I think a woman should encourage true gentlemanly manners. It's not diminutive. On the contrary, it should dissuade a man from objectifying her."

"I think you are in the minority of women, with those types of opinions."

"Probably so. It's because women have been sold the false notion that equality means they should be just like men. Our equality comes from our human dignity, not our abilities. Males and females have different gifts; it doesn't make one better than the other. It's like the study you found on wage differences. Women tend to want to be home more if they have children. That's not a weakness or society's failure at achieving equitable outcomes. It's about a woman wanting to embrace her gift of motherhood. That's something that should be celebrated and affirmed, not scorned."

"You're right," Daniel said sadly, "it should."

He shook off the melancholy from an old regret and remarked, "I have never been called a dolt or a gentleman and tonight I was called both by the same woman. That's definitely a first."

Frannie's face was a full revelation of shock. "Really? You've never been called a dolt?"

"Ha, ha, Menconi, you're a laugh a minute," he said over her fit of giggles at her own joke. "Let's go. I'll be a *gentleman* and walk you to your door."

"What time do we need to be at the train station?" Daniel asked as they approached the door to Frannie's room.

"Fifteen minutes before eight."

He looked at his watch. "Short night." He suddenly didn't care about the long train ride. His body longed for the opportunity to catch up from two nights of little sleep.

Frannie pulled her key card out of her purse. "Yep. I'll see you at seven."

A wave of awkwardness engulfed both of them.

"Good night, Frannie."

"Good night," she answered and entered her room.

Daniel moseyed down the hall to his room. Frannie was different from any girl he ever met. For a brief moment, he let himself wonder if he had met a girl who wouldn't break his heart.

❧

Daniel quickly threw his things into his suitcase. He overslept and had to rush to be ready on time. He started to lift his case off the luggage rack and froze: a small manila envelope lay on the floor a few inches from the sill.

He swung open the door and glanced up and down the hallway. It was empty.

He picked up the envelope and flipped it over. There was no name or any writing on it. When he shook it, something small could be heard jostling inside. Ripping open the seal, he let the contents fall on the bed.

Someone had given him a flash drive.

He wondered if it had been there when he woke up or if it was delivered while he was in the shower. A knock at the door made him jump. The knocker was probably Frannie but he looked through the peephole just in case.

Outside his door stood a woman with long blond hair, a silk head scarf tied under her chin, and oversized Hollywood sunglasses. His mind started racing. What if this woman wasn't working alone? What if they already had Frannie?

He grabbed a lamp off the nightstand and opened the door a crack. "May I help you?" He had one hand ready to slam it shut and was prepared to use the lamp as a weapon with the other should someone try to come through the door.

The woman lowered her sunglasses revealing a familiar set of warm green, almond shaped eyes. She pretended to speak in a German accent, "I'm here to collect Herr Fitzpatrick for train ride to Salzburg."

Daniel threw his head back and moaned. "Dammit, Frannie!" he exclaimed as she grabbed her suitcase sitting against the wall outside the scope of the peephole, and entered the room. He quickly closed the door and locked it.

Frannie gaped at him standing there with a scowl on his face, holding a lamp. "What are you doing?"

"What am I—what the hell are you doing dressed like that?"

"I brought it along just in case. Since Constantini's driver knows where we are staying and Baldy is in the area, I thought we should leave Milan in disguise."

She reached in her bag and pulled out a gray wool fedora and a pair of aviator sunglasses with silver lenses. "I have these for you to wear." Her eyes assessed him critically. "Do you have a dress shirt you could wear instead of that polo? A dress shirt with a fedora makes more fashion sense." She put a hand on her hip. "You haven't told me why you are holding a lamp."

Daniel slammed the lamp on the table. "Because this," he said with a forced calm while showing the envelope, "was slid under my door last night, which contained this." He held up the flash drive. "So when I saw a strange blond woman at the door, I wasn't sure what to think and it was the closest weapon I could find."

Frannie inspected the envelope and the flash drive. Her eyes grew wide, "Stefano!" she whispered. "Stefano said something about the morning being crystal clear. There must be information on here!"

"Let's get on the train and fire up the laptop and find out." He dug in his suitcase and pulled out a casual blazer he was going to wear when they met Cardinal Kratzer. He slipped it on over the polo and donned the hat and sunglasses. "You know, a little heads up about the costumes would have been nice."

"I figured you would have been a fuss-bucket about it."

For the first time, Daniel took a full appraisal of Frannie in her blond wig. She was still beautiful, but he liked her natural brown hair better. His frustration with her giving him a fright had dissipated.

"I probably would have," he conceded. "This time, I think it's a good idea to be incognito. How's the jacket with the hat?"

Frannie nodded approvingly. "Not bad. That fedora is a good look for you, Fitzpatrick."

He glanced in the mirror. "Hey, you're right. I look like a famous celebrity."

"Yeah. In khakis and a blazer," she scoffed, pulling her suitcase behind her. "You're right up there with Justin Timberlake."

As they left for the train station, both thought they spotted the Bald Man sitting at the café outside the hotel. Neither of them dared to look and make sure. Playing it cool, they quietly made a beeline for the train station.

Chapter 22

DANIEL SCOOTED HIS LAPTOP TO THE END OF HIS pop-up tray so he and Frannie could share the screen. He inserted the flash drive and held his breath. It contained only one file with a generic name.

"Here we go," he said, before clicking the folder.

The folder contained two files: one document and one photo.

Daniel opened the document first. It was a journal record from a private charter aircraft company documenting a round-trip flight from Rome to the capital of Slovenia. The itinerary was under the name of Cesare Constantini.

"Slovenia," Frannie whispered. "It must have something to do with Vidmar."

Her stomach turned. "I'm pretty sure this flight took place the same year he died."

Frannie grabbed her phone. A quick search for the exact date confirmed her fear. "This flight and Vidmar's death occurred on the same day."

Daniel pointed to the screen. The plane departed Slovenia at two o'clock in the morning the next day. "Why would the good Cardinal need to leave in the wee hours of the morning?" Daniel asked grimly.

He opened the photo file. The image was a page from an appointment book, on the date of Vidmar's death. Most of the notes were for various morning meetings of little consequence.

An entry for three in the afternoon read, "Fortino" and below it another at seven, "Cesare, dinner."

Frannie and Daniel gawked at the screen. They were looking at a page from Vidmar's missing appointment book.

"I feel sick," Frannie said.

Daniel abruptly closed the laptop. "Let's think this through for a minute."

"It's pretty obvious what this means," she hissed.

The pain in her eyes exposed how much the information on the flash drive tormented her. "Still," Daniel said soothingly, "let's look at all the angles. First, if the Donatis have this information, why give it to us?"

Frannie closed her eyes and exhaled slowly as if she were trying to breathe through a wave of nausea. "Maybe," she began, her steely determination returning, "they were going to give it to *Zio* but gave it to us thinking we would deliver the message to him."

"Correct. A message that would make their intentions crystal clear. You were right: they need help."

"Do you think Constantini is trying to blackmail Donati?" she asked.

"Possibly."

Frannie shook her head. "But that doesn't make any sense. If they possess hard proof on Constantini, wouldn't that turn the tables on him? What would he have to hold over their heads?"

"He dropped Donati's name to me. If he wanted me to run with it, he must smugly think no one has producible evidence," he said, pointing to the laptop. "For whatever reason, Donati wants the information to come out, but doesn't want to be the one to do it."

Frannie grabbed Daniel's arm. "Or, can't be the one to do it!" Frannie said excitedly.

Aware of her sudden outburst, she lowered her voice, "At the concert, you noticed the whole family got stiff as a board when Constantini showed up, right? What if he is threatening Elena and Giovanni? After Constantini left, Donati said something you didn't hear because it was in Italian. He made a big deal about him and *Zio* sharing the same story of caring for family members after a tragedy. Maybe Constantini knows about Donati's history with the Garones and is using it to blackmail him."

Daniel's eyes danced, "According to the Cardinal, when the young man delivered the list, he said, 'I am entrusting to you what has been entrusted to me,'" he waved his hand, "or something along those lines. I think you're on the right track: Donati is in over his head and wants help protecting his family. And, I wouldn't be a bit surprised to find Constantini is using the Garone's mafia connection to put pressure on them financially. That would explain Elena's irritation with Bald Man."

"That's got to be it!" Frannie said, still keeping her voice low. Her elation wilted and her shoulders drooped.

"There's a couple of problems," she said sullenly. "One, how did the Donatis get this information without Constantini knowing it; and two, why did they allow the Garones to bankroll the restaurant in the first place?"

Daniel let out a long exhale. "Good questions. Maybe I need to ask my underground contact to dig a little deeper into the bank information."

The train decelerated and sluggishly rolled into the railway station. "I take it this is Venice?" he asked. "Do we change trains or stay on this one?"

"Oh. Um, about that."

He furrowed his brow. "What about it?"

"I kinda messed up," she said apologetically. "We have a three hour layover before our train. Then we change again in Villach. We aren't getting to Salzburg until ten o'clock tonight."

"When did you find this out?" he asked, miffed at her lack of transparency.

"A few days ago when I bought the tickets."

"You know what will make me a fuss-bucket, Menconi?" he said harshly, "if you keep hiding things from me."

She recoiled slightly at his reaction. "I wasn't hiding it on purpose. I simply forgot to tell you!" she said defensively.

Daniel regretted being so coarse with her. He chided himself for always assuming the worst when it came to the opposite sex. Old habits were hard to break.

"I'm sorry. I overreacted. I'm tired and haven't had anything to eat. Maybe you can find me a high carb meal so I can pass out and sleep on the next leg of this trip."

Frannie's sunny nature returned. "We can share some pasta, but this is Venice. You have to have seafood!"

She passed over the restaurants on the main thoroughfare and selected a sidewalk café along one of the quiet water canals a few blocks from the train station. Boats occasionally went by, the drivers waving at the locals. Daniel hungrily dug into a basil pasta dish with seared scallops and pine nuts.

"This is incredible!" he said, taking a break from his plate to take in his surroundings. "So the canals function as the city streets?"

"Pretty much. There are a few alleys, sidewalks, and bridges and that's about it. The famous Grand Canal is a major channel and a popular attraction but I like the smaller, quieter canals like this one." Something told Frannie that Daniel would, too.

"I could live here," he said wistfully, watching a boat sputter by. "No car, just a small boat to get around. I would love it."

His relaxed candor surprised her. "Do you spend a lot of time on Lake Michigan?"

Daniel centered his gaze on the scene in front of him: tall Venetian buildings of white, golden yellow and pink. Just before a curve in the canal that ran alongside of him was an arched bridge over the water. Frannie had removed her blonde wig and pinned up her walnut brown hair with a few loose strands resting on her neck. Sitting against the charming backdrop, Frannie brought to life the most beautiful waterscape he had ever seen.

He slowly returned from his Venice daydream and reached for his glass to hydrate his suddenly parched throat. "Did you ask me something?"

"Yes, I asked if you spent a lot of time on Lake Michigan."

He nodded. "Other than Wrigley Field, it's the best thing about living in Chicago. I do a lot of kayaking in the summer."

Running and kayaking are all hobbies you can do alone, Frannie mused.

"I've always loved the water," he continued. "Growing up, I spent a lot of time at Jackson Lake, just a few miles outside of town. Georgia summers are unbearably hot so everyone flocked to the water to cool off."

"Then in the evening they came back to have a beer and listen to you sing?"

He picked up his fork and returned to his meal. "I was hoping you forgot about that."

"Not a chance! What was the name of the bar?"

"Fuller's Roadhouse. Fuller was the last name of the owner." Daniel chuckled before stuffing his face with the last scallop.

"What's so funny about that?"

Daniel leaned forward. "They had a billboard on the interstate with a beer mug and the slogan, 'Y'all come in, Fuller up and stay awhile.'"

"That's punny," she said, laughing gently.

Daniel shook his head, "I can't believe I admitted that. It's embarrassing."

"Did you like the Fullers?"

"Oh, yeah. They were really good people." His eyes twinkled. "Mrs. Fuller made the best chocolate chip cookies. They had just the right amount of toasted pecans in them. She would send me two dozen at a time when I was in Afghanistan. She would freeze them so they would stay fresh longer. I looked forward to getting her packages. It was like having a little bit of home–" He stopped. His eyes darted away from her and toward the canal.

How did she do that? She asked one question and I'm remembering there were things I actually liked about Jackson.

"If they were good people, who cares if they were a little corny?" she asked, unaware she had nudged him down a lane of nearly forgotten memories.

He didn't have to answer. The waiter brought their main courses of sea bass and shrimp.

After lunch, they walked to the end of the sidewalk and took in the view of the turquoise Adriatic Sea. Frannie sensed Daniel yearned for the open water.

"I'm sorry we can't stay. I guess now you know where to book your next vacation."

Daniel smiled weakly. He never took vacation.

Frannie pointed her thumb in the opposite direction. "Let's go back to the Grand Canal. I want to pick up a few snacks at the store by the train station. We won't have time to stop and eat at Villach."

Daniel waited for her by strolling down one of the small docks in front of the Church of Saint Mary of Nazareth, erected right by the water. He watched the water taxis pick up travelers from the train station. Many tourists went by foot to the Ponte degli Scalzi bridge to cross the other side of the Grand Canal. A band of street performers played and sang near the base of the bridge, welcoming the newcomers to the City of Canals.

Frannie appeared beside him, carrying a grocery bag. "Ready?"

"Yep," said Daniel, giving the canal a final glance.

"There's an idea for you," she said, spotting the musicians, "you could move to Venice and be one of the performers."

"Fat chance of that happening. I would have to learn Italian, then learn Italian songs. No one is coming to Venice to hear me sing Garth Brooks."

Frannie led the way inside the station. "Will you sing a song for me, when we get back to Rome?"

"No," he said flatly.

Her face fell with disappointment. "Why?"

"I don't sing for people anymore."

"You sang in the car with me the other day!"

"That was a lapse of judgement," he remarked sourly.

They boarded the train for Villach and Daniel immediately reclined his seat back. "I'm ready for my nap," he announced.

"How would you like to make a bet?" Frannie asked.

He lifted his head and studied her quizzically with a raised eyebrow. "Excuse me?"

"I will race you from Saint Peter's to the same route we ran in Villa Doria Pamphili, finishing at the top of Janiculum Hill. It will be about seven miles, give or take."

Daniel reset the chair to its upright position. He was bewildered by her proposal. "You want to race me? What for?"

"If I win, you have to sing a song for me: one of the Fuller Roadhouse crowd favorites. If you win, I guess I lose and you don't have to sing anything."

Daniel stared at her. Frannie wouldn't place the wager unless she thought she had a chance of winning. She was a strong runner; he had only beaten her to the top by a couple of steps. After running five miles his knee injury bugged him when he hit the hill, but he hadn't let on about it. A seven mile run could pose a challenge for him.

"What's the matter," she taunted, "afraid of losing to a girl?"

He was stuck. And she knew it.

"All right, Menconi. If you win, I will sing for you. If I win, I don't sing, and you take me to the restaurant in Rome with the best lasagne, where I get to order a plate for both of us. And, you buy dinner." He stuck his hand out. "Deal?"

Frannie took his hand and shook it. "Deal." Her heart was pounding from the adrenaline of sealing the bet and the touch of his hand. "Enjoy your nap, Fitzpatrick," she smirked.

Daniel shook his head. "You're a piece of work, Menconi," he muttered, and reclined his seat back. Frannie had the window seat next to him, and leaned against it. She closed her eyes, a triumphant grin resting on her face. If she played it right, Daniel would have to sing for her.

⟡

Daniel glanced up and down the ticketing area of the train station. Frannie had been by his side and now she was gone. He took long quick strides up and down the platform.

Where did she go?

A sultry voice from his past halted him in his tracks. "Hey, Danny."

Kelsay, his ex-girlfriend, sauntered toward him. She was wearing a tight black dress with a plunging neckline. She tossed her red curls over her shoulder and closed in until there were barely centimeters between them. He tried to get away but his legs and feet were suddenly cemented to the floor.

"Aren't you glad to see me, Danny?"

He pulled his head back and curled his upper lip as if he had just smelled rancid milk. "No. What are you doing here?"

"I've been watching you with Frannie and I'm here to save you from a senseless heartache. She's not for you, Danny."

She placed her arms around his waist. He wiggled to free himself but his feet were still immersed in heavy cement. "What do you think Miss Goody-Two-Shoes would think about you and me? Would she hang around after that?"

Daniel glared at her. Kelsay reacted with a heartless laugh.

"Daniel?"

Frannie had returned and looked at Daniel with hurt confusion.

Kelsay laid her head on Daniel's chest and gave Frannie a daring look.

He tried to release himself from her tentacles but they only became tighter. "Frannie," he pleaded, "it's not what you think."

Frannie turned away, nearly sprinting for the train. Daniel watched helplessly as she boarded and the train pulled away.

Daniel stood alone on the platform. Kelsay vanished in a puff of smoke, and Frannie was long out of sight.

Daniel jolted from his sleep and quickly assessed his surroundings. Two Marine tours in Afghanistan taught him how to awake and instantly be on alert. The tension in his muscles relaxed. He was on a train with Frannie and she was sleeping soundly in the seat beside him.

It was only a dream but remnants remained of panic in his chest from watching Frannie get on the train; a panic that he wouldn't see her again.

She's not for you, Danny.

He cursed silently that Kelsay could still haunt him; even in his dreams. He dug out his laptop and began to prepare the questions he would be asking Cardinal Menconi when they finally sat down for their interview. He needed to refocus his thoughts away from Kelsay and the undeniable truth: Frannie could have her pick of any guy she wanted, and she wouldn't choose someone like him. A lady like Frannie deserved better.

Chapter 23

FRANNIE OPENED THE LOCKBOX WITH THE CODE given to her by the host of the online vacation rental. She opened the door and a rush of relief came over her. She couldn't wait to climb into a bed. Daniel pulled both of their suitcases and followed her in.

They had agreed an apartment would be more comfortable to work in rather than public coffee shops and restaurants. Frannie quickly assessed the space: a couch and an oversized chair were placed around a coffee table to the right with a kitchen behind it; to the left was a half wall partition with a full size bed behind it.

Her stomach sank. There was only one bed.

"This can't be right," she said, walking over to the makeshift bedroom as if another one would appear. "The listing said there were two beds. I saw the pictures."

Daniel walked over to the couch and removed a couple of the cushions, revealing a sleeper sofa. "Bed number two is a pull-out. Did it say two beds or two bedrooms?"

Frannie felt the heat filling her cheeks. She was mortified by her mistake. "I thought it was two bedrooms with doors."

"It's okay, Frannie," he said, trying to make light of the situation. "I'll take the couch just as it is. As long as I can lay down flat, I don't care where I sleep."

She shifted her weight to one leg and slumped a little. "I'm so sorry."

"It's fine, really." He gave her a half smile. "I'm a Marine. I've slept on worse."

It had been a long forty-eight hours and there was nothing she could do about it now. "I'll see about cancelling this place and getting something different tomorrow."

They took turns using the bathroom and by the time each crawled into their respective sleeping quarters, they had passed out from sheer exhaustion.

The next morning over coffee, Frannie announced, "I found a hotel just around the corner. It has free breakfast, a bar, and a meeting area where we can work if we need it. It's going to be a little more money per night, and I only get a partial refund back on this place. Will that be ok?"

Daniel was already engrossed in his laptop and half glanced at her in between typing. "What's wrong with this place?"

Her silence made him look up again. Her cheeks were pink and he thought her eyes looked wet. It was obvious the sleeping arrangements made her really uncomfortable. He wasn't surprised Frannie held traditionalist views. What shocked him was finding a girl on the planet who had such high standards.

"If you want to move to the hotel, we'll move to the hotel," he said, giving her a reassuring smile.

Frannie's entire frame relaxed. "Thank you."

She got up and refilled their coffee cups. "Were your contacts able to uncover any more information on who is backing Elena's restaurant?" she asked, eager to forget about her epic failure in online rentals.

"They identified the company backing the loan as an angel investor: someone who invests in a start-up business when others may not want to take the risk. In return for the angel's willingness to take a gamble the business venture will be profitable, they may ask for more ownership or a higher percentage of profit return."

"That sounds like a win-win for the Garone family; it would allow them to dip their hands in the cookie jar while keeping their thumb on the business owners. Not to mention it would make an easy front for the Fratelli operations."

"Exactly. My contact pinpointed this particular company as having invested in several restaurants in Italy. In fact," he turned his computer so she could see the screen, "here is a list of restaurants whose ownership is publicly known as being part of the Garone chain."

Frannie scanned the list of over twenty restaurants and the city where they were located. She fell heavily against the back of her chair. "They are all in Rome but one!"

"Yep. One *Sotto l'Albero* in Milan."

She laid a fist against her mouth as she processed their newest finding. "It may connect the Donatis to the Garones, but it doesn't implicate Constantini."

Daniel spun the laptop around and pounded the keys. "That's why I am going to have them check to see if this angel company has ever donated to *Compassione*, or used the Vatican Bank." He couldn't believe he didn't have them do this the first time. The Cardinal had specifically told him to follow the money.

Frannie seemed to read his mind, "*Zio* mentioned money transactions at that first dinner, didn't he?"

Daniel nodded slowly.

Frannie continued to think out loud, "*Zio* wanted us to investigate the list of clergy to see why they had been grouped together. But, all we've done is open up rabbit holes: Vidmar's death, mafia connections, and Donati being the unexpected source of the list. Have we come any closer to our original task or just muddied the waters?"

"The Donati twist is pivotal. I had a gut feeling the young delivery man was important, and now we know he is Donati's nephew. We just need to keep dig—" Daniel's fingers stopped typing and strummed rapidly on the table.

"Daniel!" Frannie exclaimed impatiently. "What are you thinking?"

He snapped to attention at the sound of her voice. "I think I just went down another rabbit hole."

"Great," she said, with half an eye roll.

"Hear me out. Donati sends his nephew, a stranger, to give your uncle a mysterious list. Then, he makes sure the entire Donati family is at the cocktail party, in hopes the Cardinal recognizes Stefano." He leaned forward, intensity building on each word, "But, how did Donati know your uncle would be invited to the Milan concert? The invitation came from Constantini. Given the Donatis stiff reaction to him, I don't think they got together to discuss the guest list."

Frannie ran her fingers through her hair. "How did we miss that?"

"What if there's a mole?" he asked, ignoring her rhetorical question. "If Constantini is in with the Garone family, and the Garone family is tied to the Donatis..."

Frannie completed his line of thought, "and if the Donatis want out of the Garone affiliation, they send in a mole to find a way to get the goods on Constantini."

"Precisely."

Frannie's eyes widened. "Stefano? That would explain how he got the flight record and the picture of the appointment book."

"That's who I'm guessing."

Frannie absently bit her thumbnail, wondering how Stefano could be balancing his job at the restaurant in Milan with spying on Constantini in Rome. She would have to think about it later. The morning was slipping away.

"I'm hopping in the shower," she said. "We can drop our stuff off at the hotel on our way to meet Maureen at noon. Our meeting with Archbishop Kratzer is at three."

"Maureen is your contact?"

"Yes. She was one of the first people to work on the *Traditio* project before it was cancelled. She worked with the Archbishop when he revised a version of it to be used locally."

"And she's from America?"

Frannie nodded. "She fell in love with an Austrian man she met here and they married. We're meeting at his family's café." Her eyes danced with excitement. "I hope they serve apple strudel."

"Your obsession with food knows no national boundaries."

"Your lack of enthusiasm for cultural gastronomy is disappointing," she retorted before grabbing her bag and slamming the bathroom door.

Daniel couldn't help but be amused at her false sense of outrage. Their playful bantering teetered on the edge of flirtation. It was a means of keeping any attraction he felt for her under control. He was playing with fire, and he knew he needed to be careful. The day was going to come when they would board a plane to go back to their lives in separate cities, and he couldn't afford to let it leave a hole in his heart.

⚜

Daniel opened the door to Alder's Backerei and Café and let Frannie enter. She shot him her beaming look again and his chest swelled.

So much for being careful, he thought.

The small café was bustling with customers. It was a pleasant June day and he hoped they could sit outside on the patio. A man wearing an eye patch stood behind the counter. Daniel guessed him to be in his late fifties. He was tall with white-blond hair, and the patch only partially covered the scars that extended below his patch onto his cheek.

"Hallo!" the man said brightly.

"*Inglese?*" Frannie said in Italian, asking if he spoke English.

"*Sì, e Italiano.*"

"*Brava!*" she exclaimed and began speaking rapidly in Italian, leaving Daniel out of loop. Soon they were shaking hands and he extended his to Daniel.

"Diedrich Alder," he said to Daniel, and continued in English, "my wife has been expecting you." He placed his hand on the shoulder of a young woman standing next to him. "This is my daughter, Camille. She will take your lunch order while I tell Maureen you are here."

In one graceful move, he disappeared into the back kitchen.

Daniel and Frannie ordered their sandwiches, and to Frannie's delight, she spotted beautiful slices of apple strudel in the display case. Daniel ordered two, knowing Frannie would order one for him if he didn't.

They found a table outside, and had just taken a bite of their sandwiches when Diedrich appeared with a woman with chestnut brown hair and friendly blue-green eyes.

"Frannie?" the woman asked, extending her hand.

Frannie and Daniel stood up. "Yes, you must be Maureen. It's nice to finally meet you in person! This is my friend, Daniel."

"Nice to meet you, Maureen."

They sat down and exchanged polite pleasantries over where they were from in America.

"How do you like living in Austria?" Daniel asked.

"It was an adjustment, but an easy one. I fell in love with the city when I arrived."

"And, fell in love with one of its residents!" Frannie said. "How did you meet?"

Maureen laughed. "Right here, at the café."

Diedrich returned with two sandwiches: one for him and one for Maureen.

"*Danke*," Maureen said to him as he sat down.

Daniel watched him cross himself and lead Maureen in a low murmuring prayer, he assumed was grace in German. Daniel wasn't used to seeing men pray; Diedrich made it seem naturally masculine.

"Diedrich had volunteered to help tutor researchers for the *Traditio* project in the German language," Maureen continued. "We began seeing each other outside of our lessons, and the rest is history."

Diedrich laughed softly.

Frannie's brow furrowed quizzically.

"He's laughing," Maureen explained, "because we didn't exactly start off on the right foot. He flat out refused to tutor me at first."

"I quickly came around," he said, smiling. "It was all God's Providence."

Frannie forced herself to smile. Their tale of a haphazard beginning ending in what was undoubtedly a deep love for each other made her self-conscious. She didn't dare look at Daniel.

"How long have you been married?" she asked, hoping to wrap up and steer the conversation toward other matters.

"Four years," Maureen replied.

"Is that all?" Diedrich asked playfully.

Maureen nudged him with her shoulder. "Time flies when you're having fun."

"Mmm. Indeed." He winked at her. "I am a blessed man."

Daniel focused on his sandwich. He was beginning to think the word "blessings" and its variants were common parlance for all Catholics. Diedrich's use of Providence to describe his less-than-stellar initial encounter with his wife nearly made him choke. To his relief, Frannie started asking questions about the history of the project Maureen had worked on with Kratzer.

"Initially," Maureen explained, "the project was halted for two reasons: lack of funding and the schools sponsoring it thought they had collected enough data for a statistical analysis. Once the results were published, Archbishop Kratzer and Cardinal Vidmar became interested in polling more Catholics."

"What were they hoping to find?" Frannie asked.

"The results of the original study showed younger Catholics were more likely to attend the Latin Mass than older generations. They wanted to find out more about this group's religious practices. Such as, frequency of Confession, attendance at daily Mass, if they prayed the Rosary, if married couples were more apt to pray together, and if they had children, did the fathers lead the family in prayer, and so forth."

"So basically, they wanted to see if they were merely traditional in their worship, or if it carried into their homes as well."

"Correct. Our parish priest at Saint Sebastian knew I had worked on *Traditio*, and recommended me to the Archbishop. That's how I got involved."

"And then the study was terminated?"

Maureen's friendly eyes became troubled. "Yes."

Frannie waited to see if she would offer any more information but Maureen had suddenly clammed up. "Do you know why?" she pressed.

Diedrich placed his hand on the small of Maureen's back, as if he needed to steady her. His one piercing blue eye bore into Frannie. "What brings you here Francesca?" he asked.

"I'm helping my friend, Daniel, gather information about the project," she answered as confidently as she could.

"And yet, he hasn't asked any questions and you have little interest in the data correlations between Latin Mass attendees and their religious practices."

The table fell silent.

Diedrich was still fixed on Frannie. "Why exactly, do you wish to meet with Archbishop Kratzer?" Diedrich asked, his velvety voice becoming slightly more coarse.

"We are doing some work for Frannie's uncle," Daniel answered for her. "She's Cardinal Menconi's niece."

Daniel's voice drew the attention of everyone at the table. He had been silent, but watched Diedrich's jaw tighten when Frannie pushed about the project's termination. She had hit a nerve prompting the Austrian to become leery of her intentions. Given the Alder's friendship with the Archbishop, Daniel needed to assure him they were in friendly company.

Diedrich's eagle eye bounced back between the two Americans, then stopped. He raised his one eyebrow. "It would seem if that were so, Cardinal Menconi could arrange for you to meet with the Archbishop. They are both authors of the Letter of Opposition and therefore good friends. I don't see why you would need the help of my wife."

Frannie dug in her purse for her phone. She showed Diedrich and Maureen a picture of her with her uncle. "I promise you we are telling the truth." She looked at Maureen. "I never hid my last name from you."

Diedrich's gaze moved from the phone back to Frannie. She steadily met his direct eye contact and spoke softly but firmly, "I needed to avoid the usual channels of communication."

The gravity of her statement weighed heavily upon the couple. Diedrich took his wife's hand in his. "I see," he whispered. "Tensions have escalated."

"Even Archbishop Kratzer doesn't know why we are here," Frannie said. "We wanted to find out what we could about the closure of the project from you, Maureen. It would help us be fully prepared for our meeting with him."

Maureen took a deep breath. Frannie noticed she never let go of her husband's hand, but held it as a source of strength. "I was only helping with the project part-time," she began, "mostly helping organize the data rather than analyzing it. But, I began to notice trends. The Latin Mass goers were more likely to follow all the practices mentioned already; but they expressed their displeasure at the progressive movements within the Church. The study showed the younger generation actually preferred the Old Latin Rite, resulting in increased attendance in Latin Mass parishes."

"When you say younger, what age do you mean?" Daniel asked.

"Anyone under fifty, but mostly those in their twenties and thirties."

Daniel had never been to a Latin Mass, but he had read a little about it in preparation for interviewing Cardinal Menconi. He was thirty-two and couldn't imagine that an antiquated form of church worship would be attractive to him.

"The younger generation," Maureen explained, "described the Old Rite as authentic. If Catholics confess that the Body and Blood of Christ become present at every Mass, and the Mass is a foretaste of heavenly worship, then it should look and sound like it. For them, once they experienced it and understood it, they didn't want to go back to Mass with," she paused, choosing her words carefully. "I don't mean to sound uncharitable, or snobbish. But once the Latin Mass drew them in, a Mass with a guitar wasn't going to cut it anymore."

"It elevates you in an unexplainable way," Frannie added. "The people I know are drawn to the reverence and silence."

Maureen nodded. "I started attending after the Letter by the Archbishop and your uncle. And now, it's just home. When I first moved here, my Missal with Latin and the English translation was all I needed to follow along and pray the Mass. Other than the homily which was in German, I could understand everything!"

Daniel spoke again, "And, Cardinal Vidmar worked with Archbishop Kratzer on this restructured project?"

"Yes," she said heavily. "I know the rumors about his death, and there is nothing I can add. All I know is that Cardinal Baldano came down with a heavy hand and wanted the project stopped immediately and demanded copies of all the data. He didn't want the results published at all."

She bit her lip, obviously conflicted. Frannie watched Maureen close her eyes and waited. When she opened them, she leaned forward. "I'm the one that leaked the results to America, and let them be the ones to share it on the various social media outlets. The news eventually made its way across the ocean and back here to Europe. By then Baldano no longer seemed to care. Archbishop Kratzer was never reprimanded by the Vatican or the press."

Maybe they had a bigger fish to fry, Daniel thought.

"Your secret is safe with us, Maureen," Frannie assured her. "I can understand now why you were so nervous. I'm sorry we caused you any anxiety." She smiled. "You're very brave."

Maureen returned the smile, her blue green eyes sparkling again. "The Archbishop is the one who is brave. He encouraged me. We have strong leaders, like your uncle. They will shepherd us through these times."

Frannie sighed. "Our Mother's Immaculate Heart will triumph, right?"

"We pray her Rosary every day," Diedrich said.

A young boy with dark hair and brown eyes ran up to the table, out of breath. He started speaking in rapid German.

"Mama!" was all Frannie formally understood. She could read between the lines that he was earnestly pleading for something.

"Michael!" Diedrich scolded, then calmly reprimanded the boy in German.

"Excuse me," he said in English, looking at Daniel and Frannie, trying desperately to compose himself. "I'm sorry for interrupting you."

Frannie extended her hand. "I'm Frannie, and this is Daniel."

Michael shook their hands and introduced himself politely, "I'm Michael. It's nice to meet you."

He looked anxiously at Maureen, attempting to be patient by bouncing lightly on the balls of his feet.

Maureen responded with a list that she checked off her fingers. When she finished, Michael was nodding and very excited. Frannie heard a few German "yeses" and "thank-yous" and he turned to leave. After a few quick steps, he did an about face and came back to kiss his mother on the cheek.

"Goodbye," he said to Frannie and Daniel, gave his father a quick hug around the neck, and disappeared into the café.

Maureen gave her guests a smile. "That was our son, as you probably guessed. He has been invited to a friend's house this evening. But, he has some chores to complete before he can go."

Frannie wondered how they could have a son that age, but didn't want to be nosy.

Diedrich placed his hand over his heart. "Francesca, Daniel, I apologize for my aggressive tone earlier. I am sure you understand; I am protective of my family. Let me offer you some coffee for your strudel." He rose from the table, and entered the café's side door.

"Thank you, Maureen," Daniel said, "for answering our questions. We should have been more upfront with you. We have had some interesting experiences lately."

"When you said you wanted to avoid the usual communications, I figured as much," she said sadly.

Frannie added, "Thank you for helping us get an appointment with the Archbishop, and your hospitality."

Diedrich returned with a tray of coffee cups, then excused himself to help his daughter with closing duties.

Frannie glanced at the clock on her phone. "How far is the Cathedral from here?" she asked Maureen.

"About a ten minute walk."

"Great. We have plenty of time." She dug into her slice of apple strudel. "Oh my gosh, this is amazing!"

Maureen grinned. "I've found it is the best strudel in all of Austria."

Daniel ate his quietly while the ladies chatted about dining and living in Europe. The apple dessert was delicious, but a slice of Grandma Mae's apple pie would have given Diedrich a run for his money. From where he was sitting he could see inside the restaurant, and he watched Diedrich with his daughter. They were laughing and talking as they moved empty trays to the kitchen, he assumed for cleaning.

Daniel was intrigued by Diedrich and the way he interacted with his family. He was quick to correct his young son, but still received a hug. He asserted control over the conversation when he thought his wife might be in a hostile situation, and Maureen didn't seem to care that he was coming to her rescue. Daniel expected her to give Diedrich a look that said, "I can take care of myself" but it never came.

The Alder's reminded him of the Dawson family from Jackson, the parents of his best friend, Travis. Daniel and Travis were inseparable as kids. They played baseball on Jackson's Little League and even joined the Marines together. He considered Travis to be his one true friend. He spent many hours at the Dawson house and it became his second home.

He loved being with them and watching Mr. and Mrs. Dawson poke fun at each other and steal a kiss when they thought no one was looking. The house was filled with the noise of Travis and his brothers raising a raucous, and also full of laughter. The family members were close and although the spouses could have a temper, they genuinely loved each other.

The Dawsons provided a model of the family Daniel yearned to have. But, he had given up the dream of having a family of his own. Watching Diedrich with his wife and children brought back the longing and with it, painful memories of what he had lost.

"Ready?" Frannie asked, her voice slicing through his thoughts.

"For what?" he asked, trying to file away the emotions that had surfaced.

She lowered her chin and raised her eyebrows, "Our meeting with the Archbishop?" she asked as if it should have been clear as day.

"That's why we took the train ride," he replied, deflecting his lapse in concentration with sarcasm.

They said goodbye to Maureen, and headed to their appointment.

Chapter 24

ARCHBISHOP KRATZER SAT AT HIS DESK IN THE office of the Archdiocese of Salzburg in the Kapitelplatz building, a stone's throw from the Salzburg Cathedral. His secretary knocked on his door and entered, highly flustered.

"Archbishop Kratzer, Miss Menconi and Mr. Fitzpatrick are here to see you," she said in terse German. "I told them you were leaving at three o'clock today, but they insisted they have an appointment."

"Yes, Frida, I am expecting them. Send them in."

Frida stood at rigid attention. "I don't recall seeing them on your calendar." She knew everything about her boss's appointments and had kept him on schedule for over ten years.

The Archbishop smiled kindly at his loyal employee. "I know, Frida. I trust you will keep it that way."

"Yes, sir," the secretary replied softly. She spun on her heel and exited. When she returned, Daniel and Frannie were in tow, and she ushered them into the office.

The prelate stood up and greeted them in English, his deep voice heavily accented in German, "Francesca, it is a pleasure to meet you. I have known Nicolo for years, but I don't believe we have met."

"No we haven't, your Excellency," she replied, shaking his hand.

"And you must be Daniel," the Archbishop said to Daniel.

"It's a pleasure, Archbishop Kratzer."

The Archbishop gestured for them to have a seat in the two chairs facing his desk. He went to the door and gave his secretary some instructions in German. Daniel noticed he left his office door slightly ajar.

"Now," he said, returning to his seat and folding his hands on his desk, "you are here to find out about *Traditio?*" he asked.

Daniel asked some perfunctory questions he and Frannie had prepared to see how open and friendly the clergyman would be. To their relief, he responded with benevolent politeness. He even asked some questions about the Church in America, to which Frannie was quick to respond.

"Yes, your Excellency, there are many young families at these parishes," she said, answering his question if any young people attended the Latin Mass in America.

"It is interesting, yes?" he said reflectively.

Daniel decided to interject a question based upon what they just learned from Maureen. "Yes, sir. It is also interesting the project was shut down, given the positive data the study uncovered regarding the pious practices of this demographic outside the Sunday Mass. Why did it end so abruptly?"

The Archbishop sat up a little straighter. "Our directive came from Rome."

Daniel ignored the side step. "From Cardinal Baldano?"

There was a noticeable pause. "Yes," the Archbishop said quietly.

"Why would he have done that, your Excellency?"

Kratzer leaned back and steepled his fingers. His eyes darted back and forth from Daniel to Frannie. He settled his gaze upon Daniel. "You must have a theory, or you wouldn't have asked the question."

Daniel smiled. Kratzer was as crafty as Constantini, but without the hints of an unscrupulous character.

"Baldano's opinion and position are well known," Daniel stated. "I don't recall that he put his signature on your now famous Letter. It would appear he halted the project in an attempt to bury the results."

The Archbishop shrugged. "Appearances are just that, yes? A shadow of an impression interpreted by the other?"

Daniel held his poker face as still as a gambler raising the bet while holding nothing but a pair of deuces. *The directive may have been given by Baldano, but it originated with Constantini,* he thought.

"Appearances can be deceiving," Daniel conceded, crossing one leg over the other and leaning casually back in his chair. "Maybe he was acting under the direction of someone else."

He paused to allow the Archbishop a chance to comment, but the prelate remained silent. Kratzer's sharp eyes indicated he wasn't about to fold his cards. He was going to keep raising until Daniel showed what was in his hand.

Daniel yielded, "We have reason to think Cardinal Baldano may be reconsidering his former stance on certain issues." He glanced over at Frannie. "Actually, we have it in his own words."

Frannie had watched the polite back and forth between the two men. She took the cue from Daniel to hand over a copy of the letter Cardinal Menconi had received from Baldano. She slipped it out of her bag, looked at it, then back at Archbishop Kratzer.

"My uncle assured me it was safe to give this to you, and to tell you that he knows about this meeting. He considers you a friend," she added, before handing him the letter.

Daniel watched him read each line. His face was inscrutable. Either the Archbishop was also adept at wearing a poker face, or he wasn't one bit surprised by what he was reading.

"What do you make of it, sir?" he asked.

"It is highly irregular for a Cardinal to write such a letter. But, I agree with you. It would seem Giuseppe is changing course. Now, why would Nicolo ask you to bring this to me?"

Daniel and Frannie shared a look. Neither knew exactly where to go from here.

"He didn't," Frannie stated flatly. She zeroed in on Daniel, hoping she was sufficiently communicating to him she wanted to take the wheel. A slight shrug of his shoulders let her know he got the message.

"He asked us to look into something for him," she said, turning back to the Archbishop. "My uncle acquired a list from an anonymous source after receiving Baldano's letter. He asked us to find a pattern or reason why these people would be grouped together."

She dug out a copy of the list of clergy and handed it to him. "He said it was okay to give this to you as well."

The Archbishop's eyebrows drew together in a tightly knit line. He set the paper on his desk and placed both hands on it. "Where did Nicolo get this?"

"It wasn't signed," Frannie said, waiting to see what he would say.

Daniel's feet hit the floor and his back straightened. The Archbishop's strained face betrayed him; the list had taken him completely off guard. He saw Kratzer glance toward his office door, as if he was expecting someone to enter.

The Archbishop's eyebrows retreated and he tried to restore an unrattled demeanor. "And have you found a pattern?"

"Originally, we separated the men into either a friend or foe, based on the suggestion from Baldano's letter to know your friends from your enemies. But it's not that simple. We have found more questions than answers," Frannie revealed.

The Archbishop steepled his fingers again, deep in thought. "I see. And why did you come here? Is there something you were hoping I could answer?"

Frannie felt her stomach clench. She had a question but couldn't bring herself to say the words out loud.

"Your Excellency," Daniel interjected gingerly, "our question is controversial and rather sensitive. You were a good friend of Cardinal Vidmar. Do you have any reason to believe his death was anything other than natural causes?"

Frannie sucked in a quick breath. She hoped his face would redden and he would angrily usher them out for asking such an impertinent question based solely on rumors. But to her dismay the Archbishop's face paled; he clearly feared the rumors were true.

A voice rang out from behind, startling her and Daniel to jump and spin around in their chairs.

"You don't have to answer that, Karl."

A man in a cardinal's simar stood in the doorway. His thin gray hair and lined face testified to his advanced age. "I can answer your questions," he said.

He walked forward and stood next to the desk and gave Frannie and Daniel a tired smile.

"Francesca and Daniel, I am Cardinal Giuseppe Baldano."

Chapter 25

D ANIEL AND FRANNIE STARED OPEN-MOUTHED AT the Cardinal.

"You—you know who we are?" Frannie stammered.

"Yes, Karl informed me of your visit. When you didn't use Nicolo's connection to get an appointment we knew you must be investigating on his behalf."

Daniel's brain staggered briefly at the surprise guest but thoughts began firing at lightning speed. He glanced at Frannie, wishing he could speak freely with her.

She must have read his mind. As Archbishop Kratzer moved chairs around to get Cardinal Baldano seated behind the desk she leaned over and Daniel whispered in her ear, "I think we need to see if he knows anything about the list. Then get his assessment of Constantini. I'm not sure I want to share what was given to us in Milan."

Frannie nodded. "Go ahead," she whispered, "you start."

Daniel looked over the desk at the old Cardinal. He looked weary but his eyes revealed a sharp determination and readiness to speak candidly.

"Cardinal Baldano, meeting you here is quite unexpected," Daniel began. "If you are willing to answer some questions, I'll begin with the most obvious. Why did you choose to write the letter to Cardinal Menconi? Why not just meet him in person?"

"Because I suspect Nicolo is being watched. Word of my meeting with him would travel. Mailing the letter was safer. I asked Karl to warn him to be on his guard."

Frannie's heart grew heavy. Her uncle knew the danger he was in and didn't tell her. Daniel continued, "What did you want him to do?"

"The Church is experiencing a divergence in opinion with regard to some of her Traditions. One holds that the Church's Tradition has been handed to us from the Apostles, is rooted in Scripture, and therefore comes from the Lord Himself. The other desires change, heralding the Church should consider the changing times and culture. They believe change can bring renewal and growth."

He closed his eyes. "I was once of the latter way of thinking. I chose to ignore Saint Paul's teaching to stand firm and hold to the traditions that were taught by word or by letter."

His eyes reopened and he continued, "After I halted Karl and Jozef's extension of the *Traditio* survey and examined the data, it forced me into an examination of conscience about my ideologies and my life. I had been so certain the course I was on was the right one. It led to my own road to Damascus moment. When the scales fell from my eyes I saw the truth and the path I should take."

Baldano shifted his gaze to Frannie. "I knew I needed to call upon your uncle. He is wise and I needed his counsel. My change in position would cause my friends to spurn me; we would now share the same enemies."

Frannie spoke for the first time, "You are 'alone in your own potter's field,'" she said, remembering his letter. "A reference to the Field of Blood used to bury strangers, bought with Judas's thirty pieces of silver."

Baldano nodded. "I am both the betrayer and the betrayed. But I have confessed my sins and received forgiveness from the Father of mercies."

A heavy pause filled the room. Daniel broke the silence by softly introducing another question, "You interrupted us when we asked about Vidmar. Do you know something about his death?"

The Cardinal picked up the list of clergy names and examined it closely. Frannie had provided a copy in which she transcribed the Bible verses by each one. He smiled sadly. "My old adversary placed me in the company of the Pharisees and a brood of vipers."

"Your old–" Daniel started, "your Eminence, do you know who made this list?"

"Yes," he stated calmly. "Jozef Vidmar."

Frannie peeked at Daniel but he was riveted on Baldano. "How do you know this?" he asked.

"Before the last papal conclave Cesare Constantini began gathering people like myself: those within the College of Cardinals who supported his progressive ideas for the Church. His intention was to elect a pope that would make his ideas a reality. The conclave was fairly divided."

His eyes moved to Frannie. "Some in the College regarded Nicolo as the one to preserve the Church's teaching and stand against Cesare; he knew your uncle was a formidable opponent who would not be swayed by the changing tides of modernity. A Menconi papacy would use the teachings of Scripture and Church patrimony to steer the Barque of Peter safely along the shores of her two thousand years of Tradition.

"The conclave was at an impasse. A two-thirds vote could not be reached. Then, the next morning, the vote was cast electing our current pontiff."

Archbishop Kratzer chimed in, "Jozef Vidmar was greatly distressed over the events of the conclave. After Donati was appointed as the President of the Commission of Cardinals of the Vatican Bank, he and Constantini were regularly seen together at fundraisers, galas and the like. Jozef became suspicious."

"Suspicious of what, exactly?" Daniel asked.

"He said Fortino Donati had told him on numerous occasions that he did not trust Constantini. Yet, they were acting as old friends. Jozef tried to talk to Fortino about his shift in opinion and sudden new friendship, but was ignored. He took it upon himself to do his own investigation and the so-called feud between the two erupted."

Daniel's pulse quickened. They were getting closer to a case against Constantini. "Archbishop Kratzer, are you saying the feud was between two old friends?"

"Jozef was certain the Bank was involved in corruption. What he couldn't understand was why Donati was willing to look the other way. According to Jozef, the Donati he knew would never have lowered his moral standards in such a manner."

"Or voted for the current pontiff?" Daniel asked.

A dense silence cloaked the room. Finally, the Archbishop whispered, "No."

"I talked with Jozef the day of his death," the Archbishop continued. "He sounded shaken. He stated he didn't want to talk over the phone and would be traveling to see me in Salzburg later in the week. When I asked if he was all right, he said Nicolo would be receiving something and he might ask my help to decipher it. Then he said the strangest thing, 'It's a list of clergy that says everything and nothing. If for some reason, Nicolo reaches out to you, you will know who sent it.'"

"Do you recall what time you talked to Vidmar, sir?" Daniel asked.

"Around six in the evening."

"And the list?" Daniel pressed. "What happened to it?"

"I was able to track down his housekeeper the next morning when I received the horrible news. She was certain there were no papers of any sort on his desk."

Frannie had been silent, taking in every word. She knew exactly where Daniel was going with his questions. "And you didn't find that odd," she pointed out, "given his cryptic message to you?"

"Of course. But I did not have any hard evidence. The housekeeper mentioned he was preparing to receive a guest, but I have no idea who it was or if the person even showed up. I told the police what he told me. There was nothing more I could add."

Frannie leaned forward. "And you're sure this is Vidmar's list?"

"It matches his description and it was delivered to your uncle. When Jozef said Nicolo might reach out to me about it, he spoke as if he needed someone else to know the list existed. Like I said, he sounded nervous."

Daniel scrunched his brow. "Why did he think Cardinal Menconi would reach out to you?"

"We became good friends after the Letter of Opposition. And I can only guess he attributed the Scripture verse next to my name, 'He who has an ear let him hear what the Spirit says to the churches,' as a clue for Nicolo. In John's Book of the Apocalypse, or Revelation, it is the line that is repeated in each letter to the seven churches. It was a source of our inspiration when we wrote the Letter. Only Nicolo would know that."

Daniel waited but the Archbishop didn't offer any other information. He decided to move on and directed his question to the Cardinal. "Speaking of friendships, we didn't expect to find you and the Archbishop together in the same room."

"I respected Karl for his extensive work on the *Traditio* project. I surprised him with a visit and with my repentance. It is not public knowledge, but we are united in our mission and our friendship."

"Are you in hiding your Eminence?" Daniel asked.

The old man slumped a little in his chair. "Not exactly. No one knows I am here, at least that I know of. I announced I was leaving for retreat and prayer which I have done, tucked away here in the Austrian Alps. I will be returning to Rome soon."

There was one last thing Daniel wanted to know. "Cardinal, you said your old friends were now your enemies. If you had to choose your most staunch enemy on this list, who would it be?"

Baldano locked eyes with Daniel. Without hesitation, he answered, "Cesare Constantini. And I would consider it a favor, if you would tell Nicolo he should consider him the same."

"You said you couldn't contact Cardinal Menconi because he is being watched. Is he under the eye of Constantini?"

The old man paused. "Everyone is under the eye of Cesare Constantini. He narrows his vision on select persons from time to time. Right now, Cardinal Menconi is in his scope."

"What about Archbishop von Eichel? He's on the list yet he doesn't make many headlines."

"Germans," Baldano muttered, shaking his head. "Germans will do what they will do. Archbishop von Eichel is a follower of Constantini, but cannot vote in the conclave. Both hold ideas which are dangerous and can lead souls away from salvation. Constantini is a dangerous man because he wants power above all else. Both are wolves but Constantini is the imminent threat."

The Cardinal's face grew strained. "The Vatican is releasing little information to the public about the pope's health. Those closest to him say he is close to death. I don't need to explain the significance of the next conclave, do I? Strike the wayward shepherd that his sheep may be dispersed; or at least weakened."

Frannie's face blanched. Everything was becoming disturbingly clear. It was time for her to ask her own set of questions.

"Cardinal Baldano?" she croaked, then cleared her throat. "I wanted to ask you about something you wrote in your letter. When you said, 'Our Mother has warned us on more than one occasion,' did you have a certain apparition in mind?"

Daniel gave her a sideways glance. *Apparition? What in the world is she talking about?* To his surprise, Baldano knew exactly what Frannie was referring to.

"The ones of the last two centuries that are approved by the Church."

Frannie listed three, "La Salette, Fatima, and Akita?"

"Yes," he replied, validating her answer.

"Do you think," she stopped, gathering the courage to say her thoughts out loud and fully aware Daniel was listening. "Do you think that time has come?" she asked cryptically.

The old prelate smiled warmly. "Daughter, our Lord Himself told us no one knows the day or the hour."

"But her warnings about the clergy and mankind are reflective of our world today!" she stated urgently.

"And of our past history. There is nothing new under the sun when it comes to man's sinful nature."

"Then why would you mention it?"

"Because I dismissed her warnings as not applicable to me which placed my soul in danger. And I realized in leading others astray, I was guilty of afflicting our Lord with my sin. The Church is suffering because of it." He straightened and leaned forward on the desk. "What other message does Our Lady always leave us?"

"Penance, repentance, and pray the Rosary," she responded softly.

"And are you doing those things?"

Her stomach dropped. She couldn't remember the last time she prayed the Rosary and she wasn't consistent in fasting from meat on Fridays or doing any kind of act of penance. She shook her head slowly. "I went to confession a few weeks ago, but it had been a long time."

"Then worry less about whether the world is coming to an end and more about your own soul. Armor yourself so you may stand in the face of evil, and then you can be a light to others in these dark times."

He let out a heavy sigh. "I don't deny the times we are in are troubled. In certain ways, unprecedented. It's how we react that will make the difference. We need Catholics to rise up and live holy lives. The results of the extended *Traditio* project–the religious practices of the faithful families–made that clear to me. There is hope. For Christians, there is always hope."

Another heavy silence filled the room. After several moments Baldano asked, "Do either of you have any other questions?"

Daniel's head was spinning trying to keep up with Frannie's enigmatic conversation with the Cardinal. She appeared immersed in her thoughts so he assumed she had finished with her inquiry.

"No, your Eminence," he said. "Thank you for your openness. We will be sure to give your messages to Cardinal Menconi."

As Daniel and Frannie started to stand Baldano stopped them, "If you don't mind. I have a question for you."

The Cardinal picked up the list of clergy. "Where did you get this?"

"It was given to Cardinal Menconi a few days after receiving your letter," Daniel offered.

"By whom?"

Frannie answered, "As I told the Archbishop, it was anonymous."

Baldano's eyes darted back and forth. "And what made you want to meet with the Archbishop of Salzburg?"

Frannie spoke up, "That was my idea. Well, sort of. Based upon your letter of knowing one's friends from enemies, I was researching the men we had grouped as friends. I struck up a conversation online with Maureen Alder. Then at prayer in Adoration I felt called to come here. So, in a way, it was the Holy Spirit's idea."

Cardinal Baldano smiled faintly. The Holy Spirit, the Spirit of Truth, was guiding the Church. He needed to pray even more fervently for Nicolo Menconi.

He glanced over the list of clergy again. "I would not take the sudden emergence of this list lightly. Whomever gave it to Nicolo did so at great risk to himself. That person should be careful." He added somberly, "If you know who it was, you may want to warn them."

Daniel met the Cardinal's scrutinizing eye; Baldano suspected they knew more than they were telling. Daniel remained silent; he was not ready to share what they had learned from the flash drive or their hypothesis about Donati and Stefano.

The Cardinal stood up, signaling the end of the meeting. Daniel and Frannie shook the hands of both men, thanking them.

"You two need to be careful as well," Baldano warned. He raised his right hand in a blessing, saying some words in Latin and making the Sign of the Cross over them. "May our Lord send His angels to guard and protect you," he said in English.

"Thank you," Frannie said.

She followed Daniel to the office door. Before leaving she turned back around. "Cardinal, we will move you to the list of friends. I'm sure *Zio* will be in touch soon."

The two clergymen watched them exit. The Cardinal wiped his hands across his face. "I wondered why Nicolo hadn't called me after he received my letter. Now it makes sense; he had no idea what to make of receiving the list at the same time."

"Who would have sent it?" Kratzer asked.

"I don't know. What I do know is Nicolo has no idea of the danger he has placed his niece and her friend in, or else he would not have asked them to investigate the enemies on the list."

"I did as you asked. I warned Nicolo that trouble was brewing, and to take precautions."

"Call him again. This time, I'll do the talking."

Chapter 26

DANIEL AND FRANNIE LEFT THE ARCHBISHOP'S office and walked in stunned silence toward the hotel. Frannie came to a stop on the bridge over the Salzach River. She wished she could take in the charm of the castle fortress looming on the hill and church spires fashioning the picturesque Salzburg skyline, but her mind was elsewhere.

"I need a drink," she said.

Daniel paused mid-stride and backed up to stand next to her. "I need to sit and debrief first."

"Can you believe it?" she asked. "Cardinal Baldano. In Salzburg."

Daniel wasn't ready to admit Frannie's spiritual discernment proved to be legitimate. The odds of meeting Cardinal Baldano in the Archbishop's office were slim to none. He aimed his focus back to the information they received and not how they got to Austria.

"Can we go back to the hotel and make notes of what we just learned?"

"I think there is a place to sit outside not far from here." She spoke into her phone and looked at the map it provided. "Yep, it's super close. This way."

A few blocks brought them to Mirabellgarten, a large park with fountains, statues and luscious gardens. Flowers planted in meticulous geometric spiral curls brought the green grounds alive with color. They found an empty park bench under the shade of a long row of groomed trees.

Frannie pulled two bottles of water out of her bag. "It's not super cold, but it's better than nothing," she said.

"Thanks." Daniel didn't realize how thirsty he was until the liquid hit his parched throat. He nearly guzzled the whole bottle in one gulp. *Leave it to Frannie to think to bring water*, he thought.

He pulled out his notebook and a pen. "Okay, let's start from the beginning."

Frannie began a recap. "If we combine the Archbishop's account of the day Vidmar died with the evidence on the flash drive, Vidmar met with Donati at three in the afternoon, then penned the list to send to *Zio*. Kratzer talked to Vidmar at six o'clock, who senses he is troubled. Constantini arrived for dinner and," she stopped speaking and closed her eyes.

Daniel felt sorry for Frannie. The realization that evil lurked in the high ranks of the Church visibly shook her to the core. "And we know from the flight record that Constantini boarded a plane departing Slovenia at two the next morning," he finished for her.

Frannie continued, "Baldano said, 'Everyone is under the eye of Cesare Constantini.' He must have had tabs on Donati's every move. How else could he know to follow him to Slovenia and arrange to have dinner with Vidmar on the same day?'"

"Agreed. I think we can assume he was the one who had us followed." He smacked his notebook with his pen. "Let's go back to Donati. His sudden jump to Team Constantini helps verify our hypothesis that he is being blackmailed."

She rapidly squeezed the empty portion of her water bottle, making a crinkling noise, then stopped. "Do you think that's what Donati's meeting with Vidmar was about?"

"It seems likely. Vidmar suspected all along something was off. Maybe Donati came seeking his old friend's help and finally spilled everything about Constantini and the Garones."

"Then why would Vidmar write such a disparaging Scripture verse next to Donati's name about the love of money being—"

She threw her water bottle on the bench and started digging in her bag. She pulled out the list. "1 Timothy 6:10," she recited. "I only wrote down the first few words." Selecting her Bible app she found the full verse and read it aloud:

> For the love of money is the root of all evils; it is through this craving that some have wandered away from the faith and pierced their hearts with many pangs.

"Wandered away and pierced their hearts with many pangs!" she repeated. "I think Vidmar is connecting Donati's appointment to the Bank with Constantini. The appointment began Donati's flip flop of allegiance to someone he distrusted and has caused him much sorrow and regret. Even *Zio* said he didn't buy into the rumors Donati was involved with corruption. Like Vidmar, he considered Donati a friend once."

"Can I see the verse?" Daniel asked.

She handed him her phone. The word "evil" jumped out at him.

"All evils," he quoted. "Not just one but all." He drummed his fingers on the bench. "The Cardinal said to follow the money transactions. This is all about money; *Compassione*, the Vatican Bank, the Garones and Fratellis. Everything."

"I think there's another hint in this verse," Frannie continued. "'Pierced their hearts with many pangs' was a clue for *Zio* to know the piercing went deep. It involved Donati's family. When Mary takes Jesus to the Temple for circumcision, Simeon tells her a sword will pierce her; that's why you see her Immaculate Heart depicted in art with a sword in it."

Daniel's mind flashed to the *Pieta* again and the haunting tune from the concert. The sorrow of a mother. He absently touched his sternum area with his fingers, thinking about the medal that hung there. Not wanting Frannie to notice, he pretended to scratch an itch.

He charged forward, "We finally have a connection to the money trail and the papal conspiracy. Constantini is blackmailing Donati in order to persuade votes for the election of the pontiff, and conceal his underhanded money transactions." He paused and stared off. "The root of all evil," he mumbled.

"Vidmar's pairing of Constantini with the parable of the dishonest steward makes perfect sense," Frannie said. "The steward was a crafty one; he fixed the books to cover his own misdeeds. Vidmar wanted to draw more attention to Constantini than the others so he gave him a full parable." She flicked to the Scripture passage on her app. "The last line says it all, 'No servant can serve two masters; you cannot serve God and mammon.'"

Daniel frowned. "Baldano made it very clear that Constantini is more than just devious; he is dangerous. It must be why there is all this cloak and dagger business with letters and lists. Unfortunately for Vidmar, he found out too late." He paused a beat. "Do you think we could go back to Milan?"

"I don't see why not. You want to try to meet up with Stefano?"

He nodded. "There's still a piece missing; we don't know how he got the list. Or when for that matter. How long has he had it? Why give it to the Cardinal now?"

"I'm not sure they will talk if Mr. Baldy is lurking around. They went to great lengths to meet *Zio* covertly."

"True. I guess we can decide later." He scribbled some notes in his notebook and closed it. He twisted in his seat and hung his elbow off the back of the bench. "Frannie, what was all that stuff about apparitions and the end of the world?"

She wondered when he was going to ask. "Baldano made a reference in his letter that it was no secret that Our Mother has warned us. I knew he was referring to the apparitions of Mary. She appeared to two shepherd children at La Salette, France in the 1840s and to three shepherd children at Fatima, Portugal in 1917. In the 1970s, she appeared at a convent in Akita, Japan to a Japanese sister who converted from Buddhism to Catholicism. Fatima is the most famous since there are newspaper articles reporting the Miracle of the Sun witnessed by 70,000 people on October 13, 1917."

Daniel cocked his head to the side. He regarded Frannie as a competent and intelligent woman but what she was telling him went beyond reason. "You're saying the Blessed Virgin Mary appeared to these people and spoke to them?"

"Yes." She gave a summary of the details of each apparition, spending more time on the secrets revealed to the little shepherd children of Fatima.

He understood why Frannie would be troubled. The prophetic nature of the messages were uncanny. He desperately wanted to believe it was mere coincidence. "These warnings included predictions about the end of the world?" he asked.

"Not directly. She doesn't mince any words about wars, famine, diseases, and the like if mankind doesn't repent. It's hard not to read her dire predictions about infighting within the Church and wonder if we are living it now. As the Cardinal said, there is hope. She assured the children of Fatima that her Immaculate Heart will triumph. Meaning, those devoted to Her and Her Son Jesus shouldn't be afraid. A time of peace will come."

"And you believe these apparitions really happened?"

"Yes, I do, and they have been approved by the Church. The local bishop does an extensive investigation and ensures the message is free from theological and doctrinal error. In the case of

Fatima, the children were accused of lying and thrown in prison but refused to change their story. I don't think kids are willing to spend the night in prison for a lie they concocted. Even a Portuguese secular atheistic newspaper reported the sun became the color of dull silver and made sudden and unpredictable movements in the sky. The people described it as 'the sun danced.'"

She read Daniel's frozen and unbelieving face.

"You should know there are hundreds of claims of Marian apparitions but the number actually approved is less than thirty," she informed him. "The Church classifies the apparitions as private revelations. These are distinct from public revelation: the deposit of faith revealed in Scripture and Tradition, which Catholics are bound to believe and accept. Any private revelation is considered worthy of belief, but you can decide if you want to believe it or not." She crossed her arms and looked away. "I'm sure you think I'm crazy."

"I–I just," he stammered. "This is all new for me. Reading the verses on the clergy list is the most Bible reading I've ever done. I've been to more churches in the last three weeks than in the last fifteen years. Now you're telling me newspapers in Portugal reported a miracle in 1917, where Mary appeared to children."

Add in hearing voices at the Vatican and your call to come to Salzburg, and it's a lot for me to digest.

"I don't think you're crazy," he said gently. "I've worked with religious people but I don't socialize much outside of the office. I'm not used to being around someone like you that makes religion a part of their life."

"If you heard my confession three weeks ago you might think differently."

A sneering laugh came from Daniel's mouth. "What in the world would you have to confess? Jaywalking? You missed one Sunday Mass in five years?"

Frannie snapped around and glared at him, her eyes blazing with hurt anger. She hated being ridiculed for trying to live by a moral code. Her co-workers often made her the brunt of prudish jokes.

"I'm sorry," he said, trying to backpedal. "My sarcasm can be over the top. I didn't mean to offend you, but it's hard for me to imagine you doing anything wrong or sinful. You're one of the kindest people I've met in a long time."

He stopped himself before he tagged on beautiful, smart, and fun as additional descriptors.

Frannie's mouth parted slightly. His apology was as unexpected as the flip-flop in her stomach.

"I've done plenty I'm not proud of. And if you could see inside my head, you might reconsider."

"Are you secretly plotting my destruction?" he teased lightly.

"No. Not anymore, anyway," she poked back.

They shared a smile and her stomach did another flip. "I don't wish you harm, Fitzpatrick. But, I envy you," she stated flatly.

Daniel jerked his head back, "Envy me?" he repeated in surprise.

"Envy and wallowing in self-pity are my two worst vices." Her eyes wandered to the ground. "My parish is full of young families and I can't help but watch them. A mother has one child in her arms and one tugging on her so the husband takes the littlest one so she can tend to the other. When it's time for Communion the husband steps out of the pew and to the side to let his wife go first. It's such a simple gesture; but it speaks volumes to me."

She began fiddling with her water bottle again. "I'm not romanticizing it; I know it's not all rainbows and butterflies. But, they're living it, even though it's hard. Some are dear friends of mine: I've been their wedding shower planner, a bridesmaid, and celebrated their baby showers. They've shared their challenges with me but also the joy that makes it all worthwhile. Despite what the culture tells them they plan on having more children. And I envy them for it."

Daniel felt a connection to Frannie that went deeper than a passion for baseball. He understood her desire for a family and to want desperately what you didn't have. "Aren't you being a little hard on yourself? For merely wishing you had something you don't?"

"My envy has never led me to attempt to destroy someone. But it leads me to sadness and resentment. That's what envy is: sorrow for another's good. I felt it for my best friend, Jen. My last long-term boyfriend broke up with me two weeks before her wedding." She glanced up. "He broke up with me to go back to his old girlfriend."

Daniel grimaced, "Ouch."

"Yeah. And the worst timing ever. I was the Maid of Honor and didn't want to burden Jen with my problems. She was so great, though. She showed up at my apartment and let me have an all-out girl cry. I found out later she rescheduled her last dress fitting to do it. And despite all of that goodness, the majority of my tears on her wedding day were for me. No one assumed that, of course. But, I was drowning in self-pity that whole week."

She shook her head, pushing it away. She had confessed it all and needed to let it go. "I have to concentrate on being grateful for the blessings in my own life when I start falling into that trap."

Daniel felt goosebumps sliding along the back of his neck. Frannie had led him down the same path with his memory of Grandma Mae: the realization of the blessing turned into gratitude.

"Now that I consider it," she said, her voice infused with a lighter spirit, "I'm probably just jealous of you. I wish I had your mix of talent and courage."

"What do you mean?"

"I sort of Googled you after our first dinner and read some of your work." Her cheeks flushed. "I had already read your article about the gender wage gap, but I was too embarrassed to say anything."

His easy smile lessened her chagrin. She continued, "You're a very talented writer who picks the hard subjects and goes after them. You are balanced in your approach, letting the facts speak for themselves without promoting a particular narrative. It's unadulterated data and truth. These days, that takes a lot of courage. At least you're doing something you can be proud of with your career. I went into journalism to be a TV star." Her mouth drooped. "I don't know what my talent is in this business, or if it's even for me."

Daniel's insides went numb. Frannie didn't just respect his work; she respected *him*. He felt like a big fraud and totally undeserving to have someone like her think of him with such esteem.

She poked his arm with her elbow. "And don't forget you have a talent you don't even use: your singing voice!"

Her continued accolades only demoralized him further.

He managed a grin. "I stand by my original statement. You are a kind and gracious person. If it makes you feel any better, I Googled you, too."

Frannie covered her face with her hands. "I'm afraid to ask what you found."

"I found videos of Francesca Menconi covering the Boston news. Everything from personal stories of Boston Marathon runners, protests on college campuses, gas pipe leaks, to my personal favorite," his mouth quirked, "a dog that can waterski."

"Ugh," she groaned, slowly removing her hands from her face. "I wish I could blast that dog video into smithereens."

"All joking aside, I found the story from the Planned Parenthood clinic," he said. "Your gutsy move resulted in your best work. You're genuine, relatable, and it shines through in every news beat you cover. Some of that is raw talent, but most of it is just who you are. You're a natural in front of the camera. That's why your coworkers and Will Kelly don't like you. I would bet their envy has driven them to plot your destruction. Don't change yourself for them. You'll find your place in the sun, Frannie."

Their eyes met and her green eyes were glimmering with a warmth that caused his stomach to lurch. He tried to blame it on hunger pains and darted his glance away and out over the park.

"Are you hungry?" he asked.

Frannie suppressed a smile. The awkward teenager was back. "Yes, I was ready for a beer a long time ago."

Daniel nodded his head toward the large group gathered in front of them. "This place is a popular attraction. That's the third tour that has gone by."

"Uh, hello, this is Mirabellgarten where they filmed "Do Re Mi" for *The Sound of Music*."

"The movie with what's-her-name and the singing kids?"

She flicked her eyes upward and shook her head. "You're killing me. Her name is Julie Andrews and the children were the Von Trapp family. It's one of the most beloved movies of all time."

"Whatever you say, Menconi," he said, pretending to ignore her annoyance. He pulled the aviator sunglasses out of his pocket and put them on before rising from the bench and slinging his backpack over his shoulder.

Frannie remained seated, gaping at him. "You're really going to wear those glasses?"

"Why not?" He flashed his mischievous grin, "You said they made me look like Justin Timberlake."

She let out a mocking laugh. "I'm pretty sure you misread my sarcasm." She hated to admit he wore them shockingly well. "Come on, Fitzpatrick, let's find some beer, sausage and schnitzel."

Chapter 27

AFTER LEAVING MIRABELLGARTEN, FRANNIE AND Daniel relaxed at a small biergarten near the hotel. As part of their usual eating arrangement, they shared plates of sausages, potatoes, and sauerkraut. Daniel opted for a beef stew instead of schnitzel and a salad.

"That was really good," he said, setting his dishes to the side. He took a drink from his half-liter glass stein. "I have to admit, the beer here is totally different from Bud Light."

Frannie made a face. "Is that what you drink?"

"I don't normally drink much. I'll have a drink now and again if I meet a coworker after hours. I've definitely had more alcohol on this trip than usual. You're a bad influence, Menconi."

"It's part of my culture," she said defensively.

Daniel's phone rang. His brow furrowed at the caller ID. "It's your uncle."

Frannie reflexively checked her cellphone expecting to see a missed call. Her notifications were empty. For some reason, her uncle had chosen to call Daniel over her.

"Hello, Cardinal. Yes, she's here."

Frannie expected Daniel to put *Zio* on speaker. Instead, he kept the phone to his ear.

"We're leaving the day after tomorrow. We thought about going back to Milan–Yes, sir. I understand." Frannie noted his face grew tense with each response.

"No, I don't think you have to worry. Thank you, sir. *Ciao*."

He had barely hung up before Frannie blurted out, "What's going on?"

"Your uncle received a call from Cardinal Baldano, using Kratzer's number. Baldano didn't give him a lot of information about our conversation, but insisted that you and I needed to be extra careful. Your uncle wants us back in Rome right away."

Frannie's body was rigid, her eyes boring a hole through the table.

Daniel continued, "He doesn't want us to stop in Milan. The suggestion made him highly agitated."

"Why did he call you?" she asked curtly.

Daniel slowly shrugged and put his palms up. "Does it matter?"

Frannie slammed her hand on the table, her temper beginning to percolate. "Baldano said he asked Kratzer to warn *Zio*. You know something about the danger he's in don't you?"

Daniel calculated his response. Baldano certainly let the cat out of the bag. Frannie was too sharp not to put the pieces together. He was sure the Cardinal would understand if he told her the truth.

"At our first meeting, your uncle asked me to make sure you stayed safe. It caused me to ask if he had received any direct threats but he denied it."

Frannie was still seething. "I can't believe you kept this from me."

Daniel was taken aback by her hostile accusation. "I gave your uncle my word," he said fiercely. "I may break a lot of Commandments, but my word means something to me."

Frannie's anger dissolved into a lump in her throat. She believed him. Daniel Fitzpatrick was a man of his word; the kind of man who would keep his promises.

Daniel's voice returned to normal, "Frannie, your uncle didn't ask you here for the sole purpose of being looked after. He needed your help." He paused. "It's hard for me to admit it, but I wouldn't have gotten this far by myself."

Frannie blinked back the water that suddenly blurred her vision. Between her uncle's secrets and Daniel's appealing character that kept sneaking out, she was on an emotional roller coaster.

"I'm sorry I got so bent out of shape. It's unlike *Zio* to keep things from me. Did he say anything else?"

"No, but I think he's feeling guilty for asking us to take on this job."

"Well, that's silly," she said, her temper subsided. She fidgeted with her empty beer glass. "I guess you'll be doing your interview with him when we get back."

He nodded. "After we give him our full report."

She evaded the reality that her time with Daniel was drawing to a close. "About our race," she said, injecting a jovial mood into their conversation, "you aren't going to try to back out are you?"

Daniel laughed, relieved to have an excuse to ignore the pit in his stomach at the realization his partnership with Frannie was almost over. "I shook on it, didn't I?"

Before Frannie could taunt him further, she saw two familiar people walking toward their table. Frannie waved at them. "Oh my gosh! It's Diedrich and Maureen!"

"Hello again," Diedrich greeted.

"Hello," Frannie replied, "Won't you join us?"

"We don't want to intrude," Maureen said.

"Please," Daniel offered, gesturing for them to have a seat. He watched Diedrich pull a chair out for his wife so she could sit next to Frannie. She smiled sweetly at him.

Diedrich performed the act effortlessly. It was clear to Daniel it was a regular part of their routine. Daniel shook the incredulous stare from his face.

Another point for you and chivalry, Paolo.

The waiter came by and started speaking with the Alder's. They obviously knew each other.

"What did you have?" Diedrich asked, pointing at Daniel's glass.

"It was a pils," Frannie answered for him. "This is his first trip to Austria, so I recommended it."

"That is a good introduction. I'll order for us, yes?" Before they could agree, he was ordering in rapid German and Daniel wondered what he would be getting. The waiter took the order and cleared away the empty dishes and steins.

Frannie noticed their familiarity with the staff. "You must come here often."

"We frequented this pub when we first met," Maureen explained. "We would go for a stroll up and down the river, and always ended up here. I was renting a flat nearby so it was convenient. Sometimes we like to go for a walk and come back to our old stomping grounds."

Frannie placed her hand over her heart. "That is so romantic!"

Romantic? Daniel repeated silently. *A walk and a beer is romantic? Maybe romance isn't dead either.*

"Our son is at his friend's house for a few more hours," Diedrich said, "so we took advantage of having the evening to ourselves."

Frannie propped her chin on her hand. "I hope this isn't rude, but did you adopt Michael?"

Maureen laughed. "Four years of marriage and a twelve year old doesn't add up, does it? Yes, we adopted Michael. Just two months before we were married."

Frannie's eyes widened. "Oh, my gosh, Maureen. An instant family, a new country and language? Those are big changes."

"God brought it all together. Diedrich had helped Michael's mother try to get on her feet. She was battling a drug addiction that, unfortunately, she wasn't able to overcome. Diedrich has two children from a previous marriage but I never had any of my own. An instant family was overwhelming at first, but motherhood for me was truly a gift. I love Michael as if he were my own flesh and blood."

"What about his grandmother?" Daniel asked.

Diedrich shook his head. "There were no other family members that could take care of him. He has an aunt we keep in contact with. She comes to birthday celebrations and he sees his cousins during the Christmas holidays."

The magnitude of the blessing to have had Grandma Mae in his life washed over him again. The beers arrived, pulling him from his thoughts.

He looked at the glass beer stein that had been placed in front of him. *That sure looks bigger than what I had earlier.*

Diedrich picked up his drink and held it up. Frannie and Maureen did the same so Daniel followed suit.

"*Prost!*" Diedrich said with an enthusiastic smile.

"*Prost!*" the ladies echoed and the four clinked their glasses together. Daniel assumed "prost" was an Austrian form of "cheers."

"Which kind is this?" Frannie asked, after taking a swig.

"A hefeweizen. It's made with wheat rather than barely."

"It's delicious," Daniel said. He couldn't believe how smooth the Austrian beer was. It went down so easily.

"How was your meeting with Archbishop Kratzer?" Maureen asked.

Frannie and Daniel glanced at each other.

Maureen noted the alarm at her question. "That's okay," she said, "you don't have to answer."

"He was very gracious," Daniel offered. "We have good information to take back to Cardinal Menconi."

Diedrich leaned on the table. "We will keep praying," he said softly.

Frannie's eyes pleaded with him. "Please do."

Maureen changed the subject, relieving the heaviness that saturated the air. Soon she and Frannie were in a deep discussion over blogs and Catholic online magazines.

Diedrich asked Daniel a few questions which led to telling stories from his tour in Afghanistan. Diedrich was very interested in everything from the culture and landscape to military weapons and vehicles. Daniel wondered how an obviously well-read and highly intelligent man remained a simple café owner.

Diedrich waved at the waiter.

"Fraulein?" he asked across the table to his wife.

She looked at the time. "Sure."

"Half?"

"Please."

Diedrich turned to Frannie. "Francesca, would you like another beer?"

"No, thank you. I'm still working on this one."

"Daniel, you'll have another, yes?"

Daniel looked at his glass. It was empty. He didn't even remember drinking it.

"Sure, why not?"

The waiter arrived and Diedrich placed the order.

"Daniel," Diedrich said, placing his hand over his heart, "I am glad I got the opportunity to see you again. I wish to apologize to you as a man for my aggressiveness with Frannie earlier at lunch. I realized after you left how ill-mannered it was."

Daniel was unprepared for the formal nature of the apology. "We weren't offended."

"I am glad. As I said, I am protective of my family. When you are a husband and father, you will have the same natural instinct."

His words stung his heart. "I'm not exactly the marrying kind, my friend."

The Austrian's one blue eye riveted on Daniel, making him feel pinned down by the weight of its stare; as if he could read his innermost thoughts. Diedrich flicked his gaze at Frannie, then back to Daniel. Finally, the older gentleman gave a weak smile.

"My friend," he said softly, "do not separate yourself from the possibility of happiness. I say this as someone who almost did."

Daniel sensed the advice came from the depths of the man's heart. The last three weeks with Frannie made him wish it were that simple.

The waiter arrived carrying all three mugs of beer in one hand. When Daniel saw Maureen's glass as compared to the larger one Diedrich ordered for him, he understood why she ordered a "half." He was sure Frannie had ordered the half size with dinner.

As they drank their last round, Frannie shared stories of her trips with her uncle. Diedrich and Maureen were most interested in her trip to the Holy Land, stating it was on their bucket list. Frannie noticed Daniel had said very little, mostly nodding and laughing when socially appropriate. She shook off any concern with the logical conclusion that religious pilgrimages probably didn't interest him.

"Francesca, Daniel," Diedrich said, "this has been a lovely evening but my bride and I must go home. Our son will be back soon and work at the café begins early in the morning."

Frannie got up and gave Maureen a hug. Daniel started to stand but Diedrich held up his hand to prevent him and extended it. Daniel shook it and said goodbye.

Frannie was still smiling as they walked away. "Well, are they awesome or what? I'm ready to go, too. It's been a long day."

"Frannie, we may have a bit of a problem."

He was talking much slower than usual, and had a strange grin on his face.

She leaned forward to get a better look at him. "Oh, crap. Are you drunk?"

His response was soaked in his usually absent southern drawl, "Darlin, I'm high as a kite."

Frannie was so used to Daniel refraining from alcohol she hadn't paid attention to what or how much he was drinking. She picked up the empty liter beer stein in front of him.

"How many of these did you have?"

He held up two fingers. "Two."

Her eyes bulged from their sockets. "Two!" she exclaimed. "In addition to the half-liter you had with dinner?"

"Yup."

She smacked her forehead with the palm of her hand. "Daniel! You just drank over a six pack of beer!"

"That's impossible," he slurred, "I don't drink a six pack in six months."

"Well, you did," she scolded.

"Diedrich just ordered them, so I followed along."

"Oh good grief," she grumbled. "Beer is like water over here. You can't keep up with an Austrian."

She blew out her cheeks and exhaled. "You need to walk and get some fresh air. Luckily the hotel is only a couple of blocks away." She got up and stood by him. "Come on, Fitzpatrick."

Daniel rose a little uneasily. Frannie put her arm under his. "Bend your elbow. We'll walk like you are escorting me when I'm really the one holding on to you."

When they hit the street, Daniel glanced down at her and drawled tenderly, "Hey. This is kinda like takin' a romantic stroll."

Frannie came to an abrupt halt. Her head revolved slowly toward him, revealing a set of green eyes that were hard as steel. "Fitzpatrick, if you make a pass at me I will knock you down flat."

He drew his free hand up in a perfect military salute. "Yes, ma'am."

To Frannie's relief, they made it to the hotel without incident.

Daniel leaned his head against the door to his room. He wasn't feeling well.

"Where's your key?" she asked.

He handed her his wallet, and gave her instructions on where to find the key card. She guided him inside, and he plopped down on the bed.

Frannie's boiling aggravation had reduced to a mere simmer. Now she was vexed at wanting to take care of Daniel and yet feeling uncomfortable about crossing any boundaries. His suitcase lay open on a luggage rack. She spotted gym shorts and a t-shirt on the top of his clothes. She grabbed them and handed them to him.

"Go to the bathroom and change. I'll wait here," she ordered.

He slipped off his shoes and disappeared into the bathroom. When he came out, he had his slacks and shirt in his hands. She took them and placed them on top of the suitcase.

Daniel sat back down on the bed; his eyes were beginning to droop.

She stood in front of him. "Okay, I think my work here is done," she said.

Daniel's eyelids flew open. "You really are the kindest person I've ever met." He closed his eyes and breathed heavily through his nose. "Fallin' for you would be as easy as breathin'."

Frannie's heart vaulted in her chest.

She lightly pushed on his shoulders, so he would lay down. "You just need to go to sleep," she whispered.

As his head hit the pillow, he opened his eyes again. Despite the glossiness from his inebriation, they held her with admiration. His mouth formed a sublime grin. "The best Georgia lake sunset can't compare to your beauty."

Frannie took a step back. Daniel's eyes closed and his chest moved in the easy breaths of slumber. She closed his door quietly behind her and walked like a zombie across the hall to her room. She threw her purse in a chair and sank to the floor, resting her back against the bed and covering her face with her hands.

He's drunk, Frannie, she told herself. *It's not real. None of this is real.*

Tears fell from her eyes as she waged against the battle in her heart. She wanted it to be real. She wanted a dinner date with Daniel that wasn't built around probing bishops and Cardinals for information. She wanted him to offer his arm because he wanted to; not because they had to pretend they were a couple. Her sobs became louder as she lost her battle in the face of truth: no one ever told her she was beautiful the way Daniel Fitzpatrick said it. And she would give anything to hear him utter the words to her stone cold sober.

Chapter 28

FRANNIE SAT UP IN BED, INSTANTLY AWAKE. LOUD voices thundered in the hallway outside her door.

One of the voices was Daniel's.

She leapt out of bed and bounded into the hallway. Her feet thudded to a grinding halt at the scene playing out in front of her. Daniel was shirtless, still wearing his shorts, and shuffling in circles in the hallway. The room to his door was ajar, and an old woman was yelling at him in German.

"English?" Frannie asked her.

The woman answered in broken speech, "This man knock on my door and speak nonsense. It scare me. He must be on drugs."

Frannie stepped in front of Daniel and placed her hands on his shoulders. His facial expression was blank. "Daniel?"

He made no sign that he recognized her and appeared highly distressed. "No, please," he pleaded urgently, "I didn't. Please don't."

"I am calling police," the woman said.

"NO!" Frannie barked. "He's my friend and he doesn't do drugs. I think he's sleepwalking. I'll take care of him."

The woman muttered to herself and retreated to her quarters. Frannie put her arm around Daniel to lead him back to his room. To her relief, he was docile and allowed her to direct him easily. She pushed down on his shoulders and he sat on the bed.

"No, please," he kept repeating. "I didn't. Please don't."

She pushed lightly on his chest, hoping he would lay down and go to sleep. Daniel sprang up and began pacing the room, murmuring the same words.

Alarm gripped her. She pondered calling an ambulance but decided to give it one more try. She got in front of him and spoke gently but firmly, "Daniel."

He stopped. Placing her hands on his shoulders she guided him back to the bed again. He was still mumbling when he sat on the bed. His head started to shake, and he called out, "No, Kelsay."

Pain stabbed Frannie's chest hearing him ask for another woman. "Daniel," she said softly, "it's okay."

His head continued to shake. She placed his cheeks in her hands and pleaded, "Daniel, it's Frannie." Tears streamed down her face. "Please, go back to sleep."

His shoulders relaxed and he stopped talking. His eyelids slowly closed. She gently pushed his shoulders and he laid back on the bed. On his own, he picked his legs up and slid them under the sheet. Frannie started to pull the sheet to cover him when she noticed the chain around his neck. Her eyes wandered to the medal laying in the middle of his chest.

It was a Miraculous Medal, identical to the one around her neck. Daniel's looked old and tarnished but she could make out the figure of the Virgin Mary. She couldn't fathom why someone who knew nothing about Marian apparitions or didn't believe they were true would bother to wear a medal of the Blessed Mother. She prayed a Hail Mary for him to sleep through the rest of the night, and covered him with the sheet.

She ran her fingers through her hair. *Now what?* Her mind spun with scenarios of Daniel sleepwalking again, this time making it down the stairs and into the street. The clock on the nightstand read two in the morning. The chances of her being able to go back to sleep were slim.

An overstuffed chair in the corner gave her an idea. She darted across the hall and changed out of her cotton tank top and pajama shorts and into the modest workout clothes she wore the night they shared the apartment. She grabbed the key and shut the door behind her.

The chair was lighter than it looked and she easily scooted to his bedside. She situated herself sideways in it; swinging her legs over the arm and resting her head against the back. If Daniel were to sleepwalk again, she would be ready to stop him.

Frannie watched him for nearly an hour, the words he spoke in his sleep playing over in her mind. Was it just a nightmare? Did this happen often?

And who is Kelsay?

She could hear Jen's warning about stray dogs. Frannie wanted so desperately for this one to be different. Her eyelids finally grew heavy, and she drifted off to sleep.

Daniel awoke but couldn't open his eyes. His head pounded and his body felt like it had been run over by a truck. Flashes of memory started to piece together from the previous evening: Diedrich buying him the second beer and Frannie walking him back to the hotel.

Dread compounded the ache in his head. He cringed that he let himself be so reckless. He remembered Frannie handing him some clothes. Did he say anything stupid? She deserved an apology for his embarrassing behavior.

He slowly opened his eyes. *That's weird,* he thought, seeing his bare chest. *I swear I remember putting on a shirt in the bathroom.*

His mouth was bone dry and he thirsted for a glass of water. He moaned at the searing pain shooting across his temples and started to roll out of bed. Daniel gasped out loud, startled to see Frannie sleeping in a chair next to him.

Frannie bolted awake at the sounds coming from the bed and her feet instantly hit the floor. Daniel stared wide-eyed at her from the bed, but his expression wasn't blank like before.

"Hey," she whispered, "are you awake?"

"Yeah," he said warily. "Why are you sleeping in the chair?"

"You had some sort of sleep episode last night. I think you were sleepwalking. I was afraid you would do it again so I slept here the rest of the night."

Daniel's insides squeezed so tight he thought his ribs would break. He asked slowly, "How did you know I was sleepwalking?"

"You walked into the hallway and knocked on someone's door. The voices woke me up, and when I heard yours I came out to see what was going on."

Daniel's hands clenched into fists and he raised them to his forehead, his forearms covering his face. The embarrassment from his drunken behavior dwarfed in comparison to the humiliation that now engulfed him.

He only knew from others what his sleepwalking and sleep terrors were like. He hoped this one wasn't a full terror episode. He slowly lowered his arms.

"I'm sorry if I frightened you," he said, staring at the ceiling.

"You didn't scare me," she said gently. "I just wasn't sure how to comfort you so you could go back to sleep."

He winced. *Comfort me? It must have been a terror one.*

Frannie could tell he was mortified. "It was easy to bring you back in here," she assured him. "You were mumbling a little but I was able to get you to lay back down."

He looked at her for the first time. She was fudging the truth and he knew it.

"Frannie, I've had these before and I've been told I don't just mumble. I can be quite agitated."

She looked him squarely in the face. "Daniel, I promise, you were not uncontrollable or violent. If anything, you appeared tormented. You called me Kelsay, but that's it in a nutshell."

His face became ashen. "I could never–ever–" he whispered, "confuse you with that woman."

Frannie's heart leapt that Daniel wasn't pining over the mysterious Kelsay. Whoever she was, the pain she had undoubtedly caused still haunted him.

He said, "I'm sure all of this was uncomfortable for you. I'm fine now."

She took the hint she was being dismissed. "Ok. I'll–um, go back to my room. You want some breakfast?" she asked.

"I could use a shower and then some coffee."

"Tomaselli's is a great place. I'll meet you downstairs." She bounced up from the chair and quickly exited.

When he heard the door close he got up and headed for the shower. He stood directly under the showerhead and placed his palms in front of him, pressing on the tiled wall. The hot water fell over the top of his head and down his back, releasing the tension in his body. The stress release brought with it a stream of silent tears, and he let the water wash them away.

Daniel could no longer deny Frannie was more than just a kind person. Frannie was special: she was willing to sleep in a chair to make sure he didn't sleepwalk his way out into the streets of Salzburg, gave her best attempt to downplay how much his strange sleep disorder must have frightened her, and shrugged it all off in an effort to minimize his embarrassment.

Her words echoed in his mind: *I wasn't sure how to comfort you.* He was certain her touch, her voice, would be enough to calm him. They had been colleagues for less than a month, but he knew there was no way to avoid the hole that would burn in his heart when it came time to leave her.

She's not for you, Danny.

Frannie deserved an explanation for the events of the evening. Then, he would be able to make a clean break. Whatever respect she had for him would be gone, and there would be no doubt he was not the guy for her.

Chapter 29

"LOOK AT THOSE PRETZELS!" FRANNIE EXCLAIMED as they passed through the Alter Market on the way to Tomaselli's Café. "They're huge!"

Merchants filled the market square selling everything from pretzels, gingerbread and delectable cookies to herbs, fruits, and vegetables. She paused at a vendor to take a picture of the seller's exquisite fresh floral arrangements.

Daniel stopped reluctantly. He wanted to get to the restaurant and have the conversation he knew he could no longer avoid.

She continued merrily, "I want to come back here after breakfast and pick up some snacks for our train ride tomorrow. The fruit looks amazing, doesn't it?"

"Sure," he responded flatly.

Frannie's stomach churned. Every effort to cheer Daniel up had failed. He barely said two words since they left the hotel. She didn't want him to fret over what happened. It was over and done with as far as she was concerned.

When they arrived at Tomaselli's, it was buzzing with customers. Tables with aqua and white striped umbrellas lined the upper and lower terraces, each full of patrons enjoying the cool morning air. The waiter led them outside to the last available table, sandwiched in the middle of two other parties.

"I'm sorry, sir," Daniel said. "Would it be possible for us to eat inside? I saw a booth in the corner that was more private."

"Of course," the waiter replied, spinning on his heel to head back into the café. The walls of the classic Austrian coffee house were paneled in a rich, walnut-colored wood. Small round marble tables filled the room, with a few booths lining the windows overlooking the street. The waiter pointed toward a booth in the corner.

Frannie scooted into the cream leather seat across from Daniel. She laid her menu out on the square tan marble table. Daniel gave his a cursory look then gazed out the window.

Frannie bit her thumbnail. Whatever he wanted to talk about weighed heavily on his mind.

"What are you hungry for?" she asked, hoping to start a conversation.

"You can order something," he said, finally looking at her. "I'm ok with just a regular coffee."

The waiter returned and Frannie ordered coffees, a few Danishes, and cold meats in case Daniel changed his mind.

"Frannie," Daniel began, "I owe you an apology. Last night I put you in an uncomfortable situation not once but twice. It was irresponsible, and I'm truly sorry."

His heartfelt expression and concern tugged at her. "It's okay, Daniel. I'm not mad."

"I know," he said, as if he were disappointed she wasn't. "But, I want to explain what happened."

The waiter arrived with their coffees, and Daniel took a couple of sips before he continued. "When my mother got diagnosed with cancer, we moved in with Grandma Mae so she could take care of her. I remember bits and pieces of the day she passed away. I was sitting and talking with her, as I usually did when I got home from school. She suddenly interrupted me and asked me to get Grandma. My last memories are a haze of our priest arriving and the ambulance coming to take her. My sleep episodes started soon after.

"They frightened Grandma at first, but the doctors said they were common among children that experienced a traumatic event and I would most likely grow out of them. They were accompanied with sleepwalking from the start. Grandma Mae was afraid I would figure out how to open the front door so she put a bell over it to wake her up. As long as I stayed on a regular sleep routine, I rarely had an incident.

"By the time I entered middle school they were basically gone. One night in high school, my best friend Travis and I snuck a couple of six packs and went out to his family's barn. It was the first time either of us had tried alcohol so it didn't take much to get us drunk. I spent the night at his house and I had an episode. That's when I learned that alcohol can be a trigger, and it's why I don't drink much.

"When I decided to join the Marines, I found out the military can reject applicants with a history of sleepwalking. I started depriving myself of sleep for two weeks to test myself. I was episode free so I lied on my physical examination, hoping I had officially outgrown them. It was a risky stunt. If I would have sleepwalked, I could have been dishonorably discharged.

"I got teased a lot because I didn't party like the other Marines. Once I became the fixed designated driver of the unit, no one cared. At parties, I was an expert at carrying a beer around and pouring it out little by little to make it look like I was drinking."

Daniel was interrupted by the arrival of their breakfast order. Frannie placed it off to the side and out of the way, giving Daniel her full attention.

"About three years ago," he continued, "they came back. The same thing happened as what you witnessed last night. I went and knocked on the neighbor's door but thankfully they, too, were able to get me back to my apartment. But the second time it happened, they had to call an ambulance. I was in a full blown terror and they couldn't calm me down. After that, I put a large chair in front of the door every night which worked. I had a few nights where I woke up on the floor or in the chair."

"Do you know why they came back?" Frannie asked.

"Yeah," he said in a listless tone. This was where he would sever any possibility of a relationship with Frannie; even her friendship.

"After my first four years in active duty, I finished the last four of my commitment in the Reserves which allowed me to finish college, get a job, and move to Chicago. By the time I was twenty-eight, I was beginning to get some articles published and hoped to move from intern to contributing writer. That's when I met Kelsay," he added sourly.

"She was the friend of the girlfriend of a guy at work, and we met on a double date. We hit it off and our tumultuous affair began. After a year, it seemed the next logical step was to move in together, so we did. I tried to hide it from Grandma Mae but she figured it out." He paused, remembering the hurt in her voice when she confronted him.

"One night I came home from work and Kelsay wasn't there," he said, staring at the table. He didn't want to see the look on Frannie's face when he told the rest of his story.

"I went into the bathroom, and I happened to notice the top of a pink box in the trash can. I don't know what made me look, really. I moved a tissue that was covering it, and saw it was a home pregnancy test. Naturally, I was curious so I picked it up and there was a used test inside. It was positive."

His hands nervously rubbed his coffee cup. "I was petrified. Kelsay and I had been living together for six months and fighting on a regular basis. Any uncertainties I had about our future no longer mattered. We were going to have to figure it out."

He downed the rest of his coffee and continued to hold the empty cup between his hands so that they wouldn't shake.

"I paced the apartment waiting for Kelsay to come home. My mind was racing about whether we needed to get a bigger place, where I would look for a house, was my income going to be enough, and how soon we could get married. Slowly, the reality began to sink in that I was going to be a father. And I was happy about it."

As soon as Daniel remembered the joy, sorrow immediately suffocated it. "When Kelsay came home, she headed straight for the couch and laid down. Her face was pale and she didn't look like she felt well. I figured either the pregnancy was making her sick or she was just as nervous as I was. I told her I found the test in the trash and not to worry. I said I would take care of everything and it was going to be okay."

Frannie's insides twisted in knots. The pain in Daniel's face indicated where the story was going. An intense rage toward Kelsay flared within her. Everything Frannie desired had been at the girl's fingertips, and she threw it away.

"But, I didn't have to take care of anything," she heard Daniel saying, "because Kelsay already had. She said she didn't love me anymore, she had goals for her life, and I was holding her back. She left in the morning and the following night I had my first terror episode since the night at Travis's. They subsided within a few months. As far as I know, last night was my first in at least two and a half years."

Frannie reached across the table and placed her hand on Daniel's wrist. His eyes slowly met hers. They were as warm as her touch.

"Daniel, I'm so sorry," she whispered.

Her fingers slid from his wrist up to his hand. He let go of the coffee cup and let her hand fall in his.

"Have you talked with anyone about this?" she asked.

Daniel blinked rapidly a few times, confused by her reaction. He had expected her to recoil in disgust, not reach out in comfort.

"You and my best friend Travis are the only ones who know. I hid it from Grandma Mae. It would have killed her."

His eyes began to shimmer so she squeezed his hand to reassure him. "I'm humbled that you would trust me enough to share something so personal," she said. She wanted to say something else but hesitated. Her heart urged her on.

"Look, I know how you feel about the Church. But they have people who minister to those who have been affected with pain like yours; both men and women. You're not alone, Daniel."

Travis had given him the same advice three years ago but he never followed up on it. He looked down at her hand in his. He absently rubbed his thumb over her knuckles.

"I think the hardest thing," he said, "is not knowing if it was a boy or a girl." Half of his mouth raised in a sad grin. "I gave the baby a name: BJ," he announced proudly. "I figured he or she was in heaven with Mom and she would fill in the blanks for me; Benjamin Joseph or Bonnie Julia. It may sound crazy, but my episodes went away after I gave the name."

When he looked back up Frannie was wiping her eyes with the back of her other hand. She sniffed and shook her head. "I don't think that sounds crazy at all."

Daniel had never revealed to anyone the name of his child. Not even to Travis. It felt good to say it out loud; to acknowledge he or she existed.

He reluctantly let go of her hand. "You're probably hungry," he said, gruffly wiping his own eyes. "You should eat something."

She picked up the two plates the waiter had left and sat one in front of Daniel.

"Maybe you should join me," she said.

They ordered more coffee and loaded their plates with the meats and breads; each more hungry than they thought. They ate in silence. Frannie waited patiently for enough time to pass when he would be ready to return to regular conversation.

Pieces of events from the previous evening floated in Daniel's memory. He had a vague recollection of telling her she was beautiful.

"Frannie, did I say or do anything else last night that I should apologize for?"

She looked at him thoughtfully. *Yes, you can apologize for saying the most charming things and making me wish you meant them.*

"No. You were a perfect gentleman. I promise."

The blush on her cheeks told Daniel otherwise. "A real gentleman wouldn't have allowed himself to become intoxicated," he countered. "You, on the other hand, are a class act Frannie. And I admire that. It makes you a unique person in this world."

Frannie felt the heat from her face creep down to her neck and looked away. She hated that she was so horrible at hiding her feelings.

Daniel's phone buzzed. "Hey, I have an email from one of my contacts. I bet they have information about the angel company."

Frannie felt her skin radically cool down at the news. "Let's go back to the hotel. They have a room we can use as a work space. We'll hit the market on the way back."

"Are you really going to get one of those big pretzels?"

"You better believe it. And some jelly filled cookies. But don't worry, Fitzpatrick," she goaded, "we'll get some fruits and vegetables, too."

He laughed but secretly marveled how easily they fell back into their routine after an intensely personal conversation. As he watched her make her purchases, his stomach dropped. His plan had backfired. Frannie's compassionate reaction to his confession just made leaving her even harder. And the hole in his heart, even wider.

Chapter 30

D ANIEL AND FRANNIE SET UP SHOP IN A SIDE ROOM off the lobby of their hotel. A pair of upholstered burgundy wingback chairs and a wooden coffee table furnished their makeshift office. A sheer white curtain over the window allowed natural light to brighten the space. The room was vacant, allowing them to talk freely.

Daniel balanced his computer on his lap and verbally summarized the information from his contacts, "The angel company in question has contributed to *Compassione* multiple times, but no transactions were found with the Vatican Bank. The same firm bankrolled four of the Garone restaurants. I bet you can guess the name of one of them."

"The one in Milan," Frannie said dully, as if she were answering an easy trivia question. "I expected big deposits in the Vatican Bank by this organization. What do you think it means that they came up empty?"

"They could be funneling the cash through the Garone restaurants under another account. Or, *Compassione* is being used as the front." He leaned back in the chair. "I wish I could talk with Stefano. I'm convinced he's the one with the answers and access to the proof of Constantini's money trail."

"I have a question about Stefano. If he's the mole, and working at the family restaurant in Milan, did he come to Rome on a day off to give the list to *Zio*? Also, Baldano said *Zio* was under

Constantini's eye. Wouldn't it have gotten back to him that Stefano had passed off a mysterious envelope?"

"Hmm. You're right. It sounds like the boy is already in enough danger. Donati wouldn't risk blowing his nephew's cover." He stroked his chin. "How old do you think Stefano is?"

Frannie shrugged. "Younger than us. Twenty-three, maybe?"

"By the time I was that age I had completed two tours in Afghanistan and almost five years of military training. The military can make a man and a soldier out of you in short order. It makes me wonder if somewhere along the way Stefano has been trained to lift evidence and slip past people undetected. Something tells me he is more than a pizza delivery guy."

Frannie's eyes were heavy. The limited sleep combined with the warm sun coming through the window made a perfect recipe for a catnap. Daniel seemed eager to pursue the Stefano lead so she tried readjusting in the chair to wake up. "We can do some searches and see what we find," she suggested.

Daniel emailed his contact with a request to check Stefano's history since high school. In the meantime, he did a cursory internet search and found Stefano's social media page. The posts revealed nothing except he spent a lot of time with friends on the Italian coastline. He was about to close the page when something made him take a second look.

It was a photo of Stefano, his mother, and Giovanni sitting around a table. The description was in Italian but their formal attire suggested they were attending a wedding or gala of some sort. What captured his attention was the party sitting two tables behind them. He enlarged the photo, and the people's faces came into view.

It was blurry but he instantly recognized them: Mr. Bald Man and Cardinal Constantini.

The two men knew each well, and the photo proved it; only friends or patrons with deep pockets would be placed at a Cardinal's dinner table.

Daniel's head snapped up and almost called out to Frannie but he hesitated. She had her head propped against the side of the chair, sound asleep. Her laptop hung barely balanced on her lap.

A stab of guilt sliced through Daniel for being the cause of Frannie's poor and interrupted sleep. He downloaded the picture to his computer and put it in his backpack. Her face was so peaceful, he hated to wake her. He walked over and gently touched her shoulder. She jumped, causing her laptop to topple. He caught it before it hit the ground.

"Frannie," he whispered, "you need to go lie down. Your neck will hurt if you sleep there."

Frannie was so drowsy she didn't argue. She put her laptop in her bag. "I didn't get very far in my search."

What he found could wait. "That's okay. We can talk about it over dinner."

"What are you going to do?" she asked, yawning.

"I might go for a walk. Text me when you're ready."

"Okay," she said, and shuffled off.

Daniel dropped off his bag at his room, and headed out. He mindlessly retraced their steps toward Tomaselli's. He crossed the bridge to the west side of the Salzach River and spotted a bench under a tree. He sagged onto the seat and closed his eyes. A cool breeze off the water lightly brushed his face. Pedestrians and bike pedals clicking on the trail in front of him provided a calming white noise for him to sit with his thoughts.

He tried hammering out the triangle connecting Stefano, Bald Man, and Constantini but his mind kept wandering back to Frannie. No woman had ever captivated his heart to this degree. Heather was a first love that proved both young and naive. His relationship with Kelsay was purely physical; a fact he realized a little too late. Both women left him jaded and cynical.

He had convicted all members of the female sex as guilty before proven innocent; delivering his verdict as judge and jury based on his own witness. Frannie presented confounding evidence that cast a shadow of a doubt on his previous ruling. Her generosity and benevolence astounded him. She made his humiliating situation bearable and showed him unconditional mercy when he confided to her his deepest, darkest secret. Frannie was the woman of virtue that Paolo described; it was why he continued to open the door for her beyond the pretenses of their date at the concert. She prodded something buried within him; a part of him that desired to be set free. Whenever it bubbled to the surface, he suppressed it; he didn't want to fall in love only to be hurt and disappointed again.

Frannie had even tested his convictions about God. Either God told Frannie to come to Salzburg or she got really lucky. And if the Almighty talked to Frannie, He may have talked to him at the Vatican. The idea left him unsettled with a need to be grounded in some reality. Debunking the theory that Mary appeared to shepherd children in 1917 seemed like a quick and easy task. He dug out his phone and typed in his search engine.

To his surprise, the articles on the topic were endless. There were pictures of the crowd waiting and watching for a sign or word from the children seers. He found Portuguese news articles reporting the witnesses' claims of the sun dancing as Frannie had described. He read through the secrets and visions Mary gave to the children. At first glance, Daniel felt vindicated. The messages with an emphasis on war and hell confirmed his bias: God was vengeful and cruel and only wanted to inflict suffering on those He had put on the earth. Exploring further, however, he began to discover other messages from the Lady: her desperate urge to pray for the conversion of sinners and for peace, descriptions of God's desire to save those that are lost, predictions that came true, and the hope of triumph over evil.

His reason told him uneducated children from rural Portugal couldn't have made all of this up. There were pictures of them, too: Lucia, Francisco, and Jacinta. Their faces set like stone, ready to defend their story. Even being thrown in jail by the government couldn't make them change course. What troubled him most was the children described the woman as beautiful but sad; a woman worried about the fate of her children.

She loves you like a mother.

Was Mary concerned for the fate of his soul?

He stuffed the phone in his pocket and abruptly started walking again, anxious for something new to think about.

His legs led him back to the open air market. He paused at the vendor whose fresh flower arrangements had allured Frannie into taking a picture. A small wicker basket caught his eye: one bright white lily surrounded with pink gerber daisies, small deep purple violets, and baby's breath. Its simple beauty reminded him of Frannie. Before he knew it he was paying the woman for his purchase.

Daniel made his way back across the bridge and meandered the streets until he found himself in front of Alder's Café. The jingle of the doorbell brought Diedrich out from the back of the kitchen. The bread cases were cleaned out and Daniel stood alone inside the shop.

He greeted Daniel with a handshake, "Daniel! What a surprise! I'm afraid I am all out of sandwiches. I was just getting ready to close."

"I was actually hoping for a slice of apple strudel."

Diedrich glanced at the basket of flowers Daniel was holding and nodded. "Flowers and strudel. Francesca will forgive you. I have two slices in the back."

Daniel started to refute Diedrich's mistaken idea of a lover's spat but he had already vanished to the kitchen. This was the second time he insinuated they were a couple.

"Here you are," Diedrich said, placing a brown sack on the counter.

"Thank you."

Daniel sensed something fatherly and wise about the Austrian gentleman. He glanced around the empty café and rocked back and forth on his heels. He had wandered back to Alder's for more than strudel.

"Can I ask you something?" he asked.

"Yes."

"What did you mean last night in telling me not to separate myself from happiness? What made you say that?"

Diedrich placed his hand over his heart. "I must have spoken out of turn. I am sorry."

Daniel opened his mouth to speak but nothing came out. The formal nature of the man caught him off guard again.

He found his voice, "I'm not upset, just curious. To be quite frank, I don't think you know how to be rude."

Diedrich chuckled. "If my wife were here, she would tell you I can be quite rude if I choose to be." He gestured at a table. "Sit down, Daniel."

Diedrich locked the café door and sat at a table with the young American. He leaned back casually as if he were getting ready to chat with an old friend.

"How old are you?" he asked.

"Thirty-two."

"That is still quite young. What makes you think you are—how did you say—'not the marrying kind?'"

"It's complicated," he replied flatly.

"Mmm," Diedrich pointed to his scarred face, "I know something about complicated, yes?"

Before Daniel could attempt to apologize, Diedrich continued, "I see something in you that reminds me of myself. My old self. I see pain behind your eyes." He paused half a beat, "I am Austrian so I am very direct. Do you believe in God?"

Daniel blinked rapidly. Direct was an understatement. "Do I have to answer?"

Diedrich raised his one eyebrow. "At some point in your life you will have to answer this question. I recommend you answer it sooner than later, and in the affirmative."

He leaned forward and folded his hands on the table. "Daniel, how you answer this question determines the image you have of yourself, your definition of happiness, and how you seek it. As humans, we can make our lives quite complex and complicated. And the Enemy is right there to tell us lies about God and about ourselves; things like, 'God doesn't really love me,' 'I am not worthy,' 'I am not this or that.' These lies will corrupt your self-image and your image of God. The Enemy is also an expert at perpetrating fears. He knows what is keeping you from the fullness of life, and he will continue to taunt you with it and make happiness unattainable."

Daniel felt completely naked. It was as if the man had an uncanny insight into his most secret thoughts.

Diedrich continued, "I can say these things because I know them first hand. Only the Lord can set man free from lies, from sin," he raised his brow again, "or pain that shackles us. You have to accept Him first. Only then will you be free for happiness."

Daniel didn't doubt the sincerity in which Diedrich spoke, but he wasn't sure he could believe the words. God and happiness were hard for him to connect to each other.

"What if God doesn't want us to be happy?"

Diedrich shook his head slowly. "That is not possible," he said softly. "God may not give us an easy life, or a life without suffering and hardship. But he wants to share His blessed life with us. He made us out of love and for love."

"I think the only love I've ever really known is the love of my grandmother and a good friend who went to Afghanistan and back with me."

Diedrich began to hear with understanding; the young man had experienced considerable loss and had little family support. "It sounds like your grandmother and friend are examples of great sacrificial love. It is in self-sacrifice that we come to realize what it means to be human, and how to truly love."

Daniel thought of the sacrifices Grandma Mae made for him on a daily basis. He and Travis had presented too many folded American flags not to know the sacrifice made by soldiers on the field.

Diedrich pointed at the flowers. "You bought flowers and strudel for Francesca. Why?"

"She went above and beyond the call of duty–" Daniel stopped. *Frannie had made a gift of self-sacrifice.* He swallowed hard and continued, "And I wanted to let her know I appreciated it," he finished.

Diedrich smiled. The young man had answered his own question. He was finding out what it means to love and to be loved. "Then you should tell her," he said.

Daniel's phone buzzed. It was Frannie. She was awake and looking for him.

"I should go," he said. He pulled out a paper Euro and gave it to Diedrich for the strudel.

Diedrich held up his hand, indicating payment was not necessary.

"Please, take it," Daniel insisted. "If I don't buy it, then I really haven't given her a gift."

Diedrich took the paper bill. "You are a true gentleman, Daniel."

He was humbled to receive such a compliment from the noble Austrian. He stuck out his hand, "Thank you, Diedrich. For everything."

Diedrich returned the handshake and walked Daniel to the door to let him exit and locked it behind him.

Maureen came out from the back. "Was that Daniel?"

"Yes."

"By himself?"

"Yes."

"Is everything ok?" She crossed her arms. "I need more than a 'yes.'"

"I think it will be. We need to add them to our prayers. Especially Daniel. I think he is finding love when he least expected it."

Maureen smiled and wrapped her arms around her husband. "That sounds familiar."

He smiled. "Indeed. But, I had to give away our afternoon strudel."

She laughed. "If it was for the cause of love, I'm okay with that. Coffee anyway?"

He nodded and pulled her close, praying that one day Daniel would find the same kind of love he could hold both in his heart and in his arms.

Chapter 31

DANIEL HELD HIS FIST UP IN MID-AIR, POISED TO knock on Frannie's hotel door.

You're giving her flowers and strudel because she did something nice for you, he reminded himself.

He took a deep breath and rapped on the door.

When Frannie opened it, she burst aloud, "Hey! I was thinking we could get some coffee—"

She stopped mid-sentence when her eyes fell on the flowers.

Daniel held out the basket. "I went for a walk and I ended up back at the market. I remembered you took a picture of the flowers so I bought these for you."

Frannie took the basket and held the flowers up to her nose. "Thank you," she said, her whole face glowing, "they're gorgeous."

The way her face lit up at his simple gift caused Daniel to stammer. "And I—um—I went by Diedrich's café and got a couple of—uh—slices of apple strudel," he said, holding up the bag. "It's the least I can do for the trouble I gave you last night."

"That was really sweet of you." She smelled the bouquet one more time and placed the basket on the dresser.

"The strudel is perfect," she said. "We can enjoy it with a cup of coffee next door and start our search again."

"I found something before I woke you," he said, glad to refocus on their original venture. "You're going to be impressed."

The coffeehouse next to the hotel wasn't as richly decorated as Tomaselli's but it had a small terrace outside with round tables sheltered under the cover of large green trees. Daniel and Frannie settled in at a table in the farthest corner.

"Okay, Sherlock, what did you find?" Frannie asked.

Daniel flipped open his computer and showed her the picture. "See this table back here?"

He had only just begun to enlarge the photo when she gasped, "Holy crap! Where did you find this?"

"In Stefano's social media photos."

The image sent her mind reeling. "This is huge. It proves that Bald Man and Constantini know each other."

Daniel took it to the next logical conclusion. "And implicates Constantini as the one who had us followed." With a few keystrokes he had Stefano's personal social page up. "Does it say where it was taken?"

"Hmm. He seems like a regular Italian guy who has a lot of friends," she commented as she scrolled through the posts and pictures. She found the original post with the picture and translated it from Italian. "At a fundraiser for a children's hospital. Let me check something." Within a few seconds she was nodding. "Yep. *Compassione* is associated with this particular charity. That explains why Constantini was there. But Bald Man? You don't normally attend a fundraiser of this caliber unless you've got some deep pockets or know someone. I can't believe your people couldn't find him."

"Why would Elena and her sons be there? Would they have that kind of money?"

"Maybe Cardinal Donati was there and brought the family."

Daniel absently poked at his last bite of strudel. "It's still hard for me to imagine Donati as a victim. Based on what I read when I did my original research on the scandal, I definitely wouldn't have pegged him as an injured party."

"Lots of things aren't what they originally appeared to be." She dug out Vidmar's list. "The Scripture next to Vidmar makes more sense now: 'Behold, I send you out as sheep in the midst of wolves; so be wise as serpents and innocent as doves.' I thought it was telling us Vidmar was one of the good guys, but he was warning *Zio* while hinting the list came from him."

"We have a lot to present to your uncle, but there's still something missing. And I guess we aren't going to Milan to find out what it is," he said sullenly.

"It's a journalist thing isn't it? The desire to know the answer and feeling if you just unturn the right stone you'll find it?"

"It's bugging you, too?"

"Yes, but I guess if it's meant to be revealed God will find a way."

Daniel stared at his coffee cup. Diedrich's question returned to his mind. Did he believe in God? Frannie and Diedrich didn't just believe in a God who created the universe. They *trusted* Him. Anyone Daniel had trusted disappointed him except Grandma Mae and his platoon. How was he supposed to trust someone he couldn't see or touch?

"Daniel?" Frannie asked, breaking into his thoughts. Her fingers fiddled nervously with her napkin. "There's something I would like to know the answer to. If you don't want to explain, just say so."

His brow wrinkled. "Okay."

"Last night, I couldn't help but notice your Miraculous Medal. It surprised me, and I wondered why you would wear it."

Daniel couldn't blame her for asking. He must seem like a hypocrite to criticize religion yet wear a medal of the Blessed Mother around his neck.

He gave a little grin. "I'll explain. I'm pretty much an open book now, anyway." At this point, he didn't see any point in refusing to answer. Travis was the only person who knew more about his life than she did.

"I mentioned that I would sit with mom when I got home from school. The day before she died she talked to me about a lot of things. She told me how much she loved me and that if I worked hard I could be anything I wanted to be. I wonder now if somehow she knew—" his voice trailed off. He remembered the soft tenderness in his mother's voice and her attempt to smile while tears streamed down her face. Lost in the memory, he grasped how much it hurt his mother to leave him.

"Anyway," he continued, "that same day she gave me her medal and asked me to always keep it close. I don't wear it because I believe in anything. I wear it because it's the only personal thing I have that can connect me to her."

Frannie's eyes were steady and reassuring. It dawned on him that if anyone could understand his attachment to his mother's medal, it would be Frannie.

"I get it," she said gently. "Baseball is how I feel connected to my father. He's the one who introduced me to it. My brothers were older when we moved to the States and they traded their love of soccer for American football, but my father fell for America's favorite pastime."

Her eyes shimmered as she recalled her favorite memories. "Going to Fenway Park was something special Papa and I shared together; we loved the green of the diamond, the peanuts, and the hotdogs. Don't get me wrong, I love the game. But staying a fan is how I keep his memory alive."

He looked at her thoughtfully. "Your memories bring you comfort, don't they?"

"Yes. They had to. I struggled with depression my first year of high school. It started after an athletic awards banquet. Another girl and I were receiving our award for placing at State. After the ceremony, the other girl's father gave her a dozen roses. I was crushed. I began to run through every scenario of my life that I would have to celebrate without my dad: he wouldn't teach me to drive or be there for my high school and college graduations. The hardest one to think about was my wedding day."

She absently folded the napkin into a tiny square. "With Mama and *Zio's* help, I gained a new perspective. I learned to be grateful for the good times we had together and treasure them as blessings. I still miss him; that never goes away."

Frannie berated herself for being so careless with her words. Daniel's only memories of his mother were of her being very sick and dying. At least she could remember happy times with her father. She looked up from playing with her napkin. "I'm sorry, Daniel. I know it's not the same for you."

Her warm eyes were like a safety net. Daniel could speak his mind and receive nothing but understanding in return. "It's strange, actually," he confided to her. "I am starting to see those last days with Mom differently. The pain meds made her so tired and weak, but she would fight to stay awake when I was with her. She knew what was going to happen, but she didn't want to leave me."

She loves you like a mother.

When he was little, Grandma Mae used to tell him how much his mother loved him. He didn't fully understand it until now. The image of Mary holding Jesus' body and the loss of his own child added a new dimension to his mother's suffering.

He blinked rapidly so tears wouldn't fall. "The medal is all she really had to give me."

Frannie pinched her lower lip between her fingers. She was sure it was more than that.

"Do you know why it was special to her?"

"According to Grandma Mae, my mother always walked the straight and narrow and never got in any trouble. Then she met my father. He was from Augusta and took a summer job working on one of the farms. I guess Mom's one slip was giving in to young love and getting pregnant. Obviously, my father didn't love her enough to stick around. Grandma told me her religious devotion began when she was pregnant. Grandma used to say something about the medal protecting me but I never paid much attention."

Frannie lifted up the identical one that hung from her neck. "The images for the medal came from an appearance by Mary to Saint Catherine Labouré in France. Mary told her graces and protection would be granted to those who wear it and pray for her intercession. It's why I wear mine. I started wearing it after a trip I took to Fatima with *Zio*. On the back is a Cross and an M representing the closeness of Mary to the suffering and death of her Son. It's also imprinted with her Immaculate Heart and the Sacred Heart of Jesus."

Daniel froze. When he'd stood before the *Pieta* at the Vatican he had sworn his medal suddenly felt warm on his chest. He had shaken it off, thinking his mind was playing tricks on him. The knowledge the medal represented the close relationship of a Mother and Son—a relationship surpassing even death—suggested Someone was definitely speaking to him that day. Someone who wanted him to know She understood deep sorrow.

"Is it the heart you talked about with the sword?" he asked.

She wasn't surprised to learn he didn't know what was on the medal. "Yes, the same one."

He reached for the chain around his neck and pulled the medal out from underneath his shirt. He could make out the image of Mary despite the tarnish, but the M and the Cross on the back were barely recognizable.

Frannie noticed him struggling to make it out. "Here." She took hers off and handed him her chain.

Daniel slipped his back under his shirt and picked hers up to examine it. Everything was just as she described. He handed it back.

She fastened the clasp and let it fall back on her collarbone. "You should polish it when you get home. I've never seen one with a vintage scalloped frame before. I bet it's beautiful."

He was about to reply when a word crashed into his brain: *protection*. The medal was his mother's way of protecting him. She would have believed the promise Mary gave to the woman saint and it was the only way she could instinctively protect her child. "You're probably right," he said quietly, "I should take better care of it."

Frannie checked the time. It was still a little early for dinner. "Would you like to go for a long walk? We're going to be sitting on a train all day tomorrow."

"Don't remind me," he said, standing up and stretching. "Another walk for me would be great."

They trekked back over the bridge toward the Cathedral and ended up at the base of the castle fortress sitting on its perch above the city. Daniel preferred exercise over the funicular ride, so they made the steep hike to the top. It took them fifteen minutes to reach the terrace on the castle roof. From there, they had an unobstructed panoramic view of the city. Below them the Salzach River divided the city in half. They had a bird's eye view of the church spires and domes dotting the Salzburg sky.

The climb invigorated Daniel; it felt good to move his legs and elevate his heart rate. Standing high above the city induced an additional surge of adrenaline. He glanced at Frannie; she was leaning on her elbows against the railing. Her hair was pulled back with a few strands hanging on her face and neck. The breeze caused the wisps of her dark hair to fly around her cheeks. His eyes focused on her image like the lens of a camera, and his lids closed as the shutter, capturing the picture and imprinting it upon his memory.

"It's beautiful, isn't it?" she asked, not taking her eyes off the wide open vista in front of her.

"Yes. And the view isn't bad, either."

As soon as he uttered the words, he cursed silently. *Did I really say that out loud?* He peeked sideways at Frannie and her shy smile and wide eyes gave him his answer. *It must have been the damn adrenaline rush.*

He winced. "I'm sorry. That was totally inappropriate."

She wanted to laugh but knew it would only intensify his embarrassment.

"A girl doesn't mind getting a compliment." She held her breath and waited, giving him room to follow it up with something about Georgia lake sunsets. Daniel remained silent, refusing to look at her. She swallowed her disappointment.

"Unless," she coaxed, "you meant to say, 'Thank you, Frannie, I'm glad we followed your gut on the long train ride to Salzburg where we got to interview Cardinal Baldano.'"

She watched his lips twitch. He turned to her, wearing a big smile. "Yes, that was exactly what I meant to say."

"Let's find some dinner, Fitzpatrick."

Daniel slipped the aviator sunglasses over his eyes to conceal how enamored he was with her.

He stuck out his arm, "M'Lady? Shall I escort thee down from this stone castle?"

She laughed, half curtseyed, and slipped her arm in his. "Yes, you shall."

They had only gone a few steps when she asked, "You know when we get back to Rome we have a bet to settle, right?"

"I haven't forgotten, Menconi. I gave you my word, remember?"
She snuck a glance in his direction and grinned. "Just checking."

Chapter 32

THE MORNING STAR'S BREAKING DAWN CAST ITS rays upon Saint Peter's Basilica, painting the marble a goldenrod yellow. Daniel stood by one of the fountains in the plaza doing a few stretches, limbering up his knee for his race against Frannie. The square was quiet and still in the early Sunday hour. At five minutes before six, he saw her approaching.

"*Buongiorno!*" she said brightly, before jibing, "I hope you got a good night's sleep."

"The best," he said with confidence, but he was lying through his teeth. Although the train ride had left him lethargic and tired, it had been difficult to wind down. His mind replayed all that had happened in Salzburg; both the professional and the personal. He hoped the lack of sleep wouldn't be too detrimental to his performance.

"Great!" she said. "Then how about going double or nothing?"

He instinctively pulled his injured knee to his chest for an extra stretch. "I'm listening."

"If I win, you have to sing an additional song. A song I pick out." Frannie's eyebrows were deliberately raised, waiting smugly for his response.

"Two songs?" he repeated. He locked his eyes with hers, in a showdown to see who would blink first. She didn't flinch. If she was going to raise the stakes, then he would need to up the ante on her, too. He said the first thing that came to his mind.

"Okay," he said. "If I win, I still get the lasagne dinner, and you have to come to a Cubs home game, fully decked in Cubs gear."

Her stomach did a somersault. *I think he just asked me to come visit him in Chicago.*

She maintained her self-assured stance and stuck her hand out. "Deal."

He shook her hand and sealed the new conditions to their wager.

"You have the trail mapped out on the app I sent you?" she asked. "You know where we're going?"

"Yes, Menconi," he said, mocking her, "I know where we are going."

"Ok. I just don't want you to get lost, you know, if I get too far ahead of you."

"You wish."

She flashed her radiant smile and the pesky warm feeling that seemed to always accompany it filled his chest. He didn't detect any hesitation from her in traveling to Chicago.

Does she want to make the trip?

"On the count of three," he said. "One. Two. Three."

Daniel ran a few strides ahead of Frannie down the side streets until they arrived at the Villa Doria Pamphili recreational park, completing the first mile and a half. Once in the park, Frannie closed the gap and kept only a half stride behind him. When they came to the *Casino del Bel Respiro*, Frannie took an opportunity to nettle him.

"We're about six and a half miles, Fitzpatrick. How are you doing?"

Once again he noticed how easily she spoke while she ran. He was tired from running a longer distance than usual but he felt strong and his knee wasn't bothering him at all.

"I'm thinking about my lasagne dinner," he goaded back.

"Last stretch is Janiculum Hill. See ya at the top," she smirked, then began running slightly faster.

Daniel noticed the change immediately and increased his pace to stay ahead of her. When they hit the bottom of the hill, she picked up speed again, this time running a half stride ahead of him. He dug down deep to use all the strength he had in his legs to make the powerful strides he needed to overtake her while going uphill. Just as he passed her, his knee injury flared. He pushed harder, ignoring the pain but each time he went faster, so did Frannie.

A few yards from the top, she turned into a near sprint. Daniel's knee couldn't cooperate with the power he was trying to exert. He gave it all he had, but it wasn't enough. Frannie's sudden burst was enough for her to reach the top two steps ahead of him.

Daniel put his hands on his hips and shook his head at Frannie.

"Whew!" she said, letting out a big exhale. "You gave me a scare, Fitzpatrick. I thought for a second you were going to pass me."

Still standing, he pulled his injured knee up to his chest to give it a stretch and released it. His eyes narrowed. "Let me guess," he said in between breaths, "your athletic banquet was for competing at State in track and field."

She grinned unabashedly. "I was the anchor runner for the 400 meter relay team all four years of high school. We won the State Championship every year except my freshman year. That year we placed second."

She sat down on the ground to stretch and Daniel copied her.

"I switched to cross country in college but my training as a sprinter served me well when it came to making up ground in the last tenth of a mile. I placed third once at State and usually placed in the top ten. I still like to run races but I can't maintain a sprint like I used to."

Daniel leaned back on his hands. "You're a piece of work, Menconi. You're a hustler."

"You make me sound so devious." She stood up and offered her hand to Daniel. He took it and used it to pull himself up. A shooting pain in his knee caused him to favor his other leg when he stood and he hobbled slightly.

Frannie frowned. "Are you ok?"

"Yes, I'm fine," he said curtly. He took a few steps and then pulled his knee up to his chest again. "I just need to move my leg, that's all. Are we ready to head back?"

Frannie wasn't convinced. "What's wrong with your knee? You've been stretching and massaging it since we stopped." A thin pink scar across his patella jogged her memory. "Wait, you said you had a knee that bothered you. Is that scar from Afghanistan?"

"Yes. It's not a big deal." He walked past her and headed briskly down the hill.

She scurried to catch up with him. Daniel let out an exaggerated sigh. He knew she wouldn't let it go.

"It's just a souvenir I brought back," he explained, "some shrapnel from a land mine."

He saw her eyes widen. "It's what the military classifies as a slight wound. I was able to return to duty and I don't have any metal remnants in my knee. It didn't start bothering me until a couple of years ago. The doctor said it's probably arthritis caused by the injury. It's not debilitating and some days it gives me fits and other days it doesn't."

"And today was one of those days?" she asked.

"My knee isn't used to a seven mile run. I usually keep it around three and no more than five."

"Then why didn't you say something?" she asked, rattled that he finished the race while in pain.

"And let an old injury be an excuse for not taking you up on your challenge? No thanks. I have my pride as a guy and a Marine. I was hoping the knee would cooperate. Besides," he added jokingly, "I didn't know I was being hustled by a State Champion sprinter."

"Now you're making me feel guilty. The truth is, I knew I could keep up with you based on our previous run and I was counting on the element of surprise in my sprint. I was hoping to catch you off guard enough that I could sneak ahead and capture the lead."

"And you did. I'm not mad, Frannie. You won fair and square. But, I'm not going to lie. A part of me would like to train for a few months and have a five mile rematch."

She smiled at the thought of their relationship continuing beyond Italy. "You name the time and place, Fitzpatrick. I'll be there."

When they arrived at her apartment, he did a quick check to make sure all was clear. They had only been back in Rome for a night and he wasn't sure if Bald Man or someone else would be lurking around, scouting them out.

"All clear," he said, stepping out to the hallway.

"You're coming to *Zia* Rosa's right? To talk with *Zio* about our trip?"

"Yes, the Cardinal arranged for Paolo to pick me up."

"I was wondering," her eyes avoided making direct contact, darting between him and the door, "if you would come to Mass with me today."

She saw his mouth start to open and kept talking, "You could ride to *Zia's* with us and it would give us more time for our conversation with *Zio*." She hoped her argument for convenience and efficiency would make it difficult for him to decline.

Her request left Daniel conflicted. After hearing the results of the *Traditio* project, he was curious what all the fuss was about the

Latin Mass and why people his age and younger found it appealing. He was also apprehensive; he wasn't sure what to make of the spiritual encounters he had experienced and was reluctant to place himself directly in the pathway of another one.

Having the invitation come from Frannie amplified his consternation. Politely declining the Cardinal seemed easier than saying no to the warm green eyes that were pleading with him, and his heart yielded.

"I suppose," he said, trying to sound aloof about it. "What time?"

"Mass is at eleven. Paolo will pick me up at ten-thirty. You could be back here by then?"

He glanced at the time. It was barely eight-thirty. He nodded.

"Okay," she exhaled, as if she had been relieved of a large weight. "See you in a few."

Frannie quickly stepped inside and shut the door before he could change his mind. She took a deep breath to try and slow her galloping pulse. Earlier that morning when she entered Saint Peter's Square, something had nudged her to ask Daniel to Mass. She had dismissed it, certain he would never accept. On their walk back, the idea returned with greater intensity.

Okay, Lord, if this was from you, I asked him and he's coming. It's up to you to do the rest.

She placed a coffee pod in the coffee maker and downed two glasses of water while she waited for it to brew. With her java in hand, she sat on the couch and made sure the ribbons in her Missal were organized. She wanted to be ready in case Daniel wanted to follow along with her.

She said a prayer over her morning cup. *Lord, you know everything. You know the pain Daniel's been through. I know you see his heart. Please let him be open to your Presence. Mother Mary, I think he is drawn to you, whether he knows it or not. Lead him to your Son.*

She prayed three Hail Marys, entrusting Daniel to the heart
of the Blessed Mother, who understood better than anyone that
nothing would be impossible for God.

Chapter 33

"S*IGNORE* D*ANIEL*!" P*AOLO* CHEERILY EXCLAIMED AS Daniel and Frannie approached the car. "What a wonderful surprise! I did not know you were coming with *Signorina* to Mass this morning."

"Hello, Paolo." Daniel returned the man's smile and handshake. "It was a last minute decision. I guess it will save you a trip, anyway."

Daniel opened the car door for Frannie and she climbed in the back seat. When he shut the door he received a nod of approval from Paolo.

"Very nice, *Signore*," he said in a low voice and winking. Daniel smirked and shook his head. He had grown fond of the cupid-playing chauffeur. He walked around the car and got in on the other side.

Sitting in the front seat was a woman with chin-length straight silver hair peppered with black. She wore a black dress with a colorful scarf around her neck. Frannie was speaking with her in Italian.

Paolo interrupted them, "*Signore* Daniel, this is my beautiful wife, Sofia."

The woman turned around and smiled pleasantly at Daniel. She had friendly brown eyes and an elegant face.

"Daniel," she said, "I have heard so much about you."

He wondered what in the world Paolo would have told his wife about his occasional passenger. "It's nice to meet you, ma'am," he said, his Georgia accent escaping slightly.

Sofia said something to Frannie in Italian, provoking a light pink blush on her cheeks. She smiled politely and turned to look out the window. Daniel wondered if Sofia was as brazen as her husband at aiming cupid's arrow.

"*Signore*," Paolo said, "I will introduce you to my son after Mass. He will be there with his family."

Daniel remembered the story of Paolo's son and his recovery from addiction with the Cardinal's help. "I would be honored, sir."

The car headed along the Tiber River on the side opposite the Vatican. When Paolo pulled up to the church, Daniel was startled by the stark surroundings. They were in a tiny piazza, or square, common to the city layout of Rome. Unlike other piazzas he had been to, this one resembled a plain parking lot; there was no ornate fountain or statue of any kind in the middle. Daniel expected a church where the Cardinal celebrated Mass to be in a monumental thoroughfare, similar to Saint Peter's or the Duomo in Milan. Rather, the church appeared tucked away and boxed in among regular buildings.

Amidst the simple setting, the church architecture stood out in contrast with the rest of the property. Daniel thought it looked more like an opera house than a Catholic Church. Rich honey and rust-colored travertine blended together in the stone of the grand façade. Classic Corinthian columns created the illusion of a top and lower half of the building. Statues of the four Evangelists, Matthew, Mark, Luke, and John, sat perched in niches framed by the columns; two on the upper and two on the lower. At the top, a Greco-Roman triangular pediment crowned the structure.

Frannie paused on the steps, then stepped aside so Paolo and Sofia could pass by. Daniel watched her dig through her purse. She had a black book under her arm and was struggling to find what she was looking for.

"Here," he said, taking the book from under her arm. He glanced at the cover. It was leather and had the words *Daily Missal* imprinted in gold on the front.

"Thanks," she said, still searching, "ah, got it." She pulled a little satin pouch out of her purse.

He handed the book back to her.

Having conquered the battle with her purse, she said, "Welcome to the *Santissma Trinita Dei Pellegrini a Roma*: Church of the Holy Trinity of the Pilgrims of Rome."

"It's not what I expected," he admitted.

"It has an interesting history. Saint Philip Neri took possession of the property in the mid-1500s. He and his confraternity of brothers used these buildings to house pilgrims traveling to Rome. At one time, they were used as a hospital and a hospice for those recovering from illnesses."

"I didn't know saints were in the medical field."

Frannie nodded. "The Catholic Church and its religious orders were instrumental in the founding of the modern hospital." She quickly switched gears, "I wanted to talk to you before we went in. I want to prepare you a little for Mass."

He yanked his head back. "Prepare me? Am I going to Mass or having surgery?"

She slapped the outside of his shoulder with her missal. "I'm serious. I know you said you don't remember much about the Mass, but I bet you have more Catholic muscle memory than you think. And this Mass is a lot different from what you attended as a kid."

"Since it's going to be in Latin, I kinda figured as much," he quipped sharply.

Frannie's exuberance deflated like a balloon. "I'll have my missal open," she said calmly, "if you want to follow along. But, it is my suggestion you try to just–be."

Daniel watched the warm light in her eyes turn dull. Standing on the steps of the church made him ill-at-ease and he second-guessed whether he should have accepted her invitation. In response, he had reflexively employed his old juvenile defense mechanism of sarcasm.

He attempted to mend his offense. "What do you mean?" he asked sincerely. "Just be what?"

She perked up a little at his change in tone. "Just be in the present moment and take it all in. Don't try to figure everything out or wonder what's being said. Let the mystery of it speak for itself. I can answer any questions you have afterwards."

"I'll try."

Her lips formed a half smile, "That's all I can ask for."

He watched her open the satin pouch and take out a piece of white lace that looked like an oval, seamless, scarf. She adjusted it over her head and shoulders, letting the rest fall on her chest.

She looked up at him, "Let's go in."

Daniel couldn't breathe. Looking at Frannie with the soft white lace framing her face, he was keenly aware of her femininity, modesty, and her generous soul. The veil didn't cover up anything; it revealed to him everything that was beautiful about her. And he knew he was too wretched and unworthy to be by her side. He managed to place one foot in front of the other and escorted her into the church.

The inside of the church was as majestic as Daniel had expected. The honey-rust colored marble continued into the interior. Corinthian columns stood erect along the sides of the main aisle, supporting the ceiling arches and directing his eyes to the painted frescoes below the opening of the dome. Above the high altar hung a large canvas of the Trinity: God the Father robed in purple and gold with the Holy Spirit, represented by a dove, hovering at the Father's chest. Christ the Son was directly beneath them, crucified on His Cross with angels kneeling in adoration and sorrow at the death of the Savior of the world.

Black-veined African marble Corinthian columns framed the vertical sides of the painting. Above it, an arch stretched over a semi-dome of recessed golden panel squares created the illusion of a rounded canopy. On the high altar were six of the tallest gold candle stands Daniel had ever seen. Their height combined with the candles reached almost halfway up the Trinity altarpiece.

Daniel and Frannie entered a pew a few rows from the front, directly behind *Zia* Rosa and her family. Daniel did a quick sweep and noticed many young families with children, just as the *Traditio* project had reported. Despite his gray slacks and blue dress shirt, he felt a little underdressed; most of the men were wearing suit jackets and ties. The women, even some of the young girls, wore veils similar to Frannie's.

Frannie leaned over and whispered, "One quick thing. *Zio* will celebrate Mass facing the altar, not the people."

"He'll have his back to us?" he whispered back.

"Yes, but he isn't turning his back; he's facing the same direction as us. It's called *ad orientem*, or to the east. The posture indicates we offer the sacrifice of the Mass with him, who is offering it to God."

The tones of the organ descending from the choir loft signaled an end to their conversation, and everyone rose from their seats. Daniel, seated at the end of the pew, had an unobstructed view of the opening procession. A mix of men and boys walked reverently down the marble floor toward the altar. Most donned black cassocks under a white surplice. Two men wore intricate clergy vestments over an alb: a long white robe-like garment edged in lace embroidered with crosses. The young altar boys carried candles, and one older boy a crucifix. At the end came Cardinal Menconi, wearing his priestly vestment over a lace alb and his mitre: a tall hat of white linen and embroidered in gold thread. When the Cardinal caught sight of Daniel, one corner of his mouth tweaked up briefly in an almost imperceptible smile and he inclined his head toward him as he went by.

Once Mass started, it was hard for Daniel to, as Frannie put it, "just be." He wondered about everything: why the clergy vestments of the two men matched the Cardinal's but had sleeves; what they were doing when they knelt down next to the Cardinal while he remained standing; and why the choir sang at the same time the Cardinal read quietly from a book at the altar.

When they sat down, one of the clergy-robed men stood on the right side of the altar and began to chant in Latin from the book. Frannie touched his shoulder and whispered, "The subdeacon is chanting the Epistle and the deacon will chant the Gospel." She pointed in her missal to the Scripture readings, written in English.

Daniel glanced back up; he didn't know the difference between a subdeacon and a deacon, but he gathered it was the reason why they had sleeves on their vestments. He looked back down at her book, and intended to politely pretend he was reading. His eyes skipped over the Epistle and landed on the Gospel. The words, "boats" and "fishermen" caught his interest. He browsed through the story of Jesus telling Simon Peter to throw his net out into the deep to catch fish. Peter obeyed, but reluctantly. Daniel was astonished at Simon Peter's reply to Jesus; it sounded nearly sarcastic. He could relate to Peter: *Look, dude, we've been doing this all night and haven't caught a thing but sure, I'll go ahead and lower my net. Again. For the umpteenth time. And for probably nothing.*

But the nets became so full of fish the boats began to sink. Daniel's stomach tightened at Peter's response. The fisherman fell on his knees before Jesus and said, "Depart from me, for I am a sinful man, O Lord."

Daniel read on, expecting Jesus to rebuke Peter for his snarkiness and past sins. Instead, Jesus said, "Do not be afraid; henceforth you shall catch men." Then Peter and the other fishermen left everything and followed Him.

Frannie stood up and the choir began to chant. Daniel followed her, and saw movement from the right side of the altar: two younger servers emerged holding candles, and another carrying the gold censer of incense, and the deacon with the bookstand. The four of them fell effortlessly into a tight formation in the center, facing the altar: the deacon and subdeacon stood next to each other, the boy with incense behind them, and the two candle bearers side by side in the rear. As if on cue they all genuflected on one knee in unison, then walked to the left side of the altar. The dignity and precision of their movements reminded Daniel of a Marine Color Guard.

The deacon began chanting what he assumed was the Gospel he had just read. Afterwards they sat back down and the Cardinal began his sermon, in Italian. Daniel's mind wandered back to the story of Simon Peter.

Depart from me, for I am a sinful man...Do not be afraid.

Peter, the same man whose bones were now enshrined in the world's largest basilica named after him, felt unworthy. *Perhaps,* Daniel wondered, *even a little unwilling and nervous.* Why else would Jesus respond with, "Do not be afraid?"

His mind started bouncing from one argument to another.
What would Jesus say to me?
It's different. Peter's sins couldn't compare to mine.
Do I care what Jesus would say?
Do I believe in God?

He reflected on the question Diedrich had posed to him at the café. Deep down, Daniel knew there was a God. How or why he knew this he was unsure, but he believed it with all his...his what?

What did I use to come to this conclusion? he mused. *I haven't exactly learned much about God or read the Bible.*

Daniel cast his eyes around the grand church and his introspective query plunged further inward. The part of him that leapt when he had entered the Duomo in Milan wasn't his brain. The heat in his chest triggered by Frannie's smile wasn't from his lungs or heart. Even if neurons were activated and chemicals fired, the origin was not from a specific organ. He could deduce with his reason that human beings were more than a cerebral network of neurons that could walk and talk. He knew his child, no matter how many days or weeks old, was more than a mere clump of cells.

He closed his eyes. He came to the conclusion that this rudimentary knowledge had been planted in the depths of his being; in the place where he knew that what he knew was reality: his soul.

It was the only logical answer he could find for the unique ability of humans to write, compose music, and create works of art. The soul explained the wellspring that had filled him and his fellow soldiers with courage to risk their lives for brother and country. Daniel had never doubted that he had a soul, but had also never given it much thought: until it was pierced by the magnificence of an artist's statue and captivated by a woman of timeless beauty.

His eyelids flashed open as a new revelation dawned on him. The metaphysical attributes of his soul could not be explained by biological evolution.

Then only God could have created it.

Daniel could confidently state he believed in God. What perplexed him was Diedrich's assertion that his self-image and happiness somehow rested upon this answer, and in turn influenced his image of God. He realized Diedrich had asked him the wrong question. What Daniel couldn't answer was, *Who do I believe God is? And if I thought differently about God, would it change my image of Him and myself, like Diedrich said?*

The rustle of movement interrupted his thoughts. The congregation had risen to their feet; the Cardinal's sermon was finished and he returned to the altar. Music played from the organ and the choir resumed chanting. He glanced down at Frannie's missal. The English page began with the words *I believe in one God, the Father Almighty, Maker of heaven and earth...*

Daniel almost laughed at the irony; they were chanting the Creed, or profession of faith.

Emboldened by Peter's frankness, he thought, *Okay, God. I believe in you. I just don't know who you are, and I don't know how to find out.*

The Mass continued with the preparation of bread and wine on the altar. This much Daniel remembered, but the Cardinal and servers performed more actions than he recalled. Every movement was ordered and executed with decorum. The synchronous genuflection of the servers with the priest appealed to him.

After some additional chanting by the Cardinal, everyone knelt down. Daniel wasn't sure if he should kneel or sit. It seemed hypocritical to kneel, but it was a better option than looking out of place.

As he slid to his knees onto the bare wooden kneeler, suddenly, everything changed.

One of the younger servers rang a hand bell three times. From the side came the youngest boys in a single file: two with candles, one boy with his hands folded, then two more with candles. They stopped at the center of the altar and the boy with no candle made sure they were lined up properly. At his nod they genuflected, then knelt down. In front of them, all the other servers and clergy were in their formation. The deacon stood directly behind the Cardinal on the first step of the altar, and the subdeacon behind the deacon on the next step. Another server flanked the Cardinal's left side, and the boy with the censer of incense moved to the right of the altar. Two more servers were in front of the candle-bearers. Daniel didn't know what was coming next but whatever it was, the troops were ready and in place.

The Cardinal read inaudibly from the missal book on the altar, in the same posture as before: his back towards the people, just as Frannie had described. Daniel became aware of the choir music; their intricate vocal ranges and polyphonic sound were projected by the natural acoustics of the church. The voices from the choir loft in concert with the stillness of the troops surrounding the altar was impressive. Without warning, the music stopped. Except for the cries and murmurings of small children, the congregation was quiet as Cardinal Menconi continued to silently recite the words from the Missal.

The server on Cardinal's left knelt and within a few seconds, the Cardinal genuflected, and the boy with the bell rang it again. Simultaneously, in one fluid motion, every server kneeling around the altar bowed their head and shoulders. Cardinal Menconi stood up and elevated the Host, while the boy with the bell rang it three more times. The server on the left lifted the back of the Cardinal's vestment, so that he could lift the Host as high as his arms would allow. The server with the censer swung it so that the smoke of the incense drifted towards the Cardinal and the elevated Host. The Cardinal lowered the host back to the altar, and genuflected. All those around the altar bowed their heads low, in unison with the same precision as before.

Daniel knelt, transfixed, as the whole thing was repeated again; the genuflections, unified bows and bell ringing, but this time the Cardinal elevated the chalice. The Catholic muscle memory Frannie mentioned kicked in; the bread and wine had become the Body and Blood of Christ. He knew Catholics believed this miracle occurred at every Mass but he never thought it could actually happen.

Until now.

The Cardinal's posture of facing the altar rather than the congregation made sense to him. Every action drew his attention to the Host and the chalice. In Daniel's military mind, every server from the deacon to the little boy lining up the candle-bearers were akin to a platoon being led by a commanding officer. The officer was leading them toward something that demanded reverence and honor; something that was worth the cost of discipline and training. It was something majestic, beautiful, and worth believing in.

Daniel closed his eyes. He understood what Frannie meant by letting the mystery speak for itself. He didn't need to follow along with her missal or hear the words the Cardinal was praying; the gestures and postures said it all. He understood why people would seek out this elevated worship, magnificent on its own merit and untouched by modern inventions.

It's timeless, he thought. The Mass had the same characteristics that he appreciated about a baseball game at Wrigley Field, but even he could concede the preservation of the Tradition of worship was supernatural in a way baseball could never be. He was drawn to it; the precise militaristic movements, chants, and harmonic sounds of the choir exposed his soul to an oasis of order and peace from the chaos of the outside world.

After more prayers, chants, and synchronous genuflections, the congregation began making their way to the altar rail, kneeling down to receive Communion. Daniel had never seen Communion distributed in this manner. The priest never left the area of the altar; he simply went down the line giving the Host on the tongue to each person. He noticed no one received standing up or in their hands like in the Masses he remembered.

He noticed Frannie flipping a ribbon in her missal to a different page. In the middle was the title, *Prayer of Saint Ambrose*. He quickly discerned it was a prayer to recite before approaching the altar to receive the Lord Himself.

A certain section leapt off the paper: *To You, O Lord, I show my wounds, to You I lay bare my shame. I know that my sins are many and grievous, and hence I am afraid. I trust in Your countless mercies. Look upon me, therefore, with the eyes of Your mercy...have mercy upon me...O fount of mercy that will never cease to flow.*

The image of a merciful God flew in the face of Daniel's conception of God as a crotchety old man who was easily provoked into bringing His full wrath down upon His Creation. Apparently, this Ambrose character trusted in God's mercies despite his sins. Daniel found Peter's uncertainty more relatable.

Depart from me Lord, for I am a sinful man.

He understood where Peter was coming from. Jesus had done something good for him; a catch of fish that large was probably an exceptional day in the fishing business. The unexpected generosity led Peter to question his worthiness. Why help me? I'm a sinful man.

Frannie closed her book and turned to stand up. When Daniel rose from the wooden kneeler, he felt his knee catch.

Italians must not believe in kneeler pads, he thought dryly.

He stood to the side and let Frannie and the others in the pew pass. He knelt back down and watched Frannie kneel at the altar rail. He looked up at the painting representing the three Persons in one God. His eyes glossed over the bearded God the Father and fell upon Jesus the Son crucified; the same Jesus that Mary held in her arms in the *Pieta*. Maybe he had been so transfixed on the image of God as a wrathful and absent Father, he had missed the compassion of the Son.

Is that really who you are, Lord? A font of mercy and compassion?

Daniel couldn't deny God was compassionate enough to leave him with Grandma Mae. But he still held God responsible for his pain of growing up without parents. It was why he had turned away from all religion and lived his life as if there was no such thing as sin. It ended up costing him in the end.

What would you say to me, Jesus, if I showed you my wounds? My shame? Diedrich said if I accept you, I can be free for happiness. How do I do that? And would you let Frannie be a part of that happiness?

Frannie had returned and knelt down next to him. He closed his eyes, hoping for an answer to all the questions he had thrown up to the heavens. He neither heard nor felt anything.

He chastised himself for attempting to talk to God, *Why am I even bothering with this?*

Deep down, he knew why. The immaterial part of him–his soul–had been moved by Frannie, the *Pieta*, by watching Diedrich with his wife and children, and the Mass. He was separating himself from happiness just as Diedrich said. He wasn't free. But as much as he desired freedom, he was also afraid. He wasn't brave like Peter. He wasn't ready to leave his boat and net and follow into the unknown. He couldn't trust that happiness would be waiting for him on the other shore.

Chapter 34

CARDINAL MENCONI'S BLACK AND RED CARDINAL robes draped over a gold upholstered chair in *Zia* Rosa's living room. He sat facing a brown leather couch, occupied by Daniel and Frannie. The doors to the room had been closed; an unspoken command to the family not to disturb the meeting. The prelate digested the information being presented by his two investigators. They had given him a full account of their encounters with Constantini and Donati in Milan, and Kratzer and Baldano in Salzburg.

"What is your final analysis?" he asked.

Daniel leaned forward, resting his elbows on his knees. "In a nutshell," he began, "Constantini's your problem. According to Baldano, he's your number one enemy and has most likely been keeping you under watch. We think he is blackmailing Donati so he and the Garones can use *Compassione* as a front to funnel money through the Vatican Bank, free from taxes and prying eyes. His blackmail scheme doubled to control Donati's vote in the papal conclave so he can push through his progressive agenda for the Church."

"*Zio,*" Frannie said softly, "we have to accept the possibility that Cardinal Vidmar was murdered by one of our own. The evidence points to it. And if that's true," her voice quivered, "such a Judas cannot parade around in the cloth of a shepherd. He deserves a just punishment under the law. He is driven by power and will devour whoever gets in his way."

The Cardinal closed his eyes, rested his elbow on the arm of the chair and covered half of his face with his hand.

"You didn't tell Kratzer or Baldano about the information you were given on the flash drive implicating Constantini?" he asked, his eyes still shut.

"No *Zio*, we wanted to tell you, first."

"Sir," Daniel said, "I checked my email after Mass; my contacts were able to uncover some history on Stefano. Our friend is older than he looks. He served in the Italian Navy Special Forces. I met a few of these guys in Afghanistan and I can tell you they are an elite group of soldiers. Stefano would have no trouble delivering a letter to you undetected, or lifting evidence from Constantini."

He braced himself for Frannie's temper that was sure to erupt after she heard what he was about to suggest. "I want to go back to Milan and talk to him. Frannie would stay here, of course."

"Excuse me?" Frannie spouted loudly. "You're not going back to Milan by yourself!"

Daniel threw her a stern look. "It's the only way your uncle will agree to it. Do you want to be rid of this Judas or not?"

"It's probably more dangerous for you to go alone—"

"I am a Marine, Frannie," he butted in, "I've been trained to take care of myself."

"With what? A lamp?" she sneered.

Daniel raised his voice, "Yes, if that's all I have available to me! I can make a weapon out of damn near anything."

"*Basta!*" the Cardinal bellowed.

He watched them retreat into the couch, each retaining a stubborn look on their face. He sensed their argument had nothing to do with their male or female egos but had arisen out of concern for the other. Nothing about their behavior after Mass had gone unnoticed: the admiring look Frannie gave Daniel when he was introduced to Paolo's son and his family, the way Daniel smiled at her when he opened her car door, and the less than half inch of space separating them on the couch. Something was brewing between the two, and he would do everything in his power to protect them from harm.

"No one is going to Milan," he stated calmly. "I have already put both of you in a danger that I, myself, did not realize. I knew there were wolves in the Church; I was naïve to think they couldn't be nefarious. I need some time to pray about this before reaching out to Giuseppe Baldano. He will know the best way to contact Fortino and Stefano." He clutched his pectoral cross and mumbled, "Mother Mary, Saint Peter, pray for us."

A soft rap was heard on the door.

Cardinal Menconi spoke in the direction of the knocker, "*Sì, entra.*"

Zia Rosa timidly stuck her head in. "Dinner is ready."

The Cardinal smiled at her. "Thank you, Rosa. We will be right out." He kept his smile and let it rest on Daniel and Frannie. "I can't thank you enough. You have done a great service to me and to the Church."

He looked at Daniel. "I guess I have an appointment to keep with you for an interview." He checked his calendar on his phone. "Could we schedule it for Tuesday?"

Daniel hesitated, wanting to present another argument for seeking out Stefano sooner than later. The Cardinal's unwavering eye told him it would be futile to press the issue. "Tuesday would be fine, sir."

The Cardinal clapped his hands together. "*Brava.* I'm sure you are ready to get back to the States, but I would consider it a personal favor if you would stay through Friday and attend the gala."

"What gala?"

"An annual benefit for the Missionaries of Charity, the religious order founded by Saint Mother Teresa. It's given by a small group of benefactors that have supported them for many years and they want me to give an address. I would like you to sit at the table with Francesca and myself."

Friday was five days away. He had less than a week to say goodbye to Frannie.

"I'm honored that you would invite me, your Eminence. I'm sure I could swing staying here for a few more days."

"Wonderful!" he said merrily as he stood up. "Let's not keep Rosa waiting."

Shortly after dinner, the Cardinal approached Daniel and Frannie. "I need to go home early. Paolo is outside and will take both of you, too."

They nodded. "Excuse me, one minute," Daniel said. He walked back to the kitchen and found Rosa placing cookies on a tray. "We're leaving early, Rosa. I'll be flying back home next weekend. I wanted to thank you for welcoming me as part of your family at your Sunday dinners. You've been very kind."

"You are welcome!" She put her hands on his cheeks and gave him the double Italian kiss, then said in a low, teasing voice, "I have a feeling you will be back with Francesca on her next visit."

Daniel chuckled nervously. He had never met so many cupid-wanna-bes. "Thank you again, Rosa," he said, and turned to leave. Frannie was hanging outside the kitchen by the door. The pink on her cheeks indicated she overheard everything.

Paolo dropped off the Cardinal then drove to Frannie's apartment. "We're both getting out here, Paolo," she said.

Daniel got out and opened Frannie's door. He smiled and waved at Paolo who shot him a wink as he was pulling away.

After his usual check of the apartment, he let Frannie enter.

"Okay, Fitzpatrick. I'm ready for my personal concert."

"Let's get this over with," he groaned.

She picked up a dining chair and placed it in front of the coffee table so it directly faced the couch. Daniel noticed the wicker basket of flowers he bought her were in the center of the table. On the train, he had watched her take great care to keep them watered and protected in a paper bag at her feet. They had retained all of their vibrance.

"You can sit here," she ordered, pointing at the chair. "I'll sit on the couch. I found a karaoke app that has tons of songs for you to choose from." She handed him her phone with the app open.

He flopped down and took her phone. After a few seconds of scrolling, he announced, "All right. You wanted a crowd pleaser. This was the one. It filled the dance floor every time."

She turned on her wireless speaker, so the music would be in stereo. "I'm ready," she stated victoriously.

He sighed and placed the phone on the table. "I don't know if this will work. I'm used to singing with a live band and it's awkward not having a guitar in my hands."

"Roll with it," she said, getting cozy in her seat and propping the balls of her feet on the edge of the table.

He hit the play button on the app. A guitar played the recognizable tune of the country song, "Friends in Low Places" by Garth Brooks.

Frannie couldn't help but smile after the first two lines. Daniel's voice was amazing. By the chorus he was letting himself get into it and Frannie got an inkling of the performer he must have been on stage. His blue hazel eyes sparkled with energy and his smile was magnetic. He couldn't help but sway to the music while he sang and even gave her a few sultry looks, causing her to laugh gleefully.

When the song was near the end and the chorus began to repeat, he yelled, "Help me out, Menconi," and she joined in and finished singing the song with him. As the music faded she started clapping.

"Whoo hoo!" she shouted.

He grimaced. "Bleh. Singing with an app sucks."

"Oh, it was great. You really are talented, Daniel," she said sincerely.

"Thanks." As much as he hated the second rate accompaniment from the app, it felt good to sing again.

"Why do you hide it?" she asked.

He leaned back in the chair. "When I decided to leave Jackson, I wanted to leave everything that connected me with it; from my southern drawl to singing. I guess after everything that happened with Heather, I wanted to leave it all behind and start over. If I went home I only saw Grandma Mae and my friend, Travis.

"But, I've realized I have good memories of singing at Fuller's, and there were other good things about Jackson: the Fullers and Dawsons–" he added, clarifying, "the Dawsons are Travis's family. And Grandma Mae of course." He didn't want to admit to her they were blessings, or that she was responsible for his change in attitude.

Daniel picked up her phone and tipped it back and forth. "I think I have to sing another one. Your turn to choose." He tossed it to her and she caught it.

"Actually, my pick is on my tablet."

He squished one eyebrow. He expected to be presented with a boy band pop song from the 90s that would be easily found on the app.

She started to hand him the tablet, then paused. "You said you learned how to read music, right?"

"Yes. It's been years, though."

She handed it over. "It's my favorite hymn. Here's the sheet music with the lyrics."

When Daniel saw the title, his face fell. It was the hymn, "Be Thou My Vision."

"You want me to sing this?" he asked numbly.

Frannie hesitated, wondering if he was uncomfortable singing something he didn't know or if he didn't want to sing a religious piece. "I found an instrumental accompaniment if you need it," she offered, in case it was the former.

"I know it," he said, a slight edge to his voice. He looked up and spoke more gently. "I know the song and I don't need the accompaniment. I'll sing it *a cappella*."

He straightened his posture and took a deep breath. He closed his eyes and let the tablet lay loosely cradled in his hands.

Then he began to sing.

Frannie's mouth slowly fell open. Daniel never opened his eyes. He not only knew the melody; he knew the words by heart and sang like the song was an intimate old friend. The fun and playful drawl she heard in the country song was replaced with a serene reverence for each word. It was resonant, powerful, and sounded more beautiful than she had imagined. His handsome face reflected a warm light that could only come from a place deep within.

I see it, Lord, she spoke silently. *I know only you can truly see the human heart, but I see a glimpse of what you see. Daniel is a beautiful soul, but he has no idea who he is.*

Daniel finished the last verse and slowly opened his eyes. He set the tablet on the table, and looked intently at Frannie. Her eyes held their usual warmness, filmed with a shimmer of tears. She blinked them away.

"Thank you," she said. "That was lovely."

His hands slid down his legs to his knees. "Why did you pick that song?" he asked softly.

"It's my favorite hymn," she stated again.

Daniel stared at his feet. "It was Grandma Mae's favorite, too. She said it was an old Irish tune. She taught it to me and we used to sing it together. Somehow, I managed to sing it at her funeral."

Frannie's voice caught. "I'm sorry, Daniel. I didn't mean to upset you. I had no idea."

"I know," he said blankly. Frannie couldn't have known, but Someone else did. There was no way it was a mere coincidence, any more than it was a coincidence that his knee gave away at the perfect time for Frannie to win the bet. He was supposed to relive his childhood memories. And Someone had made sure of it.

He rose from his seat. "It's been a long day. I think I'll head out."

Frannie didn't try to make him stay. She was a little unnerved at the happenstance that she shared something in common with Grandma Mae.

She walked him to the door.

"Hey, I was thinking," she said, "we should go to dinner tomorrow night and celebrate our job-well-done. I'll take you to the restaurant that serves the best lasagne. My treat."

"You don't have to do that. You won the bet, Frannie."

Her stomach fell. She didn't care about winning or losing the bet. She wanted a date with Daniel Fitzpatrick and time was short; she only had five days left.

"But," he said, flashing his mischievous grin, "I won't pass up the opportunity to order lasagne for you. Seven o'clock?"

"Perfect."

"I'll see you tomorrow," he said. He walked out into the night, letting her radiant smile lodge itself in his mind so he could store it away. He would recollect it when he needed some sunshine on a gray and chilly Chicago day.

Chapter 35

Daniel stood on the Ponte Sisto, one of Rome's several arched bridges over the Tiber River. The lighted dome of Saint Peter's dominated the night sky, emerging above the green trees lining the street above the stone river bank. Clusters of verdant foliage cascaded down the rock wall like a vine. Pedestrians packed the bridge, using it as an entryway to the *Lungo il Tevere* summer festival. He could hear the gaiety coming from the white tents edged along the river trail.

After leaving Frannie's apartment, Daniel had gone for a walk to try to clear his mind and ended up at the bridge. He leaned on the stone wall, staring at the basilica dome. Unlike the logical scientific deductions used to determine if old bones belonged to Saint Peter, he couldn't come to any logical conclusions about what had happened to him in the last month: he had talked to God twice, heard voices, swore his medal became spontaneously warm on its own, found himself drawn to a Mass said in a dead language, and he might even believe the evidence that the Virgin Mary had appeared to children in Portugal. All of this while traipsing around Italy and Austria with a sweet and beautiful girl whose heart overflowed with kindness, who happened to share the same favorite hymn as his grandmother, loved baseball and sarcasm and was everything he could ever—

Anguish filled his chest. Frannie was everything he could ever want in a woman.

He glared at the Vatican dome. *Why would you show me something so wonderful? Why now? So you can just take her away from me like everything else?*

Daniel leaned into the wall and gripped the top with his hands. *It's like you know how messed up I am and yet you bring up the good but also the most painful memories from my past and taunt me with them.* He pushed himself away from the wall in an act of defiance. *I'm not playing your game. I'm doing this interview and going back to Chicago.*

He whirled around to storm off but almost ran into two young men who were standing still. He moved to his left to go around but there was nowhere to go. A traffic jam of pedestrians going down the stairs to the festival had clogged the bridge.

Slowly, Daniel inched his way along with the crowd. He glanced over the bridge and saw a young woman arguing with a man near the base of the steps. The woman turned away, but the man moved and blocked her. Daniel did a double take and leaned over the ledge to get a better look.

It was Lorena.

The man had cornered Frannie's cousin against the brick wall near the edge of the bridge. Daniel pushed his way through the crowd and down the steps. When he reached Lorena, she had tears on her cheeks and was yelling at the man in Italian. The man was about Daniel's age and well dressed. The fashionable clothes didn't cover up the whiff Daniel's nose picked up of an unsavory character.

Lorena was in trouble.

Daniel sauntered over to the couple. "There you are!" he huffed at Lorena. "I've been looking all over for you." He didn't care if the man knew English or not.

Lorena's eyes bulged out of her head at the sight of Daniel. "What are you doing here?"

"I travel all the way across the ocean from New York to see you, and this is what I get?" Daniel countered.

Lorena's face twisted. "What in the world are you talking about?"

Daniel placed his hands on his hips and groaned internally. Frannie would have already taken the bait and played along. He pushed the thought away.

"You told me to meet you and your friends here," he said, raising his eyebrows and giving her a look urging her to pretend and cooperate.

The Italian man inched closer to Daniel. "Who are you?" he asked in thick accented English.

Daniel gave him the once over and stood a little taller. "The question buddy, is, 'Who are you?'"

"I'm her—"

"What, Raffaello?" Lorena broke in, "you're my what?"

The man glared at Daniel but remained silent.

"I told you we were done," she said. "Now maybe you believe me."

The man spat out a cold lashing in Italian and marched off. Whatever he said made Lorena cover her face. Her shoulders shook and Daniel heard her crying.

"Come on," he said gently, "let's get you out of here."

She lowered her hands and looked desperately at Daniel. "I don't want Francesca to see me like this."

"She's not here. I went for a walk and saw you from the bridge."

"You're here by yourself?"

He nodded and threw his head in the direction of the steps. She followed him up to the street level. Daniel crossed the road and ascended the stairs leading to an old stone façade that used to be a working fountain, but now decorated a small piazza.

He sat down on one of the steps and motioned for Lorena to sit next to him. She was wearing another tight dress that was even shorter than the ones she had worn previously.

"You weren't at dinner today," he said.

"You're probably the only person who noticed. I'm not the family favorite like Francesca. Where is she?" She smiled wickedly, "Is there trouble in paradise?"

"Don't read too much into it, Lorena. You'll just be disappointed."

The blaze in her eyes fueled the crossness in her tone, "Why do you like her so much?"

"Why do you hate her so much?" he fired back.

"Because," she snarled, "she's just another perfect member of the Menconi family. You have no idea what it is like to live in a place where your family has a long history of priests, bishops and cardinals. Menconis have a lot to live up to."

Daniel wasn't surprised that Nicolo Menconi was just one of many clergymen in the family tree. "You might want to ask Frannie about that," he said. "It may surprise you that she has endured her own share of biases and prejudices because of the Menconi name."

Lorena appeared vexed by the information about her cousin but still managed an eye roll. She reached in her purse and pulled out a pack of cigarettes and a lighter. She held the pack out to Daniel.

"No thanks. I don't smoke."

She roughly tossed them back in her purse.

"So what happened down at the river?" he asked.

"The end of another relationship." Lorena stretched out her bare legs on the steps and crossed her ankles. "I'm used to it."

Daniel doubted her indifference. Whatever Raffaello said to end the affair was cruel and hurtful enough for her to break down in tears.

Without looking at Daniel she asked, "Why did you come over to help me?"

"I didn't like the way he had you cornered and backed against the wall so I intervened. I have to say, he seemed like a well-groomed scuzzball."

"I have a way of attracting those," she said dryly.

Daniel made a grunting noise.

She threw him an acid look. "What?"

He spun sideways on the step and faced her. "Look, it's none of my business what you do. But if you keep wearing dresses like that one, those are the guys you are going to attract. Trust me. I'm a guy, I know how they think."

"I suppose you think I should dress more like Francesca?"

"You're the one comparing yourself to Frannie. Not me."

Lorena shifted on the step and tugged on the hem of her dress.

Daniel wasn't sure how he got thrown into a psychotherapy session and decided to take the Austrian approach and be direct.

"Lorena, I don't know you. And I don't know your history with Frannie. What I see is an attractive young woman trying really hard to get attention, but all you're garnering is the negative kind. I think you can be Lorena, with a different sense of fashion and minus the overtly sensual flirtations."

Her chin quivered. "I know guys use me and move on to the next. I'm not stupid. I've been living this lifestyle for so long, it's hard to see myself any other way. I guess I only date guys I think I deserve. I keep hoping one day I'll meet a guy who is like me; someone who wants more out of life than this. I don't expect you to understand."

Daniel did understand. He had more in common with Lorena than she knew. His lonely lifestyle was self-inflicted so he wouldn't be hurt again. It was difficult for him to see his life through any other lens.

Lorena wiped her eyes. "I don't hate Francesca. I'm jealous of her. She knows what she is worth and she's not willing to compromise."

"Then tell yourself you deserve more. Try letting the way you dress tell men that you know what you're worth. What have you got to lose?"

She rocked her ankles back and forth. "There is a new guy at the office who seems nice. I'm sure everyone has told him about me behind my back."

"Then prove them wrong."

Lorena looked at him thoughtfully. "I guess I need to prove to myself that they are wrong."

Daniel felt like a hypocrite; her statement was his own advice coming back to him like a boomerang. He was counseling her to free herself from her past mistakes when he wasn't willing to do the same.

He rose from the steps and offered his hand to Lorena. She looked at him funny, but took it and let him help her up.

"*Grazie*. You've been very kind to me tonight, Daniel. I will give your advice some thought. If it means I could find a gentleman like you, it would be worth a try."

"I'll call you a cab," he said, quickly dismissing being called a gentleman and feeling even more like a fraud.

"No, my car isn't far from here. Thank you for helping me get rid of the—what did you call him? Oh, 'scuzzball,'" she said, smiling. "Francesca is lucky to have someone like you. You make a good couple."

The word, "couple" made his heart hurt. He knew what Frannie was worth and wanted to believe he could be deserving of her. His mind began calculating whether there was any chance he could be the guy Frannie could choose and not think she had compromised anything.

"Buona notte, Daniel."

"Good night, Lorena."

Daniel let out a deep exhale when she was out of sight. By the time he reached his residence, his body was feeling the exhaustion from the events of the day and the unexpected turn of the night. He entered the moon-lit apartment, threw his keys and wallet on the dining table, and headed to the kitchen. He needed a drink of water and then he couldn't crawl in bed fast enough. He flipped the light switch and nearly jumped out of his skin.

Someone was sitting on his couch.

"Hello, *Signore* Fitzpatrick," the trespasser said. "I assume you remember me. I am Stefano."

Chapter 36

STEFANO DE MARZO HAD MADE HIMSELF AT HOME in the middle of Daniel's couch, hands folded casually on his lap, as if he'd been invited over for a drink. His black t-shirt and black jeans were well-suited for the role of an intruder. A brown leather knapsack lay on the floor next to his feet.

Daniel's already parched throat became so dry he could barely swallow.

"Of course I remember you, Stefano," he said amiably, attempting to show he was unaffected by his surprise guest. "To what do I owe the pleasure?"

Stefano flashed a wide smile. "I knew I liked you when we met at the Duomo concert. You know how to keep your emotions hidden while your mind is analyzing everything. Our military background comes in handy, yes?"

Daniel's stiff poker face resurfaced.

"*Sì, Signore*," Stefano said, "I have done my research on you, as I am sure you have on me."

"Well, since we are like old friends," Daniel said, walking to the refrigerator and taking out a bottle of water, "can I offer you a drink?"

"No, thank you."

Daniel took a large gulp to moisten his cotton mouth and positioned himself in the armchair next to the couch. As much as he wished to fire off the questions he had burning in his mind, he wanted Stefano to speak first. "You're here for a reason, Stefano. I'm waiting."

The young man knew the American was finished with pretenses. "I am here to offer assistance. Constantini is nervous; he knows you and Francesca did not return to Rome after Milan and Cardinal Baldano has mysteriously disappeared out of sight to an unknown destination for a 'spiritual retreat.' If Constantini feels threatened with the pope on his deathbed then no one is safe. Especially my family. My uncle wishes me to contact Cardinal Menconi through you. Archbishop Vidmar assured him Nicolo Menconi could be trusted. Therefore, I trust you."

Daniel took another drink and set the bottle on the side table next to him. The admission of an alliance between Vidmar and Donati confirmed one hypothesis. "And what assistance are you offering?"

"Evidence."

"Of what?"

Stefano spoke in a near whisper, "Everything."

Daniel's heart hammered so hard it was difficult to control his breathing. He leaned back in the chair, and began to drum his fingers against his leg. There was nothing shady about Stefano that he could detect, but he needed reassurance. His fingers came to a stop.

"How do I know I can trust you?" he asked. "Or if this so-called evidence is legitimate?"

"You're too smart not to have figured out I'm the one who left the flash drive under your door. I offered it to you as an olive branch. I think when you see the rest of the documents you will see we are playing for the same team."

"Will they explain why Archbishop Vidmar clashed with your uncle over the Vatican Bank and yet advised him to trust Cardinal Menconi?"

Stefano's eyes bore into Daniel's. "Yes. I'm prepared to explain all of it."

"Mind if I take some notes?"

"Go ahead," Stefano swiftly replied.

Daniel grabbed a notepad and pen off of the dining room table and returned to the armchair.

Stefano leaned forward and rubbed his hands together. "I assume you know about my mother's history with the Garone family?"

"I know her history with Giovanni's father, Massimo Garone, and when your uncle became the Archbishop of Milan she and Giovanni opened a restaurant together. That's it."

"Were you told how Massimo died?"

"He was drunk and got in a fight with a family member who accidentally shot him."

Stefano drew in a deep breath. "A family member didn't shoot him. And it was no accident."

Daniel felt a prickle run down his spine. A bombshell of a story was about to be laid in his lap.

"The Garones were very displeased with Massimo," Stefano continued. "His antics had brought disgrace and unwanted attention to the family. They weren't bothered by his despicable treatment of my mother, or concerned for little Giovanni. They were worried it would be the end of their hidden relationship with the Fratellis. The two families had an understanding. The Garones were to remain upstanding citizens, keeping their accounting records clean and pure as snow in order to shield illegal business deals. In return, the Fratellis filled the Garone family pockets, making it possible for them to bankroll a chain of restaurants, giving the Fratellis the cover they needed. If the Fratellis wanted to separate, it would result in a disruption to the cash flow and a mafia war.

"Massimo's entanglement with the Donatis brought another complication: the involvement of the Catholic clergy. The last thing either family wanted was a priest who would cause trouble for them. Neither wanted to be put in a position where they would have to retaliate against a man of the cloth."

Daniel scoffed, "Even a mob crime boss has his limits?"

"*Sì*, they used to. Times were different back then; despite the mafia's criminal activity, they respected priests. The mob bosses may not have attended Mass every Sunday, but the women and children did. They wanted their children baptized and able to receive their First Communion. So, the Fratellis decided to send their family priest to talk to my uncle and strike a deal."

"Family priest?" Daniel repeated, unsure of what Stefano meant.

"Yes. The Fratellis also had a relative who was a member of the clergy." He let a palpable pause penetrate the air. "Any guesses who?"

Daniel wrote a few words on his notepad and looked up. "Cesare Constantini?"

"Good guess, *Signore*," Stefano affirmed softly. "Maybe I will take a bottle of water, if you don't mind."

Daniel noticed beads of sweat glistening on Stefano's forehead. Based on Baldano's warning, the young man had every reason to be skittish. Keeping his eye on his guest, he retrieved the water and placed it on the coffee table, rather than handing it to him.

"Still unsure of me?" Stefano said, chuckling. "If I were in your shoes, I would also make sure both my hands were free at all times." He took a long drink. "And masquerade note taking so I had a pen if I needed a weapon."

Daniel innocently raised his eyebrows. "I simply wanted to jot things down so I keep an accurate account of your testimony. You, my friend, are the one who is suddenly very nervous."

Stefano took another drink and replaced the lid. "Where were we?" he asked, pretending to ignore Daniel's assessment, "oh, yes, *Father* Constantini."

"How is he related to the Fratellis and how is it no one has reported his familial relation? Rumors are all over regarding your uncle's connection to the Garone family."

"The Fratellis keep their family guarded and private. Little is known about any of the members. What we do know is Constantini's father was a highly cultured and educated physician. When he met Imilia Fratelli, the Cardinal's mother, he made it known he wanted nothing to do with the family business. The family reached an agreement and allowed Imilia freedom to live separately from the Fratellis.

"Cesare, named after his father, grew up the oldest and only boy of four children in an upper middle class environment, which explains his polished charm. He and his siblings had little contact with Imilia's side of the family and the children were kept in the dark about the family's ties to the mafia. The Fratellis had little interest in Imilia and her family until they heard Cesare had entered the seminary."

Daniel interjected, "Do you know why he wanted to be a priest?"

"Imilia worried her father would try to persuade her son to join the mafia network and planted the idea of priesthood in him at an early age. By all accounts, she and her husband were quite pious and dedicated to the Church. I don't wish to dishonor her; I am sure she did what she thought was best to protect her child."

The memory of his mother handing him the Miraculous Medal flashed in Daniel's mind. He quickly pushed it away. "So he became a priest at the wishes of his mother?"

Stefano grimaced. "He was in the seminary with my uncle, though a few years behind him. My uncle claims Cesare seemed sincere about his call to the priesthood, but was never humble about it. Constantini was power-driven from the beginning and had his sights set on the highest levels in the hierarchy before he was even ordained. His charm and intelligence won over the rectors of the seminary who regarded him as a great talent and promise for the Church. You have to remember, this was in the aftermath of Vatican II and seminaries were more liberal in their priestly training. Constantini had just the charisma they were looking for."

"How did he meet up with his long lost family?"

"The Don of the Fratelli family, Filippo, sent for him to help smooth over the fiasco created by Massimo. The Don could see the hunger for power in his grandson's eyes and knew he had found an ally he could place within the Church with no one suspecting any connection to the Fratelli name. Filippo sent Father Constantini to talk to my uncle, priest to priest. Constantini offered my mother and Giovanni full separation from the mafia and protection from Massimo for her and my uncle's silence."

An offer the godfather couldn't refuse, Daniel thought.

Stefano continued, "Filippo worried Massimo wouldn't keep a low profile and would continue to antagonize my mother. He sent his eldest grandson, Bruno, one of the family protectors, and Constantini to explain to Massimo the deal they made with the Donatis. As the Don predicted, Massimo was enraged that the Fratelli family had come between him and his son and said he would not honor the pact. The next day news circulated within the mafia circles that Massimo was dead."

Daniel scribbled a few notes on his pad. "Are you saying Cardinal Constantini ordered his cousin Bruno to execute the hit on Massimo Garone?"

"Bruno or Constantini, we don't know which one. I can say with certainty Constantini didn't prevent it."

"How are you so sure?"

Stefano wiped his brow with his arm. "Five years ago, my father and Giovanni wanted to open a café near *Sant'Ambrogio*," he saw Daniel's eye squint so he clarified in English, "The Basilica of Saint Ambrose, not far from our current restaurant."

The name Ambrose instantly rang a bell with Daniel. It was the saint who had written the prayer in Frannie's missal.

"Why a café there?" he asked.

Stefano cocked his head, unsure of why it mattered. "Saint Ambrose is the patron Saint of Milan and the basilica is a popular place."

Of course he's the patron saint of Milan and would enter into this tale, Daniel thought sourly. "So what happened?" he asked.

"Our bank found an investor willing to secure the *Sotto l'Albero* so we could take a risk on opening the new restaurant."

Daniel's ears perked up at the news of the angel investor but patiently waited for him to continue.

"What we didn't know was that the backer was actually the Fratelli family." Stefano gripped his knees. "Constantini had set it all up for them," he added hotly.

"How did you find out?"

Stefano relaxed his hands. "At the last conclave," he said with forced calmness. "After the Massimo incident, my uncle held Constantini with suspicion as he rose to fame. He suspected his interference in the selection of the pope and warned some of the other Cardinals. Then he received a visit from Constantini.

"The Cardinal pressured him to change his vote or he would let the world know what happened between my mother and Massimo and that the hit on him was my uncle's idea. At first, my uncle refused. He said he was old and didn't care about his reputation. That's when Constantini revealed the Fratellis were the actual investors of the restaurant. If my uncle didn't do as he was asked, the Fratellis would make life very hard for the family. He was trapped. He knew what Constantini was capable of and couldn't let him use my mother's childhood mistake to ruin the life she had made for herself. When Mama found out she was furious. She said she would rather risk death than be a slave to the Garone-Fratelli mob bosses."

Daniel thought about the late night visit to the restaurant by Mr. Bald Man. "Are they extorting money from you?" he asked.

"Our restaurant is a go between for the sales of Fratelli illegal goods. Accountants hide the money and make it appear to go to the loan we owe. All against our will, of course."

Daniel took his phone out of his pocket and showed Stefano a picture of Bald Man.

"Frannie and I saw this man with your mother outside the restaurant. Was he there to collect some sort of payment?"

"*Sì,*" he said with disgust.

Daniel said. "Since you are spilling all this information, who is this man?"

Stefano weighed the question before responding. "I guess it makes sense you were unable to identify him. Bruno Fratelli keeps a low profile."

Daniel was unable to maintain any semblance of a poker face and let his jaw drop. "Bruno Fratelli? The same Bruno that did the hit on Massimo Garone?"

His guest slowly nodded. "Cardinal Constantini keeps his cousin close. He is also his bodyguard."

Chapter 37

A CHILL OF A DIFFERENT TYPE RAN DOWN DANIEL'S spine. This time, it wasn't adrenaline over a bombshell story. He was thinking about Frannie, alone in her apartment with a mafia gunman on the loose that could be watching her every move.

"Stefano, this man followed Frannie and I one evening. He was quite obvious about it and I lost him easily. That doesn't fit the profile of a professional and dangerous hitman."

"You're right, he isn't a professional marksman. Bruno is Constantini's bodyguard and in charge of protecting all the Fratelli operations. If he was following you, it was on orders from Constantini. My guess is he didn't think you were a big threat at first. If you gave Bruno the slip, someone else was sent in to investigate."

Daniel's memory replayed Constantini's saccharine remark in Milan at his joy to dine with a young couple in love. Bruno's report most likely made Constantini suspicious, and he dropped the bait to determine the nature of his and Frannie's relationship. When they didn't return to Rome, he probably concluded Daniel's ambition was all for show. A foreboding creeped into his stomach; Cardinal Menconi needed to hire a professional detail immediately.

Stefano confirmed his fear. "Make no mistake, Bruno is dangerous. He isn't the man they send in with a gun anymore, but he could make a kill and not blink an eye."

Stefano glanced at his watch. "It is getting late. I must finish what I have to say and make my exit." He opened his knapsack and pulled out a stack of large mailer envelopes. "My family has been waiting for the right time and the right person to tell our story. Archbishop Vidmar, *buonanima,* was going to help us but," he paused, "I underestimated our adversary."

Daniel raised an eyebrow. "You sound as if you feel responsible for his death."

Stefano rubbed the back of his neck. "My uncle suggested I approach the Archbishop on behalf of the Donati family. Unfortunately, I let my guard down and they must have followed me to Slovenia. I arranged the meeting with the two men and went to great lengths to make it look like my uncle was traveling there on Church business, but by then it was too late. Constantini had pieced together that the old friends were about to reconcile.

"I was with my uncle when he met with Vidmar and told him everything. The three of us made the clergy list for Cardinal Menconi. The plan was for me to deliver it the next week. When we learned Vidmar was meeting with Constantini later that evening, we urged him to cancel, but he refused. We convinced him to let us take his appointment book for safekeeping. I don't think he really thought a Cardinal in the Church would–" he broke off, not wanting to finish.

"What about the list?" Daniel asked, "Why did you wait so long to give it to Cardinal Menconi?"

"Uncle and I had no doubt as to the real cause of Vidmar's death; we both believe it was Bruno. We knew reaching out to Menconi would seal his fate, so we decided to wait until the proper time revealed itself. The health of the current pope forced us to act. But I had learned from my past mistakes with Vidmar, so I found a way to hack into Menconi's phone, email and credit card records." He smirked, "I knew all about you before your plane landed in Rome."

Daniel found his poker face and didn't let his interlocutor see his discomfort.

Stefano continued, "I was disappointed Cardinal Menconi had not reached out to Kratzer so I hoped he had hired you as an outside investigator. When I read Constantini's email inviting him to Milan, I panicked. We decided to show up as a family, unannounced, and steal a moment alone with him. Meeting you and *Signorina* Menconi was unexpected, but we were encouraged you were also using the element of surprise on Constantini. I knew you were in town of course, because I saw you at the restaurant. Both inside and outside."

"And you didn't stop by and say hello?" Daniel asked in mock disappointment, deflecting his unease that Stefano had covert knowledge of every move he and Frannie had made in Milan.

Stefano ignored Daniel's sarcastic comment. "I decided I would give you the flash drive connecting Constantini to Vidmar's death. I had counted on you to report back to Menconi, who I assumed would then call Kratzer. I've been in Rome for days watching the Cardinal's emails and phone, waiting for you to arrive back so I could pop in for a visit. Your detour and Kratzer being the one to call Menconi came as a surprise. I can only assume you went to Salzburg?"

Daniel gloated internally that he finally had the upper hand: Stefano was still in the dark about Baldano's letter and that Kratzer made the call at the behest of Baldano. Stefano's phone surveillance must not have included a tap to hear the conversation.

"How did you get Constantini's airline itinerary?" Daniel asked.

"That was an easy hack job." Stefano studied the American closely, incapable of being diverted. "You know where Baldano is," he murmured.

Daniel returned the stare with galvanized resolve.

Stefano snickered arrogantly. "I still like you, *Signore*. I'm sure I will read all about it later."

He picked up the pile of manila document envelopes and set them on the end of the couch. "Here are the documents you need. What is in there is enough to depose Constantini of his place of power. When it all comes out, he will know who is responsible for releasing the information. My family and I are going underground until we know it is safe. Uncle is refusing to leave with us; he won't abandon the good shepherds and feels the need to atone for aligning himself with Constantini, even if it was against his wishes. In the meantime, I have sheltered him with hired guards. To keep us protected, he doesn't know where we are going. Tell Cardinal Menconi to email you with updates. I'll see them and know we are out of danger."

"The Cardinal is scheduled to give a talk at a gala fundraiser this week. Should he cancel?"

Stefano rubbed his chin. "That is hard to say. I know they have different theological views on certain Church matters, but there are other reasons Constantini would want to get rid of Cardinal Menconi. For Constantini, it is about money and power. For Menconi, it is about the Lord and salvation of souls. That makes Menconi dangerous in the eyes of Constantini; he knows a Menconi papacy will not be compromised. Today's mafia leaders may not have the same limits their grandfathers did. The good Cardinal should be careful."

Stefano stood up and threw his knapsack over his shoulder. He looked Daniel squarely in the eyes. "And, my friend, so should you and the *Signorina*." He silently slipped out the door within seconds.

Daniel jumped out of the chair to shut the door behind his guest and turn the lock. He darted over to the stack of envelopes and began to leaf through the contents. Within minutes, he was making a phone call.

Frannie blurted out on the other end, "Daniel? It's after midnight. What's wrong?"

"We have to see your uncle right now. I'm getting a cab and will be at your apartment shortly. Please stay inside until I come get you. I'll explain later. Will you call him?"

He heard nothing but crickets on the other end. "Frannie?"

"I'm here." Her voice shook. "I'll be ready."

"Everything's all right," he said calmly. "But you're not going to believe who just left my apartment."

Cardinal Menconi laid the documents he had been studying on the dining table and rubbed his tired eyes. He had been huddled around the table with Daniel and Frannie for over an hour. Frannie was pouring over another pile of papers, her hands cradling a warm cup of tea. Daniel pounded away on his computer, organizing his notes against the evidence laid bare before them. Their theories regarding Constantini were confirmed: his money laundering through *Compassione*, embezzlement, using the Vatican Bank for tax evasion, and links to hundreds of mafia money deals.

Frannie leaned back in her chair. "There's enough here to not only laicize Constantini but to charge him in a civil court of law."

The raw anger in Frannie's voice caused Daniel to stop typing. He glanced between her and the Cardinal.

The prelate looked drained. "I need time to think this through—"

"Think what through?" she interrupted, her eyes blazing. "This man has scandalized his office and the Church, *Zio!*"

Cardinal Menconi slammed his fist on the documents. "Don't you think I know that?" He rattled on in Italian and soon they were in a heated yelling match.

Daniel held out his hands. "Hey!" he yelled. To his amazement they stopped and retreated into their chairs.

"Frannie," he began gently, "give your uncle a break. He's just been blitzed with highly sensitive information. He needs to discern the best way to proceed to keep his family and Donati's family safe. It's painfully clear that Donati was named President of the Commission of Cardinals of the Vatican Bank so Constantini could control him. These papers prove the Vatican Bank has been used as a front for funneling money for the Garone-Fratelli ring in order for them to secretly invest funds and hide cash stores to pay off scandals and church debt. With Donati as president, he would be set up to take any fallout from a scandal and leave Constantini in the clear. Not to mention what we have on him regarding Vidmar. Whatever the next step is needs to be decided carefully."

The Cardinal reached over and took Frannie's hand. "*Mia passerotta,* I am hurting, too. But Daniel is right. Cesare has weaved his web tightly. I don't want to give him any inclination that we are on to him. And I have to find a way for Fortino to have some amnesty. He didn't make the best choices but he is coming forward now at great risk to him and his family. It didn't matter what The Good Thief had done, just that his heart repented and asked the Lord to remember him."

Frannie wiped her eyes. "It's just so heartbreaking," she said softly. "I feel sorry for the Donatis, I really do. But I also wonder how many will consider this to be the last straw? How many will leave the Church this time?"

"You and I won't flee and leave our Lord," the Cardinal said. "We will stay at the Cross so that when they do come back, they'll find someone to welcome them home."

Daniel stared at the table. *I'm not leaving Peter because of Judas,* Frannie had said when they first met. He now understood her resolve went deeper; leaving the Church would be akin to abandoning Jesus. Her strong stance was logical. A bad general or commanding officer wouldn't cause him to abandon the platoon; it would make him fight harder, because there were good men who needed him. Frannie and her uncle were fighters for what they believed in. As a Marine, he could respect that.

"Frannie," Daniel said, "I think you should stay here tonight." He turned to address the Cardinal, "And you need to hire private security. You will need to take extra precautions at the gala."

Frannie yawned. "I'm too tired to argue. It's in the wee hours of the morning."

Daniel stood up and began to gather his things.

Cardinal Menconi placed his hand on Daniel's shoulder. "I have an extra room for Francesca. It would make me feel better if you stayed here, too. I admit I am feeling a little unnerved by everything. It is horrible of me to ask this of you after your long night, but would you sleep on the couch?"

Daniel could see the strain in the old man's eyes. He gave him a reassuring nod. "I'm a Marine, sir. I've slept on worse."

The Cardinal patted his cheek. "*Mio figlio,*" he whispered, then sluggishly headed to his room.

Frannie found an extra pillow and blanket and handed them to Daniel. "Thanks for staying."

"We're all tired. It's been a long night for all of us."

She glanced over her shoulder before opening the door to her room. "Good night."

Daniel collapsed on the couch and covered his legs with the blanket. His head hit the pillow, and he fell asleep almost immediately.

Chapter 38

FRANNIE YAWNED AND STRETCHED FROM HER AFTER-noon nap. She felt physically drained from the short night's rest at *Zio's* the previous evening. Daniel had escorted her home that morning and checked out the apartment as he always did. When he said goodbye, his arms made an odd jerking movement and her heart did a cartwheel at the thought he might reach out and hug her. She felt completely foolish when his hand landed on his head to scratch an itch.

The outcome of the evidence implicating Constantini was in her uncle's hands. There was nothing more she could do but pray for guidance and protection for *Zio* and the Church. She reached for her phone, scrolled through social media posts, and checked the baseball scores. Not even a five game winning streak by the Red Sox could draw her away from the one thing that filled her mind. More aptly, the one person that filled her every waking thought.

She spoke into her phone, "Call Jen."

"Hey," Jen answered. "I haven't heard from you in over a week. I thought maybe you joined a convent."

"Not even close. Did I call too early?"

"Nope. We're all up and dressed for the day."

Frannie heard the bubbly sound of Jen's two-year-old daughter in the background. "I probably picked a bad time to call. I'll let you go."

"Clare just ate so I can humor her with one of those Catholic cartoons you bought. Give me a second."

Frannie heard Jen rummaging followed by the cheery music that accompanies a child's video. "Okay," she said, "what's up with Mr. Linebacker?"

Her friend knew her too well. "He's not who I thought he was."

"Meaning?"

"He's playful, fun, and there's this side of him that's a real gentleman. He's the kind of guy that would make sacrifices for his family." Frannie didn't want to give Jen the details about Daniel's history with Kelsay. "I can't explain how I know that, but it's true."

"Do you think he's a stray?"

Frannie pondered the question. "He's injured. But there are times he seems reflective like he's trying to figure things out. And I see something in him, Jen." She told Jen about their bet and how his singing lifted the veil to his innermost being. "He has a beautiful soul. I wish he could see himself the way *Zio* and I do."

"You're falling in love with him, aren't you?"

Jen liked to cut right to the chase.

"I don't know," Frannie replied. "But I sure would like the chance to find out."

"You have no idea how he feels about you?"

Frannie hated to admit the only time Daniel gave any overt signs were in a couple of drunken moments. "He bought me flowers, to thank me for something. And there's been a few times when he's looked at me, I thought maybe I saw something." Had it been real or was she just seeing what she wanted to see?

"Oh, my friend," Jen sighed. "I want you to find your guy. And I can't understand why it's taking you so long to find him. Any man would be a fool not to see how wonderful you are. If Daniel's the one, then he'll see it."

"I wish I had the call to be a nun. Then I would know what to do with my life."

Jen laughed. "I was kidding about the convent."

"I know. I visited several communities after my experience at Fatima. It didn't feel right; it wasn't where I was supposed to be."

"I pray for you every day, ya know."

"Thanks. I need it."

"So what are you going to do?"

Frannie checked the time. "I'm going to shower and get ready for dinner. We're going out tonight. I guess I'll see what happens." She heard Clare calling out for Jen in the background.

"Well, that's my cue," Jen said. "Don't wait so long to call me."

"I won't. Give Clare a kiss for me."

They said goodbye and Frannie threw her phone to the side.

Lord, I know I've strayed away from you and I'm sorry. Help me find my path; Zio said I need to find my compass. Point my compass where it's supposed to go. Let me know if it's Daniel.

She sat quietly for a few moments working through her internal struggles. *All right, I know I can't keep anything hidden from you. I want it to be him. He's different from the other guys I've dated. But you already know that. Is that why you brought us together? Blessed Mother, intercede for me.*

Daniel sat on the couch in his apartment and tossed his phone from one hand to the other. When he finally stopped he stuck his Bluetooth in his ear, selected a number in his contacts and waited. Travis Dawson answered on the second ring.

"Fitz! How the hell are ya?"

"Oh you know me, Dawson, livin' the dream. How about you?"

"I'm good. You just caught me. I'm on my way out the door to work."

Daniel glanced at his watch. "Sorry, I didn't think about the time change. I'm in Rome."

"Rome? Italy?" Travis asked in surprise.

"Well, it ain't Rome, Georgia."

"Smart-ass." Travis shot back. "What are you doin' there?"

"On assignment. I can't really say much about it yet. How are the boys?"

"Luke's growin' like a weed and Jake's playin' in Jackson's Little League. I told him Uncle Danny could show him how to really swing a bat." Travis paused before dropping the hint, "They'd love to see you; in person and not a video call. Do I need to remind you that you're their godfather?"

Daniel flinched. "Father Donnelly made it clear he didn't approve of your choice. I don't exactly make the cut for being a good Catholic."

"Yeah, I know," Travis said, a hint of sadness in his voice. "But you were the one we wanted."

For the first time, Daniel felt empathy for Cardinal Donati and his natural desire to shield Giovanni from the Garone and Fratelli families. He couldn't blame the clergyman for wanting to protect his godson. He loved Travis's boys and the mere idea of someone threatening them was enough to make his blood boil.

Travis interrupted his meandering thoughts, "Katie's fine and it's hot and humid."

"What?"

"That's the last of the formalities: my wife and the weather. Now you can tell me why you really called."

Daniel chuckled, "Now who's the smart-ass?"

"Just keepin' it real."

"I remember the day you met Katie. We were hanging out at the lake with the usual gang, and she was in town visiting her cousin. You said that day you were going to marry her. How did you know?"

There was a palpable silence on the other end. "I thought she was the prettiest girl I had ever seen," Travis said. "Then we went for a walk along the water and I knew there was something special about her. I don't really know how to explain it."

Daniel closed his eyes. *Special. I get it.*

Travis continued, "The fact that she was Catholic made it seem like God had His hand in it somehow."

"You always were more religious than me," Daniel said.

"I'm no saint, Danny. You know that better than anybody."

"Have you ever—" Daniel started, then stopped. He knew his best friend wouldn't laugh at him, but it was still hard to get the words to come out. "Have you ever heard God speak to you? I mean, do you think that's a real thing that can happen?"

There was another long pause before Travis spoke, "What do you remember about the day the landmine went off and the shrapnel went in your knee?"

"I was driving the jeep, following behind the Master Sergeant when you told me to stop. You radioed the Sergeant and told him we needed to get off the road and go around the field. The Sergeant's driver didn't get over far enough and still tripped the mine. Other than a few minor injuries we were all okay. But if we hadn't gotten off the road..." his voice trailed off.

"Danny," Travis said slowly, "I heard a voice. That's how I knew about the landmine."

"You said something caught your eye and made you suspicious," Daniel contested. "That's what you told the Sergeant."

"I know. I lied. I was young, freaked out and I didn't know if he would believe me. It hurts me to say it, but I knew you wouldn't.

Katie's the only other person I've told. Well, and the priest on base when I went to confession for lying about it."

Daniel knew Travis was right. He wouldn't have believed him. Not back then, anyway.

"What did the voice sound like?" he asked.

"I wish I could remember. I know I heard it and that it was real. I can't remember any other characteristics. Except, it sounded like it came from your side of the jeep. It was weird because I thought it was you, but at the same time I knew it wasn't."

Daniel pinched the bridge of his nose between his forefinger and thumb. His experience at the Pieta was similar.

Travis asked, "Are you working alone on this assignment?"

"Yes and no. My work for the *Classic Journalist* is solo. I got roped into another thing and it required me to work with someone else."

"A woman?"

"Yeah."

"An Italian woman?"

"She's from Boston but has family here. She loves baseball, she's beautiful," he paused a beat, "she's special, Travis."

He heard his friend take in a deep breath before responding. "Danny, I've known you for as long as I can remember. You and I have been to places and seen things that no one else can understand. We've always considered you a member of the Dawson family. Heck, you're more like my brother than my own flesh and blood. So what I'm about to say, I say it because I love you like a brother."

Daniel waited silently on the other end.

There was a pause before Travis said clearly and evenly, "Don't be a dumb-ass."

Daniel's head jerked back, "Excuse me?"

"You heard me. In all the years I've known you, you've never asked me questions like these. Something is going on with you and whatever it is, don't be the dumb-ass who runs away from it."

He heard Travis's message loud and clear. Daniel had a history of running. He ran to Afghanistan to get away from Heather then ran from Jackson to get away from his memories. He ran away from God because he was mad at Him. He ran away from any woman that gave him a smile because of Kelsay. On the bridge he had made the decision to run back to Chicago, far away from Rome and all the emotions stirring up within him, and away from his feelings for Frannie.

"Fitz, you there?"

"I'm here. I've probably made you late for work. I'll let you go."

"You can call me later. Don't worry about the time change."

"I'll be back in the States next week. I'll plan a trip and show Jake how to swing a bat. I don't want him always striking out like his old man."

Travis understood the insult was his friend's way thanking him for his advice.

"I'm gonna to hold you to it. Or I'll come and drag your sorry ass back here myself."

"Thanks, Dawson," he said.

"Anytime, Fitz."

He slumped into the couch. The news that Travis heard a voice the day of the landmine explosion astounded him. Had the Miraculous Medal and the Blessed Mother protected them that day? Did God speak to both of them but only Travis heard Him? Why would he hear God speaking to him now? He was confused about everything: God, Jesus, the Catholic Church, blessings and Frannie. Especially Frannie. What his heart wanted was at odds with what his mind told him he deserved. But the desires of his heart were growing stronger; he had almost acted on his impulse to embrace her that morning.

He changed into his gym shorts to go for a run. He needed to clear his head before he met her for dinner.

Chapter 39

DANIEL PUT THE LAST BITE OF LASAGNE IN HIS mouth and savored it.

"That was amazing," he said, wiping his mouth with his napkin and placing it back in his lap. "Now what? Lemon drinks? Coffee? Gelato?"

Frannie let her mouth fall open and placed her hand over heart, feigning shock. "What is this? Daniel Fitzpatrick has learned the art of leisurely dining?"

"After a month with you, did I have much of a choice?" he teased lightly.

Frannie grinned widely. Her date night with Daniel had been everything she had hoped. He opened every door and even pulled out her chair for her at the table. The conversation had been light, playful, and revealed that their partnership had resulted in a mutual affinity for the other. They shelved all discussion about church scandals and clergymen and instead discussed anything and everything they wanted: from worst job experiences and baseball stats to movies and music. She was glad he wasn't ready for the night to end. There was one more door she desperately wanted him to open for her; the door to his heart.

"I vote for gelato and a stroll through the heart of the city," she suggested. The familiar ache of having to leave Italy began creeping in. "It's always hard to leave this place," she added wistfully.

After they left the restaurant, they wandered past the Trevi Fountain and Pantheon to the gelato shop where Frannie had forcibly introduced Daniel to the Italian version of ice cream. They both opted for cones and ate as they walked.

"Are you ready for your interview with *Zio* tomorrow?" Frannie asked.

"He moved it to Wednesday. I'm sure he needed some space after everything we laid on him last night. But, yeah, I'm ready."

"I got the feeling you wanted the interview to focus on the previous conclave. Now that a new story has fallen in your lap, are you exploring a different approach?"

Daniel already wrestled with the same question. So much had changed since he landed in Rome. He had developed a deep respect for the Cardinal and he would not write anything that could be construed in a slanderous way.

"I've given that a lot of thought. I can't go back without something on paper and I can't write about Constantini until the Church makes it public knowledge. So I'm going to offer the Cardinal a chance to explain his traditional views. Also, I will give him a platform to give his advice to believers on navigating through the crises in the Church without having a crisis of faith. It will set the stage for when it all comes out."

They entered the Piazza Navona and Frannie chose to park herself on a stone bench. Daniel reclined next to her, finishing his chocolate chip dessert. She looked at him thoughtfully. His story line was a different angle from the original one sought after by the nosy Daniel Fitzpatrick she first met.

"Why do you want to give encouragement to Catholics who may be having a crisis of faith?"

"I guess you could say my disdain for organized religion is less than it was. And I respect your fighting spirit for the faith and your Church."

She wondered if his anger at God had lessened, but decided not to push the issue. "Most journalists in your shoes would just break the Constantini exclusive. Why are you waiting?" she asked.

"If I wrote about it now, Constantini would probably find a way to manipulate the facts, or worse: I would place Stefano and his family in danger. It's more important to get the bad guy than instant fame. But, I can't deny I'm still a mercenary who's out for both. I'm going to propose that I am the journalist who breaks the story when he's ready for it to come out. Who knows, maybe I can turn this into a book deal."

"You definitely have all the inside information on the newest scandal to hit the Church," Frannie said flatly.

"I can understand why you would be uneasy about that. I've come to know your uncle as a good and honorable man, Frannie. I'm not going to paint him or Donati through a lens that promotes anybody's agenda. I'll write the truth and I'll be fair. You have my word."

She met his eyes and held them with hers. "Since you put it that way, I trust you."

It was the highest compliment she could have given him. Daniel forced himself to break away from her warm eyes. The sun had long since set and he couldn't use sunglasses to hide his own.

Frannie announced, "At least you have a project to work on when you get back to the States. I'm probably starting over."

Daniel whirled around. "Starting over with what?"

"I've decided to quit my job. It's bringing me more stress than it's worth and turning me into someone I don't want to be. I had a long self-examination when I first got here. Contrary to what you may think, I had quite a bit to confess. But, I've been thinking about what you said about not changing myself for the people I work with. If I went back, that's what I would have to do in order to advance at the TV station. So, I'm going to do something else."

Daniel wasn't sure what surprised him more; that she was quitting her dream job or that she had taken what he said to heart.

"What will you do?"

"I can go back to doing contract editing work to pay the bills. It's what I used to do when I was a low level intern."

"You're not the type to work just to pay the bills. You must have a greater plan."

She bit her thumbnail and squinted at him. "Promise not to laugh?"

He lowered his chin. "I lost a bet and had to sing karaoke. It can't be any more embarrassing than that."

"Good point," she said. "All right," her warm eyes had a twinkle in them, "I have this idea for a Catholic children's book series. It's about a boy named Nicolo, who travels back in time and meets famous people in history. For example, the title could be "Nicolo goes to Rome" and he encounters the early Christians in the catacombs. Or "Nicolo goes to France" and meets Saint Joan of Arc, or to Mexico to meet Saint Juan Diego. In each story, Nicolo would have an adventure that would also teach something about a saint or an event in Church history."

"Hmm. A historical fiction-adventure series?"

"Exactly. I'm thinking of targeting the middle school age group. There's a lot of details I haven't ironed out. I've been thinking about it for two years now but I keep pushing the idea away so I've never tried to fully develop it." She shrugged one shoulder. "Who knows. If I can get one book published, maybe I can put my toe into the Catholic journalism circuit while I write another one."

Daniel leaned toward her. "I think it's creative. You should go for it."

She wrinkled one side of her nose. "Really? You're not just saying that? You can tell me if it's stupid."

"I don't think it's stupid. Your days as a tour guide give you a unique advantage. I've learned more about Catholicism through art and music in a month from you than in all the classes at church I took as a kid. Nicolo definitely should travel back to when Peter was buried and placed in the graffiti wall. Maybe the portal that sends him back in time is near where the event took place. Like back in that room where Peter's bones are."

Frannie's eyebrows knit together and she tilted her head. "That's not a bad idea," she said hesitantly.

"I've been known to have a few," he replied smugly.

"What? Bad ideas?" she smirked.

"Ha ha, Menconi." He stood up and without thinking held his hand out.

Frannie placed hers in his and he lifted her from the bench. The touch of her soft skin filled his chest with warmth. He lowered his hand and let hers slowly fall out.

"Ready?" he said, with his teenage awkwardness.

She nodded and they slowly made their way back to her apartment.

Daniel went in first. Rather than waiting outside, Frannie slipped inside and closed the door.

"All clear," he said. Even though he knew he would see her Friday at the gala, there was something about their dinner tonight that felt final. She was wearing the pink dress she wore at the café when his lips had almost brushed her cheek and he learned that she smelled of jasmine. He needed to start preparing how he was going to say goodbye. The same panic he felt in his dream when she jumped on the train crept into his stomach.

Frannie spoke first. "So, I guess this is it."

"I guess so," he said, taking a small step toward her.

"I think we made a pretty good team," Frannie said, stepping even closer.

They were like two magnets being pulled together at the poles by their natural attraction.

"If you're ever in Chicago—" his words stuck in his throat but his feet took another step toward her.

"You'll show me Wrigley Field?" she finished for him.

They both took the last step that closed the gap between them so that their faces were inches apart.

"Sure," Daniel said, not remembering exactly what Frannie had asked. Her green eyes were even more hypnotizing up close.

Frannie wasn't sure who made the first move but their lips found each other and she fell into his arms. This wasn't like Salzburg; this time, everything about Daniel was real. Her prayer had been answered and her internal compass was pointing directly at Daniel Fitzpatrick. And by the way he was kissing her, she believed he felt the same way.

Her bliss was interrupted without warning. Daniel placed his hands on her shoulders and abruptly pushed her out of the warmth of his embrace.

"I'm sorry," he whispered, and turned away.

Frannie stared at his back, bewildered by his reaction. She had responded to his touch with abandon. How could he mistake her for being offended?

"I'm not sorry," she said, "I'm actually wondering what took you so long."

He kept his back to her. "This is really difficult."

An ache began to form in the back of Frannie's throat. "What's difficult about it?"

"It's not what you think."

"I think you kissed me, Daniel," she said, dread beginning to fill her chest. "Are you really going to stand there and pretend it was some ordinary kiss?"

She waited for him to answer but he was silent.

It felt like all the air had been compressed out of Frannie's lungs and replaced with sharp glass. She had finally found the man she had been waiting for and he was about to reject her.

She covered her mouth with her hands and mused out loud, "I can't believe this. I just can't believe it."

Daniel finally turned around. His face was pained and his eyes tormented. "Frannie, it's not you. It's me."

The familiar words hit her ears like nails on a chalkboard. Her hurt blinded her from seeing his anguish or hearing the haunting agony in his voice. The shock had worn off and she was consumed with prideful anger. She laughed derisively.

"Really, Daniel? That's the best you can come up with? Like I've never heard that one before!"

She thought she saw him flinch slightly but she didn't care. This stray dog had hurt her more deeply than any other, and she let her accusations fly with acidic blows, "I thought you were different. But you're just as wishy-washy and cowardly as the rest."

Daniel looked away. He had no rebuttal.

Frannie crossed her arms. "I guess you'll get your interview and book deal," she hurled at him scornfully. "That's what you came here for." She marched over and threw the door open.

"Goodbye, Daniel." Her eyes were riveted on the floor so he couldn't see the hot and bitter tears that were filling her eyes and about to spill down her cheeks. When she saw the blur of him pass by, she slammed the door.

Daniel bolted out of the apartment and to the street. He clenched his hands into fists, wishing he could erase Frannie's betrayed and crumpled face etched in his brain. He broke into a run to let out his pent-up frustration and didn't stop until he reached Saint Peter's. He ran up the stairs, two at a time in a near sprint, ignoring the throbbing in his knee. When he got to the top he flopped down on the step.

This was a first; he was running away from someone he had hurt, not someone that had hurt him. He bent his injured knee and let his forehead fall on top of it.

You really don't deserve her. You are a coward. And a dumb-ass.

Chapter 40

CARDINAL MENCONI GREETED DANIEL AT THE door. "Hello! Come in, come in. Can I get you something to drink?"

"No, thank you, sir."

The Cardinal gestured at the couch. "Have a seat. I cleared my calendar, so we will not be interrupted."

Daniel positioned himself so he had room for his notes, laptop, and voice recorder.

The prelate lowered himself in his chair and smiled politely, "I am ready when you are."

"Then let's begin. Do you mind if I record you?"

"Not at all."

Daniel picked up the recording device and poised his thumb over the button. His thumb hovered in mid-air for several seconds, unable to press it. He threw it to the side along with his notepad.

"Cardinal," he said, "I have prepared a list of questions to ask you, all geared to fulfill the job I was sent here to do as well as boost my career. But there's only one question that matters to me: How can I get another chance with Frannie?"

Cardinal Menconi closed his eyes and leaned back in his chair. Francesca had called him yesterday morning, wilted in tears. She had planned to book the first flight back to Boston she could find. He was so worried about her leaving in such a state, he called Alessandro who had just returned to Rome from his retreat. Alessandro went to her apartment and was finally able to console her. He even convinced her to stay long enough to attend the gala and offered to be her escort.

Daniel wasn't sure how to read the Cardinal's silence. "Sir, I'm sure Frannie told you everything. I wish I would have handled it better."

The Cardinal's eyes flicked open. He looked intently at the young man. "Then, you do care for her?"

Daniel's eyes were watery. "Deeply," he replied.

Cardinal Menconi exhaled. "I thought you did. However, she is certain you have rejected her."

"I wasn't rejecting her, I was—" he ran his fingers through his hair. "I thought I was helping her reject me. She deserves better than a guy who is confused and broken. I need help," he said fervently. "I need help sorting out all the stuff in my head because I've been running from my past for so long, I'm afraid I just let my future slip through my fingers."

A lone tear escaped down Daniel's cheek. "Please," he pleaded, "I need another chance, Cardinal. I don't want to be apart from her."

Cardinal Menconi said a quick prayer. He wasn't going to be a high ranking church official doing an interview today; he would be living his vocation as a priest and shepherd. "Tell me about this past you are running from."

Daniel gushed forth his life story, beginning with the death of his mother. From there he moved to Heather, then to Kelsay, and allowed himself some tears over BJ. He was taken aback by how comfortable he was with the Cardinal, and how patiently the clergyman listened. The man's fatherly eyes never judged; they were full of empathy and kindness. Encouraged by his compassion, Daniel continued to unload the baggage he had been carrying for years.

"The hardest part about BJ, and my greatest guilt, is that I wasn't able to protect my own child. I left BJ fatherless and abandoned, just like me. All because I chose to be with a woman out of convenience and pleasure rather than love. I have to accept responsibility for putting myself in a situation without any thought to the consequences. With a past like mine, how can I even consider that I could deserve someone as wonderful as Frannie?" He shot up from the couch to pace the small living area and his heartfelt confession quickly morphed into ranting.

"Which brings me to the next thing," he said sharply. "Why is God taunting me with the woman of my dreams? The God who left me without parents suddenly wants to notice me? And talk to me? After all of these years?"

Cardinal Menconi nodded knowingly. *Now we're getting to the crux of the matter,* he thought. *This is his stumbling block.*

"What did God say to you?" he asked gently.

Daniel stopped, whipped around to face the Cardinal and braced himself behind a chair. "I think he spoke to me at the *Pieta,*" he replied, and recounted the whole event.

When he finished, the Cardinal rubbed his chin. "I see," he said. "If Mary loves you like a mother, do you think God can love you like a Father?"

"How can I say yes to that?" Daniel retorted. "He didn't give me a father and took my mother away from me when I was seven years old."

"You are angry at Him," the Cardinal stated.

"Shouldn't I be?" he shouted angrily. "I'm sorry," he whispered, regretting his outburst.

"You have had much sadness and heartache in your life, Daniel. It is a lot to wrestle with. But it appears God is wanting to get your attention."

Daniel walked back to the couch and dropped down on it. He rubbed his forehead and looked at the Cardinal out of the corner of his eye. "All He has done is stirred up the most painful memories of my past. So if this is His idea of reaching out, how can I see it as an act of a loving Father?"

Cardinal Menconi folded his hands and rested them on his stomach. "Over the last few years, I have found myself being drawn to the life of Saint Peter. I have come to think of him as a friend," he added with a smile. "There is a story from Peter's life that has always inspired me. It occurs after Jesus' Resurrection. Peter decides he is going to go fishing, and some of the other disciples decide to join him. They fish all night and catch nothing. Jesus appears on the shore, but they don't recognize him. He tells them to cast their nets on the right side of the boat. They do so, and the nets fill with so many fish they couldn't haul them all in. The disciple John remembers this same scene from when Jesus first called them. He knew immediately it was Jesus. Peter, being ever impetuous, jumps out of the boat and swims to the shore to meet his Lord."

Daniel's stomach clenched in a knot; the Cardinal's story choice coincided with the calling of the disciples from the Gospel on Sunday. He recalled how quickly he related to the brassy fisherman.

The Cardinal continued, "Now when Peter got to the shore, there was a charcoal fire burning. This too, had a memory. Unlike the happy memory of the first catch, this was a painful one for Peter. The night Jesus was arrested, Peter was warming himself at a charcoal fire when he denied he knew Jesus not just once, but three times.

"On the shore, the Lord asked Peter, 'Peter, do you love me?' not once, but three times. It is written that Peter was grieved that Jesus asked him the third time. It must have been like pouring salt on a wound: Peter had wept bitterly for abandoning his Lord only hours after swearing he would die before denying Him. But here was Jesus asking him the question, and telling him to 'feed His sheep.' He was reminding Peter he had been called to something more; something greater."

Daniel gave him an angled look. "So, God has a habit of rubbing people's noses in their past mistakes?"

The Cardinal shook his head. "No, no. He wants to enter into those memories and heal them. He wants to release you from pain, free you from shame so that you can be made new; to realize who you are in His eyes."

"I don't know what any of that means," Daniel said dully.

"Tell me again what you heard at the *Pieta*."

"She loves you like a mother."

"What do you think those words meant?"

Daniel leaned forward with his elbows on his knees. "Frannie and I have talked about a lot of things and what has become clear to me is that my mother didn't want to leave me."

He swallowed the emotion that was welling up in his throat. "She loved me. Like a mother should love her son. What struck me about the statue was Mary. She was sorrowful, yet resigned to the reality of her situation. That was my mom." He pulled the medal out from his shirt and held it up. "And she gave me this as a way to protect me. I couldn't see any of this before but I see it now."

"And you see it, because the memories have been revisited?"

Daniel closed his eyes. He had never felt more at peace about his mother. He even felt closer to her. Like a piece of her heart had been revealed to him. He couldn't hold the emotion back and it trickled down his face.

"Yes, sir," he choked. He wiped the water off his cheeks. "But it doesn't solve my problem with God."

The Cardinal sighed heavily. "God may have helped you come to terms with your mother's death but you want to know why He had you grow up without any parents."

Daniel looked at him with wide eyes, marveling at how well the prelate understood him. He nodded slowly.

"*Mio figlio*, I cannot answer that question. We live in a broken and fallen world because of sin and death. There is sickness and there is suffering. It's how we understand suffering that makes the difference."

"How am I supposed to understand it?"

"Suffering can be a means to get our attention, to teach us to depend not on ourselves but on God; it can make us stronger and it can make us wise. I look at you, Daniel and I see a young man who has known from an early age that life is not easy. You had to grow up fast. Your trials have allowed natural masculine characteristics to cultivate within you: courage, sacrifice, and protective instincts. In your work as a journalist, it has made you unafraid to tackle hard topics with unbiased truth. Your willingness to join the military rather than pursue a music career was a sacrifice for the greater purpose of providing for a family you hoped to have. Although I cannot condone your choice to live with a woman outside of marriage, you were ready to make the sacrifices necessary to provide for your child. All these things have been working within you; you just didn't know it was God who was molding you."

The Cardinal's character assessment made Daniel uncomfortable. He thought back to the park bench at Mirabellgarten when Frannie affirmed his courage and talent for writing.

"It's remarkable," he said, "how you and Frannie see things in me I don't see in myself. She has this ability to ask me a few questions and suddenly my perception changes. It's like I'm looking at my life through the same lens but new slivers of light are shining upon it differently. Parts of my life I thought were sad and awful actually had things that were good about them."

Cardinal Menconi smiled faintly. "The Lord is always blessing us whether it be in times of trial or rejoicing." He got up and walked to his bookshelf and pulled down a book. He returned to his seat, opened it, and read, "'I lift my eyes to the hills. From where does my help come? My help comes from the Lord, who made heaven and earth. God will not allow your foot to slip, your guardian does not sleep. The Lord will keep your going out and your coming in from this time forth and for evermore.'"

"Is that from your book, *From Whence Comes My Help*?"

The Cardinal closed the book and showed him the cover. It was the same book Frannie was reading when he met her.

"Yes. It is from Psalm 121. It is a song to the Lord our guardian, whom we trust in times of trouble. The Hebrew word, *shamar* appears in the Psalm six times; it means to guard and protect."

Protect. Daniel's reason led him to conclude Grandma Mae, Travis, and his mother's medal were all instruments of protection in his life. Could he believe that God was behind it all? And if God protected him then, could he trust and have faith that God would continue to protect him now?

"How am I supposed to trust God? Aside from Grandma Mae, He has taken everything I have tried to love from me: my mother, Heather," he swallowed back the tears and whispered, "and my child."

He had other reasons for pushing Frannie away. "I am afraid that with Frannie, I will find a happiness I have never known, only to have God yank it away from me."

The Cardinal gazed upon the young man thoughtfully. "Is that what you meant by God 'taunting you?'"

Daniel nodded.

"One of the paradoxes of the Christian life is our definition of happiness. Your happiness cannot come solely from Francesca. It can only be found when we realize our vocation: the calling God has for us in this life. Our primary vocation is to do the will of God and live a holy life. That is how we find our fulfillment, our purpose.

"I cannot discern for you whether God is calling you to marry Francesca and have a family. As with any vocation, marriage can bring you great happiness and joy; but not without heartache and sorrow. But when you surrender your life to the will of God, a peace and happiness will abide within you that can only come from the Lord. This, too, helps us understand suffering; we depend on him because He alone is our help. He will guard us and never sleep."

Daniel could only dream of one day placing a ring on Frannie's finger. He had so much harm to undo and overcome. And there were many things he had yet to understand.

"Sir, when we looked at Saint Peter's bones, you told me faith and reason work together. I can reason that God exists. How do I get faith?"

"Faith isn't something to be 'gotten.' It is an active response, made in pure freedom of our own will, to assent our reason to God who has revealed Himself to us. It is accepting His invitation to know Him."

"I don't know who God is," Daniel admitted.

"He is made known to us in Jesus Christ, His Son. Jesus is the One asking to get in your boat; for you to cast your heart into the deep waters of His mercy. He is asking you not to be afraid to trust Him; not to be afraid to give Him your heart. All you have to do is throw yourself at His feet and confess you are a sinful man and let His love and forgiveness make you new."

The reference to Peter and Jesus struck him hard in the chest. He was Peter: a sarcastic man who couldn't imagine Jesus had anything of significance to give him. Peter didn't think he, a professional fisherman, needed any help. But he threw his net into the deep anyway. And caught more than he imagined.

"How do I do what you're asking of me? I've only talked to God two or three times in my life, and all were in the last few weeks."

The Cardinal picked up his book again and flipped through the pages until he found what he was looking for.

"You were drawn to the *Pieta*, yes?"

"It is the most beautiful piece of art I have ever seen. It touched a place deep within me. I can't explain it, or any of the other weird things that have happened to me on this trip."

The Cardinal smiled faintly. The Holy Spirit was stirring within the soul of the young man. All Daniel needed to do was respond.

The Cardinal glanced back down at his book. "Did you know Michelangelo carved it out of a single block of marble?" he asked.

"Frannie mentioned it," Daniel replied.

"It is said Michelangelo could see the images in the raw material before he started working on them. It reminds me of a poem by Saint Edith Stein I used in one of my chapters. She was a Jewish convert to the faith, became a nun, and died at Auschwitz. At age thirteen she gave up on God and prayer and before her conversion was a respected philosopher in academia." He paused a moment to let the similarities in the saint and Daniel's contentious relationship with God sink in.

"The poem she wrote," he continued, "is titled, "I Am Always in Your Midst." I'll let you read it for yourself."

Daniel took the book from him and read the page.

Of course, the Lord leads each on her own path,
And what we call "fate;" is the artist's doing,
The eternal Artist who creates material for himself
And forms it into images in various ways:
By gentle finger strokes and also by chisel blows.
But he does not work on dead material;
His greatest creative joy in fact is
That under his hand the image stirs,
That life pours forth to meet him.
That life that he himself has placed in it
And that now answers him from within
To chisel blows or quiet finger strokes.
So we collaborate with God on his work of art.

Daniel reread the poem a second and third time. The words sank into his bones. They came from the depths of a heart that had been searching on a path all of her life for happiness. And she had found its Source. He had so many questions but all he knew was he wanted to meet the Artist the saint had met.

"What do you understand about the poem, Daniel? The Cardinal finally asked.

Silent tears streamed down Daniel's cheeks. "I'm the block of marble. I've been hammered by the chisel blows and the gentle strokes. But there is something that stirs within me that I cannot run away from any more."

Cardinal Menconi leaned forward. "God is waiting for the stirring to become a response to His invitation in faith; so you can collaborate with His grace and love to be the masterpiece designed by His hand. You asked how to get a second chance with Francesca. You have to allow yourself a chance with the Lord, first. This is it. Let yourself be the man God created you to be. Francesca can see who you are within the marble. Come to Christ and see yourself the way He does."

The Cardinal's phone buzzed. He waved his hand, "Ignore it. Whoever it is can wait."

Daniel was about to speak when the Cardinal's phone buzzed again repeatedly. "Maybe you should just see who it is, sir."

The Cardinal picked it up off the table. He jumped slightly and quickly answered. Daniel watched with growing concern as the color slowly drained from the prelate's face. His worst fears about Bald Man finding Frannie played in his mind. He mindlessly dropped the book beside him on the couch.

"Your Eminence, did something happen to Frannie? Is she all right?"

"No, no," he answered, holding up his hand. "She's fine." He crossed himself and muttered a prayer under his breath.

Daniel waited patiently for him to finish.

"The pope has passed from this life to his eternal reward. He is gone."

Daniel fell back against the couch. Given the unresolved situation with Donati and Constantini, this couldn't have happened at a worse time.

"When will the conclave start?" he asked.

"Fifteen days. Twenty at the most."

Thoughts swirled in Daniel's head. What would Constantini do now that Baldano wasn't in his camp? Would he threaten the Menconi family? Who would protect Frannie?

"Sir, there's a lot to be considered here."

"I know. But we need to go back to our conversation, Daniel. If it be God's will for me to be the next Vicar of Christ," he shook his head, "if you only knew how terrifying it is for me to say those words." He drew in a deep breath. "If that be God's will, it will change everything. I will not be as readily available to Francesca as I am now. It is time for her to find a man who will stand by her," he paused, "and love her."

Daniel's mouth went dry. "I thought you couldn't discern—"

"I cannot," the prelate interjected. "But I will not be unhappy if it is you."

"Do you think it's possible she will forgive me? If she doesn't, I'll have a hole in my heart forever."

"You may be hurt but there is only One who can fill the God-sized hole in your heart. What is even more important than you and Francesca is what is going on between you and our Lord. You said you could not run away from the stirring of your heart. How can I help you run toward Christ?"

Daniel stared at the cover of the book next to him. He was sitting with Cardinal Nicolo Menconi, who might possibly be the next pontiff of the Catholic Church. The possibilities of interview questions were endless.

His future was on the line and he knew what he needed to do.

"Cardinal, I know this is bad timing and you probably need to get to the Vatican. But, will you hear my confession?"

Tears of joy filled the old man's eyes. "*Mio figlio*, it would be my honor. The timing is perfect, because it is God's timing."

He retrieved a purple stole from his credenza, kissed its center, and placed it around his neck. Returning to his chair, the Cardinal made the Sign of the Cross out loud and prayed, "May God, who has enlightened every heart, help you to know your sins and trust in his mercy."

Daniel slid off the couch and onto his knees. He paused, "I don't remember how to begin or what I'm supposed to do."

"Not to worry. I'll help you."

Daniel's stomach dropped at the reality of what he was getting ready to do. He was about to trade a professional interview for the most intimate of all interviews: pouring out his heart to Christ Himself.

"I've told you some of my past but, there's more. This is going to be really ugly."

The Cardinal saw the tears already filling Daniel's eyes and gave him a fatherly, kindly smile. "Jesus will replace your penitent tears with grace and leave behind his masterpiece. It will be beautiful."

Chapter 41

D ANIEL PACED BACK AND FORTH IN FRONT OF THE entrance to the Church of the Holy Trinity of the Pilgrims of Rome, rallying up the courage to go inside. He had arrived at seven in the morning, fifteen minutes before the weekday Mass began. The church's website listed daily Masses as *Messe basse,* Italian for "Low Mass." After some online research, he learned the Latin Mass he had attended with Frannie and the Cardinal was a Solemn High Mass. The Low Mass he would be participating in today would be absent of music and incense. Any responses would be made by the altar server rather than the people. It didn't matter to Daniel; he didn't know what to say anyway. He figured his best bet was to follow everyone else and take Frannie's advice to "just be." He checked his watch and slowly ascended the stairs leading up to the large doors he had entered with Frannie on Sunday.

Although he felt awkward stepping into the church again, especially on his own, a profound need to return urged him on. Upon entering, the beauty of the interior caused the familiar leap in his soul. This time, he embraced it, letting it envelop him in a warm welcome.

The church was quiet and still with a small number of attendees: a mix of men and women catching Mass before work and older retirees. He walked down the main aisle and chose a row near the back. He started to enter the pew, but backed up to bend his knee to the Lord who resided in the tabernacle in the high altar. It had been years since he genuflected; he doubted he even made the gesture at Grandma Mae's funeral. He entered the pew and knelt down, his eyes fixed upon the large canvas painting of the Trinity. The depiction of God the Father no longer resembled the image of a wrathful old man. His arms and hands were open as if to say, "See how much I love you? I sent my only Son to forgive your sins." Daniel's eyes remained glued to the crucified Christ. He took up the conversation he had started on Sunday.

Hello, Jesus. I'm back. The Cardinal said prayer is just me talking with you. He added something more eloquent about lifting my mind and heart to you. So, here it goes. I showed you my wounds and exposed my shame. I've never cried that much before. But, I believe you have forgiven me. I feel pounds lighter; it's like my heart and soul have wings and could fly right out of my chest. A "thank you" seems a little anticlimactic considering all I've done.

He took a deep breath as he continued to take in the Crucifix; the arms of Christ now seemed stretched out wide in a personal invitation.

The Cardinal said I can give my thanks by living my life in a way that gives glory to You. I'm not sure I really know how to do that, yet. I have so many questions and I wish I could talk to Frannie about all of this. Please Lord, give me another chance with her. I know I just jumped on this Catholic train and I'm already asking for stuff but the gala is tomorrow night and I don't know what I'm going to say when I see her. I'm finally free from the tentacles of my past and I am ready for whatever my future holds. And I would really like it to include Frannie.

The tinkling of a bell interrupted him and everyone rose from their pews. Daniel did the same and finished his prayer.

Okay, Lord, I'm going to try to "just be" now. Oh, I forgot…I'm supposed to depend more on you. Can you help me "just be?" Tell Grandma Mae and my mom hello for me. I don't know if they can see me or not so could you tell them I'm at Mass? They will be really happy about that. Thank you, Lord. I promise I'll get better at this prayer thing. Um, Amen.

The Mass began with the priest and only two altar servers which slightly decreased the military feel as compared to the Solemn Mass from Sunday. It still held the same reverence and precision, drawing Daniel in once again to the timelessness of the ancient worship. His mind drifted a few times to Frannie, wishing she was beside him, but he returned his focus back to the altar.

At the elevation of the consecrated Host, he bowed his head. It was suddenly easy to believe that bread and wine could become the Body and Blood of Christ. If the Lord could fill his heart with the desire for confession and then flood it with a peace he had never known, the miracle of the Mass seemed like an easy thing.

When it was time for Communion, the men and women in the pews rose and began to line up in the center aisle. For a moment he faltered, and wondered if he should really go up to receive the Holy Eucharist; surely a type of boot camp retraining should be required first. He reminded himself of the Cardinal's assurance he was fully received back into the arms of Mother Church, and therefore back to Christ, Her Head. The sins that blocked his access to the grace of the Sacraments were gone. Cardinal Menconi had encouraged him to attend Mass as soon as he could.

He exited the pew and processed forward. When his turn came to approach the altar rail his heart thrashed in his chest. His eyes never rested on the priest's face; only the Host that was about to be placed on his tongue. After he received, he numbly stood up and went back to his pew. He knelt down and covered his face with his hands. The sounds of moving people, creaky pews and kneelers melted away and it was just Daniel and his Lord.

Surrendering to the present moment, Daniel realized what it truly meant to just be. To just be in His Presence; to just be and feel His love.

The deepest and innermost place of his being that had been tugged and stirred over the last month began to swell and he had no desire to run from it. A spring of gratitude poured out and words he never thought he could compose came forth from his soul.

O Lord, my God you are my guardian, my help, and the font of all mercy and goodness. How long I have foolishly ran from you and yet you never stopped seeking me. Please accept my song to you, my Father in Heaven.

In his heart, he silently sang the hymn, "Be Thou My Vision." When he got to the second verse, the gratitude flowed from his eyes.

> *Be thou my wisdom, and thou my true word*
> *I ever with thee and thou with me, Lord*
> *Thou my great Father, and I thy true son*
> *Thou in me dwelling and I with thee one*

Daniel had a Father. A Father who had always been with him and loved him like a son. A Father who welcomed him back with open arms. His image of God had changed and along with it, the image of himself. On bended knees in his confession, Daniel found his dignity in Christ. He was not defined by his past mistakes, but by the love of the One who made him.

He continued praying through the rest of the verses to the favorite hymn of his grandmother and Frannie. A smell tickled his nose, causing his eyes to flash open. He looked around but he was alone, except for the priest who was extinguishing the candles on the altar. He didn't even realize Mass had ended.

He took in a deep breath through his nostrils, but smelled nothing. A month ago, he would have thought he was crazy. Now, he believed anything was possible. He was certain he had smelled roses but had no idea what it could mean. It was one of many things he would have to ask Frannie, if she was willing to give him the time of day.

Daniel exited the pew, genuflected, and left the church. He had a lot to do between now and tomorrow's gala. The Cardinal and Daniel had reconvened over dinner for the official interview and to strategically plan its release to break the Constantini story. Daniel's boss was growing impatient; he would be pounding away at his laptop all day to get the article ready for submission.

Most importantly, he needed to rent a tux for the gala. Tomorrow night he would find out if he would be leaving Italy brokenhearted or with the woman of his dreams.

Chapter 42

THE BLACK SEDAN SLOWED AS IT TURNED TO PASS through a tall, black, wrought iron gate. Flowering shrubs bordered the rock walls along the cobble and pebble stone driveway. After a couple of curves lined with Rome's iconic tall umbrella pine trees, the Villa Aurelia came into view.

"Wow. This is the place?" Daniel asked.

"*Sì, Signore,*" Paolo replied.

Daniel peered out the window at the ivory seventeenth century Baroque structure. Paolo and Daniel had scrutinized the floor plans that morning when they consulted with the Cardinal's security detail on proper safety measures for the event. Daniel had paid more attention to entrances and exits than the actual look of the venue.

The grand two story building was a mix of tall square and arched windows. Framing the windows were columns and half domes ornamented by reliefs of shells and garlands. Jutting forth at the end of the structure was another wing, annexed at a right angle, with potted palm plants dotted along its terraced roof. A checkerboard garden of green and white turf-like squares decorated the patio in front of the villa. Lemon trees planted in terracotta pots occupied each green square.

"I didn't realize this was so close to Janiculum Hill," Daniel said. "I think Frannie and I jogged right by the gate."

"*Signore,* I was surprised when I was instructed to pick you up by yourself. Why didn't you ride with *Signorina?*" Paolo asked.

Daniel decided to tell his cupid-playing friend the truth. "I messed up, Paolo. I'm here tonight to try to win her back."

Paolo chuckled. "Ah, now I know why he was with—" he broke off and waved his hand. "You will succeed. Her eyes are sad, *Signore*. She will be happy to see you."

Paolo got out of the car leaving a puzzled Daniel in the back seat. *Who is "he?"* His door opened and he stepped out.

"Thanks for the ride, Paolo. You're staying in the back as planned?"

"*Sì.* I'll be with a couple of the men working security."

Daniel shook his hand. "See you in a few hours."

Paolo jumped back in the car and pulled away. Daniel stood in line with the other guests arriving at the main entrance. A man at the door checked off each person's name on the approved list of attendees and waved them through.

Daniel followed the crowd through the rooms of the main building toward the L-shaped annex and the Sala Aurelia room, where the gala was being held. Daniel was well acquainted with its floor plan: there were three doors along each side of the wing, and the security detail had stationed a guard at each one. Three of the doors faced the checkerboard lemon garden, and the other three opened up to a terrace.

After passing through the last room before the Sala Aurelia, he paused in an open-air breezeway. Both he and the head of security detail had expressed their dislike for this area of the villa. The unobstructed access to the gala drew concern; someone could sneak in and enter without being checked off at the front. He glanced and saw two guards stationed under the archways, just as they had recommended. Everything looked like it was going according to plan.

Now it was time to execute his own plan and ask Frannie for a chance to explain himself.

Twin French door entrances led down two separate short hall-ways to two identical curtain doors that opened into the ballroom. The tall glass paned doors that opened to the terrace were open, letting a cool breeze flow through the area. Daniel had memo-rized the layout.

The podium where the Cardinal would make his speech was to his right. Round tables covered with white tablecloths and floral centerpieces filled the rest of the chamber where the benefactors and their guests would be seated for dinner. The table placed directly in front of the podium was reserved for the Cardinal, Frannie and his guests. His eyes landed there immediately and upon the most beautiful woman in the room.

Frannie's dark brown hair was styled in chunky braids that twined into a bun at her neck. A few wisps of hair hung in loose curls, framing her face. The bodice of her red cap-sleeve dress glimmered with sequined floral lace that stopped at the waist. The red flowing skirt was full enough to be modest, but did not drown her thin figure. The same floral lace in the bodice adorned the hem that fell below her knees. She was holding a wine glass and visiting with one of the Sisters of Charity. She smiled at something the sister said and turned, and their eyes met.

Frannie's lips parted in disbelief. Daniel Fitzpatrick had come to the gala and was making a beeline in her direction. She groaned internally. His tux fit him like a glove, and the pain of his rejection seared through her with great intensity. She closed her mouth and tried to erase any evidence that his presence affected her.

"Hello, Frannie."

"Hello, Daniel," she responded blandly. "I expected you to be halfway back to Chicago by now."

Her bristled tone and stony stare reminded him of their first conversation in the airport. *So much for her being happy to see me.*

"I wanted to talk to you." He glanced toward the doors that led to the terrace. "Could we step outside?"

"Sure," she replied, trying her best to sound detached.

Daniel held out his hand. "After you."

Frannie clenched her jaw. He was just as intoxicating as he had been in Milan. Had he come here to twist the knife in further? Could she dare hope that he had come back for her?

They stepped onto the terrace. There was still another hour before the sun completely set, but it had disappeared behind the building, cloaking the terrace in shade. Outdoor lamps in the corners provided a soft light, so Daniel could see every feature of Frannie's delicate face.

Frannie's heart skipped. The way he was looking at her gave her a sprig of hope.

Just tell me you made a mistake Daniel, and we can start over.

A voice with an Italian accent startled them, "Francesca, are you going to introduce me?"

"Oh, uh," she stammered, "Alessandro, this is Daniel Fitzpatrick."

The handsome young man stuck his hand out and smiled amiably. "Daniel, it is good to meet you."

Daniel's neck twitched. The man said his name with familiarity; as if he knew who he was and everything that had happened between him and Frannie. Daniel looked him right in the eyes. They were the same height, but Daniel quickly assessed he was more brawny than the Italian. He straightened to make himself look taller and more intimidating.

He reluctantly took Alessandro's hand and squeezed it firmly, but didn't offer a greeting in exchange.

Alessandro turned to Frannie and whispered rapidly in Italian, "Forget your pride, Frannie. I told you if he shows up, he's 'the one.' Give him a chance."

"Maybe when you become a priest you'll stop lecturing me about my love life," she quipped in Italian.

Alessandro smirked before walking away.

Daniel watched the interchange between them and his stomach turned. This man must be the "he" Paolo had mentioned. Whoever he was, he wasn't someone she had just met. They had a relationship with each other that went beyond casual. Paolo had gotten this one wrong. Frannie's eyes weren't sad; he may have hurt her briefly but she'd clearly gone running into the arms of an old boyfriend. God may have given him a second chance, but Frannie wasn't going to. She had moved on.

"What did you want to talk to me about, Daniel?" Frannie pressed.

A hole began to burn in Daniel's heart. He was too late.

"The interview went really well," he said robotically. "I didn't get a chance to thank you for your help and kindness. I sincerely wish you the best, Frannie."

She blinked away the deer-in-the-headlight look from her face. "You came here to thank me?"

Frannie felt the flush of humiliation creeping its way from her neck up to her cheeks. She scolded herself for being so easily led into the promise of false hope.

"Let me get this straight," she said, her voice shaking. "You came here tonight to tell me about the interview and to thank me?"

Daniel stood completely still, held in place by a set of green eyes that drilled into him.

She threw her hands out to the side then let them fall. "I thought for a moment you came back—" she stopped, held her hands up and shook her head. "No, it's not worth it."

Stung with indignation, she brandished her tongue like a weapon.

"You're the same dolt I met at the airport," she said harshly. "I don't know if you are cruel or clueless or both, but I can't do this," she choked. "Go back to Chicago, Daniel."

She spun on her heel and stormed back inside.

Daniel staggered to the back of the terrace and leaned his hands on the railing. Frannie's reaction didn't add up for a girl who had moved on. What did she think he came back for?

She thought I came back for her.

Old habits of assuming the worst had wormed their way into his mind and tricked him. He should have known better than to think Frannie could be so fickle.

There was still the question of What's-His-Name. Daniel gritted his teeth. His stupidity and cowardice just pushed her even further into the old boyfriend's arms.

His resolve and backbone stiffened. *You are a Marine! Act like it!*

Adrenaline began coursing through his veins as if he were getting ready for a military exercise. Frannie was the girl of his dreams and he wasn't giving her up without a fight; old boyfriend be damned. He would march back inside the ballroom and tell her the real reason he had come to the gala.

He whirled around, took two steps, and froze in his tracks.

Mr. Bald Man, Bruno Fratelli himself, was speaking with the guard stationed by one of the doors. The guard waved him in, and gave the others a nod to begin securing the doors.

Daniel sprinted over but was detained roughly by the man who let Bruno Fratelli enter.

"Sir," Daniel said, "I'm a guest. My name is on the list—"

"No one is allowed in after seven-thirty. No exceptions."

Daniel cursed under his breath. He knew the protocol. It had been his idea.

He watched helplessly as the doors closed, shutting him off from Frannie who was barricaded in the ballroom with Cardinal

Constantini's mafia bodyguard. He spotted a staircase that descended down from the terrace. His feet flew down the steps and around to the back of the Villa Aurelia.

Paolo was leaning against the Cardinal's sedan visiting with Remo, the senior officer assigned to the Cardinal's detail. His eyebrows shot up at the sight of Daniel.

"*Signore*, why are you—"

"Paolo, you've got to get me back into the gala," he blurted urgently, "Cardinal and Frannie are in danger. Bruno Fratelli is here. I was on the terrace and watched him go in." He glanced at the senior officer. "Either he got in using a fake name or the Fratellis found a way to turn one of your employees."

Remo conferred with Paolo in Italian. Daniel clenched his hands into fists. They were wasting precious time. Frannie and the Cardinal were unprotected. Bruno wasn't here to spy; something big was about to happen. He could feel it.

Paolo placed his hand on Daniel's shoulder. "I told Remo to trust you."

Remo spoke to Daniel, "*Signore*, I do not want to cause panic. I know who the Fratelli brothers are. They are known for their money laundering, black market rifles, and being hired hitmen. Why would they be the ones behind the letters the Cardinal received?"

Daniel held his tongue. The security company had merely been informed that the Cardinal received some suspicious letters and wanted extra protection. Cardinal Menconi did not want anything about the Constantini back story to be revealed.

With all the calmness Daniel could muster, he said, "With all due respect sir, I know Bruno is here to cause harm. The news of the pope's death and speculations of a tense conclave are on every media outlet. They're already predicting factions and schisms. You must know Cardinal Menconi is being hailed as a front runner for the next pontiff."

Remo flinched slightly. Daniel continued, "I can't tell you any more than that. I agree Bruno Fratelli isn't your hitman. But he's planted one somewhere."

Remo consulted in Italian again with Paolo, then looked at Daniel thoughtfully. "I suggest the three of us stand at the two curtain entrances in the back. It's the best view of the room and all the doors."

Paolo nodded. "I will stand on one side and you and Remo on the other. If I see movement by Remo or you, I will take care of the Cardinal." He gave Daniel a hard stare. "You take care of *Signorina*."

Daniel knew he could be placing Paolo directly in the line of fire. The steel determination in the chauffeur's eyes told him there would be no negotiation.

"I hope I'm wrong, Paolo," he said.

Paolo crossed himself and the three made quick strides around the front by the lemon tree garden to the breezeway. The guard moved quickly aside and let his senior officer pass with his escorts. When they arrived at the hallway, they passed by waiters bringing out the dinner food trays.

Remo had a team monitoring the kitchen staff. He said something into his wireless transmitter, then translated for Daniel, "I told the kitchen staff not to come and clear the tables until after the Cardinal was done with his speech."

Daniel nodded and stood concealed by the curtain, gathered by a rope tieback. He peeked around it and surveyed the room for Bruno. He found him at a table in the back, close to one of the doors that led to the terrace. Bruno had finagled the perfect seat; in two steps he could be out the door and lost in one of the lush gardens on the property.

Daniel pointed this out to Remo.

The officer responded affirmatively, his concern a little more heightened. Remo spoke again into his receiver. The two men watched as a new guard took the place of the one who let Bruno in.

Remo speculated, "That should tip him off that we are watching him. He may think twice now before executing any plans." The guard being removed looked disturbed but quietly relinquished his position. Bruno pretended to lean back and casually glance in their direction, but appeared indifferent to the change, and continued to eat his dinner.

"The first guard's wireless has been taken offline," Remo stated. He raised the device to his mouth, alerting his security team to where Bald Man was sitting.

Daniel turned his attention to the Cardinal's table. There were three Sisters of the Missionaries of Charity, Frannie, and an empty seat next to her. His eyes danced around wildly for What's-His-Name, and finally located him at a table primarily of priests. The young man was in deep discussion with one of them. Why wasn't he sitting next to Frannie?

His stomach dropped. The empty chair was his.

The Cardinal had probably saved it for him, expecting him to be fully reconciled with his niece. He wondered if Frannie had told her uncle about their incident on the terrace. Daniel had asked the Cardinal not to tell Frannie anything. He wanted to be the one to tell her about his conversion and coming back to the Sacraments.

He couldn't think about that now; there were more pressing matters that required his attention. One of the Sisters was moving to the podium, and Daniel assumed she was getting ready to introduce their guest speaker.

Through the glass of one of the side doors opening to the terrace, Daniel spotted movement. A waiter was speaking with the guards.

"Remo," he whispered, "didn't you tell the kitchen staff to wait until after the speech to come back?"

"*Sì.*" Remo spoke into his wireless. Daniel waited for him to translate the back and forth communication. "Someone has a food allergy to something on their plate. He's delivering an exchange."

"That's a little convenient," Daniel muttered. "Which guest?"

Before Remo could ask, the attendees erupted into a spontaneous applause. The two men hesitated, watching closely as Cardinal Menconi approached the podium. The prelate caught sight of Remo standing in the doorway and Daniel hiding behind the curtain. His surprise caused him to pause briefly. He made eye contact with Daniel who nodded slowly. He hoped their silent communication was enough for the Cardinal to be on alert.

When he arrived at the platform, one of the sisters was roused by her enthusiasm to stand up and continue clapping, prompting the rest of the crowd to give the Cardinal a standing ovation.

Daniel cursed under his breath. "Now we can't see." He pulled the curtain back further and caught sight of the waiter entering through the door carrying a plate with a silver food cover dome. He was headed directly for Bruno's table.

"Remo, I'm telling you that's not a waiter," Daniel insisted over the din of applause. "We need to get the Cardinal out now!"

Everything happened within seconds. Bruno got up from the table and darted out the side door. Adrenaline immediately flooded Daniel's veins preparing his muscles to react. When the waiter removed the food cover, a Glock pistol lay on the food tray.

Remo was already yelling commands into his wireless speaker. Daniel heard himself shouting, "Gun! Everyone down!"

He broke out in a sprint running in front of the podium. Out of the corner of his eye, he saw Paolo heading for the Cardinal.

At the front table, Frannie watched the scene unfold in slow motion. She watched in horror as Paolo dived in front of her uncle. She heard a familiar voice call out, "Frannie! Get down!"

When she turned, she saw Daniel Fitzpatrick running headlong toward her. He crashed into her, and amidst the screams, sounds of bullets, and breaking glass, they fell to the floor.

Chapter 43

THE SOUNDS OF COMMOTION AND CHAOS SWIRLING around Frannie faded into the distance, dissolving into a muffled rumble. She lay flat on her back, pinned under the weight of Daniel's body. Having the wind knocked out of her made it difficult to breathe, and she gasped for air.

"Daniel?" she whispered. She didn't recognize the sound of her own voice. It was strangled and shaky.

He rolled to his right and propped himself up on his hand. The gunfire had ceased but he glanced to the back of the room. The gunman was nowhere in sight and Remo's men were securing the area. Assured of their safety, he turned his attention to Frannie.

"Are you all right?" he asked.

She looked at him with wide eyes filled with fright. "I don't know."

He looked her up and down for any sign of injury and saw none. He placed his left hand on her head, and pressed his lips to her forehead.

"I couldn't let anything happen to you," he whispered.

Frannie froze in shock. She couldn't make sense of what just happened. All she knew was Daniel Fitzpatrick had risked his life to protect her. The sound of police sirens brought her back to some fuzzy form of reality.

Zio!

"Daniel!" she said, attempting unsuccessfully to roll out from underneath the other half of his body. "*Zio!* I have to get to *Zio!*"

Daniel put pressure on both hands to push himself up, then cried out in pain. Fannie was able to sit up and pull her legs out from under him. Daniel fell back on his rear, and grasped his left shoulder with his right hand. He instantly felt warm and sticky blood on his hand, leaking through his suit coat. When he pulled his hand back, Frannie yelped.

"Daniel! You've been hit!" She jumped to her feet and called out for help in Italian.

The physiological effects of the fight or flight syndrome blunting his pain were wearing off and his arm began to throb.

"It's probably just a graze," he said to calm her down. He grabbed a napkin that had fallen on the floor and was getting ready to apply pressure to his wound when What's-His Name appeared, knelt down beside him, and started cutting the arm of his coat with a pair of scissors.

Daniel tried to jerk his arm away but Frannie stopped him. "It's okay, he's an EMT. He's going to help you." Tears spilled down her cheeks. "We need to get him to the hospital," she said tersely.

"Francesca," Alessandro said soothingly, "I need to assess the injury first." He carefully removed the pieces of clothing he had cut away and examined the wound. "It looks like, uh, *escoriare,*" he said, not sure of the English word, "but a rather deep one." He applied pressure with gauze.

"A bullet graze?" Frannie repeated.

"*Sì,*" Alessandro replied. "The bullet only grazed him. He's going to be fine," he said gently to Frannie.

"See? That's what I said," Daniel reiterated, demonstrating he didn't need any help from the old boyfriend. He tried not to wince in pain from the pressure being exerted on his arm.

"Thank you, Lord," she whispered. She placed her hand on Daniel's cheek and opened her mouth to speak but was interrupted by Remo. He appeared disheveled and out of breath.

"*Signorina,* the Cardinal is asking for you." His attention turned to Daniel. "*Signore,* were you–"

"Just a graze, Remo," Daniel said dismissively. "Is the Cardinal ok?" he asked urgently.

"*Sì,* I'm supposed to bring both of you to him."

Alessandro shook his head. "He is going to the hospital. His wound needs to be cleaned and treated."

"Remo," Daniel said, "what about Paolo?"

The officer lowered his voice. "He was taken to the hospital. That's all I know."

Daniel groaned out loud. Images of Paolo's wife and son flashed in his mind. *Lord, let him be ok. Please.*

Alessandro stood up and shouted something to one of the other EMTs who came running with a stretcher.

Daniel instantly objected, "I can walk."

Alessandro waved the EMT away and offered his hand to Daniel, who ignored it and got to his feet without assistance. Alessandro placed his hand under Daniel's arm to lead him to the ambulance parked outside.

Frannie grabbed Daniel's hand. "I'll meet you at the hospital. After I see *Zio.*"

He allowed himself to cast his eyes upon her with his heart, without hiding behind his past or a pair of sunglasses. He was truly free; and the warm almond shaped green eyes he fell into gave him hope. His resolve to win her back returned and he squeezed her hand.

"I'll wait for you, Menconi."

She let go of his hand, letting her fingertips linger briefly, before hurrying off with Remo to her uncle.

Alessandro loaded Daniel into the ambulance. He grabbed Alessandro's forearm as he was about to walk away.

"I'm going to fight for her," Daniel said, giving What's-His-Name full warning of the battle that was about to come his way.

A smile broke across the young Italian's face and he chuckled. He placed his other hand on Daniel's shoulder, as if they were old friends. "I know."

Daniel was perplexed by his response; it was almost like he was happy about it.

Alessandro closed the doors and Daniel watched him walk away through the back window before the ambulance pulled off and raced to the hospital.

Remo led Frannie to a room in the Villa that had been converted into a makeshift communications center. Italian police and national security officers were making calls and meticulously sifting through security videos to try to get an ID on Bruno and the gunman. Cardinal Menconi was in a chair being examined by a physician. When Frannie entered the room he stood up, much to the dismay of the doctor. Frannie rushed into the arms of her uncle and he squeezed her tightly.

"*Mia passerotta*, praise be to God that you are not hurt."

The full gravity of what happened fell upon her. Her body began to tremble, and she collapsed into sobs. She could have lost *Zio* and Daniel tonight. If Daniel hadn't been there to push her out of the way, she may have lost her own life.

The Cardinal continued to hold her in a secure embrace until her trembling and tears subsided. When she pulled away she asked, "Are you really okay, *Zio*?"

"Yes, I'm fine. I've provided all the answers to the authorities that I can. Now I need to get to the hospital; I need to tend to Paolo and anyone else that has been injured tonight."

"Daniel was asking about him. How bad is he?"

"All I know is he took the bullet that was meant for me. He was unconscious when they left here. Daniel is ok?" he asked.

"Yes, but he's on his way to the hospital. A bullet grazed–" emotion welled up in her throat. "He saved my life, *Zio*."

"I know," he whispered. "He saved both of us. Remo said he was the one that alerted them about Bruno."

Frannie's thoughts spun about like a merry-go-round. A fundraising gala turned assassination attempt; Daniel's insipid, "I wish you the best" to a one-eighty, "I couldn't let anything happen to you," and a tender kiss on the forehead. Nothing made sense.

The Cardinal's phone rang and he dug it out of his pocket. "It's your mother," he said, handing it to Frannie.

Her shoulders drooped. "News of this must have reached America already." She would need to text Jen.

"Can we leave for the hospital?" she asked, taking the phone. "I'll talk to her on the way."

"I'll get Remo. He is going to escort us."

***

It didn't take Frannie long to find a nurse who could take her to Daniel. He was the only American brought to the emergency room from the Villa.

"The doctor is with him now," the nurse told her.

Frannie followed her to the patient treatment area. Each open-air room had a short half wall on either side of the bed, providing a little privacy. Frannie saw a pair of legs wearing tuxedo slacks and black shoes laying on a bed. She pointed and the nurse nodded. When she made it to the end of the bed, her knees buckled.

The doctor was sewing up the laceration in Daniel's arm. Daniel was calmly watching him as if it were a woman sewing a quilt.

When he saw her, he smiled and stirred slightly.

"Sit still, please," the doctor ordered.

"Sorry," Daniel muttered.

Frannie rolled a stool over and sat as close to the bed as she could. She grimaced. "Does it hurt?"

"No. They injected me with anesthetics. I can feel some pressure but it doesn't hurt. I'm a Marine. I've endured worse."

Her frown turned into an involuntary chortle. "So you keep saying."

"Any word on Paolo?" he asked anxiously.

"He's in surgery. But they're hopeful."

"Was anyone else seriously injured?"

"Thankfully, most are minor injuries. One of the sisters sitting with us, Sister Agnes, she—she didn't make it."

"I'm sorry."

"*Zio's* blaming himself." She shot a glance at the doctor then back at Daniel. He understood. The Cardinal wished he would have exposed Constantini sooner.

Her eyes glistened. "If it hadn't been for you, it could have been a lot worse."

"She is right, Daniel." The two looked up to see the Cardinal standing at the foot of the bed. "I will never be able to express my gratitude. To you or to Paolo."

Daniel's face brightened. "He's out of surgery? And he's okay?"

"*Sì.* He is resting. I just came from anointing him."

Daniel closed his eyes. *Oh, thank you Lord*, he prayed silently.

"I am here to anoint you, too, *mio figlio*."

The Cardinal wasted no time praying the words of the Sacrament of the Anointing of the Sick. He opened a small sterling silver vial and dipped his thumb on the opening and placed the oil on Daniel's forehead in a cross with his thumb.

Frannie marveled at Daniel's reaction. Daniel Fitzpatrick had the appearance of a man at prayer. He even reverently made the Sign of the Cross at the Cardinal's blessing.

The Cardinal closed the vial and placed it in his pocket. "Much to the dismay of Remo and the authorities, I am staying to anoint my flock. The wolves have scattered; and now the sheep need tending."

"Scattered?" Daniel repeated. "Bruno escaped?"

"They have the gunman and are searching the area. All we can do now is wait. Rosa is insisting you will need help caring for yourself and is expecting you at her house tonight. There's no use arguing with her." He added, "Francesca, she has prepared a room for you, too."

"That's very kind of her, sir," Daniel said.

He smiled. "You are family. We will catch up tomorrow." He spun around and was off to pastor the injured.

The doctor stood up. "I am finished. It will take us some time to draw up your discharge orders. Someone will come get you when they are ready."

Finally alone, Daniel sat up and swung his legs over the side of the bed. He scooted down, making a space next to him. Frannie instinctively sat next to him on his uninjured side. There was so much he wanted to say to her, he didn't know where to start.

"How are you doing?" he asked.

She shrugged. "I don't know. Numb. Confused. A little jumpy."

Daniel's military tours had taught him firsthand about traumatic events. "Sounds pretty normal. You're tough and have a strong faith; it will take some time but it will get easier."

Frannie sat up a little straighter. *Did he just say my faith will help me through this?*

"I'm glad I didn't hurt you when I knocked you to the floor," he said, still avoiding the elephant in the room.

"I'm pretty used to your linebacker moves by now."

He started to chuckle at her witty sarcasm but stopped when he saw her chin quivering.

Frannie couldn't hold it back any longer and broke down. "Daniel, I'm so sorry I called you a coward. I'm so sorry," she repeated in between her sobs.

"I deserved it Frannie," he said, gently wiping her tears with his thumb. "I know I've been a dolt, but I'm not the same guy you met at the airport. So much has happened; I went to confession and to Mass—I even received Communion. There's a lot I don't know or understand but I do know one thing: if you give me a second chance, I'll *never* run from you again."

Frannie's entire body went limp. She couldn't believe what she was hearing.

The gates had opened and Daniel's true feelings were unrestrained, rushing forth like a stampede. "You saw something in me I didn't see in myself. But, I'm ready now—I'm ready to be the man you deserve. I'm sure I will fall short, but I give you my word, I'll try."

He paused just long enough to grab her hand and lock his eyes with hers. "Frannie, you're everything I thought I would never find. That's why I came back tonight; to ask you for a second chance."

She slumped forward, cupped hand over her mouth, and wept. Daniel hadn't rejected her, he just needed time. He had found

Jesus and in the process had discovered who he was; the man she knew him to be.

Daniel pulled back at her reaction. *She must be upset at having to choose between two guys. I need to warn her I'm not giving up easily.*

"I'm not sure who Mr. EMT is," he said, "but I'm not going to just roll over. I'm going to fight for you. And I told him so," he added defiantly.

Frannie's muffled weeping stopped, then morphed into giggles. She removed her hand, revealing a smirk across her face. "And what did he say when you told him that?"

"Nothing really. He said, 'I know.'"

Great. Alessandro will never let me live it down that he was right; Daniel is the one.

"Mr. EMT's name is Alessandro. We've known each other since we were little kids. He is my best friend. And," she paused for dramatic effect, "he is entering the seminary."

Daniel's head jerked. "To be a priest?"

Frannie's smirk grew larger. "Mm-hmm."

His mouth fell open. *A priest? That meant—*

"Wait, the unmarried kind?" he asked, knowing the Church was still quibbling over the matter.

"Yes. He will take a vow of celibacy."

"That's good," he said happily. Recognizing how overjoyed he sounded, he retracted a bit, "I mean, it's good, right? We need more priests?"

"Yes, it's wonderful he has found his calling. So, you can put your sword back in its scabbard, Fitzpatrick, and save the fight for another day."

Daniel grinned. The playful banter had returned. Just to be sure, he asked, "Is there another rogue I should keep my sword out and ready for?"

She scooted even closer and planted her hand more firmly in his. She looked at him intently. "No. There's no one else, Daniel."

He closed his eyes and sighed. Frannie was giving him a second chance.

He softly touched her cheek. "I never even told you how beautiful you look tonight."

"Bah," she scoffed, "my hair is all unraveled and my face is probably one gigantic make-up smudge."

Daniel shook his head slowly. "The best Georgia lake sunset can't compare to your beauty."

Her wide eyes prompted him to quickly apologize, "That must have sounded really lame."

Frannie's eyes misted. "Not at all. It's the sweetest compliment anyone has ever given me."

She leaned in and he met her for a kiss. When they parted, she rested her head on his chest. He held her as tightly as he could with his uninjured arm. With Frannie at his side, Daniel knew God had blessed him beyond measure–leading him to Rome and to the interview of a lifetime.

Chapter 44

DESPITE HER EXHAUSTION, AND THE SECURITY OF knowing Daniel was a few doors away, Frannie didn't sleep well. In the early hours of the morning she tiptoed into Rosa's kitchen to make a cup of chamomile tea, but her efforts at being quiet failed. Daniel appeared, having heard the rummaging, and he sat with her for a time. His presence comforted her, and she managed to go back to sleep for a few hours.

Rosa was in a dither the next day, constantly fussing over Daniel, waiting on him hand and foot. She would randomly burst into tears blubbering, "You saved my family, *la mia famiglia,*" and kiss both of his cheeks.

"Will she be over this by tomorrow?" Daniel whispered to Frannie, after Rosa had propped a pillow under his injured arm.

She chuckled. "I wouldn't bet on it. Maybe in a year, if you're lucky."

In light of the night's developments, Daniel spent the day reworking and editing his article, an exclusive for *The Classic Journalist*, detailing the attempt on the Cardinal's life and the Constantini-Fratelli-Donati triangle. Cardinal Menconi had given his approval, saying he would be able to release it within a day or two. Daniel wasn't able to type due to his injured arm, so he dictated his words for Frannie to enter into his computer. She was grateful to have something to do and keep her mind distracted.

The following day Daniel and the Menconis went to Sunday Mass. Daniel and Frannie left early so they could stop by and visit

Paolo in the hospital. He was in good spirits, and promised he would be back in the driver's seat in no time.

Remo tried to convince the Cardinal to celebrate Mass in private, with only family and few trusted friends, but he would not consider it. Police stood guard all around the church of the Holy Trinity and monitored the street. It was Daniel's first time attending with Frannie since returning to the Church. His heart was full of anticipation for the music and elevated worship of the Solemn High Mass. When she covered her head with her veil, any feelings of unworthiness were gone. All he felt was love; love for Frannie, love for his Lord who forgave him and gave him his new life, and love for the Woman and Mother who first tugged at his heart to make it all possible.

Mass was both beautiful and blissfully uneventful, and they passed safely through security on the way out to head back to Rosa's. Daniel and Frannie received extra hugs from the family as they gathered together for Sunday dinner. Frannie tried to help but was shooed out of the kitchen with instructions to take care of Daniel.

She joined him on the back patio and handed him a bottle of water. "Rosa sent me out here to make sure you don't need anything."

"Oh, good grief! I need to have a talk with her."

"In other news," she said, skipping to another subject, "Maureen reached out to me. She said you have been in their prayers and they would be praying and fasting for the conclave."

His conversation with Diedrich seemed like a lifetime ago. *I should write him a letter, letting him know I finally have an answer to the question he asked me.*

"That was nice of her. I'll have to tell you about the talk I had with Diedrich when I went back for the strudel."

She was about to question him when Lorena ran up and threw her arms around her. "Francesca! I'm so glad you are okay. And you too, Daniel!" she said, embracing him next. "I couldn't believe what I was watching on the news."

Frannie gawked at her cousin, completely dumbstruck at her transformation. Lorena had traded in her tight and revealing clothes for an elegant and modest navy blue dress with white flowers. The dark, caked on makeup was replaced with a light and natural look, allowing her genuine beauty to be seen rather than hidden.

"Thanks, Lorena," Frannie said mechanically. Her eyes moved to the handsome man standing next to her cousin.

Lorena introduced him, "This is Luca. He works at my office in one of the other departments. Luca, this is Francesca and Daniel."

Daniel was the first to offer his hand. "Luca, nice to meet you."

Frannie numbly exchanged a greeting.

"I've heard a lot about both of you," Luca said.

Frannie noticed something non-verbal being communicated between Lorena and Daniel.

"I'm going to introduce him to *Zia* Rosa," Lorena said. "Don't leave Rome without saying goodbye." She gave her cousin another hug, and walked away.

"What just happened?" Frannie asked, popping her hip to the side. "She looks fantastic and that's the first normal guy I've ever seen her with." She squinted at Daniel. "Why do I get the feeling you know something about this?"

"It's another conversation I haven't told you about."

"Well, we certainly have a lot to discuss on our flight back to America."

With his one good arm he grabbed her by the waist and pulled her close. "We certainly do."

Daniel knew he would be leaving Chicago and looking for an apartment in Boston. He had already begun negotiations with his boss regarding working remotely from the main office. His life was about to change forever, and he couldn't wait for it to start.

After dinner, Frannie and Daniel met the Cardinal in the living room. They took the couch and he melted into a chair.

Frannie eyed him carefully. "Have you slept at all, *Zio?*"

"A little. I will sleep better tonight. Bruno Fratelli was arrested about an hour ago."

Daniel leaned forward. "They found him?"

"Yes. The Fratellis underestimated the Villa's security cameras placed throughout the gardens. The police were able to get a license number on the car. The Fratellis have brought in their team of lawyers but the evidence against him and Constantini is strong. I will probably be calling you later tonight with the green light to submit your article."

"I talked with Remo at the church this morning," Daniel said. "They suspect the Fratellis made a donation under a fake name to secure an invitation to the gala. The wait staff said Bruno switched seats with someone so he could be at the back table. He bribed one of the guards ahead of time to let him in."

The Cardinal remarked, "Remo is furious, naturally. He's offered to give me some of his best men to work solely for me."

Daniel continued, "Remo went on to say the gunman admitted that changing out the guards messed with their plan. The bribed guard was going to pretend to struggle with him after the shots were made and help him escape. The gunman is denying he knew Bruno was a member of the Fratelli family, probably out of fear. But he was happy to hang him out to dry for darting out and leaving him to take the fall."

"And as for Fortino Donati and Giuseppe Baldano," the Cardinal said, "they are ready to give their witnesses once Constantini is in custody. I turned over all of Stefano's evidence. Stefano and his family will return once they know it is safe."

"Constantini is a big fish," Daniel noted. "I bet they're hoping to get the Fratelli ring while they're at it."

He noticed Frannie was unusually quiet, staring at the floor. Daniel rubbed her back, causing her to look up.

"*Zio*, with Constantini out of the conclave, you know the chances are high you could be elected."

"Yes, I do," he whispered.

"It will change how often I can see and talk to you, won't it?"
He bowed his head.

Frannie wiped her eyes with the back of her hand. Her voice cracked, "I feel like I'm losing you."

The Cardinal sighed heavily. "It's time to confess a secret I've been keeping."

Frannie leaned into Daniel's shoulder to brace herself. "What secret, *Zio*?"

"Daniel's request for an interview came across my desk the same day I received Giuseppe Baldano's letter. Given the gravity of its contents, I didn't have time to think about an interview with an American journalist, so I tossed the request aside. When I did, I heard the words, 'He will protect her.' I wasn't sure what to make of it, so I put it in my desk drawer. The next day, Stefano delivered Vidmar's list. I sat at my desk, reading the Scripture passages over and over. Then, I heard it again: 'He will protect her.' This time, I smelled roses."

Frannie gasped. The Cardinal looked at Frannie and nodded. Each knew what the other was thinking. Frannie voiced it out loud, "Fatima."

Daniel's eyes bounced back and forth between the Cardinal and Frannie. "Is smelling roses a thing that usually happens?"

"It's not common, but quite possible," the Cardinal answered. "Sweet fragrances can be present in moments of prayer and can indicate the presence of a saint, or most commonly, the Blessed Mother herself."

"It happened to me when *Zio* and I went to Fatima," Frannie explained. "I was sitting in the Chapel of the Apparitions, where Mary appeared to the shepherd children. I was fifteen and still recovering from my bout with depression. I asked Mary to pray for me, that I could be grateful for my good memories with Papa. The Scripture passage, 'Mary pondered these things in her heart,' came to me. I thought about how Mary must have gone back to those early days with her Son—the shepherds and Wise Men, losing Him at Passover and finding him in the Temple—to get her through the days of His ministry and Passion. But I began to wonder if she recalled other memories not written down: His first steps, first words, and learning the Torah. All the memories a woman would place in a baby book, Mary kept in her heart; and they must have brought her comfort.

"Then I received a message: 'I will protect your family.' I was stunned and didn't know what it meant. I closed my eyes and that's when the smell of roses came. I consecrated myself to the Blessed Mother when I got home, and thought maybe she was telling me to be a nun. I visited several communities but discerned it wasn't my calling."

She smiled at her uncle. "I've been on a wrong path, but Mary, Star of the Sea, has protected me and placed me on a path to find my compass again." She dabbed at her eyes. "Last night she kept her promise. She protected all of us."

The Cardinal returned her smile. "You can see now why I couldn't share with you why I asked you to fly here and work with Daniel. You were already so annoyed at him, you would have fought it even harder."

Daniel snorted a laugh. "Don't be too hard on her, sir. She had good reason for thinking the idea was obnoxious."

The Cardinal clapped his hands together. "All is well now. It was better to rely on the Holy Spirit to lead you to each other, if it be God's will," he concluded.

Daniel twisted in his seat. "About the smelling roses thing. I think that happened to me at daily Mass this week."

Frannie did a double take. "What?"

"After Mass, I was," he paused, hesitant to expose his ignorance. "First off, I'm still new to all of this. I'm not sure what to do or say when I'm praying so I'm winging it at this point."

Frannie took his hand. "We're not going to laugh at you, Daniel."

He gave her soft hand a squeeze. "I tried your advice: to 'just be' at Mass. And when I got back to my pew after Communion, it happened. I was in the present moment and full of peace to be there. There was no thought about getting back to the apartment and the work I needed to get done that day. I've never felt anything like it.

"The joy caused me to start singing—" he faltered a moment, hoping he didn't sound too weird, "I started singing, "Be Thou My Vision" silently to myself. When I finished, I smelled it."

"Sounds like a perfect prayer of thanksgiving to me," she said.

"Yeah, but I wasn't talking to Mary at all." His face slowly lit up. "I asked God to tell mom and Grandma Mae that I was at Mass. Maybe the smell was from them, letting me know they could see me."

His face immediately fell and his eyes darted away. "I don't know if they can do stuff like that: see me from—you know," he stammered, feeling foolish.

"Daniel," the Cardinal said gently, "I can't say why you smelled the roses. But I am certain that the Blessed Mother and our Lord saw you. And they wanted you to know that."

Frannie threw her arms around him. She knew something the Cardinal didn't; the special connection between the hymn and Daniel's grandmother. She whispered in his ear, "I think it was all three of your mothers." He squeezed her tightly in return.

Cardinal Menconi closed his eyes and gave his own prayer of thanksgiving to the Lord, who had given him a great gift. He had allowed him treasured moments with the young man who would be taking care of his little sparrow.

"I hate to interrupt you two," he said, rising from his chair, "but I have a lot to do before the conclave begins."

Frannie and Daniel pulled away, a little embarrassed at their show of affection.

The Cardinal asked them to rise. "I want to give you a blessing before I go." He took Francesca's hand, placed it in Daniel's, and covered them with both of his hands.

He began to pray,

"I lift up my eyes to the hills.
From whence does my help come?
My help comes from the Lord,
who made heaven and earth.
He will not let your foot be moved,
He who keeps you will not slumber.
The Lord will keep
your going out and your coming in
from this time forth and for evermore."

He followed the Psalm with a blessing in Latin, making the Sign of the Cross over them both.

Frannie met her uncle's eyes and understood the meaning of his gesture; he was leaving her but not before giving her to someone he trusted. She embraced him, thanking him through her tears for always being there for her, and telling him how much she loved him.

The Cardinal turned to Daniel, who gave him as tight of a hug as he could with one arm. "Thank you, sir. For everything."

"No, thank you, *mio figlio.*"

A few tears escaped Daniel's lids. He was saying goodbye to the only person who had been like a father to him; the only person to have called him a son.

"I guess it would be wrong to pray that the Holy Spirit picks someone else, wouldn't it?" Daniel asked, half-jokingly.

The Cardinal chuckled. "Yes. Saint Paul was wise when he said, 'No one comprehends the thoughts of God except the Spirit of God.' Who knows? Perhaps the Spirit has someone else in mind."

He smiled and patted their cheeks, gave them a parting look, and turned away so they wouldn't see his tears as he left the room. The Lord had graciously blessed him with the peace of knowing that his niece had a guardian here on earth; someone who would care and protect the garden of his family. Should he, Nicolo Menconi, be the one chosen to guard the Bride of Christ, the Church, he had to trust that God would lead him in such a mission.

On the way back to his apartment in Borgo, he prayed, *Lord, I cannot ask that you protect me from suffering; that is not the way of the Cross. But protect me from evil. Fill me with fortitude but most importantly, fill me with your grace. That is sufficient, I need nothing more. Saint Peter, pray for me.*

Epilogue

Three years later

A BLACK SEDAN PULLED UP IN FRONT OF SAINT Peter's Basilica. The sun was just beginning its ascent in the sky, casting its light upon the dome and statues of the Apostles, Christ, and John the Baptist, perched on the top of the façade. The square was vacant save a few priests scurrying in to pray and celebrate their daily Mass before the tourists arrived.

"Thanks for the ride, Paolo," Daniel said, reaching behind the back seat to pat his friend on the shoulder. "You're coming, aren't you?"

"*Signore*, I wouldn't miss it for the world. *Signora*, I'll get the door for you."

Paolo jumped out and opened the driver's door for Frannie.

"Thank you, Paolo," she said, grabbing the large bag at her feet. Daniel leaned into the passenger side, unbuckled a car seat, and lifted it out. A little gurgle came out from under the blanket. Frannie did a quick inspection and smiled at the little face with blue eyes smiling back at her.

Frannie still wore her smile when she looked up at her husband. "Ready?"

"Yep. And, I'm ready for dinner at *Zia* Rosa's later. She made her famous cookies."

"I have no doubt she baked them just for you."

"I saw that eye-roll, Menconi."

"Just stating the obvious, Fitzpatrick. You're her favorite."

Daniel took a few steps and stopped. The Bernini columns of the basilica stretched out like arms welcoming him home. He took a deep breath and exhaled. "It feels good to be back, doesn't it?" he mused.

Frannie drank in the majestic view. "Always."

Daniel placed a hand on his wife's back and gave her a kiss. When they reached the top of the steps to Saint Peter's, a woman with dark hair greeted them with a chastisement, "It's about time! We're almost ready to start!"

"We're here, Ma," Frannie said blandly. "Like we don't know we're on a tight schedule," she grumbled to her husband.

Frannie's mother ignored her daughter's remark and cooed and made faces at her grandchild in the carrier.

They followed each other inside the large basilica doors and stood at the entrance. A blond-haired woman came over and gave Frannie a big hug.

"Lorena! It's so good to see you. How's married life?"

"Fabulous!" she said, her face glowing.

"We really wanted to be here for the wedding," Daniel said. "It was tough knowing that Frannie couldn't travel that close to her due date."

"I know," Lorena said, waving her hand. "Your live video toast at the reception meant so much to Luca and me." She lowered her voice, "I want to ask both of you something before we start. Are you really sure you want me to be the godmother?"

Frannie placed her hands on her cousin's shoulders. "Lorena, you are exactly who we want."

"You're going to be a great witness," Daniel added. "Even Alessandro, despite his seminary studies, doesn't have the same experiential understanding of the mercy and love of God as you do. That's why we chose you."

Lorena wiped her fingers under her eyes. "I am truly honored."

As if on cue, Alessandro darted through the door, dressed in a black cassock.

"Speak of the devil," Daniel said.

"Devil? Where?" Alessandro said, looking around, "Better call an exorcist!"

Frannie laughed and gave her childhood friend a hug. "I was worried they weren't going to let you leave the seminary for this."

"It helps having friends in high places," he said with a wink. "*Ciao*, Daniel."

Daniel gave him a friendly smile and slap on the shoulder. "*Ciao*, Alessandro."

"Aha! There's my godson!" Alessandro said, bending down to peek in the car seat. "You might as well let me hold him now since the godparents hold the child during the Rite of Baptism when celebrated in the Extraordinary Form."

Daniel reached into the carrier to pick up his son, and handed him to Alessandro. Frannie fussed over him, making sure Alessandro held him according to her standards. The echoing sound of shoes clicking on the marble floor made them all turn. They all stood reverently still as Pope Pius XIII, smiling broadly and flanked by two cardinals, approached them. He reached Daniel first and offered his hand.

"Holy Father," Daniel said, bowing his head and kissing the pope's ring, also known as The Ring of the Fisherman.

Pope Pius XIII went down the line and all greeted him the same—until he reached Frannie.

"Holy Father," she said, with a crack in her voice. She kissed the ring, then broke all protocol and threw her arms around him. "You look tired, *Zio*," she whispered.

The bags under her uncle's eyes revealed the toll of steering the Church back from the Constantini scandal, internecine feuds, and divisions. Besides restoring the Church's traditions to a male clergy and celibate priesthood, the pope had worked with the Congregation of Divine Worship to ensure a liturgical reform. He asked the Congregation to compose specific liturgical directives for the *Novus Ordo;* for it to be fully enriched by the Extraordinary Form with beauty, reverence, and the sacred. By correcting liturgical abuses and not abrogating either form, he hoped to bring an end to Catholics labelling themselves based on Mass preference and reunify as one Church praying as she believed.

The pope patted her hand. "I'm fine, *mia passerotta*. My heart is full of joy today to see you and Daniel." He leaned in and whispered in her ear, "I'm sneaking over to Rosa's for dinner. The guards aren't happy about it, but I have some say in the matter," he added jovially.

Given the attempt on his life prior to being elected the Bishop of Rome, Vatican security took extra precautions with the pope. The pontiff constantly battled with his detail, and was known for his impromptu visits to hospitals and schools. He was planning a trip within the month to Jerusalem to visit the holy sites and walk a portion of the Via Dolorosa, or "The Way of Suffering" that Jesus walked on His way to Calvary. "I must show the flock the Way of the Cross is the way of Christ; it is the way of the Church," he said in a public statement. "Anyone who wishes to follow Christ, must take up his Cross, and follow Him. To echo our pope of happy memory, 'We must not be afraid.'"

Now, tending to his beloved family, the pope motioned for everyone to gather at the door. He began the prayers for the Rite of Baptism at the entrance, signifying the child was not yet a member of the Church. After exorcism prayers to command any unclean spirits to depart from the child, he placed exorcised salt in his mouth, with a prayer he may have an everlasting taste for wisdom. Then Pope Pius led Alessandro, who was still holding the baby, Lorena, and the rest of the family, including Paolo, to the baptistery, immediately to the left of the basilica's entrance. Daniel stole a glance to his right; the *Pieta* was directly across from the baptism chapel. He would stop by the statue for a moment of prayer afterwards.

They gathered around the font, made of red porphyry, centered in front of a large painting of Jesus being baptized in the Jordan by Saint John the Baptist. The pope continued with the prayers of the Rite: another prayer for the exorcism of unclean spirits, asking the mouth and nose to be opened as the Lord had healed the deaf and mute man, and an anointing with oil.

Daniel and Frannie moved even closer to the font. He put his hand on his wife's shoulder, and she reached up and placed her hand on top of his. They had both longed for this moment; for a family of their own. Daniel was still in awe he was a father to the most perfect and beautiful boy he had ever seen. It was equally surreal that his son was being baptized by the pope at the Vatican.

He couldn't help but grin. *Mom and Grandma Mae must be dancing a jig up in heaven today.*

The moment had come for the actual baptism in the name of the Holy Trinity. Pope Pius reached down in the basin and poured water over the baby boy's head: "Nicolo Daniel, *Ego te baptizo in nomine Patris,*" then pouring water a second time, "*et Filii,*" and a third pouring, "*et Spiritus Sancti.*"

A single tear leaked from the corner of the pope's eye. He was the successor of Peter and leader of the Catholic Church; he could canonize saints, issue papal encyclicals, and speak to world leaders by phone in a matter of minutes. But baptizing his namesake and his precious niece's little boy was the greatest honor and deepest joy of his vocation to the priesthood.

Once the Rite was completed, Frannie took her son in her arms and followed her uncle to the side altar next to the baptistery, the Presentation Chapel, for the Blessing of a Woman After Childbirth and of Her Child. Frannie knelt down and looked up at the altarpiece, a painting of the Presentation of the Virgin Mary in the Temple, showing her being consecrated to divine service by her parents. Her eyes drifted to the body of Saint Pope Pius X, lying in full papal robes in a crystal and bronze casket under the altar. She was not surprised her uncle chose the name Pius after this great saint. Saint Pius X was a staunch defender against modernism and for the promotion of beautiful liturgies, calling for the restoration of sacred music and chant in the Mass. Pope Pius XIII regularly called upon the intercession of his predecessor.

After the Blessing, Daniel joined her and they walked to the next side altar, the Altar of the Immaculate Conception, to consecrate their child to the Immaculate Heart of Mary. Knowing firsthand the power of the protection of the Blessed Mother in their own lives, they prayed the act of consecration, "We offer him to you that you may present him to your Divine Son, that you may take him under your loving, maternal protection…"

When the prescribed prayer was finished, Daniel and Frannie took a few moments to pray their own personal prayers of thanksgiving. They didn't know what trials and storms of life were to come, but they were certain they would never be alone. They could place their trust in the protection of Mary's mantle, the loving arms of the Heavenly Father, the mercy of Christ, and the guidance of the Holy Spirit. Daniel looked down upon his wife and child and smiled.

Yes, Mary, you love us like a mother.

Acknowledgements

To God be the Glory!

To my editors, Megan Hjelmstad and Tracy Brend: You have enriched this book beyond measure. Thank you for taking the time to read it and provide your honest and constructive feedback. It made all the difference.

All my love to my husband, Robert, who read the first draft, and continues to support me in my new hobby.

When I set out to start writing this story, I knew how it would begin and how it would end. I had a few other scenes mapped out, but most of the middle was yet to be determined. I had planned Daniel's moment of surrender to occur at the "interview" which would end up being his confession–the true interview of a lifetime. How all the dots would be connected during Daniel's conversation with the Cardinal was still unknown. I wish to acknowledge where my inspiration came from in helping me complete the chapter.

As the time grew closer for me to begin writing that part of the story, I received two articles from two online Catholic email subscriptions. They came ten days apart from each other.

The first was, "The Charcoal Fire," by Grace Abruzzo, from www.spiritualdirection.com. It is this article that provided the insight that just as Jesus led Peter to return to the painful memory of the charcoal fire of his betrayal, Jesus also desires to enter into our own painful memories, where He wants to walk with us. The article also connected it to the happy memory of the first catch. I had already written and assigned the first catch as the Gospel reading for the Sunday Mass Daniel attended with Frannie! The timing and connections with memory were astounding, as I had also already written extensively of Daniel's memories–the good and the painful. In addition, I had assigned Saint Peter's role in the story as well: the Saint that both the Cardinal and Daniel would identify with, for different reasons.

The second was an article written by Elizabeth Mitchell from *The Catholic Thing*: "The Masterpiece of the Divine Artist." In this article, Ms. Mitchell used the *Pieta* and Michelangelo's talent of seeing the image inside the block of marble as an analogy for God seeing His masterpiece in us. She also used Edith Stein's poem to bring home her point: that we must collaborate with God's grace for His work in us. By this time, Daniel's experience at the Pieta had already been written and woven through the chapters. Needless to say, my heart raced when reading this article. It was the second connection I needed.

I can only hope my reception of these articles were not "coincidental" and the story of Daniel and Frannie will have an inspirational message for (as well as entertain) whomever reads it.

For more information on the remarkable story of Saint Peter's bones, see The Bones of St. Peter by John Evangelist Walsh, 1982, found on the Vatican website: http://stpetersbasilica.info/Necropolis/Scavi.htm I also highly recommend the fascinating book, *The Fisherman's Tomb* by John O'Neill. Thank you, Andrea Ruccolo for my copy!

The effects of abortion on men are not often reported. Resources, retreats, and counseling for men and women who are hurting from an abortion (whether they participated willingly or unwillingly) are available through Rachel's Vineyard. For help with this book, I used Kevin Burke's blog that can be accessed via https://www.priestsforlife.org/kevinburke/. Ironically (or maybe not) he uses the repentance of Saint Peter as a model. He wrote a book for the recovery of men wounded by abortion titled, *Tears of the Fisherman.*

Mary, Star of the Sea and Saint Peter, pray for us!

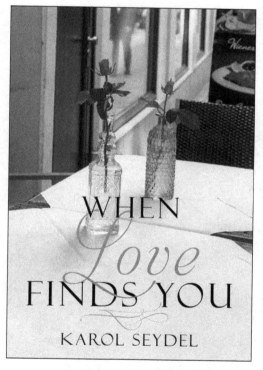

Maureen Simmons, still heartbroken from the loss of her husband, leaves her life in America behind to find a fresh start in Salzburg, Austria. Diedrich Alder is a brooding cafe owner with a scarring past. When Maureen crosses the threshold of his small cafe, they both discover the unexpected: a love that will redefine their story in ways neither could imagine.

Printed in the USA
CPSIA information can be obtained
at www.ICGtesting.com
JSHW010241280723
45536JS00003B/7

9 781662 841705